The Streets Made Me 2

Larry D. Wright

Lock Down Publications and
Ca$h
Presents
The Streets Made Me 2
A Novel by *Larry D. Wright*

Larry D. Wright

Lock Down Publications
P.O. Box 944
Stockbridge, Ga 30281

Lock Down Publications
Like our page on Facebook: Lock Down Publications
@
www.facebook.com/lockdownpublications.ldp
Cover design and layout by: **Dynasty Cover Me**
Book interior design by: **Shawn Walker**
Edited by: **Lashonda Johnson**

Stay Connected with Us!

Text **LOCKDOWN** to 22828 to stay up-to-date with new releases, sneak peaks, contests and more…

Thank you!

Submission Guideline.

Submit the first three chapters of your completed manuscript to ldpsubmissions@gmail.com, subject line: Your book's title. The manuscript must be in a .doc file and sent as an attachment. Document should be in Times New Roman, double spaced and in size 12 font. Also, provide your synopsis and full contact information. If sending multiple submissions, they must each be in a separate email.

Have a story but no way to send it electronically? You can still submit to LDP/Ca$h Presents. Send in the first three chapters, written or typed, of your completed manuscript to:

LDP: Submissions Dept
P.O. Box 944
Stockbridge, Ga 30281

DO NOT send original manuscript. Must be a duplicate.

Provide your synopsis and a cover letter containing your full contact information.

Thanks for considering LDP and Ca$h Presents.

ACKNOWLEDGEMENTS:

My pen has been a faithful companion through indictments, jury trials, solitary confinement, tragic losses, heartbreak, and utter chaos. My light could not have illuminated darkness without Apolonia and Ciara who provided the spark that ignited the movement. Colossal thanks to Ca$h and Lock Down Publications for putting me on. Major thanks to Dynasty Cover Me, Shawn Walker, and Lashonda Johnson. My entire team has been patient and professional.

Much love to all my fans and supporters. Bless up Big Dana, Michael Brown, Tabu, Shako, Key, Shawn, Eric 'ESPN' Johnson, Charger Gurl, Wink (falling stars), Eucalyptus Street (Movin'), Fifty Second Street (Groovin'), Tracy ('til the moon melts), Kitty Brown (courage), and Diaab Sanders.

I'm forever grateful for my three kings: Jeshurun (Rest In Paradise), Larry Jr. (future billionaire), and Troy (I promise to make up for the lost years). Lighters up to my comrades behind the wall. Bulletproof love to my shooters. Teflon slugs for my haters. Baller Belly Entertainment 'til death do us or the Feds unglue us! God is great!

ABOUT THE AUTHOR:

"Writing is my passion," explains crime novelist and entrepreneur Larry D. Wright. Mr. Wright is the founder of Baller Belly Entertainment and author of "The Streets Made Me." He holds a Microsoft Certified Systems Engineer certification and is currently pursuing a Bachelor of Science degree. He signed with Lock Down Publications in 2019 and continues to find success with his raw, provocative, and unapologetic style of writing.

A native of Los Angeles, Wright has had a kaleidoscope view of the violence and deprivation that afflicts the inner-city. "My real-life experiences enable me to paint vivid portraits of the streets and the infamous characters who live in them," he reports. Through his intriguing novels and thought-provoking essays, Mr. Wright has become an inspiration to young men and women across the U.S.

What's next for this talented writer? "I'm working on a book project, developing content for a web series, and creating Street Lit Magazine to give incarcerated authors a marketing platform," he says with enthusiasm.

Blood Out

"For what will it profit a man if he gains the whole world, and loses his own soul?"

Mark
8:36

Larry D. Wright

CHAPTER 1

Blood In

My intuition forewarned me that it was going to be a gloomy day. A mass of ghostly, gray clouds lurking in the heavens and casting an ominous shadow over Los Angeles greeted me when I stepped out of my stash house. Thunder rumbled and lightning illuminated the dark sky as a black cat superstitiously crossed my path. That should've been my warning of impending danger, but I ignored the furry feline, strolled pass the neatly manicured hedges lining the perimeter of my two-story, Italianate, stucco townhouse, and chirped the alarm to my Maserati, bad mistake.

The sound of swift footsteps demanded my attention, but before I could reach for my heat, a young shorty ran up on me. He held his banger sideways and squeezed off six shots. All six rounds ripped through my flesh. I stumbled to my Maserati and reached for the door handle, but the velocity of the seventh slug struck me in the back, driving me to my knees, pushing me closer to my death. Gritting my teeth in agony, I looked down at my bullet-riddled body in disbelief.

"Damn, ain't this 'bout a bitch?" I wondered who had set me up. *Was it, Sosa? Was it, Nella? Was it the Feds?* The truth eluded me.

Dark, red blood oozed out of the quarter-sized holes and saturated my favorite white button-up shirt. The gunman could not have been more than sixteen-years-old. A blue bandana covered his nose and mouth like a bandit, but it did nothing to conceal his narrow, slit eyes. In them, I saw pain, utter chaos, and a complete absence of hope. He reminded me of me. I knew my days were numbered. I just didn't expect to get murked today. Last night I made a decision to repent for all my sins and was on my way to God's Temple in order to ask for forgiveness. That's right, me of all people was about to square-up, but it was too late for redemption now. A solitary tear trickled down my cheek as I thought about the missed opportunity to broker a peace treaty with my maker.

The determined shooter kneeled next to me. His merciless pupils were darker than the barrel of his gun. I could tell that he was about that life.

"Fuck it, let's get it over with!" I said, and disrespectfully spit a wad of phlegm and thick blood in the young assassin's face.

The slimy saliva dangled from his eyelash. An evil snarl formed at the corners of his lips and his bushy eyebrows contracted into a frown. He crammed the steel barrel of his cannon into my mouth, cracking two of my front teeth. The pain traveled from my gums to my big toe. His index finger curled around the trigger, twitching, squeezing until yellow flames spewed from the barrel.

Blocka! It was a wrap, game over!

Ain't nothing poetic about dying, homie. I didn't go out in a blaze of glory waving a machine gun and taunting my adversaries like a coked-up, Tony Montana. I stay strapped, but to keep it one-hondo, I didn't foresee this coming, I was slippin'.

Standing over me, shorty removed the nickel-plated Taurus Millennium from my waistline. He ignored the black diamond Jesus piece draped across my neck as well as the fat knot of gwuap in my pocket, opting to blast me in the face with my own gun instead. This wasn't a robbery, it was a hit. Trust me, dawg, that bright light at the end of the tunnel ain't a neon welcome sign cordially inviting sinners into heaven. I staggered toward the end of the tunnel but realized at the last moment that the brilliant white light was actually the flickering flames of hell.

Satan, his eyes fire red, beckoned me to jump into the blazing inferno. I turned and ran in the opposite direction, screaming as the radiant heat singed the hair on the back of my legs. In my haste to escape Lucifer, I stumbled and fell like white people do in horror movies.

As I laid flat on my back, a familiar face came into view. It was my Nefertiti, my earth, my wifey. Nella rapidly pressed on my chest, but I couldn't tell whether she was attempting to give me CPR or trying to smother me. I panicked and swung my fist violently, finally calming down when she screamed my name.

****

"Najee wake up! Wake up, baby!" Nella shook Najee until he woke up from a deep sleep. Beads of cool, sweat bubbled on his clean-shaven head, and his chest heaved as he struggled to catch his breath. She gently wiped the perspiration with the palm of her hand. "You okay, honey?" Nella inquired her voice laced with concern.

Najee rubbed the crusty sleep from the corners of his eyes and squinted at the alarm clock. The blurry red numbers read, 1:37 A.M. The vivid nightmares had returned, but this time they were different. Instead of reliving the day he was forced to watch his first love get brutally raped and his parents get gunned down, he was now having premonitions of his own death. He shook the graphic images out of his mind before speaking.

"Yeah, I'm good, bae," he lied and pulled Nella closer. He needed to feel her warm body next to his.

Nella snuggled against her man. Now that she had Najee back in her life, she promised to never let him go. It seemed like just yesterday she thought he was dead, only to find out he had faked his death. Initially, she was heated, especially when she learned that he also underwent facial reconstruction surgery courtesy of renowned Beverly Hills plastic surgeon, Renee Brooks. However, one look at the compassionate fire gleaming within his familiar brown eyes made the edges of her frozen heart instantly thaw.

She adored everything about Najee. He was a double scoop of chocolate Häagen-Dazs with a muscular physique. Standing at 5'7, he was short in stature but well respected in the streets as a goon with colossal power and influence. Nella loved bad boys, and Najee was the epitome of thug passion. Just thinking of him made her panties moist.

She laid her head on his broad chest and listened to the *thump-thump* of his beating heart. He was more relaxed now. She smiled thinking about how complex of a black man he was. Najee was a perfect imperfection. He was cocky, yet humble, cunning, yet loyal, vulnerable, yet fully confident in his manhood. Sharp barbwire guarded his thoughts and emotions, however, he handled Nella as delicate as the wings on a butterfly, except in bed, of course. He was a beast between the sheets, and she loved the way he beat it up.

Her only wish was that he'd forget the past and embraced the future. They had each other, a successful non-profit organization called Alive 365, which helped disenfranchised inner-city youths, and racks on racks stacked up from robbing drug dealers.

On the contrary, Najee wanted more. The desire to hunt down Benzo Al, the ruthless Latino kingpin responsible for the brutal slaughter of his family, consumed him. His obsession with revenge was driving a wedge in their relationship.

"Whatchu' thinking about, babe?" Nella lazily raked a long fingernail across Najee's chiseled abs as she rested on his bare chest. "A woman can tell when her lover has something deep on his mind," she continued.

Her finger traced a circle around the large bullet wound on his stomach. A similar mark was in the same spot on his back. He had received the battle scars when he was fifteen, the same night Los Cinco Diablos massacred his family.

Najee looked toward Nella's empty wheelchair, then he softly kissed each of her eyelids. Although she was defying the odds of paralysis and starting to feel sensation in her legs again, guilt ate through his flesh like a colony of termites. The three hollow points that hit her spine were meant for him. His mind was on retaliation.

Najee's primary target was Benzo Al, but Nella's shooter wore an iced out BBE medallion, so he also had a slug with Sosa's name on it. Nella, however, disagreed with the decision and persuaded Najee not to green-light Sosa until he was absolutely sure of his involvement. She liked Sosa and was convinced that Benzo Al had set him up.

"Answer me, baby. What's going on in that mind of yours?" Nella continued to pester, shaking Najee from his thoughts.

14

Najee sighed. "Why do some females ask so many dang questions? Let's build on something else," he suggested, trying to change the subject.

Nella wasn't having it. "First off, Negro—" she rolled her neck with divatude. "—I'm not *some* female. I'm your future wife. Secondly, I care about you. I love you, Najee, but all you think about is murder, murder, and more murder. When are you gonna start thinking about us?"

"Here we go again," Najee groaned. "Those muthafuckas took away everything I had, baby girl. They left me an orphan to these streets. I thought you had my back?"

"Don't even go there. I literally have the scars on my back to prove that my loyalty is royalty. I just want us to live a normal life. We've been puttin' it down ever since I met you, and we still haven't been able to knock, Benzo Al. He's untouchable, my King. Can't you see that?"

Najee's pupils turned as black as a turbulent monsoon. "It's you who don't understand. This ain't just about revenge, it's about redemption. My whole family was murked because of me. It was my fault," his voice cracked and trailed off.

Nella felt Najee's body go rigid. "Whatchu' mean, it was your fault? Talk to me, baby. I'm not your enemy."

Some things were not meant to be spoken about, but if Najee owed anyone an explanation for his murder expedition, it was his lover, best friend, and confidant. Pulling Nella's body close, he granted her rare access into his past.

"Boulevard was a mack, and my adopted mother was his bottom woman. When the pimp game dried up, Boulevard started flippin' yayo. Benzo Al liked Boulevard's hustler ambition and eventually fronted him ten bricks. Around that same time, I discovered that Boulevard was pimpin' out my mother. I used to get into all kinds of shit at school because the other kids teased me and said my momz had a white sugar daddy. It seemed like everyone knew except me, so out of anger, I flushed the ten keys down the toilet—"

15

Najee paused and his shoulders tensed up. "Anyhow, momz left the life, and we moved, but one day, Boulevard tracked us down and followed me home from school. He didn't realize that he was being followed as well. Cheddar crashed through our front door dumpin'. No words, just gunshots. I wanted to help, but I just stood there like a coward listening to Boulevard wheeze air through a collapsed lung." Najee stopped talking and became distant.

"Go on, I'm listening," Nella encouraged.

Najee took a deep breath and continued, "Cheddar turned his gun on my momma next and shot her in the back. I watched her fall, watched her bleed, watched her die. I finally got the courage to rush Cheddar, but his accomplice, Lil' Wack, slugged me over the head with a sawed-off shotgun and tied me up. When I regained consciousness, Cheddar was tryna' rape my girlfriend, Angel. Our eyes met, and I silently encouraged her to be strong, but she looked away from me and cried. Before they left, he shot her in the face at point-blank range, then shot me in the back. Ever since then, I've had this unquenchable thirst for murder in my heart, and I won't be satisfied until Benzo Al feels my pain!"

Nella shivered at his cold words. Going against the almighty Diablos was a suicide mission, and she was afraid he would meet the same unfortunate fate as his family. "I respect your gangster," she said, letting her curious hand snake its way inside of Najee's Polo boxer briefs. She wrapped a warm hand around his manhood, her fingers unable to touch because of its thickness. "And I respect how you ride for your people, but you caught, Cheddar. You sent him to hell, so why are you so obsessed with, Benzo Al?"

"Benzo Al didn't pull the trigger, he gave the order. To me, that's even worse. That coward gotta go, straight up!"

Nella shook her head at Najee's stubbornness, however, when she spoke again, her voice was soft, sweet, and full of empathy, "You're turning into a monster, baby. The malice in your heart is gonna destroy you. It's gonna destroy us. How long are you going to harbor this absolute hatred and spite in your heart?"

"Until my casket drops!"

"But, honey!"

"Shhhh," Najee placed a finger against Nella's lips. He didn't want to poison the mood any further with his venomous thoughts. Ignoring her inquisitive questions, he focused on her delicious treats.

Nella shivered when Najee's lips touched her Hershey kiss shaped nipples. Her vagina muscles spasmed when his middle finger breached the elastic of her pink panties and caressed her slippery slit. She screamed when he used the tip of his tongue to spell his full government name on her clitoris. She came when he pushed his stiff tool deep into her flaming hot juice box.

He was rock hard, Nella could feel him in her stomach. Each time Najee put it down, the sex was deeper, harder, better. That's the type of man he was. He did everything with raw intensity. Nella's manicured fingernails dug into the crucifix tattoo on his back as he ravished her body like a starving wolf.

"Oh, God, oh God, ooohh Gawd," she moaned the Lord's name in vain.

Najee stroked deep into the pussy, hitting all the right spots and whispering all the right words into Nella's ear. "No matter what happens in the future, always remember that I need you. I cherish you. I adore everything about you."

Najee was raised by some of the most charming pimps and cunning hustlers the game had seen, so he knew the importance of getting into a woman's mind. To a female, the words, *I need you* are more potent than saying, *I love you*. However, Najee was not running game. His words were sincere. Nella was his oxygen, and he would soon find out just how essential she was to his survival.

After two hours of acrobatic lovemaking, their bodies glistened with sweat. They remained locked in an intimate embrace until Nella drifted into a peaceful slumber. When she began to snore lightly, Najee eased out of bed and sat at the maple desk situated in the corner of their luxurious hotel suite in Amsterdam. Having nothing more than a sliver of moonlight shining through the parted curtains, he retrieved an ink pen from the top drawer and began to write the realist shit he ever wrote.

His soul bled between the lines of paper. He passionately expressed his love with poetic syllables until the sun peeked over the horizon. Once complete, he folded the fancy stationery and stuffed it inside an envelope. He had gotten everything off his chest, yet his shoulders still carried a heavy burden.

He was having second thoughts about leaving Nella, but it was the only way to keep her safe. Benzo Al had put a green light on Najee and everyone he loved. Los Cinco Diablos would not rest until their mission was complete. They had already tried to murk Nella once, and Najee wasn't going to give them another opportunity.

The need to explain that he would never abandon the woman who he would one day marry compelled him to open the letter. He ripped the seal with a sharp, gold, envelope opener and passionately expressed his love with poetic syllables.

Once complete, he licked the saccharine tasting glue to seal the envelope and quietly placed the finished letter on the pillow lying next to Nella. For a moment, he admired her angelic features as she slept. She was a beautiful, mulatto redbone with tiny brown freckles sprinkled on her slender nose and high cheekbones.

His eyes slowly traveled from her shoulder-length, jet-black hair, to her succulent D-cup breasts. His gaze lingered on the contours of her voluptuous thighs before ultimately resting on her pretty feet. It was safe to say that Nella was a bad bitch. She was a stomp down murder Mami, and he was going to miss her.

Najee ignored his nagging conscience, leaned forward, and planted a gentle kiss on Nella's forehead. He hoped she would understand the reasoning behind his sudden departure. At the door, he looked back at his wifey one last time, pulled a dark blue hoody over his head, and bounced out. A tragic destiny awaited him.

CHAPTER 2

Rancho Hacienda: Acapulco, Mexico

Lounging on the terrace of a secluded villa in Mexico, Juice enjoyed the picturesque view of the shimmering ocean. The gleaming yellow and orange sun beamed its tropical rays on the private seaside of Hacienda and created an alluring ambiance. He had demolished a large plate of carne asada enchiladas, Spanish rice, and refried beans. Now he was in need of a fat Afghan Kush blunt and some bomb pussy. He let out a loud burp and rubbed his full belly while checking out the bangin' curves on the naked Latina who happily fussed over him.

Juice's lips curled into a naughty grin. "Come get some of this big black Mandingo, Mamacita!" he offered lustfully and reached out to smack the colorful butterfly wings tattooed on each of her ass cheeks. Her round booty jiggled, making it look as though the butterfly was flapping its wings. Juice chuckled and silently thanked Benzo Al for letting him hideout at the cozy villa. He was enjoying the good life, and the names of Najee and Nella never crossed his feeble mind. He was positive both of them had met an early demise.

The looming presence of Benzo Al snagged Juice out of his thoughts. Benzo Al stepped outside onto the patio and took a seat across from Juice. He looked like a Mexican version of *Suge Knight*. Even when he smiled, a permanent scowl disfigured his face. The top two buttons on his red silk shirt were opened, revealing a gold cross nestled between a thick patch of gray and black chest hairs. He did not speak, he leaned back in silence, crossed his legs, and stared at Juice with contempt. The hot, orange ashes on the tip of his Cohiba glowed brighter with each puff.

Juice swallowed a lump of nervousness and squirmed uncomfortably in his seat. "Is everythang straight, boss?" The words felt like sandpaper scratching his tonsils.

Benzo Al expelled a squiggly stream of white smoke in Juice's face. "I'm afraid not. You fucked up big time, homes! That chica is still alive!" He was referring to Nella.

The statement knocked the wind out of Juice. He knew the consequences of fucking up a Diablo mission. "That's impossible," he declared adamantly. "I caught Nella slipping at Najee's funeral and let her have it on the church steps. Blood was everywhere, B. Trust me, that bitch is toast."

"Why should I trust a Chango like you?" Benzo Al called Juice a monkey in Spanish. "You betrayed your own friends. At least Najee had morals. I hate rats, and I hate mistakes even more." He dropped his $100 cigar into Juice's beer bottle. The flame sizzled. Juice stood up to plead his case, but Benzo Al's booming voice paralyzed him. "¡Sientate!" he commanded Juice to sit down. "Your words mean nothing to me. In this organization, we don't tolerate fuck ups. ¿Entiendes? Do you understand?"

Through his peripheral, Juice caught a glimpse of the naked Latina quickly approaching him. Her cordial smile had evaporated. She wrapped a piano wire around his neck and twisted it into a firm knot. She was a Sicario, an assassin. She loved the thrill of the kill. After her first murder as a child, she never looked back.

Known for killing her unsuspecting victims with a technique called the Spanish guillotine, the female assassin was an expert at her craft. She gritted her teeth and tightened her lethal grip until Juice's lungs were deprived of oxygen. The harder he struggled, the more difficult it became for him to breathe.

Juice threw up his last meal and suffocated in his own vomit. His limbs twitched violently before his world dimmed into eternal darkness. A pitiful yellow stain appeared where he had pissed in his pants.

Benzo Al's savagery was not complete. He wanted to send his friends as well as his enemies a clear message. "I feel like having swordfish tonight," Benzo Al announced. "Chop off Juice's dick, put a hook through it, and use it as bait." Even his brutal assassin cringed at his cruelty but did not hesitate to follow orders. She went inside and reappeared with a sharp machete.

Benzo Al watched the blue waves crash into the white sand-banks. His power and respect were growing immensely amongst his syndicate peers. Los Cinco Diablos was one of the deadliest and most profitable criminal cartels in the Western hemisphere. Los Cinco Diablos translates into The Five Devils in English. It received its name because the members had their hands into everything from drugs, prostitution, gambling, counterfeit goods, murder, and money laundering. Their power and influence reached from the bowels of the darkest corners of the underworld to the Oval Office of the White House.

Just as a human hand has five fingers, Los Cinco Diablos has five board members, each with equal authority. Yet, even with all of their street power and political might, they were not immune to difficulties. The Border Patrol had recently confiscated five tons of cocaine, causing an oppressive drought in hoods across the U.S. Then there was a potentially dangerous feud brewing between their ranks.

Benzo Al's stepbrother, Carlos Manuel Guzman, was also a well-respected Diablo member and Benzo Al's biggest critic. Carlos felt that Benzo Al's extravagant lifestyle, senseless murders, and brushes with the law were bringing unwanted heat and attention to the organization.

Benzo Al was enticed by the game at a young age, and he used murder, ambition, and hustle muscle in order to claw his way up the ladder of success. His struggles made him resent his father and illegitimate stepbrother.

****

Benzo Al stood on the patio gazing at the choppy waves with a bad feeling rumbling in his stomach. Another cartel war was on the horizon, and there were signs that Najee was still out there.

The chime of his Motorola satellite phone jolted him from his deep thoughts. Only a select few had the ultra-secret number. He switched phones as frequently as he changed underwear. He flipped up the thick, black antenna and growled into the receiver with the confidence of a seasoned boss.

"This better be good news, Oscar. I was right in the middle of something important," he stated with authority.

"Si, señor," the excited voice answered with respect. "We located that chica, Nella. She's laying low at the Sofitel Hotel in Amsterdam." Oscar was posted up across the street from the hotel, positioned under the canopy of a café. He had an unobstructed view of the front entrance.

Benzo Al raised a skeptical eyebrow. "Amsterdam? Is that puta alone, Ese?"

"No, El Jeffe," he looked around nervously. "She was laid up with a mayate. This vato is real paranoid. He just left the hotel with a hoody pulled over his head and is looking over his shoulder to make sure he ain't being followed. I got one of my shooters tailing his shadow. Just give me the green light and his bitch ass is dead, Ese."

A rush of icy adrenalin surged through Benzo Al's veins. He stroked his salt and pepper goatee, recalling that Najee's remains could not be positively identified. "Describe this vato to me, mi amigo."

Oscar flicked his cigarette butt on the curb and tapped the menu icon on his cell phone. He scrolled to the picture he had snapped of a man exiting the hotel wearing a blue Akoo hoody. "No problem, I'm texting his pic to you now, carnale."

Benzo Al's satellite phone beeped when the transmission came through. He examined the image closely. The shifty-eyed man in the photo was stocky and dark-skinned with a square chin and hollow cheeks. It was not Najee. Benzo Al expelled an audible sigh of relief. "Muy bien, compadre. You did an excellent job tracking that puta down. This proves that nobody, no matter where they run, can hide from the almighty Los Cinco Diablos." He rolled a string of rosary beads between his fingers, a common practice amongst Latino drug lords who worshipped Santeria. They believed the Catholic deities provided power, protection, and prosperity.

The caller smiled, showing off his fucked-up grill. Two of his front teeth were missing. The rest were crooked with brown tobacco stains. "What do you want us to do with the bodies, Ese?"

"Burn them just like her and those banditos burned my cocaína!" Benzo Al green-lighted Nella and her anonymous companion, but then he paused to reconsider his last order. For him, it was all about stacking chips and emptying clips, however, his stepbrother Carlos was scrutinizing his every move, so he needed to show some discretion.

"On second thought, I have a better idea," Benzo Al grinned mischievously. "Let the vato go free and concentrate on the pinche puta."

"Are you sure, homes? This might be our only opportunity to murk both of them," Oscar pointed out.

"I feel you, but if you sneak in and sneak out quickly and quietly, he will have been the last person who was seen with her. The policía will pin the body on him. Entiendes?"

Oscar nodded his head with understanding, impressed with Benzo Al's shrewdness. "That's a clever idea, homes. I feel you."

"And, Oscar," Benzo Al spoke in a somber tone. "Don't fuck this up. Make sure that black cunt has a painful death, but do it professionally," he warned through clenched teeth and pressed the end call button without waiting for a reply.

Larry D. Wright

CHAPTER 3

Sofitel Hotel: Amsterdam

The sound of hushed whispers conspiring outside of her hotel room door jolted Nella awake. She sat up in bed and listened intensely trying to decipher whether the voices were benign or life-threatening. Two Diablo hitmen were arguing in Spanish.

Nella did not speak their language fluently, but after living and trying not to die in Los Angeles, she had picked up a few words of Español. Her heart thumped in her chest when she heard the word pistola. They were having a heated debate over who would get the privilege of putting a bullet in her head. In the end, they flipped a coin.

Nella's eyes immediately became acclimated to the darkness. She focused on the shadows at the bottom of the door. Two sets of shoes loitered on the other side. "Psst, Najee, wake up, bae!" she whispered.

Oscar jiggled the door handle. Fear slithered down Nella's spine. She reached out to shake Najee awake, but his side of the bed was empty, he was gone. She instantly jumped into G-mode. Najee always slept with his heat cocked and unlocked, so she reached under his pillow. In doing so, she inadvertently knocked his unread letter on the floor without seeing it. She frantically groped under the pillow searching for his strap but couldn't find it.

"Shit!" she cursed when she remembered that she had told Najee that she didn't want to be around any firearms while they were on vacation. Now she regretted her foolish decision.

She scanned the room for a weapon. Anything heavy would do. The only object she saw was a sharp, gold letter opener lying on the desk. She also noticed that Najee's backpack was gone. Confusion riddled her mind.

Oscar slid the credit card-sized hotel key into the door handle. The distinct *chic-chic* sound demanded Nella's attention. She swiveled around in time to see the small red light on the door handle turn green. The lock clicked open. Oscar eased the door ajar slowly and quietly.

Nella needed to move, and she needed to do it fast. She struggled to get out of bed, but her legs wouldn't cooperate. The drive-by shooting had left her legs paralyzed. Although she was beginning to feel stimulation in her toes, she still needed months of physical therapy. Improvising for her handicap, she used her hands to swing each of her legs over the edge of the bed. She bit her bottom lip, ignored the pain in her joints, and stood on her own two feet. She felt like a baby walking for the first time. She took a brave step forward, however, her brittle knees buckled under her body weight. She collapsed next to her wheelchair, hoping, praying.

The door creaked open. Two hulking figures towered over her. Nella could smell the odor of stale cigarette smoke in their clothes and cheap tequila on their breath.

"Help!" she yelled, but Oscar roughly covered her mouth, the palm of his callous hand muffling her scream.

"Shut the fuck up, bitch!" He grabbed a fist full of Nella's hair and snatched her to her feet.

His accomplice, a tatted-up cholo named Joker, slammed the door shut. He earned the name Joker because his facial features resembled an evil clown laughing. Imagine a piranha smiling at you. He retrieved a .380 from the small of his back, screwed an Armalite silencer onto the barrel, and racked a Teflon slug into the chamber.

Nella's teary eyes begged for mercy, but her assailants knew nothing of leniency. Oscar reached back like Rick James and slapped the taste buds off her tongue. Nella's legs wobbled like boiled spaghetti. She fell backward, banging her head against the nightstand, the hard collision almost knocked her unconscious. Oscar drew back and viciously punched her in the mouth before she could recover. His steel knuckles busted her lips.

"Please don't hurt me," Nella begged. "If it's money you're after, I'll give it to you." She had fifty bands hidden in the cushion of her wheelchair seat. Unfortunately, her offer was rejected.

Another blow drew blood from her nose. The pain was unbearable.

Joker belched out a wicket laugh. Misery was his amusement, however, he was more focused and disciplined than his crime partner. He was strictly about that gunplay. He watched Oscar bash Nella once more, then he tapped his homie on the shoulder. Nella's lip was split, and her left eye was swollen shut.

"That's enough, Ese. I won the coin toss, so let me pop a cap in this puta so we can be out." He clicked his banger off safety.

Oscar had other ideas. His lust-filled eyes molested Nella's naked body. He licked his chapped lips while staring at her round, brown areolas and perky nipples. His unwanted glare gave Nella the creeps. She recoiled and folded her arms across her bare breasts. In doing so, she left the smooth triangle between her legs exposed.

Oscar stooped down, rubbed her bikini waxed slit, and then sniffed his middle finger. The musky-sweet aroma of her vagina gave him a stiff erection. Repulsed, Nella snapped and smacked the shit out of him. She countered with a ferocious right hook to the jaw. If she was gonna die, then she was going out like a rider, she decided. Her sharp claws raked across Oscar's face leaving his bloody flesh under her fingernails. Oscar covered his eyes with both hands and screamed.

"Who's the bitch now, you punk muthafucka?" Nella grabbed the heavy, old fashion telephone off the nightstand and smashed Oscar upside the head. The force of the blow made his ears ring.

Joker laughed and shook his head in disappointment. *'If only people knew how much of a fuck up Oscar was,'* he thought to himself. He glanced at his watch and tapped his foot impatiently.

Rage overtook Oscar. He lashed out with a backhand across Nella's bruised cheek and then threw her on the bed. "You like to dish out pain, huh?" he asked with malicious intentions. "By the time I'm done with you, you're gonna beg me to put a bullet in your forehead," he promised. He ripped open his shirt and unzipped his blue jeans. The butt of a Taurus nine-milli protruded from his waistline.

Nella ignored the gun and zoomed in on the black hand tatted on his chest. Every Los Cinco Diablos soldier had the same tattoo branded over his hearts. Nella's mouth dropped open in disbelief. *"How did they find us?"* she wondered.

The goons were not there for money. They were there for murder. In a clandestine underworld where millions are made over overnight, the only currency that mattered to Benzo Al was death.

Oscar looked over his shoulder and made eye contact with Joker. "Ay, homes, leave us alone for a minute. I need to teach this chica a lesson."

Joker shifted uncomfortably. He knew what Oscar had in mind. Rape was morally offensive and went against everything Los Cinco Diablos stood for. Punishment for such a hideous crime included torture before castration and then finally, death.

"I know whatchu' thinking, Ese, but I can't let it go down. We live by sacred codes, homie. Raping a chica could get us both killed," Joker explained.

Oscar twisted his lips into a sour frown. "Ay, Ese, I know the devil ain't tryin' to preach to the choir," he shot back. "The code also says don't get high off your own supply, but that don't stop you from powdering your nose. Does it, homes?"

Joker sniffled. The monkey on his back had grown into a gorilla. He wavered for a moment, then laughed his demented laugh. Before turning to leave, he tapped the face of his watch. "Hurry up, Ese, I got next."

Nella knew what was about to pop off. She was scared, she was helpless. Above all, she was angry with Najee for not being there when she needed him most. A salty tear rolled down her cheek and rested in the crease of her quivering lips.

Oscar grabbed Nella by the throat, squeezing her neck tightly as he pointed his heat between her eyebrows. "We can do this the easy way, or we can do this the hard way, it's up to you."

Nella looked down the dark barrel of the nine-mill. She was prepared to fight, but the lethal cannon was the equalizer and gave Oscar the upper hand. She surrendered. She stared up at the spinning blades of the ceiling fan with a blank look on her face as her attacker climbed on top of her. She cringed at the sight of his fucked-up grill. She would never be the same again, never!

Oscar stumbled to the bathroom in order to wash away the evidence of his perverted crime. A loud crash in the next room caused him to rush out and investigate. Nella had fallen off the bed.

"Wus good, mamacita, you want some more?" he remarked sarcastically.

Nella laid on the floor next to the large maple desk with one of her hands concealed behind her back. She opened her legs, enticing Oscar to come closer. He kneeled and Nella attacked brandishing the sharp, gold plated letter opener that Najee had earlier. She swung with the strength and rage of a woman who had just been violated. The tip of the blade plunged into Oscar's right eye. Before he could react, she pulled it out and stabbed him in the left pupil. Bright, red blood gushed out of both eye sockets like crimson tears. Oscar lashed out blindly. Falling to his knees, he clutched his face in the palms of his hands and squealed like a filthy pig.

Joker was posted up by the ice machine trying to look as inconspicuous as a coked-up criminal could. He glanced up and down the hallway before placing his ear to the door. *Blocka! Blocka!* Loud gunshots beat on his eardrums.

Inside the hotel room, Oscar looked down at his crotch. If he could see, he would have seen two deep craters where his testicles used to be. *Blocka!* Nella drilled him once more in the gut. Oscar toppled over and died with his limp dick hanging out of his zipper.

Joker frantically fumbled with the hotel key card, finally sliding it into the lock. He waited for the red light to turn green, and then he burst through the door with his heat extended. Murder greeted him. Lying flat on her belly, Nella double-tapped the trigger. Joker caught the Teflon coated shells with his teeth. The back of his head exploded, staining the fancy wallpaper in the hallway. A half-naked hotel patron peeked out of the door, saw the carnage, and wisely retreated into his room content with minding his own business.

After watching Joker's frail body tumble backward, Nella turned the pistol on herself. She squeezed her eyes shut and pressed the hot barrel against her temple. Oscar had robbed her of her most precious possession. No matter how many times she killed him, she could never get back what he took. She didn't want to cry, she wanted to die. Her index finger applied pressure on the trigger, but someone appeared in the doorway.

"Mademoiselle are you okay?" the friendly, chubby, French maid who cleaned the second floor inquired softly. She cautiously eased into the suite being careful not to step in any of the blood that soaked the plush carpet. The gruesome sight of two dead bodies did not faze her.

She spotted Nella holding the strap to her dome. "Madame don't do it! Don't go out like this!" She pried the murder weapon out of Nella's trembling fingers, draped a robe over her shoulders, and helped her into her wheelchair.

On the way out of the door, Nella hocked a wad of spit in Oscar's face. "You sick, bastard!" she screamed.

The chubby French maid pushed the wheelchair to the freight elevator. "Hurry, hurry! We have to move quickly." Once in the lobby, she rolled Nella out of the front entrance unnoticed just as several police cars pulled up.

Nella rejuvenated at the maid's two-bedroom flat for a month. In exchange for her hospitality, Nella broke the maid off twenty racks before secretly returning to Los Angeles while the maid was at work. The maid never got a chance to give Nella the love letter that she had recovered from the hotel room. There was also another secret that she could not reveal. The secret nibbled on her conscience and would come back to haunt her.

The chaos in Nella's world amplified when she got back to Cali. She couldn't locate Najee. He was MIA and so was her period. She discovered that she was pregnant but didn't know if the baby belonged to Najee or the rapist. She was in a catch-22 and needed to decide between keeping the baby or having an abortion.

CHAPTER 4

Atlanta, Georgia

Sosa's extravagant mansion sat upon five acres of lush, green land. The six-bedroom terra cotta abode on Belair Lake Drive was a far cry from the concrete battlefield he was born and raised in. Normally, the serene suburban neighborhood with its uber-rich residents was a quiet and tranquil community, however, tonight the spot was jumping like a jam-packed club.

In typical BBE fashion, celebrities, famous athletes, musicians, and drug dealers mingled under one roof. They all came to pay homage to Sosa and bid him farewell. Magnums of expensive champagne and silver platters brimming with lines of powder cocaine circulated liberally. Gray clouds of cannabis smoke made the mansion look like a dim pool hall.

The High-Intensity Drug Trafficking Area task force, a joint venture between the local PD and the DEA, had the house and its colorful patrons under heavy surveillance. The pictures the HIDTA snapped could have easily appeared in an issue of Hip Hop Weekly.

For several summers, Sosa had the game in a headlock, but now he was on a new page. He had gracefully bowed out of the game caked up and with his good reputation intact, a feat every street nigga dreams about.

Sosa could not have chosen a better time to make his exodus. U.S. Customs had intercepted tons of Los Cinco Diablos cocaine at Texas, Arizona, and California borders, driving coke prices sky-high and sending the D-Boys into a frenzy. In addition, his Block Boy Empire crew was the target of a Continuing Criminal Enterprise investigation, a charge that guarantees a minimum sentence of twenty years. CCE indictments are primarily used against narcotic traffickers who operate elaborate, long term, corrupt organizations that function like a business, and BBE most definitely functioned like a corporation.

Sosa stood by his brick fireplace watching everyone rotate through blunted eyes. Reality TV stars mingled with Hip-Hop moguls, Pro athletes tossed it up with flashy niggas, and the coke boys were lurking in the darkest corners. Their gold grills gleamed like metallic bottles of Ace of Spades.

A bad, high-yellow, Dominican bitch eyed Sosa from afar. She rolled a crisp one-hundred-dollar bill into a straw, sniffed two lines of blow off the platter, and rehearsed her lines before sliding up on Sosa, shaking him out of his thoughts. She seductively snaked her pink tongue across her tantalizing lips and said, "This is your special night, Sosa. Why are you posted up in the corner by yourself?" her Dominica accent made her drip with sex appeal.

Sosa's eyes started at her neatly painted toenails and paused at the wide gap between her legs, then lingered on to the stiff nipples proudly protruding through her BCBG blouse, and stopped at her dazzling, hazel eyes. She had gold digger written across her face, but Sosa didn't care. He was buzzin' off Purple Harem, throwed off Louie, and wanted to smash something with a big butt and a cute smile.

Adjusting his platinum and black diamond crucifix, he responded smoothly, "I'm not hiding, I just like to lay low. Feel me? Sup with you tho', what's your name and who you with?"

"My name is, Katrina," the bad, yellow-bone blushed excitedly. "And I'm with you for as long as you want me." The high-quality yayo had her pussy moist.

Stepping closer to Sosa, Katrina put her hand in his front pocket and rubbed his dick through his slacks. His long, thick manhood rose to the occasion. She knew who Sosa was and what kind of paper he was working with. If he wanted her to she would have dropped to her knees and bossed him off, right there.

Sosa wrapped his strong hands around her small waist and whispered, "I'm finna take you up to my room, slip an ecstasy pill up yo' ass, and beat that phat monkey 'till it's funky. You rollin' with a nigga or what?" Sosa always kept it real, blunt and to the point.

"I thought you would never ask." She continued working his stiff dick, excited that she could not wrap her fingers around his thickness.

Katrina was a true hustler. She came to the star-studded affair hoping to use her voluptuous goodies in order to entice a hood-rich nigga or an up and coming rapper. However, she did not expect to catch a baller of Sosa's caliber. A plethora of conniving schemes percolated in her head.

"I have to go to the ladies' room first," she announced. "So, don't run off with none of these thirsty bitches I see scoping you out. Ain't none of them thots flexible and double-jointed like me."

"Damn, gurl, you got it like that?" Sosa's dick stiffened and grew another inch.

Katrina winked and made her way to the bathroom. Sosa was watching her round booty wobble like a bowl of Jello when a BBE trooper named Ice approached him.

Ice, a twenty-five-year-old hot boy, coveted Sosa's vacant leadership position. Towering at 6'2, with smooth, dark skin the color of black olive, he earned his street cred by clappin' his steel, jacking out of town studs, and throwing them thangs like Mayweather. Although Ice had potential, he was racing toward a catastrophic collision with hell or a federal holding cell.

As a teen, Ice had a kaleidoscope view of hard times and heartache. The whereabouts of his deadbeat father were a mystery, his mother was hooked on the pipe, and her abusive boyfriend was hooked on the needle. Hunger pangs and the threat of eviction were common occurrences in his world.

Two months prior to meeting Sosa, Ice came home early from school and caught his mother on her knees in the middle of the living room sucking the landlord's dick in lieu of the late rent. Her pathetic boyfriend was locked in the bathroom. His hand shook badly as he held a Bic lighter up to the bottom of a dirty spoon. The flame made the water and Heroin sizzle. His filthy syringe anxiously awaited a vein between his toes.

Outraged, Ice looked for something he could use as a weapon, but the small apartment was bare because his mom and her dope fiend boyfriend had sold everything that wasn't nailed down.

Feeling defeated, Ice backed out of the apartment with tears rushing down his cheeks. He ran and ran until he literally ran into S-Dizzle and Fly, the neighborhood thugs. They had seen Ice around the block stealing bikes and hitting petty licks, so they took him in figuring he would make a good lookout and errand boy.

One rainy night, they were on the Ave pitching nickel and dime rocks when S-Dizzle spotted a familiar hype hobbling up the street. "Ay, my niggas, there go, Renetha Lee, the clucker with no front teeth. I'm finna see if she'll suck my dick again for a dime piece." He pointed to a skinny, forty-something woman who had seen better days.

"On what?" Fly asked in disbelief. "That bad breath bitch charged me two dubs for that throat. I can't lie though, her head game is bananas." He chuckled and high-fived S-Dizzle.

Hearing his mother's name being defamed pushed Ice to the brink of insanity. Raindrops pelted his face as he strained to get a better look at the woman. For a moment, he was relieved. The frail zombie staggering up the block looked nothing like his mother. His joy, however, was short-lived. The woman passed under the glow of a street-lamp, and Ice got a clear view of her features. Gone was the beautiful woman he remembered and loved. She had lost twenty pounds since the last time he saw her, and two of her front teeth were missing.

Ice turned to S-Dizzle. "Let me see yo' gun, Dawg!"

S-Dizzle sucked his teeth. "For what, lil' nigga? You ain't no killa, youz a paper soldier." He puffed on a stale blunt packed with Bobby Brown and blew a foul-smelling blast of weed smoke in Ice's face.

Ice grew impatient. "Just let me see yo' ratchet. I need to sweat somebody." He looked over his shoulder, his mother was crossing the street.

S-Dizzle peeped the serious look on Ice's face and pulled a blue steel .32 from the pocket of his leather Pelle. He passed it to

Ice with a warning, "Don't fuck 'round and get my pistol ganked. Who you 'bout to sweat anyways?"

"You, nigga!" Ice pulled the trigger.

Blam! Blam!

S-Dizzle folded over, smoke rose from the bullet holes in his Pelle. Fly attempted to flee, but Ice drilled him in the legs, back, and head. His twisted body landed half on the curb half in the street. Heavy rain washed his blood into the gutter. Ice stared at the dead bodies, his feet unable to move until he heard a voice coming from the window of a black Jag.

"Hurry up and get in!" Sosa yelled out of the window. Ice hesitated before accepting the invitation. Once the car twisted off, Sosa passed him a blunt. "Relax, my dude. You safe with me. Those fuck niggas was short stopping my custies. BBE could use another soldier like you."

Over the years, Ice had forgotten most of the sordid details that occurred on that rainy night, but the disapproving look on his mother's face was a sorrowful portrait that remained painted in his mind. She wasn't concerned with his health or safety. She wasn't mad that he had run away. She was angry because she had to find a new dope man.

****

Sosa was still watching Katrina's backside when Ice jarred him out of his lustful daydream. "What it is, big homie?" Ice greeted with a handshake and a shoulder bump. His diamond-studded smile revealed the origins of his nickname.

"Same shit, different toilet, my dude. What's poppin' with you and the crew?" Sosa probed with genuine concern. He now spent most of his time floating between the Durty and the West Coast.

"Shizz, keepin' it one-hondo, Ahki. It's been all bad." Ice sniffled while wiping cocaine residue from his nostrils. "We still beefin' with them Baton Rouge niggas. The knockers been smashing through kicking indoors, and we can't find a plug for some heavyweight. Benzo Al got that A-1, but he won't even return my phone calls."

Sosa cringed at the mention of large quantities of coke. The game was dead, and he didn't want anything to do with selling drugs. He put a brotherly arm around Ice's shoulder and led him to a quiet corner away from the turned-up partygoers.

"Lem' me chop it up with you for a sec, nephew. Be careful what you say and who you say it to," he spoke with a calm authority, his body swaying side to side like a cobra. "The game is cold. Loyalty, betrayal, love, and murder are spoken in the same sentence. That's why I retired, I got tired of the bullshit. Make sho' you move with caution, my nigga. The Feds can make a hundred mistakes, but if you make one wrong move, it's a wrap. Ya' heard?" Sosa said his peace, mobbed off and found Katrina in the bathroom just as she was about to send a text message.

"Damn!" Katrina cursed in frustration. She heard Sosa coming through the door and quickly stuffed her iPhone into her Gucci clutch, aggravated that she was unable to hit the send button. Sosa bent her over the sink, pulled down her tight shorts, and tugged her white thong to the side. Forgetting to slip on a Magnum, he plunged his entire 11-inch monster into her wet pussy in one long stroke.

Katrina gripped the sink and gasped, "Ahhh, dang, daddy! Take it easy on a bitch." Her vagina muscles squeezed his instrument as she came. The pungent smell of weed smoke lingering in the air camouflaged the fishy odor coming from between her legs. Sosa held on to her yellow hips and pulverized her tight pussy with his tool. Her ass cheeks rippled like waves with each stroke.

Ice was left fuming. Sosa's wise words went in one ear and out the other. "I hear you, alright. I hear you loud and clear, nigga." Resentment began to incubate in his heart.

CHAPTER 5

Blood on The Money

8 Months Later

Tropical sunshine, tall palm trees, and sandy beaches camouflage the treacherous barrios of Los Angeles. However, lurking beneath the glitz and artificial glamour of Tinsel town lie the city of Hawthorne. Once a thriving, mostly Caucasian community, poor Hispanics, struggling black folks, and chaos now plague its grimy blocks. These rough streets were Najee's stomping grounds and the place where a slim, Haitian, D-Boy named Stix foolishly decided to set up shop.

Lounging in his sparsely furnished trap house, Stix poured himself a drink and split open a Blackwood cigar with his long fingernails. He took a sip of Ciroc before emptying the brown tobacco into an ashtray filled with old cigarette butts. He replaced the tobacco with sticky nuggets of Grape Ape.

The mid-level street pharmacist had dark, acne plagued skin and nappy dreadlocks that were dyed blond on the tips. He sparked the fat blunt, took a deep toke, and admired his operation through blood-shot red eyes.

Two skinny white girls sat at a round kitchen table, chain-smoking Marlboro Lights and stuffing large stacks of currency into money counter machines. The rapid flutter of dollar bills was music to Stix's ears.

His Enforcer, a Haitian refugee who migrated to the U.S. after a devastating earthquake rocked Port-au-Prince, was doing exactly what he was paid to do—be quiet and look mean. He stood in the corner of the kitchen with his python sized biceps folded across his white wife-beater.

Everything was moving smoothly. Stix had met a sexy bartender at the King of Diamonds Strip Club in Miami, and after giving her some hard, Haitian dick, she plugged him in with a Cuban hustler who was connected to Los Cinco Diablos. After her introduction, Stix literally went from serving pieces to pushing weight overnight. His hustle had slowed down due to the drought, but thanks to the Diablos, he was still getting paper.

The secret to Stix's grind was his cold whip game. He could cook crack and make the work jump back with extra grams. He would serve the perfectly shaped cookies straight from the Pyrex, the added water weight tipping the scale in his favor. His only fault was bumpin' his gums too much.

His gwuap wasn't long enough to be fucking directly with the boss, yet that didn't stop Stix from stuntin' hard and running his mouth. Every time he tossed it up at trendy nightclubs or cashed out on a new whip, he let it be known that he was getting it in with Benzo Al. His flashy indiscretions earned him a visit from Najee.

Najee crept up to the trap house on Freeman Street with the stealth of a walking nightmare. He was cloaked in a black hoody, black Timbs, a black Jason hockey mask, and a black cloud hovered above him. His menacing attire matched his attitude.

Haitians are born killers, no doubt, but the loud Caribbean music blasting from an open window and the lack of surveillance cameras lining the perimeter of the house immediately let Najee know that he was dealing with a clique of amateurs. He took a deep breath and racked a slug into the cavity of his heat. Although he had a body count as long as Martin Luther King Boulevard, he still got nervous before each hit. Sweat lathered his palms.

Inside the smoky spot, Stix lounged on a leather couch, with a blunt dangling from the corner of his mouth and his eyes glued to a 65-inch flat-screen imagining he was Mad Max from the movie Shottas. Translation, he was slippin'.

Najee kicked in the front door waving the four-four. "Er'body get down before I lay you the fuck down!" he demanded, his eyes quickly surveying the scene.

The splintered door hung on one flimsy brass hinge. The startled occupants froze, eyes wide, hearts pounding. Realizing the intruder was not the po-po conducting a raid, Stix lunged for his chopper.

Najee upped a second .44 magnum and warned, "Pump yo' breaks, fuck boy!"

Stix wisely put his hands in the air, but the Enforcer raised his thumper and popped off three rounds in Najee's direction. His aim was off. The stray bullets knocked chunks out of the drywall above Najee's head.

Najee dropped to one knee and let both cannons bark. Two bullets hit the Enforcer in the chest. The armor-piercing ammo made an exit through his back, splattering a huge pile of dollar bills with speckles of blood. As the Enforcer's ankles buckled, Najee aimed one of the burners at Stix and the other at the petrified white hoes.

"Alright, mufuckaz, let's try this shit again. Get down before I lay you down!" Najee ordered. The trio immediately laid flat on their stomachs with their hands laced behind their heads. Neither of them put up resistance as Najee wrapped gray duct tape around their wrists and ankles.

"Gimme this blunt, nigga." He snatched the half-smoked blunt from Stix's lips and took a deep pull. The potent ganja circulated through his lungs, raced to his brain, and put a satisfied grin on his lips. He flicked the gray ashes off the tip, unzipped a large, black Nike duffel bag and removed another bag. He worked quickly and methodology, filling the first sack with cash.

Najee stepped over the so-called Enforcer's corpse and scraped a pile of stained bills off the kitchen table, into the second black sack. "Now this is what I call blood money," he commented coldly and zipped each bag.

Stix struggled to break free. "Youz ah dead mon. Do you know who'z money ya' dealing with?" His Caribbean accent was velvety.

Najee frowned at the gaffled up Haitian. "Yeah, I know exactly whose dough I'm fucking with, and I'm gon' keep fucking Benzo Al over until I get close enough to twist his cap off." Najee wasn't in the game for the money. He was the ghetto version of Robin Hood. He stole from Benzo Al's hood-rich drug lords and gave the loot to the inner-city poor.

"That's where ya' wrong, bloodclot," Stix kept talking, hoping to distract Najee while one of the skinny white girls worked to wiggle her scrawny wrist free. "Nobody gets close to, Benzo Al. He iz ah ghost. Even I no meet tha boss," he spoke the truth. Benzo Al wasn't trying to meet anybody new.

"So, let me get this shit straight. You tellin' me that you're counting all these stacks, but you ain't never met, Benzo Al?"

Stix nodded his head in confirmation. "A few racks don't mean nothin' to, Benzo Al. He wipes his ass with this type of chump change. In order to meet tha boss, ya' must push major weight. Dere no other way."

"Fuck what you talking 'bout. I don't believe you." Najee pointed both burners at Stix. "I'm going to untie one of yo' hands so you can call Benzo Al. Tell him that you got his paper ready, but you need to holler at him in person."

Stix laughed. "You no listen, Benzo Al is a ghost, and you're a dead mon. By tomorrow morning, dem Los Cinco Diablos boyz have ya' head. Dem feed you to piranhas."

Najee grew impatient. "Where is Benzo Al, nigga?"

"Go to hell, pussy, Boi!"

"You first." Najee held the strap sideways and knocked Stix's noodles loose. A stream of dark red blood oozed out of the ugly gash in his temple.

Next, Najee turned his weapons on the two weeping white girls. Their blue eyes pleaded for a pardon. He knew that compassion was a bitch with sharp teeth, and his actions would eventually come back to bite him on the ass.

'*It is what it is,*' he told himself. He had already drug too many non-combatants into his war with Benzo Al. The trigger has no heart, however, Najee decided to let them live.

He strolled out of the ram-shacked home, looked both ways, and slung the heavy bags into the back of a Porsche Cayenne. The loud wail of police sirens blared in the distance. He wished Nella was by his side puttin' it down, he missed her immensely. Nella kept Najee balanced. Without her in his life, his equilibrium was off, and he was spiraling into a deep abyss. He started to drink heavily, and his weed habit was off the chain. Trying to fix the past was jeopardizing his future.

He pressed the gas pedal and the Porsche's dual exhaust purred like a hungry feline. The rugged voice of the *Pancake Man* rapping over a thunderous beat rattled the 15" Solar Baric woofers. Najee's crafty mind was so occupied with articulating his next move that he did not peep the two Caucasian DEA agents discreetly parked down the street in a tan Crown Victoria. One of the agents jotted down Najee's license plate number as the other snapped pictures with a long lens Nikon camera.

"Shouldn't we respond to the Code-1 that just came over the scanner?" asked Special Agent John Sullivan, a young crime-fighter who was a third-generation cop.

His partner, Special Agent Steven Rossetti, stuffed his ink pen and note pad into the breast pocket of his suit. "No, let the local PD handle the shots fired call. We've been investigating Los Cinco Diablos for far too long to blow our cover. Besides, I wanna know more about this new character in the Porsche." The seasoned DEA agent twisted the key in the ignition and merged into traffic.

Special Agent Steven Rossetti was a veteran with seventeen years on the force and as crooked as they came. Cats in the streets gave him the nickname Blondie because he had pale white skin and a head full of golden hair. He was notoriously known for planting narcotics on suspects, illegal wiretaps, perjury, robbery, and outright corruption.

Federal prosecutors and judges tolerated his draconian, strong-arm tactics because he produced incredible results. The cases Blondie investigated had a 98.8% conviction rate, and to a frustrated government that was losing the war on drugs, the ends justified the means. The bad guys were behind bars, the crime rate was low, and hopes for re-election were high. Blondie was not an outlaw, he was their hero.

Najee obeyed the strict speed limit and cruised North on the 110 Harbor Freeway nodding his head to the hardcore rap lyrics. He had dropped off one of the duffel bags, making an anonymous donation to a struggling performance arts school in Watts. Now he was headed to the badlands. The badlands are home to the homeless, hopeless, and heartless. Murder, prostitution, robbery, drug dealing, and absolute lawlessness abound, making this square mile of treacherous concrete the most dangerous slums in America.

In the early 80s, in an attempt to stop the Tsunami like crime wave from spilling over into the nearby downtown business district, the government erected a five-story brick mansion notoriously known as the Bungalow Projects. The city camouflaged their attempt to sweep the problem under the rug by calling the poorly built compound affordable, low-income housing. Despite the Housing Authority's efforts, the crime rate soared. The Bungalows became so savage that even the police feared patrolling its boundaries. Najee, however, had hope.

He had dreams of using his ill-gotten funds to clean up the dilapidated projects. His plans included building a recreation center for the poverty-stricken kids and a computer lab and job placement office for the disenfranchised adults, but his war with Benzo Al kept his visions from coming to fruition. He contemplated the incomplete items that lingered on his bucket list as he switched lanes, sped up, and pushed toward the Bungalows with a bag full of money.

Blondie gripped the steering wheel and smiled. "Watch and learn, rookie! Watch and learn! The most effective way to follow someone is to not follow them at all. I like to coast in front of them like we're doing with this suspect. Criminals are so occupied with looking over their shoulders, they don't pay attention to what's right in front of them."

Agent Sullivan sat in the passenger seat and soaked up game.

****

Najee drove until he found himself trapped between two worlds. To the West, majestic steel pyramids with shiny-mirrored windows and luxurious corner offices stretched into the stratosphere of downtown L.A. However, to the East, a crumbling, five-story brick building plagued the improvised landscape like a rotten tooth. A rickety sign outside of the decaying structure cordially welcomed visitors to the Bungalow Projects as if the poverty-stricken section of town was an attraction at Disney Land.

Najee swooped up being extra careful not to scrape the chrome Asanti rims on the curb. His next lick was at a Cinco Diablo chop shop, so he needed the SUV to be in pristine condition.

A black iron gate surrounded the tall building, making it look like a maximum-security prison. The expensive Porsche truck appeared out of place amongst the graffiti-covered walls, broken down cars, and malnourished dope fiends loitering about and plotting on their next fix. Najee, however, showed no fear or trepidation. He was raised in an environment that was just as toxic.

Tucking his burner in the small of his back, he stepped out of the SUV with a duffel bag full of gwuap slung over his shoulder. The local gang bangers and thirsty street corner hustlers took notice and huddled into a group. Whispers of stripping Najee of the Porsche truck and money circulated.

"That nigga sweet," remarked a rugged looking, twenty-six-year-old hot head named Sincere. He upped his TEC-9 and toyed with the trigger. Sincere had dipped to Cali because he was on the run from some killers who ran the Trey's in Milwaukee. "I say we split this boy's wig, then split the money. Feeling me, fammo?"

The congregation of hardened criminals murmured their agreement. Sincere yanked the shaft back on the TEC and a slug sprang into the empty chamber. "Just say the word, Fam, and I'm on that ass," he instigated.

Gotti, a soft-spoken, twenty-seven-year-old drug dealer who was born and raised in the Bungalows held up his hands to calm his crew. "I feel you, Sincere, but we don't know who this cat is. He could be plugged. The last thang we need is some more drama." His rough neck demeanor did not match his soft voice.

"That square ass nigga ain't plugged, he crazy for thinking he could come up in the Jects without an escort," Sincere grilled Najee with murder in his pupils.

"True dat, true dat," Gotti agreed as he thought about the candy paint and 30-inch DUB floaters he recently slapped on his '73 Caprice thanks to Najee. "But think about this, my nigga, every time dude comes through and play Mr. Big Shot, the hypes bring the money directly to us. It's like the first of the month all over again." He chewed on the end of a worn toothpick.

Gotti's point was valid. Sincere had no choice but to agree. His freshly painted Audi A8 squatting on 24-inch Forgis was killing shit. "I guess you right, B, but I still think we should body that nigga on GP. He making us look bad comin' through the hood giving out gifts like he Santa Claus."

"I don't appreciate niggas coming through the projects unchecked either, but dude is good for business. Remember our motto, Money Over Bullshit?" A toothpick dangled at the corner of Gotti's mouth. He turned and spoke directly to Sincere. "Besides, if we look bad, it's because we trick off more than we help our people. That's supposed to be us feeding our community, not him."

"What, you tryna' kick knowledge, fammo?" Sincere brushed off the truth. The two men used to be as thick as thieves, but Sincere felt that Gotti was going soft. "I'm beginning to think that G in yo' name stands for, Good Boy. We ain't saints, nigga, we street pharmacist. I help my people by servin' them this bomb medication for the low-low." He laughed and high-fived the other thirsty troops. They were just as lost as he was.

Gotti shook his head and sparked a wine flavored Black N Mild as he watched Sincere and the clique light a sherm stick and crack a bottle of Remy. Gotti was on a different level than they were and hated to see his friendship with Sincere suffer.

Hard years of survival in the projects had made Gotti grow up quick. His mama wasn't shit, and if he knew who his daddy was, he figured he probably wasn't shit either. He dreamed of moving out of the hood and raising a family somewhere in the burbs away from the stench of the Bungalows, yet, every time he was ready to make that move, something or someone pulled him back into the bucket.

Najee grilled Sincere and Gotti as he strolled through the black iron gate and whistled to a group of ghetto residents. The three men exchanged mean mugs until Sincere backed down and looked away.

"That's right, keep it movin', nigga. You don't want these problems," Najee mumbled under his breath. His cold stare, however, did not ravel Gotti.

Gotti continued to throw fiery daggers through slanted eyes. Najee knew then that Gotti was a gorilla. The rest of the zoo was just a bunch of monkeys.

An old-timer named Spade was begging for spare change. Upon hearing Najee's whistle, he perked up. His lips parted displaying a row of yellow gapped teeth. "Hey, everybody, there go Sinatra!" He beamed brightly, pointing a dirty fingernail toward Najee. Najee used several aliases, but he preferred Sinatra the most. It sounded slick, and the ladies loved it.

A throng of hungry and hopeless men and women rushed Najee as if he was a famous movie star. They cheerfully greeted the ghetto celebrity with crooked smiles and daps on the fist. They knew every time Sinatra came to the Bungalows he came bearing gifts. Today was no different. The haters looked on from the sidelines with jealousy boiling in their blood.

"A'ight, everybody, form a line," Najee instructed. "I got a lil' sumthin' sumthin' for y'all."

The eager crowd of pitiful black faces and poor white trash scrambled to get in line. A large homeless man with a scruffy, gray beard and tattered clothes shoved an eight-month pregnant prostitute out of the way.

Najee barked, "No pushing or cuttin' to the front of the line. If y'all can't do this shit right, then I'm closing up shop." His warning settled everyone down.

The long line stretched down the block. Najee unzipped the duffel bag, reached inside without looking, and pulled out a random greenback. The pregnant prostitute rudely snatched the money out of Najee's hand and frowned at the measly ten-dollar bill with detest.

45

"What am I supposed to do with this?" She placed a hand on her wide hips and complained. "And then you got the nerves to have dried up blood on the money. Who does that?"

Najee ripped the money out of her ungrateful grip. "Move around! If you don't like it, I know somebody who'll love it."

The large homeless man was next in line. He gladly accepted the ten-dollar bill. Spade was next. They called him Spade because his skin was blacker than midnight, which allowed him to blend in with the darkness. He somehow knew everything that went down in the projects. He balanced his bad leg on a wooden cane and waited patiently. Najee blindly reached into the bag and fished out a crisp C-Note.

Spade accepted the money with gratitude and shook Najee's hand enthusiastically. "The game needs more real brothas like you, nephew. I bet if you wanted to, you could take over the Bungalows. Them young boys is killers, but they ain't thinkers. They been lost ever since Bumpy got kilt."

Najee paused when he heard the comment and looked towards the decaying project building. Hardened black eyes stared back at him. He had no desire to take over the Bungalows, yet for some strange reason, he filed the info into his memory bank and completed his mission. In a matter of minutes, he had handed out $14,300, giving the improvised inhabitants of the slums a temporary moment of hope.

The pregnant prostitute sashayed her way up to Najee as he prepared to depart. She batted her false eyelashes and displayed the sexiest smile she could muster. Despite her efforts, she looked pathetic. Najee leaned against the Porsche truck and folded his muscular arms, eager to hear what kind of bullshit game she was about to run.

"What it do, shorty?" he asked dryly, looking at his watch.

Ol' girl cleared her throat. "Hi, Sinatra! Sorry 'bout catching a 'tude earlier." She moved closer and seductively rubbed against him. Her large boobs leaked breast milk. "If you break me off some real dough, I'll break you off some of this wet pussy. And you already knowin' what they say about pregnant pussy!" She finished her solicitation with a wink-wink, and one of her fake eyelashes fell off.

It was rare that Najee showed compassion, but her offer broke his heart. He studied the black queen who had just offered her priceless jewel with such ease and realized that she was his old flame from Hawthorne High School. He had given her the pet name Tam Tam. Tammy was sitting in the passenger seat of the cherry red low-rider when Najee murdered Cheddar the merciless gunman who killed his mother, Boulevard, and Angel.

In spite of being a hype, trips in and out of the county jail kept Tammy thick as oatmeal. Unfortunately, dark rings circled her hollowed-out eyes, and her cracked chapped lips made her look as though she had been eating powdered donuts. White, dried-up cum stains decorated her pink halter-top. A dingy bra strap hung over her left shoulder, and her frizzy, platinum wig was a hot mess.

Tammy was tore up from the floor up, but Najee looked past her outer appearance. As with all black women, he saw the essence of her inner beauty, the possibility of her hidden potential. He gently lifted her chin with a delicate finger.

Tammy's knees buckled and she damn near came when she gazed into his attentive brown eyes. There was something familiar about them, but she was spaced out on crack and couldn't put her finger on it.

Najee spoke smoothly, "Overstand this, my beautiful sista. I can't afford the precious diamond you possess between your legs. No man can. Evaluate your self-worth and get your shit together. If you don't do it for you—" he paused and pointed at her swollen belly. "—do it for the baby you're carrying." He reached into his pocket, peeled off two big faces, stuffed them into her palm, and mashed out. Revenge was on his mind and he had more body bags to fill.

Gotti watched the Porsche truck spin-off, then he issued instructions to one of his young minions. "Yo, Remy, I need you to holla at cha' peoples in Carson and yo' relatives up in the Yay

Area. See if anybody know who this Sinatra nigga is? I wanna know if he's plugged or is he a renegade."

Remy immediately got on his cell phone to carry out the mission. The hypes formed a new line in front of Gotti. Spade spent the whole hundred. Gotti hesitated to serve a pretty, green-eyed teenager. She was a trick baby mixed with black and Asian.

"What I tell you about fuckin' with this shit, China?" Gotti looked her up and down. She had lost weight since he'd last seen her. Although she did not have anything in her mouth, she moved her lips like she was chewing gum.

"I know, I know. I'm gonna get my shit together, but I'm sick, right now." She squirmed like she had to take a piss. "Hook a bitch up." She handed Gotti the fifty she had just gotten from Najee.

Gotti reluctantly accepted the cash and handed her three small rocks.

"Hell naw! Sup' with these dimes?" China stopped squirming and moving her jaws when she saw that she was about to get played on the dope. "I gave you a fifty, I ain't taking no shorts!"

"I know what yo' monkey ass gave me. You forgetting we in a drought. That's how shit gotta be for, right now. Give it back if you don't want it."

He reached to take the cavi back, but China gripped the rocks in her hand like they were the last life jacket on the Titanic. Gotti watched her shuffle away. He would later use the money to buy her and her little sister some groceries.

Sincere caught Tammy trying to creep off. "Say, bitch, come holla at a player for a minute." He beckoned with a wave of his arm.

"What, Sincere?" Tammy asked, hand on her hip, agitation in her voice.

Najee had left her with a wet spot in her panties and something deep on her mind. She had never been checked so eloquently. Now she hated that she was so rude to him in the beginning.

"Don't what me, bitch. Whatchu and that nigga talk about?"

"No—nothin'," she stuttered.

Sincere twisted his lips. "Nothing my ass. Didn't I tell you the next time ol' boy came through on that stuntastic shit, I wanted you to throw the pussy at him and set him up? Did you at least try to lure the nigga into the projects?"

"Yeah, I did, but he ain't no trick. I think you should leave him alone, Sincere. He's different, he got this dangerous vibe that scares me."

"Is that right?" Sincere rubbed the stubble on his chin. "Alright, cool, you don't have to help me set him up, but dig this, hand over that dust he gave you."

"I need this money to buy some food for my kids," Tammy objected. "We don't have nuthin' to eat."

"Bitch, I don't care if you need the money for a heart transplant! Yo' punk-ass owes me three-hunnit dollars for the dope you smoked up on credit."

Tammy looked down at her cheap flip-flops. The red nail polish on her big toe was chipped. Sincere was potentially the father of her baby, but he still treated her like shit. Her breasts heaved and salty fluid seeped from her tear ducts as she handed over the money.

Sincere stuffed the two crisp Benjamins in his front pocket and ran his tongue across his top lip while eyeing the puffy pussy imprint in her cutoff denim shorts. She had the top button unbuttoned and her pregnant belly hung over the zipper. "I know how you can make this money back." He vulgarly grabbed his crotch with his offer.

"I'll pass," Tammy declined and walked away holding on to the last bit of dignity she had left.

Agent Sullivan snapped pictures of everything that went down. Blondie started the engine and maneuvered into traffic, carefully positioning the Crown Vic two cars ahead of Najee.

Agent Sullivan drifted into deep thought as they dipped in and out of lanes. Most criminals he had encountered were only concerned with self. They were quick to blow money fast on strippers, Ace of Spades champagne, and flashy whips, but they were slow to give back to the broken communities from which their riches came from.

Agent Sullivan sensed that the suspect under their surveillance was cut from a different cloth. Blame it on being young and naive, but he was impressed with Najee's generous philanthropy.

On the contrary, Blondie was not remotely influenced. He became even more determined to find out who the stranger was and what he was up to. "Get on the wire and call headquarters." Blondie unwrapped a stick of Wrigley's Juicy Fruit and stuffed it into his mouth. "Have Cindy down in the Intelligence Department run this perps mug through their facial recognition software and compare it with any social media profiles. I've never witnessed a crook brave enough to hit a Los Cinco Diablos stash house by himself in broad daylight, then have the balls to go into one of the toughest neighborhoods in the nation and give the money away. In-fuckin'-credible. I gotta know who this schmuck is, pronto."

Najee unknowingly led the Feds to his posh high-rise in Pacific Palisades. Each lavish condominium had a picturesque view of the beach. Najee rarely splurged on material things, but the ocean was his tranquilizer.

As Agent Sullivan took surveillance photos of the condominium, Blondie noticed a powder blue and black Bugatti sports car swerve out of the carport. The vanity license plate proudly boasted the initials BBE. Blondie could not believe his luck. The driver of the 1.2 million-dollar whip was none other than Sosa.

Sosa had been on the Feds radar for years, but law enforcement officials could not catch him red-handed with any coke or link him to the dozen or so murders purportedly committed by the Block Boy Empire organization. Each time they built a seemly solid case against him, the star witness would either recant their story or mysteriously disappear.

"Get ready for a wild ride, Agent Sullivan," Blondie remarked as he dialed the number to a confidential informant. "We know that Benzo Al supplies BBE, but this new guy is a mystery. We need to find out how he's connected to Sosa and Los Cinco Diablos."

CHAPTER 6

Mo' Money, Mo' Problems

Sosa made a habit of being familiar with his environment. He laid in the cut and watched a candy painted Porsche SUV spinning on 30s swoop into the carport and park in space 15A. The driver drove with a hustler's swag. Sosa had never seen the flashy SUV before, and the black limo tent prohibited him from seeing the player behind the wheel.

The buzz of his iPhone distracted him for a hot second. He smiled at the phone number on the screen. It was his homegirl, Nella. After her man got murked, Sosa made it a priority to check up on her to make sure she was straight. He provided a shoulder for her to cry on, but ever since she came back from Amsterdam, she had grown cold and distant. He wondered what happened to her over there.

Before he could accept the call, a car alarm chirped, drawing his attention away from the phone. He quickly looked up, but the driver of the Porsche was stepping into the elevator. Sosa only got a slight glimpse of the man's face and shaved head as the elevator doors closed.

"Damn!" He wanted to see if he recognized ol' boy.

He was already running late, so he decided to holla at Nella later. He made a few mental notes and pressed the start button to his Bugatti. The voracious engine roared like a well-tuned NAS-CAR. He slipped on his gold-framed, Louis Vuitton aviator shades and swerved out of the secured carport. Years in the streets had conditioned Sosa to smell a pig from a mile away, and he immediately noticed a tan, Crown Victoria parked inconspicuously under the shade of a huge palm tree.

He didn't know if the Alphabet Boys were watching him or the mysterious owner of the Porsche Cayenne. Either way, it was time to move around. He had some B.I. to handle in the ATL, but once he got back to Cali, he vowed to find a new spot to lay his head. Better to be safe than sorry.

His black and red Yeezy's mashed the clutch while his iced-out wrist worked the stick shift, the needle on the speedometer quickly reaching a buck fifty as he pushed up the empty highway. He checked his rearview mirror and was relieved that the dick heads were not pursuing him. He relaxed, blazed a blunt, and turned up the music.

Blondie smiled, he didn't need to chase the Bugatti. His CI didn't know where Sosa lived, but he did know where Sosa was headed. The zealous DEA agent radioed into headquarters and booked a flight to Atlanta. To a cop, informants possessed a treasure trove of information. To a hustler, a snitch is kryptonite.

****

Hot-Lanta, GA

The plush G5 Gulfstream jet taxied across the runway and released its VIP passengers at Gate 12. After retrieving his Louie luggage from the baggage concierge, Sosa casually mobbed through the terminal at Hartsfield International. He was aware that all eyes were on him. Standing 6'3, with peanut butter-colored skin and lustrous cornrows braided in a zigzag pattern, he looked more like a professional athlete than a professional drug dealer. In addition to being rich, handsome, and charismatic, Sosa exuded an air of confidence that attracted the opposite sex like a moth to a flickering flame. Normally, he would have fraternized with the sexy flight attendants who threw flirtatious smiles and sexual innuendoes his way, but today business occupied his thoughts.

The sizzling heat greeted Sosa when he stepped outside. He inhaled a gulp of fresh, down South air and blinked his eyes in the bright, summer sun. Out of all the places he had hustled, he was feeling ATL the most. New York was too crowded, Detroit was too cold, and L.A. was too fast. The tempo and temperature in the A were just right.

A glacier, white Bentley GT slithered up to the curb. Loud reggae music thumped out of two 15-inch, JL Audio subwoofers, and the powerful aroma of high-grade marijuana seeped through the tinted windows. Sosa opened the passenger side door and got in.

"You late, my nigga, and what's that funny smell?" he sniffed as he tossed his bag in the back seat and shook up with his man Ice.

"My bad, I just filled up at the Amoco and fucked around and spilt some gas." Ice handed Sosa a perfectly rolled Garcia Vega stuffed with Afghan Kush.

"Good lookin'." Sosa took a hit. "What's been poppin'?"

"Shizz, you know what it is. Cop it, cook it, whip it, and flip it. Block Boy Empire 'till death do us or the Feds unglue us!" His country grammar was slow and syrupy.

Sosa let out an audible sigh. "You gotta get yo' mind out the gutter, bruh. Outlaw told me you took yo' Shahadah and turned Muslim. That's the type of positive shit you need to be on, especially with them peoples breathing on us." He looked in the side rearview mirror and took a mental snapshot of the cars behind them, old habits die hard.

Ice chuckled. "Don't believe everythang you hear, dawg. I ain't tryna' be praying fifty times a day. Plus, I love codeine, white women, and pork chops too much to be on that Farrakhan shit. I just needed a new twist to keep the DEA off balance. Sorta like you doing with that businessman act." He used a wooden brush to stroke the deep waves in his hair. He had a habit of brushing his hair when his devious mind was calculating a plot.

Sosa let the comment slide. No one believed he had squared up, not even after gracing the covers of Jet and Black Enterprise Magazine. Each publication did an exhaustive exposé on his life and applauded the success of his string of drive-thru soul food restaurants called Mama Merls. The franchise was named after his deceased mother, a thoroughbred money getter and one of the baddest bitches in high heels that ever blessed the game.

Sosa took a toke off the spliff as Ice put the Bentley in gear and zigzagged in and out of the evening traffic. The bomb ganja filled Sosa's chest and instantly helped him unwind. Seeing the

Feds posted up by his condo had him on 'noid, plus a slew of problems had suddenly plagued his restaurants.

Someone was secretly praying on his downfall and trying to sabotage his success. The hater had already cost him two mil-tickets, so Sosa was in the ATL to do damage control before the situation forced his company into bankruptcy.

Another blast off the sticky bud had Sosa's eyes slanted low like an Asian. "This is some fiyah ass weed, my nigga! Bank make a left-right here, and take me to the Mama Merl's spot across the street from Victoria's Steakhouse," he instructed, handing the thick blunt back to Ice.

Ice took a long drag off the Vega as he accelerated past a black and white patrol car with no regard for the law.

"Chill, nigga," Sosa warned. "There go one-time!"

"Fuck the police! The world belongs to us!" Ice proclaimed and expelled a cloud of smoke through his nostrils. He was young and reckless.

Ice examined Sosa out the corner of his eye as he maneuvered the whip. The coke drought was affecting ghettos across America, and the streets of Atlanta were thirsty ever since Sosa had left the game. Ice knew it was only a matter of time before his hustle dried up as well.

There was a rumor circulating through every barbershop, car wash, and nail salon in the hood that the Mexicans on the West Coast were deliberately sitting on several tons of blow, but Sosa could solve his dilemma. Sosa had a plug with the Cholos in Cali, the Puerto Ricans in Chicago, and the Dominicans and Cubans on the East Coast. Ice was desperately trying to lure Sosa back into the game, but so far, nothing was working, Sosa was retired.

"Yo, Sosa," Ice began, "I heard you copped that new Bugatti joint with the Mansory carbon fiber exterior. You be shitin' on the game with dem' big boy toys, dawg. When I get my weight up, I wanna be just like you," Ice complimented in a woozy, Dirty South accent.

"Thanks for the love, my dude, but don't try to be like me, be better than me," Sosa encouraged. "I fucks with you the long way because you have the potential to turn the street corner into a corner office, but you gotta stay on your deen, move in silence, and formulate a solid exit plan. Ya heard?"

Instead of soaking up game, Ice was temporarily distracted by a thick breezy. The caramel cutie in tight denim jeans openly eye fucked his 26-inch Forgiato rims even though she was sitting at the bus stop with her man. Ice blew a kiss and a cloudy halo of THC smoke her way. The boyfriend peeped game and glared at the passing Bentley and its disrespectful driver. He regretted not having his strap but got a good look at Ice as he muffed his bitch in the face with a stiff palm and checked her for being out of pocket.

Ice laughed and turned his attention back to Sosa not realizing that he had just created a new enemy. "I hear you, big homie, I hear you. But fuck that nine to five square biz. I'm tryna' get my pockets paid and my whips candy sprayed. Kna'mean? When is a gladiator-like yourself gettin' back in the arena?"

"I told you a hunnit times, my nigga, I ain't getting back in the game. Them Caucasians would love to indict my black ass. So, I'm doing the suit and tie thizzle, feel me?"

"Stop frontin', Sosa. Dis' me you talking to." Ice pinched the blunt between his fingers. "This street shit runs through yo' veins. It's in yo' blood. It's all niggas like me and you know. Besides, the team needs you back in the kitchen, Ahki. This drought got us out here starving like Marvin."

Sosa scanned the hand-stitched pomegranate color leather and rich wood grain accents that lined the cockpit of the British automobile. It didn't look like Ice was hurting for dough, but Sosa knew where the young hustler was coming from. There was a time when he was just as hungry and ambitious. All he needed was the right connect. It was Benzo Al who stepped in and changed his life.

As if reading Sosa's thoughts, Ice turned down the reggae music and spoke in a sincere tone. "You're like a big brother to me, and I'm proud of you. You flipped the game and now you out here legit ballin'. But I gotta keep it hot with you. I'm in love with the coco. It's all I know. If you done with the game, cool. I can't knock yo' hustle, but at least link me up with yo' old plug so me and the crew—"

Sosa was shaking his head no before Ice finished the sentence. "You my nigga and all, but I can't make no introductions. This is indictment season, bruh. We could catch a conspiracy charge just for talking 'bout this shit. Ya heard?" He gazed out the moon roof and did a double take. An Atlanta PD drone zipped through the sky above them. He watched the new age ghetto bird until it drifted into the horizon.

"C'mon, Ahki," Ice pleaded. "Everybody can't be a big-time businessman like you. You made it out of the hood, but what about the rest of us? We stuck in the slums and gotta get it how we live. What I look like going to a job interview with all these jewels in my grill and jailhouse tattoos on my face? I come from a different world, big homie."

Sosa looked at the black heart and teardrops tatted on his face. Ice had a point. "I feel you, nephew. Let me think about it for a couple of days, a'ight?" He checked the side rearview mirror again. The conversation was making him paranoid.

Ice smiled displaying two rows of platinum and diamond slugs. "Now that's the Sosa I know! Till death do us." He banked a left onto Peachtree Street and waited for Sosa to finish the Block Boy Empire slogan.

"Or the Feds unglue us," Sosa finished the mantra half-heartedly. He was desperately trying to exit the game and end the perpetual cycle of sleepless nights, deadly shoot-outs, and court dates. However, his people needed him. He was trapped between two worlds.

Sosa and Ice bent the corner and spotted a large crowd of curious spectators and police officers congregating in Mama Merl's small parking lot. The restaurant was engulfed in a ball of orange flames. A billow of black smoke rose from the roof and formed a dark, mushroom cloud in the sky. Gray ashes and the smell of ether polluted the summer air.

This was the third Mama Merl's location that had mysteriously caught on fire. Sosa rushed out of the car just as a parade line of fire engines, police cars, and ambulances descended upon the carnage.

Sosa and Ice frantically forced their way through the thick crowd in order to get a better view, but yellow tape prohibited them from moving closer. The stench of burning flesh assaulted their nose. Part of the roof collapsed, trapping an elderly woman under a steel beam. Her shrill scream echoed from the restaurant.

Sosa turned his attention back to Ice. "This shit finna cost me some millions," he sadly admitted.

Ice patted him on the shoulder. "The streets will always be here for you, dawg," he said with a smirk, hoping Sosa's failing business and rising misfortunes would pull him back into the dope game.

Sosa did a doubletake. He thought he spotted Blondie questioning one of the spectators, but when he moved in for a closer look, the DEA agent was gone.

Another badly burnt victim was pulled from the smoldering restaurant. An EMT worker covered the body with a white sheet. The corpse belonged to a sixteen-year-old girl named, Ty. Her disfigured face was barely recognizable. The fire had melted away her nose and lips. Sosa stumbled away from the gurney with tears blurring his vision. A tight knot formed in the pit of his stomach. He folded over and threw up the club sandwich he had eaten on the airplane.

He had personally hired the young woman five months ago. When he met her, she was hustling hard on Auburn Avenue selling pussy, weed, and her condemned soul in order to provide for her two-year-old son. Sosa got her off the streets, helped her get back in school, and gave her a job as a cashier. She felt safe and protected under his tutelage. Now she was dead, and her shorty was an orphan.

Sosa thought about her as he sat in the Bentley next to Ice. His fists were balled tight, causing his fingernails to dig into his palms.

The vile taste of vomit in his mouth was replaced with an unquenchable thirst for vengeance.

He turned toward Ice and looked him square in the eyes. "Keep yo' ears glued to the streets. Whoeva behind this shit gon' die slow." His bottom teeth were grinding against the top. "Touch his mama, his baby mama, his grandmama, and everythang else he loves. Ya heard?"

Nodding his head in agreement, Ice pulled the long barrel of his Desert Eagle from his waistband and sat the instrument of death in his lap. He lit another blunt with the car's cigarette lighter, passed it to Sosa, and peeled out of the parking lot. Ghetto streets from coast to coast were about to run red with bloodshed.

CHAPTER 7

Compton, CA

Najee was back on his grind. He sported black Dickies, black Timbs, and his favorite black hockey mask. As usual, a black cloud hovered above him. He tucked his cannon in the small of his back and snatched the blindfold off his latest victim's eyes.

"Where tha fuck am I?" Juan, a Los Cinco Diablos drug runner with a raspy voice and rotund belly, demanded.

"In your casket," Najee's haunting words bounced off the walls of the dark, dank garage in Compton.

Juan's eyes adjusted to the darkness. The last thing he recalled was scratching lottery tickets in front of his chop shop on Wilmington Avenue when a Porsche truck pulled up and the driver jumped out. Beyond that, the throbbing knot on his head made his memory foggy.

He glared at Najee contemptuously. "You fucked up, Ese. I'm a validated Cinco Diablos soldier! Untie me, and I'll just kill you, not your whole familia!"

Juan was confined to an uncomfortable metal chair. His arms and torso were duct-taped, making him look like a mummy. Najee searched his eyes for a sign of weakness. Despite Juan's unpleasant predicament, the high-ranking Cinco Diablos affiliate blatantly returned Najee's obstinate stare.

Whack!

Najee viciously backhanded Juan across the right cheek like a St. Louis pimp.

"Fuck you, puto!" Juan lashed out through a busted lip and spit blood at Najee.

"Another tough guy, huh? We gon' see about that." Najee powered up an industrial-sized battery charger.

The machine stalled, then sputtered to life. He walked over to Juan in a zombie-like daze, unbuckled his Gucci belt buckle, and yanked his jeans and Hanes briefs down to his ankles. Juan's shriveled up genitals were exposed and vulnerable.

Larry D. Wright

"What tha fuck are you doing, Ese? Are you loco?" Juan asked in a jittery voice.

Najee answered by touching the red side of the jumper cables against the black. Hot yellow sparks rained on Juan's hairy thighs. Najee clapped the jumper cables together again, enjoying the way Juan squirmed when the sparks burned his naked flesh.

Juan screamed, "Aaaghh, shit! Look, homes, I got coca, mucho coca! Let me go and I'll give it to you. I put that on everything."

Najee belched out a cold, heartless laugh. "A minute ago, you was acting like Tony Soprano. Now yo' bitch ass wanna cop a plea? Fuck you and your dope. I'm not here to steal your poison." He clapped the battery cables together again. More sparks, more screams.

There was no peace between lambs and wolves. Juan was used to being the wolf. Now he found himself on the other side of darkness. "Wait! Wait!" he begged. "I got ten bricks and a hundred bands in the office. Remove the vent cover that leads to my secret escape chamber and take it. It's all yours."

You cannot negotiate with a lunatic. Najee reached down and savagely clamped the positive charge of the jumper cables onto Juan's flaccid dick. The sharp, copper teeth bit into his genitals and drew blood. Next, Najee retrieved a red gas can from the Porsche. Juan read the yellow and black label, and the whites of his eyes bulged like two golf balls.

WARNING: *HIGHLY VOLATILE AND FLAMMABLE LIQUID COMPOUND. KEEP AWAY FROM HEAT.*

Juan did the math in his head. Hot sparks plus flammable liquid equaled fire. This was no time to play brave. He pleaded for his life, "Okay, okay! You proved your point. It's a drought, but I can get you more dope and more fetti. Untie me, and I will take you to it. I promise you won't be disappointed," he sounded desperate and pathetic. Salty droplets of sweat trickled from his forehead and ran down the sides of his temples.

Najee grinned at his hostage. "Like I said, dead man, I don't want your money or your work."

"Then what do you want?"

"I want Alonzo Guzman!" Najee's deep growl sounded like Batman.

"Benzo Al? Why, what did he do to you?"

Najee slowly peeled back the black hockey mask and revealed his new face. His jaw muscles twitched as he spoke. "Benzo Al sent two of his goons to my house when I was a shorty. One of them murdered the only mother and father I've ever known. After that, he raped and murdered my fourteen-year-old girlfriend. So, as you can see no amount of money can satisfy me. I want Benzo Al, and you're gonna tell me where the fuck he's at."

Juan shook his head. "I can't do that, Ese."

"Yes, you can, and you will."

The men stared each other down until Juan averted his eyes. "You might as well smoke me now, homes. Because if I flip on El Señor, I'm a dead man anyways."

Los Cinco Diablos did not tolerate snitches. A swift execution awaited members who broke the Ometra, the law of silence. Najee appreciated Juan's loyalty, but he had a mission to accomplish and no person or organization was going to stand in his way. He held the gas can over Juan's head and unscrewed the lid.

"This smells like gasoline, but its ether," Najee began. He shook the canister and drenched Juan's immobile body. "Ether is more flammable than regular gas, and it burns hotter."

He got directly in Juan's face, their noses almost touching. Najee's voice grew deep and malefic, "Everybody gotta clock out one day. The choice is yours how you want to go. You can tell me where Benzo Al is at and take your chances with the Cinco Diablos. Or I can make barbeque out of yo' punk ass, right here, right now."

It did not take long for Juan to weigh his options. Death before dishonor and other poetic Mafioso quotes were quickly forgotten when one's life hung in the balance. When a real nigga stick that Glock in your mouth or the Feds threaten you with football numbers, the primal instinct of self-preservation kicks in.

Juan saw the determined, deranged look in Najee's dark eyes and began to sing like Luther—the fat Luther. He was jaw jacking so fast, it sounded like he was speaking in tongues.

Najee held up his hands to interrupt. "Hold up. Slow down for a second. You said that Benzo Al is in Mexico. It's too risky trying to make it back across the border, especially with the drug cartels at war. So, why is he down there?"

Juan swallowed to wet his parched throat, then continued betraying his organization. "The heads of the five families are having a secret meeting. Each of them are putting two million dollars in the pot in order to fix the election and get one of our guys elected as the governor of Los Angeles. We're also about to form an alliance with the Nogales Cartel. The peace treaty will make Los Cinco Diablo unstoppable."

"Whoa!" Najee took a step back. Los Cinco Diablos and the Nogales Cartel linking up was equivalent to Facebook and Twitter merging. Their partnership would send ripples through the underworld. "When is he coming back to the U.S.?"

"Your guess is as good as mines, Ese."

Najee exploded, "You still want to play with my intelligence? You're one of his top lieutenants. You know his every move."

"Me and Benzo ain't as tight as we used to be. The only person he trusts now is that crazy chica who he uses to kill his enemies."

His answer was not satisfactory. Najee clamped the negative charged jumper cable onto Juan's balls. The sharp, scissor-like copper teeth chewed into Juan's scrotum, and he squirmed in pain. The jumper cable attached to his balls rubbed against the cable clamped on his dick, causing sparks to shoot into the air and land on his crotch. His ether soaked pubic hair instantly combusted into flames. The fire rose quickly.

Juan yelled, "I swear to God, I'm telling you the truth! Benzo Al is a ghost! I don't call him, he calls me. All I know is that the ten mil will be kept here along with a big shipment of dope. You gotta believe me!"

The Haitian also referred to Benzo Al as a ghost, but Najee kept pushing. "I want to know where he lays his head at night. I want to know how I can reach out and touch him."

"Water! Please, I need water!" Juan's voice was a painful whisper.

"So do people in hell." Najee was without sympathy. He was driven by the images of Boulevard taking a slug to the chest, his mother being savagely gunned down in the kitchen, and the look in Angel's tearful eyes as Cheddar stole her virginity.

He poured more ether on Juan's squirming body. The fire spread down Juan's thighs, and the pungent aroma of burnt flesh filled the chop shop.

Juan made one last, urgent, plea. "What part don't you understand? Benzo Al is a ghost. He's untouchable. You can't go to him. If you want to get into his circle, start moving a lot of coca. That will get his attention, and he will come to you," his raspy statement was barely audible, however, Najee heard him loud and clear.

His words confirmed what the Haitian and many others had already told him, yet Najee struggled with the thought of becoming a D-boy in order to lure Benzo Al out of the shadows. He vowed never to sell yayo. He had witnessed firsthand what drugs did to the black community, and it was counterintuitive to what his non-profit organization, Alive 365, stood for.

On the other hand, hunting down Benzo Al had proven to be fruitless. The elusive kingpin was well insulated by faithful captains, loyal lieutenants, and ruthless foot soldiers. Najee had officially hit a dead end. Instead of looking for Benzo Al, he needed to make Benzo Al look for him and allow himself to be found.

Now that Sosa was in retirement and Juan and the Haitians were out of play, there was a big void in the dope game. Najee needed to fill the empty slot and penetrate the core of Los Cinco Diablos.

Juan's moans pulled Najee out of plot mode. He rushed to the loading dock and grabbed the pressure washer that he spotted when he was casing the joint. He was not going to let Juan burn to death. Such heinous crimes are unforgivable. Contrary to popular belief, Najee was not a killing machine mindlessly prowling the ghetto in search of his next vic. There was a method to his madness, a purpose for his savagery.

He sprayed down Juan's smoldering body, dialed 911, and asked God for forgiveness as he made a quick exit with the ten kilos and a hundred bands in his duffel bag. He used to warn his old crew about removing dope from the scene. Now he was going against the grain and becoming the type of person he despised. He had a bad vibe about the whole situation and would soon regret his decision to let Juan live.

****

Nightfall found Najee in a state of solitude. He sat in his lonely condo with his broad shoulders slumped, a grape Swisher Sweet in his left hand, a bottle of Hennessy in the right, and depression gnawing away at his soul. He wondered what happened to the bright-eyed, innocent teenager who loved Hip-Hop, math, and playing Pop Warner football at Jesse Owens Park. Those nostalgic memories were relics of the past.

Now when Najee looked in the mirror, he did not recognize the reflection staring back at him. It wasn't because he had his face reconstructed. It was deeper than that. It was because he had become a monster. Nella was right, she was always right.

Thinking about wifey was painful. He loved Nella with all his heart. His cell phone rested on the glass coffee table amongst a pile of old newspapers, urban magazines, and junk mail. The phone beckoned him to pick it up. It dared him to stop being stubborn and call his Boo.

He took a sip of Henn and chased the strong cognac with a long hit off the Swisher. He held the smoke in his chest until his lungs protested, causing him to hack and cough in a pleasant way. He threw his head back and took another swig of yak. The liquid fire burned his throat as it descended into his belly and gave him that tipsy sensation.

He flicked the stereo remote, then Tupac and Scarface serenaded the opulent condo with their rebellious brand of poetry. Pac and the Texas rhyme veteran traded heat-felt bars over the track, "*Smile.*" Yet, not even their thug motivation could elevate Najee's mood.

He stood up and paced back and forth on his plush, Persian rug until he found himself gazing out of a large panoramic window. An array of twinkling city lights dotted the terrain. They looked like hundreds of curious eyes staring back at him. If his brain wasn't so fogged up by Kush smoke and yak, he would have realized someone was definitely watching him from below.

Instead, he took a stroke of the half-smoked blunt, poured another drink and grabbed his cell phone. He reclined in his white, leather sofa, scrolled through his contacts with his thumb, and highlighted Nella's digits. It was time to make that call.

Larry D. Wright

CHAPTER 8

Wins and Losses

Nella wrapped her hair in a tight bun, leaned back, and submerged her tense shoulders into an ocean of hot Jacuzzi water. The soothing whirlpool jets along with lavender-scented oil from *Bath & Body Works* caressed her curvaceous body. The soulful melody of *Sade* streamed through her Beats Pill. The sultry R&B singer was harmonizing about a broken heart. Nella's cell phone laid face down on the hot tub's marble ledge. She was lip-synching to the song when the buzz of her vibrating phone interrupted her bliss. For the last nine months, Nella's concerned friends had been trying to cheer her up to no avail.

Nella dodged their phone calls and made up a slew of excuses when they wanted to come over to see her. Nella figured it was her BFF, Lala so without checking the caller I.D. she swiped the ignore icon and sent the call directly to voicemail. The only thing she wanted to do tonight was light a few aromatic candles, listen to some music, and drown her sorrows with a chilled bottle of Moscato.

She turned up the volume when her favorite song came on. "Heyyy, 'dis is my jam, sweet as taboooo," she sang the Sade lyrics with a heavy heart.

Nella had a legitimate reason for being stressed and depressed. Being raped by someone you hated and abandoned by someone you loved all on the same night would leave anyone psychologically fucked up. Then to learn that you were pregnant and didn't know who the baby's daddy was would make you feel like a demolition crew was dismantling your life with a wrecking ball.

After learning that she was eight weeks pregnant, Nella left the hospital in a fireball of confusion. What if she had an abortion and the baby belonged to, Najee? However, what if she kept the child and the baby belonged to the rapist? Those were the complicated questions doing somersaults in her head. Either scenario would be devastating. In the end, she did what was best for her.

Now as she soaked in the Jacuzzi, she was experiencing a combination of emotions. On one hand, she missed Najee like crazy. Her body yearned to feel his skilled fingers and talented tongue sensually exploring her most secret places. She desired for him to make love to her mind with his philosophical conversation. She needed him to appear on her doorstep, pull her into his embrace, and reassure her that everything was going to be okay.

On the other hand, she was a pissed-off sista, a woman scorned. She called Najee every kind of black and ashy nigga there is and stole the money he had stashed in lockers at Greyhound bus stations scattered throughout L.A., leaving a dead rose in its place.

Finally, she poured bleach on all of his gear. The only item of clothing she did not destroy was his favorite, white, button-down dress shirt. She kept the cotton garment as a souvenir and slept in it every night. The musky-sweet scent of his Yves Saint Laurent cologne was all she had left of him.

Once again, the persistent buzz emitting from her Samsung interrupted her grove. Irritated, Nella snatched the cell phone off the marble ledge of the hot tub and examined the caller's pic. "Oh, now you wanna call me back!" She unconsciously ran her eyes across the caller's handsome features.

His low-cut beard was trimmed neat and crispy, and he had those *LL Cool J*, pussy-eating lips. A lovely smile formed on her face. She swiped the accept call icon and said, "Hello," her voice was soft and sweet like cotton candy.

"Wassup, ma, it's me, the one and only, Sosa," his voice was rich and deep like a rhythm and blues singer.

"Boy, I know who this is and stop trying to sound all sexy like you, Barry White, knowin' damn well you more like Chris Brown," she joked playfully.

"Whateva." Sosa was trying not to laugh. "Listen though, I was calling to see if you heard from what's-his-name?"

"Who?"

"Deezz Nutz!" Sosa burst out laughing. He was chillin' in a large suite at the W Hotel in downtown Atlanta and smoking on some good.

"Oh, you got jokes, huh?" Now it was Nella's turn to stifle her giggle. She poured another glass of Moscato and took a sip.

Sosa's cheerful mood was contagious. It felt good talking with someone who had also been through a lot. They ribbed each other with yo' mama so ugly jokes until there was an awkward silence on the line.

Sosa spoke first, "Is everythang straight?" his voice was strained with concern.

Holding on to the towel rack for support, Nella carefully stepped out of the Jacuzzi. She had worked hard to regain the ability to walk again. Once out of the water, she looked at her figure in the full-length mirror that hung on the back of the bathroom door.

She had gained weight, she massaged her breasts for cancer lumps and marveled at how full they felt. Her hands slowly rubbed her stomach. No stretch marks, she was thankful for that. Even in her early thirties, she was still looking good.

"I asked was everythang straight?" Sosa repeated a little louder.

"It's all Gucci. What's up with you, tho'? I hear a little bit of stress in your voice." She cleverly deflected the conversation back on him.

Sosa grabbed an ashtray and flicked the ashes off the tip of an obese blunt. His hotel room was clouded with cannabis smoke. "It's that obvious, huh?"

"A woman can always tell when her lover—" Nella began but caught herself. She used to tell Najee that a woman could tell when her lover has something deep on his mind. She couldn't explain why her subconscious feelings escaped while talking to Sosa. Blaming it on the Moscato she cleaned it up, hoping Sosa didn't detect her verbal error. "—a woman can always tell when a friend is having problems."

Sosa caught Nella's slip, but let it ride. It wasn't even like that. He viewed Nella as a little sister or a close homegirl. They could chop it up about anything. She was easy going, knew what it was like to be knee-deep in the game, and a certified gunslinger. He had witnessed her in action dodging bullets and dumpin' that iron like a G.

He had to admit he'd never met a true ride or die chick like her before. Any street nigga would be enticed by her rare qualities. Plus, she was thicker than a frozen Snicker. Ass like pow, titties like damn! Still, Sosa kept it one-hundred. Najee had asked him to look out for Nella, and he was determined to be a stand-up guy and honor the fallen soldier's request.

Nella's sexy voice jarred Sosa back to their discussion. "Are you even listening to me? Which one of those ratchet thots got you trippin'?" she quizzed.

Sosa sensed a little jealousy in Nella's voice and chuckled. "I stopped fuckin' with strippers and gold diggers. The last thing I need is for one of them shiesty ass hoes to set me up. I'm ready for a real woman. Besides, I ain't stressing over no pussy; I'm trippin' off something else," he confessed.

Nella dried herself off and slipped into Najee's favorite button-up shirt with no panties or bra. Her erect nipples pressed against the soft fabric and stuck out like NO. 2 pencil erasers. "So, holla at cha' gurl. What's bothering you then?"

Sosa blew weed smoke in the air. "Somebody torched another one of my restaurants a couple of days ago. I'm in the ATL handling the paperwork and trying to find out what the fuck is going on. This is the third Mama Merl's spot that got hit. The shit is costing me major bread, fa' realz."

"Won't your insurance cover the damage?" Nella understood why Sosa was so upset. She felt sorry for him.

"All-State is buggin'. Those crackers think I set the fires for the insurance money. I would never put one of mines in that type of danger for a lil' bit of change—" He paused to hit the blunt, expelled double streams of smoke through his nose, and kept speaking, "When I find out who's behind this shit, I'ma—"

"Oohh, shit!" Nella moaned, cutting Sosa's words short. "My water broke!"

"Here I am telling you my life story and you worried about yo' water. You need me to call a plumber or something?"

"No, I need to you call nine-one-one. I think I'm about to have my baby."

Sosa choked on the bud smoke. "Baby? How? By, who?"

"It's a long story," Nella panted. Her heart raced a hundred miles per hour, her saliva glands became dry, and her cervix began to dilate. The first-time mother panicked, but the feelings she was experiencing were normal. Her body was instinctively preparing itself for childbirth.

Sosa stepped up and took control like the leader the streets had made him. "Listen, Mami, I need you to sit down, take a deep breath, and relax. Everythang is gonna be okay," his voice was calm and reassuring. "When we get off the phone, I want you to pack some clothes and whatever else you may need. One of my niggas will be there in fifteen minutes to scoop you up. When he gets there—"

"But shouldn't I just call nine-one-one?" Nella interrupted.

"Nine-one-one is a joke. You're better off calling a taxi than an ambulance, ya heard?"

"Yeah, I hear you." Nella settled into a comfortable armchair and tried to remain calm.

"A'ight, now check this out," Sosa continued. "My mans, Brazy, is gonna drive you to Cedars Sinai Hospital in Beverly Hills. Register under a fake name and then have the receptionist page, Dr. Clayter. She's my people and will take good care of you. You got all of that?"

"Yes, I got it," Nella uttered between moans.

Sosa crushed the tip of the blunt in the ashtray and quickly stuffed his clothes and shaving kit back into his suitcase. "Just relax and don't forget to breathe. I'm catching the next thang smoking back to Cali. It's only a fo' hour flight, so hopefully, I'll be there before the baby is born."

Nella sniffled back the river of salty tears dribbling down her cheeks. She was grateful to have someone like Sosa in her corner. She felt so alone and so ashamed when she went to the abortion clinic in Leimert Park. An old white doctor handed her a thin, blue, hospital gown and callously instructed her to undress. She did so and climbed onto a cold, sterile gurney.

The doctor crudely stretched her thighs wide and placed her legs into a pair of nickel brushed stirrups. He left the room, allowing Nella to examine his tools of trade. A pair of stainless-steel tongs rested on what appeared to be a metal lunch tray. A clear suction hose was connected to a diabolical looking vacuum. The vacuum was attached to a black tube that ran to a red and white container marked, *Bio-Hazard Waste*. It would serve as a disposable casket for the fetus.

Nella could not go through with the abortion. She ran out of the clinic and burst through a crowd of radical Christians holding up picket signs boldly stating, "Abortion Is Murder."

Nella had witnessed so much death, now she was about to give life. For once, her tears were tears of joy.

****

Just as promised, one of Sosa's BBE soldiers arrived in fifteen minutes. Brazy was a large, hulking figure with a no-nonsense scowl on his face, but underneath the carbon shield, he was actually a mellow brotha. He gently chaperoned Nella to his dragon red Escalade swagged out with cranberry red suede guts and red 30-inch DUB rims. They raced through the city and made it to Cedar's in record time.

Dr. Clayter arrived, white coat flapping in the wind, radiant smile illuminating the dreary emergency room. A team of nurses escorted Nella to a huge, private suite. Brazy mobbed to the snack shop while Nella filled out the appropriate paperwork. It wasn't until he heard Nella's cell phone ring that he realized he still had her large Birkin carryall bag. He ignored the first call, but when it persistently rang several more times, he decided to answer.

'*Who knows, it could be one of her family members,*' he reasoned.

"Yo, hello," he said.

Silence.

"Hello! Hello!" Brazy repeated.

Smoke fumes oozed from Najee's eardrums. "Who tha fuck is this?" he demanded.

"Niggah, you called this number. Who da fuck are you?"

"Don't worry 'bout it. Just put Nella on the line, homie."

Brazy's anger subsided, but just a little. "Dig this, patna, I don't know you. I don't know Nella, and I most definitely don't argue with insecure niggas over the phone. My mans Sosa just asked me to bring the sista to the hospital, feeling me?"

"The hospital?" Najee stood up in his condo. "For what; is she okay?"

"It's all good, she's about to have the baby."

"Have the baby?" Najee's drink slipped out of his grip and splashed on the plush white carpet. "What baby are you talking about, Cuzz?"

"First off, don't *fuzz* me, nigga! Second, I ain't 'bout to put another man's bizness in the streets. Obviously, it takes nine months to have a baby, so if Sosa and Nella wanted you to know about it, you would be up on game by now."

Najee lost it. "Hoe ass nigga, I know you ain't tryna get disrespectful!"

Click!

Brazy pressed the end call button. He didn't know that Sosa and Nella were not a couple. He merely assumed she was one of Sosa's many 'round the way girls and that Sosa was the baby daddy because of the urgency in his voice when he called.

Oh well, Brazy kept it moving and sat at a corner table in the back of the cafeteria. He destroyed a large plate of chili cheese fries while waiting for Sosa's next order.

****

Najee stood at the large windowpane overlooking the ocean and a number of beachfront properties. His handsome features were a distorted African mask, mouth skewed into an artic frown, nostrils flared like a charging bull, and an icy veil covered his eyes. His heart did not simply break, it crumbled into a thousand jagged pieces.

He couldn't take the hurt. Not only had Nella given away his pussy, but she also let another man skeet all up in her and get her pregnant as well. That was the ultimate betrayal. He grabbed the 8x10 photo of them hugged up at the Niagara Falls and slung it across the living room. The gold frame collided with the wall, its glass face shattered on impact.

As if on cue, Tupac began to chant, *"You wonder why they call you bitch. You wonder why they call you bitch."*

Najee pulled out his .38 revolver with the lemon squeeze grip and emptied all the bullets onto the coffee table. Using a black Sharpie marker, he wrote the names of Sosa and Nella on two of the copper slugs. He seriously contemplated adding a bullet for their baby, too, but quickly pushed the devilish thought out of his mind and reloaded the iron.

A snub nose revolver is the perfect apparatus for committing premeditated murder. It's easy to conceal, you don't have to worry about incriminating shells ejecting from the chamber, and the short barrel makes it difficult to match ballistic marks on the slugs.

Najee tucked the heat in the small of his back and decided to hit the Crenshaw strip. He pulled his New Era, L.A. Dodgers fitted cap low so no one could see the pain in his eyes, grabbed his keys, and bounced. Cruising down the 'Shaw always helped him get his mind right. Ironically, the Crenshaw strip would also be the place where fate and opportunity collided, bringing him one step closer to murdering Benzo Al and two steps closer to his own demise.

CHAPTER 9

No, Love No Loyalty

Blondie slammed a confidential informant named Alex Munoz against the hot hood of his unmarked squad car, grabbed him by the collar, and wagged an accusing finger in his face. "Listen up, you refried bean eating schmuck. I helped you out of a jam, now it's time for you to help me." Five clear vials packed with crack cocaine were scattered on the ground by the informant's feet.

Alex couldn't believe his ears. "You helped me, how?" he asked with a hint of sarcasm. "You just planted some bogus evidence on me. I don't even sell hard." He referred to the vials of ready rock lying in the street.

Blondie snatched the CI by the collar, bent him over the hood of the car, and twisted his right arm behind his back. "That's it, smart ass, I'm taking you in. Who do you think an all-white jury is gonna believe? A decorated officer or a low life thug who's facing his third strike?" He clamped a pair of handcuffs on Alex's wrist.

Soaring at 6' with a buzz haircut and a thick, black goatee, Alex was a handsome Latino who bounced from New York, Philly, and Atlanta setting up drug distributors for the Feds. He had the look, the walk, and the talk down pat, but lurking behind his street cred was a cunning snake.

"Alright! Alright!" Alex grimaced. "Take it easy, yo. I think I might have something for you."

"I'm listening." Blondie hated dealing with snitches. They had no morals, therefore, they lacked the ability to be loyal. Even so, they were a necessary evil. Sometimes Blondie would employ two informants from the same crew but would not disclose their identity to each other. This ensured that the intel he received was accurate. "Start talking. Whatcha' got for me, Alex?"

"I got this cat on my line who tryin' to cop some weight. I can set him up for you," Alex spoke in rapid-fire broken English like Billy Blanco from the Bronx.

"Not interested." Blondie opened the backdoor of the sedan and shoved the CI inside. "Watch your head, asshole." He cautioned but deliberately rammed Alex's head against the car.

"Wait! Wait!" Alex pleaded. "Dude is tryna' cop some major weight, yo. Don't you at least wanna check it out?"

Blondie slammed the rear door and sat behind the wheel. "Big fuckin' deal. Some schmuck wants to buy some dope. We take him down and two more drug dealers take his place. I want a whale, not a goldfish." He put the ride in gear and pulled away from the curb.

Alex began to talk fast, "You not hearing me, yo. This cat is from BBE. He and Sosa used to be tight, but word on the streets is that there is some kinda friction within the clique. That's why ol' boy tryna' link up with me. He talking 'bout coppin' ten bricks, yo. If he gets knocked with that much yayo, he's gonna flip like Gabby Douglas and hand you Sosa on a prison platter. Trust me."

At the mention of Sosa, Blondie hit the brakes, looked in the rearview mirror, and made eye contact with the informant. "Now you got my attention, keep talking."

Blondie pulled onto a quiet, residential street to assure that they were not seen and listened intensely. By the time the informant finished blabbin' his mouth, Blondie had scribbled down the names, known hideouts, and vehicle descriptions of key Block Boy Empire crewmembers. This was information his other Atlanta snitch failed to disclose. Blondie's trip to Georgia was turning out to be promising. Snatching up Sosa would lead him directly to Benzo Al and give him the ammunition he desperately needed in order to crack the biggest case of his career.

He uncuffed Alex, but before letting him go, he had a few more questions. He pulled his ink pen from behind his ear and asked, "Do you know who's responsible for burning down Sosa's soul food restaurants?"

The informant rubbed his sore wrists and shook his head. "Man, that shit is mad crazy, yo. I haven't heard nothin'. Sosa has been off the radar lately, but I'll keep my ear to the pavement."

"Okay, you do that." Blondie turned to leave.

"Hold up doe'. This might not mean nuthin', but the news said that Sosa's spots were being torched with ether, right?"

Blondie nodded his head. He cursed the Atlanta PD for leaking vital information to the press. Alex continued, "Well, remember that stick-up crew in L.A. called the Body Snatchers? They were runnin' up on niggas, taking all their dough, and blazing the dope with ether before they bounced."

"Right, I remember that, but most of that gang is dead. In fact, one of them just washed ashore in Mexico. Do you think there is a copycat crew?"

"I don't know, but I did hear about a Diablo chop shop out in L.A. that was recently torched with ether too. So, do the math, yo."

Blondie jotted down a few more lines in his notebook. "You might be on to something. I'll check it out. In the meantime, work on setting that deal up. Don't try any backdoor shit either. Once you get this guy on the hook, call me immediately."

In the beginning, Alex had flipped from D-boy to rat out of necessity. It was either cooperate with the Feds or allow his mother to get indicted for money laundering. As a straw buyer, she used her name to cop jewelry, cars, and two fixer-up cribs for her son. Each item was procured using drug proceeds, and none of the retailers filed a federal form 8300, paperwork required for purchases over $10,000.

In the end, Alex agreed to wear a diamond faced Jacob's watch that housed a recording device. With his help, the DEA, in conjunction with the ATF and FBI, took down a ruthless chapter of the Latin Kings in New York. The Attorney General conveniently redacted all mentions of Alex's real name from the discovery paperwork, referring to him only as CI-three. Alex got a downward departure sentence reduction under provision 5K1.1 and vamped to Hot Lanta hoping to make a fresh start. However, once the Feds got you, they have you for life.

Alex bid Blondie farewell with a middle finger and flagged down a yellow cab to take him back to where he left his Aston Martin. "Why do ten when you could tell on a friend," he justified his actions and dialed the digits of his next vic. The mark picked up on the fourth ring. The CI grinned. "What up, Papa? It's ya boy, Mr. Sixteen-Five aka Alex!"

The cab driver ears perked up. His occupation gave him a telescope view of the world. He saw everything and heard even more. He had witnessed Alex speaking with the federal agent, so he tuned in and monitored the phone conversation closely. In his line of work, information was a valuable commodity. He put the cab in drive and listened intensely, hoping that Alex dropped a name.

CHAPTER 10

No Honor Amongst Thieves

2-Chainz spewed out of the state-of-the-art audio system at Magic City gentlemen's lounge. "I'ma be fresh as hell if the Feds watchin'."

The earsplitting bass had all the dope-boyz turned up and throwing bands at the strobe light stage. A bad Dominican stripper named Katt dropped it low, brought it back up, and made her phatty jiggle like Jello. Not to be outdone, the porn star Pinky slid down a brass pole, got on her hands and knees, and made each of her famous booty cheeks clap to the rhythm of the thumping beat.

The testosterone-charged crowd roared with applause and more stacks rained on the stage with reckless abandon. The D-boyz tricked off their re-up money, and those who worked a steady nine to five fucked off the rent.

DJ K-Slay was on the ones and twos. He changed the track and *Rick Ross* serenaded the club with his baritone voice and caviar laced lyrics. "I think I'm Big Meech, Larry Hoover."

The Block Boy Empire clique went berserk and chanted along with the hustler's anthem, "Whippin' work, hallelujah!"

Big face bills were tossed in the air and drizzled on the floor like confetti. Although the streets were in a depression, BBE made their presence known. Goons and ballers wearing black Tee's with the initials BBE splashed across the front and their battle cry, '*Till Death Do us or the Feds Unglue Us*, silk-screened on the back, reigned supreme. Tabu and Shako, two of Milwaukee's finest, got lap dances from Thicky Minaj and Roxanne 50-Bandz.

Ice and two of his closest cronies occupied the VIP. Gutter and a BBE henchman named Escobar were sipping Goose, smoking loud pack, and enjoying the scantily clad models from *Straight Stuntin' Magazine*. The super thick women were competing for attention.

Ice ignored the sideshow. His mind was strictly focused on making money, not spending it. The coke drought was getting worse, and he who controlled the supply controlled the streets. Ice wanted to be that nigga, but he needed a solid plug first.

The Cholos he was dealing with out of Arizona were not consistent. He thought he had found a reliable coke connect named Stix, but the Haitian drug dealer got wet up by an unknown assailant out in Cali. Ice's only hope was Sosa, and even he was giving him the runaround.

"What it do, Ice? What's on yo' brain, my nig?" Gutter inquired.

Gutter was 5'11", light-skinned, and wore his long hair pulled back into a frizzy ponytail. Number XXV J-Bones adorned his feet, and the ice cube sized diamonds in his earlobe sparkled like his green eyes. He dressed fresh to death but was not a pretty boy by far. Heavy hitters in the streets knew what time it was, and he never hesitated when it came time to clap that iron.

Ice cursed himself for allowing his stressful thoughts to be so obvious. He had never been good at concealing his emotions. It took all of his strength to force an artificial smile. "It's all Gucci, I'm just thinking 'bout which one of deez ratchet hoes I'm gon' run-up in tonight." In reality, he was anxiously waiting for Sosa to hit him on the hip.

"Fa' sho'!" Gutter and Ice locked fingers and performed their nation's ritualistic handshake. Pinky twerked her ba-dunka-dunk like it was on steroids.

"Check this, my nig, we should see if we can run a train on that porno star bitch," Gutter suggested before tilting back a tall bottle of Grey Goose and taking it to the head.

"Ah, man, ol' gurl ain't going." Ice sprinkled three point five grams of fireweed with no stems or seeds into a mango-flavored blunt wrap. Everybody in the club was fucked up off one drug or another.

"That's the same thang you said when we flipped that punk bitch from that reality show. I told you, my nig, 'dem bands will make her dance."

Ice smiled, reminiscing. "You wasn't lying, cuzzo, that hoe turned out to be a boss freak. I never would've thought in a million years that she was getting down like that." He licked the ganja filled mango wrap to seal it and ran his lighter across the seam in order to dry the saliva.

Escobar changed the subject, his mind was on getting money, too. "Did Sosa hit yo' line yet? It's damn near one-thirty in the morning. You said he was supposed to contact you 'round midnight, right?" Escobar was a fat, black, greasy nigga, but he dressed dapper, had the gift of gab, and could talk the panties off a mannequin.

Ice raised his wrist and looked at his Patek Philippe. Escobar was right, it was pushing two in the morning and still no word from Sosa. He was beginning to believe that the big homie was spinning him, but didn't want Escobar and the others to know, so he played it off smooth.

"Sosa, prolly busy. He gon' holla, though. So, y'all just chill the fuck out." Ice passed the blunt to Gutter, leaned back on the velvet couch in the VIP, and brushed his waves.

Another BBE affiliate named Outlaw stuck his head into the VIP area and asked, "Did Sosa call yet?" A Block Boy Empire medallion littered with gleaming black diamonds hung from a chunky platinum rope that was looped around his neck.

Ice rolled his eyes. "Damn, y'all niggas act like some little kids. Are we there yet? Are we there yet?" he mocked. "When the big homie call, y'all will be the first to know. I'll even let one of y'all niggas hold my dick while me and him chop it up."

Laughter exploded and everyone's mood lightened. Outlaw playfully smacked Ice on the back of the head. "Whateva', 50 Cent looking, ass nigga." He flopped down on the plush couch next to Ice.

Outlaw was tall, dark, and deranged. The words *PAY ME* were tatted on the palms of his hands, and *GAME OVER* was inked on each of his eyelids. He and Ice were best friends. "Aye, Gutter, pass the bud before you smoke up all the weed with those big ass fish lips," he continued the friendly banter.

Ice doubled over in laughter. Seconds later, his phone rang. It seemed as if the DJ had pressed the mute button in the club. The four men eagerly waited in silence hoping it was the call they had been expecting. They wanted to ball hard and continue living the extravagant lifestyle that they had become accustomed to. Sosa and his Rolodex of cocaine suppliers was the key.

Ice did not want to seem anxious, so he played it cool and answered on the fourth ring. "Wassup, holla at me."

"What up, Papa? It's ya boy, Mr. Sixteen-Five aka Alex!" The slippery confidential informant had his plan laid out. All he needed was for Ice to bite the bait.

The two hustlers politicked and negotiated. They finally settled on $14,500 for each birdie. Ice hung up the phone with a broad grin on his lips. His VS1 diamond grill twinkled like a chandelier.

"Wuz that him?" Escobar inquired. He needed to chop it up with Sosa about a rumor he heard about Ice while getting his box Chevy detailed at the car wash.

"Nope, it was that Spanish cat, Alex. He was finna serve us ten of them thangs, but the numbers is looking lovely, so I'm 'bout to catch twenty of them pretty white bitches. We back in business, baby! 'Till death do us!" Ice shouted and raised his bottle of Spades in the air.

"Hold up, hold up, fam," Escobar interrupted and raised a curious eyebrow. "How much is this Spanish cat finna tax us?"

"Sixteen-Five a unit," Ice retorted. He ignored the way Escobar looked at him side-eyed and chanted, "Till death do us!"

"Or the Feds unglue us!" Gutter and Outlaw sang in unison and raised their bottles for a toast.

Ice never stopped to consider why Alex agreed to such a low price during drought season. He was only concerned with pocketing the extra forty bands he added onto the ticket. More blunts were rolled and more alcohol flowed. Gutter's game wasn't strong enough to pull Pinky. In a drunken stupor, he called her all types of bitches and hoes and accused her of having AIDS. Ever the consummate professional, Pinky took it in stride and strolled backstage to count her loot.

Katt chose Ice, they worked out a deal while she was gyrating her wide hips on his crotch during a steamy lap dance. She was a fresh face on the scene. She grew up in Milwaukee but migrated to Como, Mississippi after her baby daddy got indicted with the Murda Mob. Those country boys eventually ran her out of Como, so she drifted to L.A. and finally the ATL.

The bar closed and a legion of foreign automobiles mounted on oversized chrome rims and drippin' House of Kolors candy paint caravanned out of the parking lot. The entourage of expensive whips looked like a moving exotic car show.

Two Porsche Panameras, an S550 Benz, and a cocaine white Bentley GT remained in the dark lot. These luxurious chariots belonged to BBE. The only other vehicle left behind was a charcoal gray Dodge Magnum that belonged to one of the bouncers.

Ice rubbed Katt's phat booty while leading her to his ride. Her hazel contact lenses almost popped out when she saw what he was pushing. She had been clocking Ice all night. The jewels on his neck, wrists, and teeth told her he had a little money, but she did not figure that he had $249,000 Bentley money. By the time he opened the passenger door, she was already creepin' on a come up.

Ice escorted Katt to his whip and then huddled up with Gutter, Outlaw, and Escobar. He had his plan all laid out. "Alex wants to meet early in the morning," he began. "So, I'm finna go to the stash tonight and snatch up that paper we been stackin'. Once everythang go down, we gon' meet up at Gutter's crib, stretch the twenty chickens with Pro Scent, and recompress 'em with a 5-ton floor jack. Everybody gon' get an even split. When we finish with that load, we gon' put all of our cake together again and keep on bubblin'. Feel me?"

Escobar wasn't feeling him. He hit the automatic start to his Benz, and asked, "What about the stripper hoe? You sho' you wanna have all that skrilla around a bitch you just met? We don't rock like that."

All heads swiveled towards Katt. Her shoulder-length weave was on point, and she was killing the game in her snug-fitting Emilio Pucci denim jeans. She noticed the men looking her way and flashed an innocent smile. Nothing about her docile demeanor and cute, Chinese looking eyes seemed threatening.

Ice shrugged his shoulders. "Nah, she straight." Gutter and Outlaw foolishly agreed. A cocktail of weed, sizzurp, and Molly clouded their better judgment.

Katt damn near pissed on herself when the four, well-known thugs looked her way. She thought one of them might have recognized her. She was prepared to hop out of the Bentley and run, but when they resumed talking, she relaxed. She held her cell phone low in her lap and typed a quick text message. She tapped the send button just as Ice opened the driver's side door and eased behind the wheel.

He pressed start engine, and *Bryson Tiller's* new joint leaked through the speakers. It was late and the traffic was light. No one was on the streets except the hypes and the vampires.

Katt unbuckled Ice's Gucci belt, unzipped his designer jeans, and pulled out his rock hard, magic stick. A clear drop of precum oozed from the tip. Katt used it as a lubricant and jacked him up and down.

"Damn, daddy, you working with a monster!" She stroked his small dick and his big ego at the same time. Finally, she clamped her soft lips over the head of Ice's penis and twirled her tongue around the crown. Ice swerved and damn near hit a light pole.

He regained control and kept one hand on the wood grain steering wheel and used the other to wrap her honey-blond weave around his fist. He groaned and pushed her head deeper into his lap. His balls were on her chin.

Katt expertly deep throated the remaining inches with ease. Ice moaned and his eyes rolled into the back of his head. Katt came up for a gulp of air, spit on the head of his dick, and swallowed him again. She bobbed her head, twisted her neck, and bossed him off like Monica Lewinsky.

Ice rewarded her efforts with a mouth full of thick white cum. A geyser of hot sperm shot from his dick and hit her tonsils. Katt gagged but managed to guzzle it all. The intimate encounter meant nothing to her. A trick was a trick in her book. Her soul had been hardened long ago by the streets of North Side Milwaukee.

"That's just a teaser. The best is yet to come," she promised, wiping her sticky lips with the back of her hand. She looked in the side rearview mirror and strapped on her seatbelt.

"Fa' sho'!" Ice cheesed from diamond earring to earring. "I'ma tear dat pussy up all night!" His eyes were glued to the phat camel toe imprint between her legs as a black cargo van swooped in front of the Bentley and cut them off. The driver of the van braced himself and mashed on the brakes. "What the fuck!" Ice saw the van's red taillights flash and pressed his own breaks.

A Dodge Magnum swooped up from behind. The gold teeth driver accelerated and rammed the back of the Bentley. The horrendous collision caused Ice's neck to snap back. He lurched forward and banged his forehead on the steering wheel. The Bentley careened out of control, jumped the curb, and smacked a large cedar tree. The airbags deployed and cushioned the blow, but Ice was still dazed. The back doors of the cargo van swung open. Ice thought he was seeing double visions but quickly realized that the two goons charging towards him were not a mirage. Their murderous AR-15's craved blood.

Regaining his equilibrium, Ice reached under the driver's seat for his piece and came up dumpin'. He popped off two slugs before Katt jumped on his back, causing his unsteady aim to miss its mark.

"Get off me, bitch!" He slung her off his shoulders.

The distraction was all the time the jackers needed. The first goon opened the Bentley door, and his partner bashed Ice in the face with the rigid butt of his assault rifle. Ice saw white stars and then absolute darkness.

Katt stood bowlegged over Ice's unconscious body with her hands on her thick hips. "What took y'all niggas so dang long?" she grumbled. She could still taste the after taste of Ice's salty cum.

"Stop complaining and let's groove outta here. Did you touch anything, bitch?" The club bouncer asked from behind a black wool ski mask.

Katt smacked her lips with attitude. "How many times have we pulled this same lick? Naw, I ain't touch nothing. You know me better than that."

"Wipe that joint down anyways, then hop in my Magnum. Lay low at the telly, and I'll call you when it's time to implement phase two of the operation." He patted her on her fat ass, sending her on her way.

Katt jumped inside the Magnum and sped off. Her plan was coming together nicely.

The three masked hooligans dragged Ice by the arms and slung him into the back of the van. His limp body landed with a nasty *thud*. The jackers jumped in, and the black van merged with the night.

****

"Wake yo' bitch ass up!" Twin, one of the masked men who snatched Ice up, splashed him in the face with a pitcher of ice-cold, grape Kool-Aid. Ice snapped awake, but he was groggy, and his vision was still blurry. It took a second to realize that he was in an unfamiliar setting and sitting in a chair with his hands securely tied behind his back.

Twin moved aside, saying, "Wake this fuck boy all the way up, Wiz."

"Awww, man!" Wiz shook his head in utter disapproval and exaggeratedly flopped his arms. "Why the fuck you say my name, Twin?"

"Yo' dumb ass just said my name too, fool." The two young criminals began to bicker and fuss like the Three Stooges.

Trey, the bouncer at Magic City, barked his frustration, "Both of y'all clowns shut the fuck up." He was a tall, almond-colored roughneck with penitentiary muscles bulging out of his shirt. "We ain't here to play games. Let's handle this bidness and keep it groovin'."

He pulled a Sig-Sauer P228 9mm from his waist and aimed it at Ice's dome. "Open yo' mouth, nigga!"

Ice did not register fear. Defiantly, he clenched his lips and mean mugged his abductors. Trey raised his pistol high above his head and smacked Ice across the ear with a powerful blow. Painful currents traveled through his eardrum, down his spine, and terminated in his big toe. Ice cried out in anguish, and Trey jammed the barrel of the gun into his open mouth.

Trey applied pressure on the curved, steel trigger. "I only got one question. Where the money at?" He was a man of few words, but when he did speak, his voiced hinted of the evil that resided in the vacant space where his heart used to be.

Ice remained mute and his blood boiled in anger. The possibility of getting stripped by the jack-boys was one of the hazards of the job. He was mad at himself for allowing a snake bitch to catch him slippin'.

Trey leaned closer, his face was wicked like a nest of blood-thirsty bats fleeing a dark cave. Ice could smell onions and pepperoni on his breath when he spoke. "You know the drill, nigga. We wearing ski masks. Tell us what we need to know, and you get to live another day and make back everythang we take. But if you ready to die, then we might as well take these hot ass masks off."

The implications were clear. If they kept the masks on, Ice had no way of identifying them. However, if they took the masks off, he could see their faces and therefore have to die. Ice wasn't ready to die. He told the stickup crew what they wanted to know hoping they would not renege on the deal.

Trey and Wiz dashed off to the address Ice gave them while Twin held down the spot. Ice studied everything about him, from the slight limp he noticed as Twin paced nervously back and forth, to the scent of his cheap cologne. There was also a greasy box from Sal's Pizza sitting on the living room table. Sal's only delivered within a five-mile radius. That was info Ice could use.

Twin took offense to the way Ice was grilling him. "What da' fuck you staring at, bitch made nigga?" He stopped pacing the filthy rug and turned to Ice. "I could give two fucks how you feel or what kind of revenge you plotting. Matter of fact." He broke protocol and pulled off the ski mask, tossing it to the side. Long, skinny braids with white beads on the ends of them hung wildly in his face. He swiped them aside, giving Ice a better view of his face.

Ice sized up his opposition. Twin had scrawny arms, round shoulders, and a glass jaw. There was something familiar about him, but Ice couldn't recollect where he had seen the face. "What, am I supposed to be scared because you took off that punk-ass mask? My heart don't pump milk, nigga. This BBE 'till I die!"

Whack!

Twin slapped Ice in the mouth. Ice grimaced and tasted salty blood coming from his top lip. Twin held his chopper at waist level and lifted Ice's chin with the barrel. "Look at me real good because my face is the last one you gon' see. This ain't just business, it's personal. You disrespected me by blowing a kiss at my BM while we wuz at the bus stop. That was a foul move. Thinking with cha' dick is how you got caught up in the first place."

A flicker of recognition registered in Ice's pupils. His Adam's apple bobbed as he swallowed a wad of spit to wet his dry throat. He recalled picking Sosa up from the airport and blowing a kiss at a super thick dime piece who was eye-fucking his 26-inch Forgiatos. You cannot outrun Karma. Ice's dirty deeds and shiesty character had finally caught up to him.

There was only one way to play the situation. Ice continued to mug Twin, seeking out a weakness, any weakness. Finally, Ice pulled his hoe card. "Real killas don't give long speeches before they squeeze the trigger. If you gon' shoot, then shoot, nigga!" He held his breath, hoping that his instincts were not wrong.

Twin's heart thumped like a pair of 15-inch strokers. His index finger curled tightly around the black, metal trigger. He raised the AR and aimed it squarely at Ice's forehead.

Whack!

Twin viciously clobbered Ice over the head with the stalk of the AR-15. The creaking sound of Ice's skull cracking was sickening. The rickety chair tumbled backward. Ice was unconscious before his body violently hit the shag rug. Blood drained from the laceration and pooled around his head.

Twin heard a set of tires crunching on the gravel driveway. The van's engine stopped, the headlights blinked out, and two heavy doors opened and shut. Wiz and Trey were back. Twin used two fingers to peek out of the vertical blinds and then opened the door for his associates. The corners of their lips curled into jubilant smiles.

Twin hurled a barrage of questions at them. "Did y'all get the dough? Was this nigga holding?"

"Hell yeah, he was holding. We up, fool! We finna shit on the whole city!" Wiz gave Twin some dap on the fist. They celebrated Ice's misfortune with sheer enthusiasm.

Always observant, Trey noticed Ice stretched out on the floor. "Whaddup with dude, whatchu' do to that nigga, Cuzz?" He eyed the motionless body and small circle of red blood.

Twin held his head high and stuck his chest out proudly. "That nigga got a slick mouth, so I shut him up."

Trey was surprised. "Like dat? I didn't think you had a killer bone in your body." He raised his black and chrome ratchet and aired Twin out.

Flacka! Flacka! Flacka! He drilled Twin in the chest with a three-piece.

Wiz gasped in shock. He and Twin had run the streets together since they were shorties, and even though they argued constantly, they were tight. "What tha fuck, Trey? Why you kill, Cuddy? That wasn't part of the plan." He started creeping back towards the door. "I thought we was supposed to double-cross Katt, not Twin?" he sadly assumed.

"That nigga was a liability. He said yo' name, he took off his mask, and he murked the hostage. What if ol' boy was playin' us and we didn't get the loot? A dead man can't talk. We would have been assed out." Trey pointed out, not realizing that when Twin stated that he shut Ice up, he only meant that he had knocked him unconscious.

Wiz wisely agreed. He would exact his revenge later, he promised himself. "You right, my nig, he was gon' fuck 'round and get us popped off. Besides, that just means mo' money for us."

"Naw, nigga, that means mo' money for me!" *Flacka! Flacka! Flacka*! Trey drilled Wiz in the gut. Wiz stumbled and tripped over Ice. Trey was right on him.

Wiz held up his hands as if his palms could stop a speeding .9mm bullet. "No! Please, no!" he begged.

Flacka! Flacka! Trey stood over him and let off two more rounds, striking Wiz in the wrist and just below the eye socket. The game is cold but fair. Trey scrambled out of the house and called Katt. She was right around the corner already making a call of her own. When she clicked over, Trey said, "Come scoop me up, bitch. The plan worked out perfect. We headed to the Bahamas, baby!"

Katt and Trey were a team. They traveled from coast to coast and city-to-city stalking ballers at strip clubs, fashion malls, and celebrity events. Katt would lure them in, and Trey would lay them out. The dollars were stacking up, but so were the bodies and her reputation. After nearly getting murked in Mississippi, Katt decided that she wanted to hit one last lick and retire some place warm and sunny. When she met Ice, the jewels, the Bentley, and his braggadocios mouth told her that she had met the ultimate mark. Enticing him away from the security of his crew turned out to be easier than she expected.

Trey tucked his iron and retrieved two oversized lima bean green Army bags out of the van. He draped one over each of his broad shoulders and smiled when Katt eased up in his Dodge Magnum.

"Hurry up, boy, you moving too slow." Katt popped the lock to the hatchback and watched Trey through the rearview mirror.

Trey slung both bags in the trunk and swiftly made his way to the passenger side of the whip. As he reached for the door handle, an Atlanta PD squad car screeched around the corner and lit up the Magnum with sirens and twirling red and blue lights.

"Impossible!" Trey whispered as his smile melted. Even if the neighbors had reported gunshots, which he seriously doubted considering what hood they were in, it was still impossible for the police to arrive on the scene that fast. Something didn't fit right, but he had no time to figure it out.

He pulled on the chrome door handle, but it was locked. "Open the doe, Lil' Mama!" he pleaded frantically and pounded on the window. "Open the doe, bitch! The one-time is behind you!"

There is no honor amongst thieves. Katt made no effort to unlock the door. Their eyes met, and for the first time, Trey saw the slithery rattlesnake in the woman he loved. Betrayal knew no boundaries nor pledged its allegiance to any man. Katt laughed coldly and peeled off, making the Hemi engine roar.

Trey drew down and dumped at the Magnum. The back window exploded. Katt lost control, swerved, and sideswiped two parked cars. She yanked on the steering wheel to regain control of the whip and pressed her Christian Louboutins on the gas pedal.

"Freeze!" The police demanded before opening fire on Trey, cutting him down in a blizzard of burning bullets. He died exactly how his mother predicted—in the streets.

Larry D. Wright

CHAPTER 11

Murder Mami

The egg yolk yellow sun had descended, and a silver oyster moon illuminated the night sky. Najee trotted down five flights of stairs to the underground carport. Once in the secure garage, he strolled past parking spot 15A and walked to space 10E. Spot 15A was a decoy, Najee actually lived on the tenth floor.

He snatched the dust cover off his low rider and gazed at the six-foe Chevy Impala with admiration. For a moment, he forgot about Nella, Benzo Al, and the price tag on his head.

Najee cranked the 350 Crate engine and the Holly carburetor growled like a Pitbull with bronchitis. He hit the garage door opener and eased out to the carport with West Coast gangsta rap wangin' out of the three 15-inch Kickers that were mounted behind the back seat. There was no room for music in the trunk. The trunk housed ten deep-cycle batteries and three gold plated CCE hydraulic pumps that powered the Impala's sixteen switches.

Najee mashed down his quiet block and immediately spotted a suspicious work truck with the slogan S&L Heating and Electric painted on the rear quarter panel. The truck was parked two buildings down from his condominium. Several cigarette butts piled up by the driver's side door, indicating that the truck had been in the same spot for a while.

Keeping his head straightforward, Najee quickly scanned the interior of the vehicle out of his peripheral. Two Styrofoam Star Bucks cups rested on the dashboard. Red-orange embers glowed on the tip of the driver's half-smoked cigarette.

"Fuck!" Najee banged on the wood grain Nardi steering wheel. "First I find out Nella pregnant, now this shit!" He wondered if the Alphabet Boys were clocking him or the owner of the flashy Bugatti.

Making a slow right turn, he watched the truck's movements. The truck's headlights popped on, and the driver crept into traffic. To be cautious, Najee did a 1-2-1 counter surveillance maneuver.

One right turn, two left turns, and another right. He was well versed on how the fuzz operated and knew how to elude them.

He made the last right turn, checked his rearview while fumbling with his cell phone, and put his contingency plan into effect. The person he called answered the line with a brusque but jovial voice.

"Hujumbo, my warrior friend," Jahiem greeted Najee in Swahili. He resembled Bookman from the sitcom Good Times. Hot water splashed into a yellow mop bucket and a small FM/AM radio whistled jazz tunes.

"Cijumbo, comrade. Habri za Kazi?" speaking in Swahili, Najee asked him how was work.

"I don't like slavin' for the man, but it pays the bills the righteous way. I'm 'bout to mop the lobby, then I'm outta here. What's hap'nin'?"

Jahiem was the night janitor at Najee's condo. At one point in life, he was a top-notch player and used to get it in with Freeway Rick. However, age and one too many prison stints had caught up to him. Having no education or work experience, he found himself mopping floors for a living, a dim fate that many hustlers faced.

Najee switched lanes and checked his mirror again. "I'm glad you're still at the condo. I got two devils stepping on my shadow, and I need yo' help. Remember when we were building on Supreme Mathematics number Eight?"

This was serious business. Jahiem turned up the radio to drown the conversation and closed the utility closet door. "Word to life, I remember, God. We had a cipher on Build/Destroy. You called it operation Hiroshima." The code name was fitting. Hiroshima was the target of the first atomic bomb. The Japanese seaport was totally destroyed.

Najee looked over his shoulder. The Feds were coasting several cars back. He sparked a chubby blunt and took a deep hit. "Make it happen!" he instructed through a miasma of weed smoke. "There is an incentive waiting for you in the freezer. It's enough for you to start your own commercial cleaning service like you've always dreamed of."

No further words needed to be spoken. Jahiem knew his task and was confident that he would be rewarded handsomely. Slipping on a pair of latex gloves, he grabbed the red canister Najee had supplied him with weeks earlier. Taking the back steps, he sprinted to the tenth floor and pulled the lever on the fire alarm just as Najee had instructed. A piercing bell rang in the hallway.

Half-naked residents spilled out of their units. Jahiem directed the frightened tenants to the emergency exit. When the coast was clear, he carefully moved to Najee's door, looked both ways, and punched in the code, 0-4-2-9.

The lock clicked open, Jaheim rushed inside and worked quickly, wiping down the entire unit, including the buttons on the microwave. Next, he put several used spoons, cups, and plates into the dishwasher to strip away any DNA. Finally, he doused everything with the foul-smelling liquid in the canister. Before making a fast exit, he struck a book of matches, watched the yellow flames rise between his fingers, and then tossed the fire into the trashcan.

Poof! The condo ignited into a blistering inferno. The fire would eventually destroy everything, including the ten birds that Najee took from the chop shop.

Najee's cell phone buzzed. He tapped the accept icon on the first ring. "Talk to me."

Jahiem made his way through the front lobby with a bundle of money stuffed into his lunchbox. "It's done!"

Najee was relieved. "Ashanti, comrade," he thanked Jahiem.

"Sikitu, you're welcome, God."

Now it was time to shake the jakes. Najee crushed the tip of his blunt in the ashtray, swerved over the yellow lines dividing the street, and raced into oncoming traffic. His Air Max pressed on the gas pedal, sending the steel Impala barreling down Pacific Coast Highway in the wrong direction. Cars turned sharply to avoid a head-on collision and honked their horns in protest to Najee's reckless driving.

He looked back and laughed. The Feds were stuck in limbo. The frustrated driver's face turned tomato red. Najee threw up a middle finger. The oncoming headlights aided his escape and parted like the Red Sea, allowing the Impala through unscathed. At the first intersection, Najee busted a left turn and dipped down a maze of back streets until he found himself at the corner of Century and Crenshaw.

****

As usual, Sunday night on the 'Shaw was crackin'. Lambos, Cadillac trucks, low-lows, and sightseers in hoopties took over the lanes causing bumper-to-bumper traffic. The Crenshaw strip was one of the only venues in Los Angeles where hard-working civilians and hardcore gang bangers congregated with a common cause. For the most part, everyone cruised the strip to have fun and meet someone new. Angela Rodriguez was on such a mission. Her hair and make-up were on point, her tight jeans clung to her sexy hips, and her Benz was flossed out.

Najee made a left turn going north and joined the convoy of souped-up cars and tricked out motorcycles. At the red light on Crenshaw and Slauson, a magnetic force tempted Najee to turn his head to the left. In that same moment, an alluring power compelled Angela Rodriguez to look to her right. She was feeling Najee's smooth dark skin, seductive stare, canary yellow stones in both earlobes, and the swaglicious way he wore his fitted cap pulled low. Their eyes locked. The attraction was irresistible, the chance encounter was inevitable.

Angela swept a stray strand of lustrous black hair away from her comely face to get a better view of Najee. She was a twenty-eight-year-old Latina from Boyle Heights. She inherited her sun-kissed bronze skin from her ancestors who picked avocados in the hot fields of Mexico and got her bangin' body from her momma.

Najee gave her a quick once over and approved of what he saw. Her chestnut-colored eyes were bright and inviting, and her slender nose merged into a pair of luscious, lip glossed lips that would put Angelina Jolie to shame. She held Najee's gaze, not wanting to be the first to blink, however, a silver and blue Rolls

Royce Ghost gliding on 26-inch chrome Lexani rims pulled up next to her black on black, 600 Benz.

The driver possessed a charming smile. He rolled down the passenger side window, leaned over, and asked, "Iz that cho' fly ride, boo, or iz you out flossin' in yo' man's whip?"

Angela rolled her eyes and rolled up her window. His game was lame, and the chauvinistic remark was insulting. She was a boss. She was Queen Kong shittin' on bitches and broke niggas. The brand new Mercedes was just one of her many toys.

She dismissed the nonbeliever and turned back to the clean-cut, chocolate brother whose handsome looks and bad boy mystique captivated her attention, but Najee had lost interest. He gave her the deuces and banked a right turn onto Slauson heading east towards Van Ness.

"Gee-wiz, it's like that, Papi?" Angela pouted and made an illegal right turn in order to catch up with the classic Impala. She loved a good challenge.

"Bitches!" Najee grumbled to no one in particular. He was tired of getting his feelings hurt by women. Falling in love went against all of the ism players like Pimpin' Ken and John Divine had instilled in him as a youngster, yet Nella had somehow penetrated his armor. "Bitch!" Every time he thought of her, he got angry all over again. He vowed to never trust a hoe again.

Angela caught up to Najee as he crossed Van Ness headed towards Normandie. She pushed up to his rear bumper and flashed her high beams on and off. She was a woman used to getting what she wanted, and she wanted Najee.

Najee peeped the two flashes in his rearview but kept rolling. He was still salty that ol' girl lost focus when the ballin' nigga in the Rolls Royce pulled up. He hated gold diggers just as much as he hated snitches.

At the red light on Normandie, Angela's 600 slid up on Najee's driver's side. He tried his best to continue bobbin' his head to *School Boy Q* and act like ol' girl was invisible, nevertheless, her powerful magnetism willed him to look in her direction. He cut his eyes to the left just to get a little peek, but she caught him looking and pierced his heart with her breath-taking smile. Najee smiled back and Angela's thong combusted into fire and desire. For both of them, it was lust at first sight.

"What's ya' name, beautiful?" Najee asked through his open window.

"Angela. What's yours, Papi?" She spoke clear English with a hint of a Mexican accent.

"My name is Sinatra," he hit her off with his suave sounding alias.

"I like that, it's sexy. Is it your real name?" Angela probed through sexy lips.

"Nah, I just do things my way," he spit one of *Frank Sinatra's* most favorite lyrics.

A cherry red, '77 Cutlass with four shadows inside pulled up to the light as well. Each of the young thugs wore red fitted caps. In that area, they could have been from either Six-Deuce Brims or Van Ness Gangster Bloods. Both sets were deadly.

Angela recognized game. "Let's get out of traffic. Follow me, Sinatra."

Najee hesitated, he had heard too many horror stories about niggas getting caught up over a female, but the temptation was unconquerable, plus the bangers in the Cutlass were grillin' him like he was in the food chain.

He looked Angela dead in her eyes and warned, "If this is a setup, I'm blasting you first." He held up his snub nose trey-eight and clicked the metal hammer back to add emphasis.

Angela smirked. "Aww, that's cute," she complimented his gun like it was a little puppy. "I stay strapped, too." She reached in her lap and came up clutching a huge, Smith & Wesson Desert Eagle. The chrome shaft glistened under the full moon.

Najee caught a case of pistol envy. He wished he had brought one of his bigger guns. The light turned green. Angela mashed the accelerator and burned rubber through the intersection.

"I hope you can keep up!" she yelled out of the moon roof. Her flirtatious words were encrypted with a double meaning and dripped with sexual innuendo.

Little mama was just Najee's type, beautiful and dangerous. Common sense nudged at his conscious, but Angela's mysterious and enigmatic personality made him stomp on the gas and pursue her. The onyx black paint and matching black 24-inch Giovanna rims made Angela's Benz look like a stealth bomber gliding across the asphalt. Both cars blew through the red light on Figueroa and headed towards the 110 Freeway.

Najee found himself following Angela up several squiggly roads that ascended into the Hollywood Hills. She stopped at an iron-gated mansion on Mulholland Drive. *Julia Roberts* lived on the same cul-de-sac, and *Steven Spielberg's* massive ranch was nearby. Angela stuck her arm out of the window and punched in her security code. Najee carefully watched her hand movements. After all, he was a jack boy. Within seconds, the nine-foot, black gothic gate rolled back, giving Najee a view of Angela's magnificent fortress. It was a vogue, split-level, stone palace.

Angela drove through and parked next to a black Range Rover. It too was swagged out with black Giovannas and pink suede seats. Najee pulled in and parked in a spot that gave him a quick get-away if needed. He got out of his ride and mobbed-up the cobblestone walkway towards Angela.

Standing 5'6' with long, jet black hair, Angela's milkshake definitely brought all the boys to the yard. Her face was pretty, her C-cup breasts were perky, and she had a phat ass like *Ice-T's* wife, *Coco*. A $5,000 Hermes bag hung from her petite shoulder.

"Welcome to the bat cave," she playfully welcomed him into her home. "I have some vicious dogs, so watch yourself." As she discharged the ADT alarm system, she could feel Najee's eyeballs scanning her curvy body like a security guard with a metal detector wand.

Angela opened the door and stepped into a beautiful, contemporary furnished living room with a domed ceiling. Her two dogs dashed from their cages. Najee was half expecting to see a pair of menacing Pitbulls with sharp, gnashing teeth, however, the two small frisky Pomeranians jumped into Angel's arms and greeted her enthusiastically.

She turned to Najee. "Meet my two bodyguards. The golden one is, Jackson and the black one is, Princess."

Najee followed her into an impressive kitchen where she refreshed the dogs' water and replenished their food. He took the opportunity to admire her round derrière as she bent over. The tour came next, they walked hand in hand as she led him on the journey. Her house looked like it belonged on MTV Cribs. Marble, expensive art and high-end electronics populated each room. The spacious backyard boasted a swimming pool, a large Jacuzzi, and a wooden sauna shack. The green ceramic tiles on the bottom of the pool were custom made. Upon closer inspection, Najee realized that the green tiles were a picture of Benjamin Franklin with a black bandana covering his face like a crook.

Angela was definitely plugged with some heavy hitters, and whatever kind of hustle they were into, they were definitely runnin' it up. Najee was impressed with her stylish tastes, but what really sparked his curiosity was the fact that Angela didn't have any family photos on the walls. That made his spider senses tingle.

The grand tour ended on the lower level. Najee was glad he got a chance to inspect her spot. He didn't see any signs of her having a man and the jack boys didn't jumped out of the closet. This temporarily pacified his paranoia, but, there were two doors on the lower level she avoided. Danger could lurk behind either one.

Najee's inquisitiveness got the best of him. He let go of Angela's hand and asked, "What up with those two rooms? Whatchu' hiding in there?" He pointed towards the huge, wooden doors at the end of the hall.

Angela smiled at him, her teeth were perfect. "That's where I keep the dead bodies." She saw Najee stiffen. "Gee-wiz, just kidding. Why are you so serious all the time, Sinatra?" She moved closer to him, their lips almost touching.

"I don't know. I guess it's because I've been through a lot of shit."

"I can tell."

"How?"

Angela scrunched her cute face into a mock frown. "You're always mean muggin'."

"Is this better?" Her antics earned Najee's warm smile. His pearly white teeth complimented his dark skin.

Angela's reply came in the form of a kiss. First one, then two. Finally, Najee cupped her soft ass in his palms and pulled her closer. His big dick was harder than Chinese arithmetic. Angela could feel it throbbing against her, straining to burst through his Robins Jeans. He pressed his hungry lips tightly against hers, and their tongues performed a salacious slow dance.

Angela broke the steamy embrace. She took off Najee's hat and put it on her own head. He liked the crazy, sexy, cool look. Next, she peeled his shirt off. She wasn't surprised that he was rocking a bulletproof vest. Everything about Najee screamed bad boy. His swag made her clitoris tingle.

She unfastened the Velcro straps and let the body armor fall into the growing heap of clothes. Her hands slowly massaged his broad chest. His chiseled pictorial muscles and gunshot wounds made her mouth water. Her eyes followed the thin line of silky hair that traveled down his stomach and disappeared into his Polo boxer briefs. A low gasp escaped Angela's lips when she grabbed his bulge to feel how many inches he was working with.

"Mmmm, Papi Chulo." She stroked him through his blue jeans and moaned her approval.

That was all Najee could take. He pushed Nella out of his mind and pushed Angela against the wall. He pulled her black Alexander McQueen blouse over her head and worked her tight pants over her thick hips until they dropped at her ankles. Angela stepped out of them. Her firm ass and grapefruit-sized breasts spilled out of a red Victoria's Secret thong and matching lace bra. Her fingers fumbled with Najee's belt. She unzipped his trousers and unleashed his Zulu spear. He appeared to grow longer and harder right before her eyes.

Grabbing two hands full of her phat ass, Najee lifted her 137-pound frame in the air with ease. His strong arms and powerful legs supported both of their weight. Angela pulled the crotch of her panties to the side, giving Najee unrestricted access to her cleanly shaven, phat monkey. His pulsating member pushed into her slippery slit, every black inch driving into her tight canal. He pressed her against the wall and bounced her up and down on his pole.

"Si, Papi Chulo!" Angela's first orgasm made her body shudder. Her next earth-shattering orgasm came when Najee gently laid her on the rug, placed both of her bronze calves over his shoulders, and dove into her sex pool like the Olympic gold medal swimmer Michael Phelps.

During each tantalizing stroke, he pulled all the way out until only the head of his penis lingered in her opening, then he slammed balls deep into her pussy again and again and again. Angela bit her bottom lip and took the dick like a big girl.

"Ohhh, damn, Sinatra, that's my spot! I feel that dick all in my back." Her lips nibbled on his ear. "Fuck me harder. I can take it," she encouraged.

Najee pounded into Angela's velvet vice grip for sixty exquisite minutes before holding her ankles wide apart and thrusting his iron rod deep into her one last time. His body stiffened, his teeth bit into her neck, and his pulsating missile detonated in her pussy. Angela's claws raked across his tattooed back as she talked dirty to him in Spanish. Najee kept stroking slowly until she came for the sixth time, and then he rolled onto his back with a smile.

Angela was out of breath. "D-damn that was nice!" Her pussy was sore, but it was that good kind of pain. She ran her middle finger up and down her swollen slit before dipping the tip inside. She removed her wet finger and licked it clean, savoring the sweet taste of her peach and Najee's gooey cum.

Najee stood up and fished in his pocket for a dub sack of Kush. "You smoke?" he asked. He stood in front of Angela, his semi-erect penis glistened with her feminine juices.

"Yes, but first I wanna smoke this big, black, blunt between your legs." Her sexy mouth parted and took his circumcised head into her warm throat. Her talented lips continued their expedition down the length of his pole until her nose pressed into his wiry pubic hair. She gagged and released his saliva-coated dick. After catching her breath, Angela blew bubbles and then proceeded to give him a sloppy blowjob.

Finally, she rose from her knees, took Najee by the hand, and led him into one of the closed doors. It was her bedroom. Like the rest of her huge casa, this room was also beautifully furnished.

Najee laid her on the California king size mattress and opened her thighs. Her vulva was smooth and plump. He returned the oral favor and his tongue made a slow pilgrimage across each of her pointy brown nipples, down her flat stomach, and finished its journey at her sacred temple. Angela clutched the sheets, arched her hips to meet his tongue, and came for the seventh time.

"Ohhhh, hell yes! Don't stop, that's my other spot!" She held onto his ears and wrapped her legs around his neck. "Eat this panocha!" Najee devoured her vagina like a vegan eating BBQ ribs for the first time.

They didn't make love, they made lust. The sexcapade ended two hours later with Angela face down, ass up, and biting the pillow as Najee beat it up from the back. She had a colorful butterfly wing tatted on each of her booty cheeks. When her butt jiggled, it looked as though the butterfly was flapping its wings. Najee was so hypnotized by the tattoo he didn't notice the newspaper clipping sitting on the nightstand. Angela had cut out a newspaper article describing Juice's horrendous execution. There was also a hit list next to the article. Unbeknownst to Najee, his name was at the top.

Larry D. Wright

CHAPTER 12

Grady Memorial Hospital: Atlanta, GA

Ice woke up with a massive headache. His pupils slowly took in the unfamiliar surroundings. Medical equipment announced their mechanical presence with rhythmic beeping sounds, and an older model Zenith color TV was bolted to a metal stand. The metal stand was mounted high on the wall as if the outdated, 32-inch television was in danger of being stolen.

There was a patient to his left, and a patient to his right. Both were at Mama Merl's soul food restaurant when it mysteriously burned down. The victims suffered significant first-degree burns, and their bodies were wrapped in white gauze-like deceased Egyptian Pharaohs. Painful moans and groans were their only form of communicating.

Ice grunted a moan of his own. The last thing he recalled was a blurry figure in a black ski mask stalking his way and gripping an AR-15. His hand instinctively reached for his head. It was wrapped tightly in a bandage. A circular bloodstain marked the spot of his wound. Seeking answers and pain medication, he pressed the call button for a nurse.

After a twenty-minute wait, a slim, mocha-skinned sista casually strolled in wearing light blue hospital scrubs and pushing a medication cart. She stood bow-legged by his bedside.

"I'm glad you're finally awake. How do you feel?" she articulated her words like a country girl who had been educated in a big city.

Ice groaned, "Keeping it trill, I feel like shit."

The nurse examined his chart. "You'll be fine. The medication is wearing off, that's all. The doc has you on a high dosage of Vicodin. Let me check your sutures." She waltzed to the side of the bed and unwrapped the soiled gauze bandage from the crown of his head. "You have ten stitches. Dr. Petty did a great job sewing up the incision, but you'll probably have a permanent scar on your forehead."

"How many times did I get shot?" Ice questioned, feeling blessed to be alive.

The nurse twisted her lips and rolled her eyes and neck. "Shot? You wasn't shot. You got knocked the fuck out. The police found you unconscious with your hands tied behind your back. You lucky they got there when they did. One of the guys that kidnapped you turned on his boys and murdered them. You were probably next, but the police showed up and gunned his crazy ass down."

"What?" Ice asked in disbelief. "How do you know all of this?" She handed Ice the morning edition of the *Atlanta Journal-Constitution*. He scanned the article quickly, shocked at what he was reading. "How come it don't say nothin' about me?"

The nurse wrapped a black strap around his bicep and checked his blood pressure. "I can only assume that they're keeping some of the details about the investigation under wraps. Plus, you didn't have any ID on you, so the police don't know your identity yet. Best believe they'll be back to question you, though."

Ice snapped alert at the mention of the knockers. He needed to raise up, ASAP. He looked down at the flimsy white hospital gown and then back to the nurse. "Do you know where they put my clothes?"

The nurse eyed him for a moment, and then her features softened. "Listen brotha, I know you rock with BBE. I used to dance at the ONYX, but your mans, Sosa, helped me turn my life around. I was lucky enough to get it together and get out of the game. Who knows, if it wasn't for him, I'd probably be locked up or strung out on powder—" She paused as if to reflect on an unfortunate demise. "Anyhow, I was supposed to alert my shift supervisor when you regained consciousness so she could notify the authorities, but I'm gonna let you get a head start. I put your belongings in a bag." She reached under the medication cart and fished for a plastic Wal-Mart bag. "Here you go, and hold on to these pills, it's pain medicine. Vicodin's are very strong, so take one every four hours, no more than that. Now hurry up and get dressed before the po-pos come back."

Ice accepted the bag of clothes and the brown bottle of pills with gratitude. He rummaged through the sack frantically looking for his $30,000 Patek Philippe timepiece and iced out Block Boy Empire medallion. They were gone. Stolen! Small bits of the abduction started to come back to him. He remembered getting bossed off by—*'Damn, what's that hoe's name? Oh, yeah, Katt or some shit like that.'*

The newspaper didn't say anything about the money being recovered, so he figured Katt came out a winner. He needed to locate her so he could be reunited with his jewels and the crew's money. The knot on his head throbbed harder just thinking about how he let himself get played. He looked at the face of his cell phone as he walked through the hospital corridor. The low battery indicator flashed, and he had twenty missed calls. Nineteen of them were from his baby mama, Qnesha.

She was straight up ghetto. He macked up on her because she had the biggest booty on the block. By the time he realized she was also the biggest flipper on the block as well, it was too late. She was already pregnant. He pressed the call button and braced himself for her gettofied attitude.

"Which one of dem' stankin' ass, hoodrat's pussy was good enough to make you stay out all night, huh?" She was breathing fire through the phone.

"Dang, bae, no hello? No how are you doing, I'm glad you're alive?" Ice asked.

"Nigga, pleeze! I'm tired of yo' bullshit. If I leave, then little Ice comin' with me."

"There yo' ratchet ass go. Why you always tryna' use my shortie as a weapon?"

Qnesha bit a big pickle with a cherry *Now-N-Later* in the middle and smacked her lips. She was one of those weave wearing, section-eight getting, boosting clothes on the side, loudmouth bitches who loved to start fights in public. She knew where all Ice's nerves were and loved to pinch each one.

"Like I said, Ice, I'm sick and tired of you fucking these nasty little hoochies and making me look like a damn fool. Lakesha's boyfriend told me yo' ass was at the strip club last night, and that Katrina was all up in yo' grill."

Ice straightened up and became attentive. "Hold up. Who you say was in my face?"

"You heard me. It was that bald-headed, home-wrecking bitch Katrina who do hair over at the Pampered Diva. And don't try to front 'cause I know it's true." Qnesha was fucking Lakesha's boyfriend on the low, and all he did was pillow talk.

It all became clear to Ice. He figured he knew Katt from somewhere. She was the buss down that was all over Sosa at his going away party. Half of the mystery was solved. "Good looking out, bae. Take Lil' Ice to my momma's house. I'll be at the crib in a minute."

He hung up in her face and looked at the other missed call. It was his new connect, Alex. They were supposed to have met over an hour ago. Ice couldn't afford to tell Alex or his team that he tricked off the re-up money, so he needed to track down Katt and torture her until she told him where the paper was.

Outside the hospital, Ice hailed down a yellow cab and climbed in the backseat. The driver was a short, Palestinian man with a thick beard and a black kufi hat perched on top of his head. A slab of clear Plexiglas separated the passenger from the driver. The commercial license posted on the dashboard stated that the operator of the cab was named Abdullah.

"As Salaamu Alaikum," Ice greeted him in Arabic. The morning sun was already beaming.

"Wa Alaikum Wa Salaam," the cab driver returned the blessing and started the meter.

Ice settled in and called Sosa. He was confident that Sosa would understand and help him out of his fucked up predicament. The line rang several times, but Sosa did not answer. His voicemail was full, so Ice couldn't even leave a message.

He hung up salty, his bitterness towards Sosa continuing to grow sour. Cursing under his breath, Ice hit Alex on the hip. Now that he knew who was behind the set-up, he vowed to catch up with her trifling ass by sundown.

"Holla at me!" Alex grumbled.

"What it do, Alex? Dis ya' boy, Ice." He chewed one of the Vicodin pills with no water and stuffed the bottle back into his pocket.

The shady informant set down his cold bottle of Corona and waved the female who was massaging his shoulders off like a fly. "You tell me, yo. I hit cha' line earlier but got your voice mail."

Ice didn't have a brush, so being careful not to touch his wound, he used the palm of his hand to stroke his deep waves. "My bad, my nigga. I had a wild night. You know how BBE gets it in."

"What up, tho'?" Alex asked between swigs of beer. "We still on or what?"

Ice hesitated for a moment and then went with the flow. "Fa' sho'. Of course, it's still going down. Why wouldn't it be? Dig this though, meet me at the Waffle House 'round ten tonight. We can make it do what it do then. Feel me?"

Tilting his head back, Alex drained the Corona while contemplating the logistics. Hustlers typically wanted to do deals on their own terms. If a cat said meet him at the Amoco at 3 O'clock, you would tell him to meet you at the BP gas station at 4 O'clock.

"Why so late, bro? Let's get this shit out the way as soon as possible," Alex countered.

Ice thought fast. "I dig what you sayin', but I was out partying all night. I still gotta swing by the trap and grab that cake for you."

The mention of money eased Alex's nerves. In addition to being shifty, he was also greedy. "A'ight, bet. I'll be there 'round eleven-thirty. Make sure you come alone."

"Bet that!" Ice confirmed. The extra hour and a half worked in his favor.

The two parties disconnected. The wheels were in motion. Out of habit, Ice looked at his arm to check the time. His naked wrist reminded him that the jackers had not only stripped him of his merch but of his dignity as well. He raised his head and caught the Middle Eastern taxi driver staring at him through the rearview mirror. The look made Ice nervous.

"Say mane, swing by the Pampered Diva," Ice directed. Abdullah switched lanes and picked up speed. They made it to the Pampered Diva in record time. "Keep the engine running, and be ready to move fast when I come back," Ice instructed.

As usual, a hive of beautiful queen bees filtered in and out of the upscale salon and spa. Ice accidentally bumped into a redbone stallion as he walked through the tinted glass doors. The redbone resembled the urban model, Cubana Lust. She looked Ice up and down but didn't see any sparkling jewelry or a flashy car at the curb, so she disregarded his existence and kept her Red Bottoms marching.

Ice caught a glimpse of himself in a large mirror and felt disgusted. He didn't have on his chain or watch, the neck of his shirt was stretched out, his jeans were dusty from being dragged on the ground, and he had a blood-stained gauze bandage wrapped around his head. He was beat up from the feet up.

The owner of the salon, a heavyset black woman in her early fifties, adjusted her shabby wig and accosted Ice in the lobby. "Sorry, brotha, but you can't come in here selling fake purses and bootleg DVDs," she warned.

"What, bitch?" Ice felt offended.

The owner pointed one of her long, ghetto-fabulous fingernails at a black and white sign taped on the wall. "See that sign? It says no solicitors. That means we don't want the hustle-man bothering our clientele. Try the barbershop up the street."

Ice became infuriated. "Dig this, fat bitch! I don't sell DVDs, I sell keys. Don't get it twisted!" His platinum and diamond grill shined in all of its glory.

The shop's proprietor stepped aside, and Ice strolled over to Lakesha, his baby mama's hairstylist. His eyes roamed back and forth looking for any signs of Katrina. He didn't have a plan. He was simply going to snatch her up by the weave and drag her outside gorilla pimp style.

Lakesha was rinsing shampoo out of a client's hair when she spotted Ice and gasped, "Oh my gosh! What happened, boo?" She gently touched the bandage on his head. "Do it hurt?"

He wanted to say, '*Bitch, what do you think?*' Instead, he said, "It's a long story, shawty. Come here, let me holla at you for a second." He grabbed her by the elbow and led her to a quiet corner.

He was fuckin' Lakesha on the low, but today he didn't have time or patience for small talk. "I'm looking for Katt or Katrina, whatever the fuck her name is. Where's her booth at?"

Lakesha copped a 'tude. "You got nerves, nigga, comin' up in here asking for another hoe. I thought you and me was supposed to do the dang thang, but I haven't heard from yo' ass in two months."

Ice looked at her sideways. She was the type of unscrupulous female who would stay out at the club all night, go home to her man with dick on her breath, and tongue kiss him without even having the courtesy of brushing her crooked teeth. He couldn't phantom her as his wifey, but he needed some 411, so he played nice.

"Why you trippin', gurl? You know damn well I miss that phat monkey, but Qnesha was getting suspicious, so I had to let things cool off." His fingers massaged up and down her spine as he ran game.

Lakesha blushed like a little girl. "I'm sorry, big daddy. I just want you all to myself. That's why I'm glad Katrina packed her shit and hit it. I don't need any extra competition."

Her words deflated Ice's hopes of retrieving his money and jewels. "Whatchu mean, she hit it? Where did the bitch go?"

"I don't know. The bitch said she finna' open up her own salon in New York, but that's a lie."

"Why do you say that?"

"She was a nervous wreck when she came in this morning, that's why. She packed all her shit and was out of here in a flash. I think she's running from something or somebody, and when a person who is on the run say they're going down south, that means they're going up North. If they say they're going to New York, you can prolly bet that they going to—"

"California," Ice completed her sentence.

Lakesha popped her gum loudly as she threw salt on Katrina. "I don't see what you see in that thot anyway. She ain't poppin'. And I heard the bitch booty ain't even real. The bitch prolly got silicone injections. Now me, my thickness comes from eating buttermilk cornbread and colla' greens. That's right, nigga." She slapped herself on the ass. "Neckbones and black eye peas."

Ice stomped out of the salon leaving Lakesha rambling to herself. On his way out, he spotted an empty salon chair and a booth with a *For Rent* sign. He sat in the backseat of the cab with a daunting look on his face and a sullen disposition. Once again, he caught the cab driver staring at him through the rearview.

This time, Ice spazzed out, "What tha' fuck you looking at, dawg?" He angrily punched the Plexiglas partition.

Abdullah eased into traffic and calmly said, "Cab drivers and bartenders are in a unique position. We hear everything. I think I can help you." He looked in the rearview and his eyes locked with Ice's.

"Do you know a chick named Katrina?"

"No, but—"

"Then you can't help me," Ice stated bluntly, and instructed the driver to make a left turn.

Abdullah banked a left and dipped into the gutter lane. "I beg to differ. I hear many things. Things that can keep you out of jail. Things that can keep you alive."

Ice's head was pounding. Disregarding the nurse's instructions, he twisted the childproof cap off the pill bottle and popped another Vicodin. "Look, Ahki, it don't take a dime to stay outta mines. Just keep those nosey eyes of yours on the road and make a right at the light."

"Okay, cool, suit yourself, but there's something you need to know about, Alex." The inside of the cab became extremely silent. Just as anticipated, Ice was all ears.

Abdullah cleared his throat and began to debrief. "I don't know Alex, but I know that Blondie cop very well. He was on the Anti-Terrorist Task Force after Nine-Eleven. He was known for harassing anyone wearing a turban. The Holy Quran does indoctrinate death to all infidels, but, not all Muslims are suicide bombers."

Ice rolled his eyes. His patience was running thin. He knocked on the Plexiglas to interrupt Abdullah's rant. "Skip the Jihad rhetoric, Mack buddy, and tell me what the fuck you know about, Alex."

"Okay, okay, last night 'round one a.m., I was taking my break when I spotted a dark blue, undercover police car with no hubcaps. Blondie was driving, and he had a skinny Mexican cuffed in the backseat. They talked for about twenty minutes, then Blondie uncuffed him and let him go. That's when he flagged me down for a ride."

"What the fuck does that have to do with me?"

Abdullah continued, "When I heard you speaking to someone named Alex this morning, I put two and two together. I don't think it's a coincidence that he was secretly speaking to a federal agent, and then openly talking about coke prices with you a few minutes later, so be careful. Your next drug buy could be a drug bust."

Ice brushed his waves with his palm as he pondered the situation. Despite being woozy from the pills, his mind traversed at peak speed. "A'ight, I hear you. Ol' boy smelled like crawfish from the jump. You just confirmed my suspicion. Make another right at the stop sign."

BBE kept several hideouts with colorful code names tucked away in suburban neighborhoods throughout the ATL and other cities across the country, but this spot was in a seedier part of town. The Bluff, located off the old Bankhead Highway on the West Side, was a withering pit of urban decay. Ice loved it here.

"Pull through the alley and park next to that green garbage can," Ice directed. The cab came to a halt. Ice got out and stuck his head through the passenger window. "I'ma run in the house and grab some cash. How much I owe you?"

Abdullah looked at the meter with a sly grin. "The ride was free. It's up to you to decide how valuable my information is. I see and hear a lot of things, so this could be the beginning of a beneficial relationship for both of us."

Ice shook Abdullah's hand, went through a chain-link fence, and cut through a backyard. His spot was actually on the next block, but he would never let someone like Abdullah know where he lived. Abdullah had no morals or loyalty. He would auction his soul to the highest bidder.

Ice burst through the front door of the stash spot eager to assess the damage. A part of him hoped that the jack boys didn't find the loot, however, his hopes quickly metamorphosed into despair. The living room was ram shacked.

Ice moved towards the kitchen. The robbers had moved the stove aside, ripped up the linoleum, and pried the wooden floorboards loose with a crowbar. The metal trunk containing the crew's $500 racks was gone. Fuming mad, Ice tugged open the oven door, grabbed his hidden strap, dipped back through the neighbor's yard, and out of the chain-link fence.

Abdullah drummed his fingers on the steering wheel impatiently waiting for Ice. He was beginning to believe that Ice had stiffed him but was relieved to see his meal ticket shuffling his way. Abdullah rolled down the window and relaxed. Consequently, he did not observe the peculiar transformation in Ice's demeanor.

Ice stood in the alley on the driver's side of the taxi. "How much did you say I owed you?" His right hand dug into his pocket.

"Whatever's clever," those would be his last words.

Buck! Buck! There was silence, then one last shot. *Buck!*

The Heckler & Koch hit Abdullah twice in the chest. His limp body slumped over the steering wheel. The last shot burned through his kufi hat and left a grotesque gash in his left temple. A choir of neighborhood dogs barked loudly. Ice scanned the alley for witnesses, tucked the smoking tool, and casually strolled off. One block over, he hopped into his 73' Chevy Caprice sitting on 30-inch Davins and called Alex to change the meeting time again. He was in trife life mode, and letting Abdullah live would be detrimental to his freedom.

CHAPTER 13

The Trap House

After another brief conversation with Ice, Alex hung up the phone with a big decision to make. Should he call Blondie and set Ice up right away, or should he pull a shiesty do-low, pocket the money, and dip out of town. Once again, Ice had changed the time and location of the meeting, so he had to come up with a verdict quickly. He turned off the loud mariachi music so he could centralize his thoughts and formulate his next move. Fifteen minutes later, his conundrum became clear.

He made a run to a nearby Piggly Wiggly grocery store and copped the ingredients he needed in order to whip up twenty fake kilos. He rushed back to the trap and set up shop in the kitchen. He carefully weighed up twenty ounces of Bisquick, eight ounces of vitamin-B, and eight zips of granulated sugar. The sugar crystals gave the phony dope that sparkly, fish scale look. Next, he poured a can of 7 Up into a spray bottle and lightly sprayed the batter so that when the concoction locked up, the flour and sugar would crystallize and harden into a solid block. Finally, he scooped the mix into a clear Seal-A-Meal bag, shaped it like a brick, and wrapped it in gray duct tape.

"Not bad at all," he complimented his handy work and repeated the process nineteen more times.

The ticket was fourteen-five for each bird. There was no way in hell he was going to let the Feds confiscate two hundred and eighty bands and leave him high and dry. Besides, he concluded, if the quick come up scheme didn't pop off proper, he would simply abort the mission and set Ice up at a later date. Maybe even throw in a dirty pistol or two for good measure.

Having his first problem resolved, Alex grabbed his burn-out and called his cousin out in L.A. The drought was affecting everyone, but if anybody knew where to find some work, it was them. He planned to burn Ice and Blondie, vamp to Florida, and re-up with the stolen money. He could already imagine himself cashing out on a new whip, lounging at the beach, sipping colorful drinks with little umbrellas, and mackin' to some Cuban mamacitas.

Alex cracked his knuckles and got down to business when they answered. "What's up, primo, Como Esta el tiempo?" he asked how was the weather?

"El tiempo esta caliente. The forecaster said it prolly won't rain for another month."

Alex and his cousin were talking in code. Asking about the weather was a covert way of asking do you have any coke. Replying that the weather is hot and that it probably won't rain for another month, meant that the border patrol had seized several large shipments, and the drought was still on.

Alex was disgruntled by the news. "Damn, yo'. This shit is killing me," he admitted. His safe was on E, and his pockets were running on fumes.

"Shit happens. That's why I always tell you to keep two jobs. It's never wise to keep all of your eggs in one basket. Entiendes?" His cousin admonished him for not having a legit side hustle. "But I'll tell you what, primo, your checks have never bounced at my store. So, I'll see what I can do. However, familia or not, I gotta have all mines. The price tag is veintiuno for each book. Take it or leave it!"

Alex didn't hesitate, he took it. Twenty-one thousand a key was much more than he was used to paying; however, the coke was being fronted and his people always plugged him with that A-1 yayo. He could stretch the work with Benzocaine, an additive used to cut cocaine, and still easily pass the price increase to his clientele. He suspected that his cousin was connected with Los Cinco Diablos, but he knew better than to ask and was not foolish enough to mention it to Blondie.

Another issue now settled, he strapped on a Rhino bulletproof vest and packed the twenty neatly wrapped bricks into his custom-made stash box. He obeyed the speed limit and traffic laws while driving to meet Ice.

****

Ice made it to the meeting spot early and checked everything out. The isolated spot on Peachtree used to be a jumping nightclub called iCandy. Sosa owned the popular joint along with a slick-talking pimp named Prince. The club was eventually shut down due to one too many shoot-outs between rival crews. Now a dollar store chain called Wow-A-Dollar was renovating the building. Changing the time and location of the meeting gave Ice a strategic advantage. He fired up a doobie and rehearsed his plan in his head.

Drug dealers made moves at their own leisure and had a reputation for being fashionably late to every engagement. On the contrary, Alex was punctual. He arrived on time and cringed when he pulled into the parking lot. He spotted Ice in the corner waiting in a fuchsia-colored Dunk. The humongous, 30-inch chrome rims looked like shiny mirrors, and weed smoke seeped out of the tinted windows.

Alex shook his head in astonishment and disgust. He wondered how someone so stupid and indiscrete lasted so long in the game without catching a case. He parked his low-key Honda Civic in the slot next to Ice. The old school Chevy was suspended in the air by a Gorilla lift kit and dwarfed the compact vehicle. Both hustlers stepped out of their rides and met by the trunk of the Caprice. Alex swung a large Gucci duffel bag over his right shoulder. Ice never took his eyes off the merch. It held his destiny.

Alex examined the bandage on Ice's head. "Damn, son, what the fuck happen to you?" He and Ice shook up and gave each other a friendly shoulder bump. "Do it hurt?"

Ice exhaled a halo of ganja smoke. "You the second person who asked me that dumb shit. Is shark pussy wet? Hell yeah, it hurt, my nigga." He passed the blunt.

Alex accepted the spliff and laughed. "Calm down, kid. I was just fuckin' with you. I heard how yo' baby mama be putting hands on you," he joked, trying to put Ice at ease.

"It's a long story, I'll tell you about it later. Right now, we need to handle this biz so I can put this merch on the streets. This punk-ass drought got niggas starvin'."

"I feel you, I'm in a rush, too." Alex hit the blunt. "First things first, tho' show me the money."

"Show me the dope," Ice rebutted.

Alex chuckled nervously. "Don't take it personal, yo. It's just business. Money on the wood makes the deal good."

Ice knew that it was going to come down to this sooner or later. He huffed resentfully and got in Alex's grill. "What kinda bullshit you on, mane? You tryna' say BBE money ain't good? Fuck it, I'll go cop from the Miami Boys," he bluffed and walked away. He deliberately fumbled with the Chevy door handle, allowing Alex to change his mind.

Alex watched the Lambo doors rise. He couldn't afford to let a sweet deal go sour. Before Ice climbed into his whip, Alex gave in and called him back. "Slow up, son. I know you ain't on no thirsty shit. Let's make this happen, captain."

He unzipped the duffel bag and flashed the twenty keys of dummy coke very quickly. The duct-taped blocks looked authentic. "I showed you mines. Now let me see yours," Alex requested.

"No problem, my nig." Ice stood to the side and used the remote on his key ring to pop the trunk. "Take a look, it's all there."

Dollar signs gleamed in Alex's eyes. He licked his lips, raised the trunk and peered inside. His visions of grandeur living in South Beach, Miami, rapidly faded.

Outlaw was in the trunk. He came up aiming a sawed-off double barrel. Alex looked like a deer caught in the headlights of a speeding semi-truck. He wanted to run, but his Bally's felt like heavy cement blocks. He wanted to scream, but his vocal cords were paralyzed with fear.

Outlaw grinned sadistically and squeezed the trigger. The full force of the blast gave Alex a checkup from the neck up. His bulletproof vest was useless. Steel pellets ripped through his face without mercy and knocked him flat on his back.

Outlaw climbed out of the trunk and brushed the dust off his Levis. "Get the bag and let's move, Cuzz."

Ice stood over Alex's motionless body and stripped the duffel bag off his shoulder. "Don't take it personal, it's only business, yo!" he mimicked the dead man's words, almost throwing up from the ghastly sight.

"C'mon, nigga, stop playin'; we gotta ride out." Outlaw wiped down the sawed-off and grabbed Alex by the feet. "Help me with the body."

This was not the first homi that Ice and Outlaw had pulled off. Both men were ghetto stars from the same block. When Sosa first met them, they were literally hungry. Their gourmet diet consisted of white bread, boloney, and government cheese. They entered the game starving and stayed that way.

They hoisted the mangled corpse into the trunk of the Honda, then jumped into the Chevy. Ice mashed out of the parking lot but drove smoothly once they hit traffic. Two blocks away, he pulled up next to Outlaw's Bentley truck.

Outlaw left the coke on the passenger seat and got out of the car. "Damn, Ice, I'ma ride with you 'till the wheels fall off and the tailpipe is draggin', but why we have to do, Alex? Papa was the only nigga in the city with that butter," he said before climbing into his luxury SUV.

"I'll put you up on game later," Ice promised, and quickly changed the subject before Outlaw asked about the crew's money. "Swing by the GNC store and pick up some of that mix we use to cut cocaine. We gon' turn two into foe and foe into mo'. I'll swing by my BM's house and grab the blender, some molds, and the hydraulic jack so we can recompress the coke into bricks. Post up at Gutter's crib, and I'll get up with y'all tonight."

Outlaw seemed reluctant to leave. "Those crazy-ass Mexicans ain't gon' take this laying down. Shit is 'bout to get real ugly, Cuzz."

Ice shrugged his shoulders. "It is what it is, till death do us."

"Or the Feds unglue us," Outlaw replied, and peeled off.

Ice mashed to his baby's mama house in Bankhead. All they did was fuck and fight. The habitual quarrel ignited as soon as he walked through the door. Qnesha talked cash money shit, put one of his tires on flat, and interrogated him about the hoes on his Instagram page.

Ice slapped the shit out of her, ate her pussy real good, and dicked her down. Afterward, she fried him some chicken wings. Their relationship was a match made in ghetto heaven. Ice had a hectic night, and after a stressful afternoon dealing with Qnesha and popping Vicodin pills like Skittles, his eyelashes felt as heavy as lead. He retrieved the 20 kilos from his ride but dozed off before he got a chance to inspect the yayo. His dreams were peaceful, however, a federal nightmare lurked on the other side of his nocturnal bliss.

CHAPTER 14

Loyalty Is Royalty

An ancient urban legend proclaims that when one person dies, another person is born. Nella labored for eight excruciating hours and ushered a healthy baby boy into the world just as Abdullah expelled his last breath and perished.

Doctor Clayter clipped the umbilical cord, wrapped the newborn in a powder blue blanket and gently placed him against Nella's bosom. Nella was apprehensive about looking at the infant's facial features. Would he look like Najee or the rapist? She deliberated in agonizing suspense. Finally, she summoned up enough courage to examine her baby.

"Yes, my baby," she whispered proudly. "He's my baby, and I will love him regardless."

Nella appraised the slope of his nose, the contour of his lips, the structure of his cheekbones, and the color of his skin. She was left speechless and wept until she ultimately cried herself to sleep. Two hours later, she woke up feeling surprisingly refreshed and found herself surrounded by a room full of colorful flowers, congratulation balloons, and a small mountain of gifts, all courtesy of Sosa.

She noticed Brazy lurking in the corner like a salivating guard dog. Sosa loafed in the plush chair next to her bed. He had a serious look on his face and wore the same wrinkled clothes from yesterday. Nella was touched. He had stayed by her side all night.

Hearing Nella stir, Sosa was prodded from his thoughts. "About time you woke up, sleepyhead." His tone was cheerful, yet there was a hint of anxiety in his voice.

Nella reached for Sosa's hand and expressed her sincere gratitude, "Thank you for having my back. I don't know what I would've done without you."

"Don't sweat it, shawty, loyalty is royalty." Their eyes met and loitered for an unanticipated moment. Their interlocked fingers lingered longer than necessary.

Sosa was the closest thing that Nella had to family. She had to abandon everything she loved because she was wanted by the Feds, street niggas, and a league of Mexican criminals more powerful than the Italian Mafia. She couldn't afford to expose her friends to that type of danger, so she begrudgingly kept her distance from them.

An upbeat Korean nurse appeared in the doorway holding the bundled baby. "Uuhhmmm." She cleared her throat to get Sosa's and Nella's attention. Her presence broke their spell. "He has a slight temperature, but nothing abnormal," the nurse said and placed the newborn in Nella's arms. She nodded her head hello to Brazy and Sosa before leaving the room.

"Hey, Sosa, want to hold him?" Nella offered.

"You sho' you want me to hold him? I'm not a good role model. Fuckin' with me, little dog gon' be on the block poppin' tags and countin' money bags," Sosa joked.

Nella chuckled and rolled her eyes. "Stop playing. My son is gonna be a God-fearing lawyer, not a hustla," she proclaimed proudly.

Sosa accepted the baby from Nella. "Shit, lawyers and pastors are the biggest crooks and pimps in the game. Who else you know get to dress fly, talk slick, and take people money?" Brazy and Nella conceded with his point and mumbled their agreement.

Sosa did not have any shorties of his own. When asked why he would tell people that he didn't want to give his enemies any ammunition to use against him. However, truth be told, it was because he hadn't found a woman who was worthy enough to have his seed.

He lived a life of fast money and fast cars. Along with that came fast women and cheap thrills. The females in the game are just as thirsty as the men. They will set you up to get stuck-up, poke holes in condoms to get knocked-up and leave yo' ass if you get locked-up. Sosa was hip to their conniving ways and guarded his heart like an armored truck.

However, holding the newborn in his arms felt natural. Sosa drew the tightly wrapped blanket back to get a better look at the baby's face and did a double-take. He looked from the baby to Nella, then from Nella back to the baby. The shorty had the same Afro-American nose, thick lips and intense brown eyes as Najee.

Something ain't right. Sosa pondered to himself as he began calculating the number of months that Najee had been dead.

Nella broke his train of thought. "What's good, Sosa, you straight?"

Sosa shook off the initial shock of the baby's resemblance to Najee. He sensed that something was amiss, but couldn't put his finger on it. "My bad, I zoned out for a hot second," he apologized and checked the face of his icy watch. "I got a call early this morning from the condo association. My building caught on fire last night."

Nella sat up in bed. "Another fire? What's going on, Sosa? First the restaurants, now your spot. I'm ready to ride on whoever!"

"Nah, nah, calm down, Al Capone. Thankfully, it wasn't my tilt that burned up. It was prolly one of those rich white bitches on the tenth floor trying to boil an egg or sumptin'. But I'm still 'bout to raise up and relocate. I think dem' Alphabet Boys is watching this new stud who just moved in my building. He kinda reminds me of Naj—"

Before Sosa could elaborate, two female visitors appeared in the doorway. They were Nella's best friends. Glenda was a beautiful forty-eight-year-old butter pecan colored diva. Younger men flocked to the sexy cougar because she was a successful lawyer, kept her slender body tight, and had a girlish charm about herself.

Lala was the tall, black Barbie type with legs longer than the Underground Railroad. The twenty-six-year-old aspiring model, slash wannabe actress, graduated from Spelman College with a degree in marketing, yet she had not put her diploma to good use. However, despite not having a job, she still pushed a Land Rover and stayed Dougie Fresh.

Lala squealed happily when she saw Nella. "Bitch, how you gon' have a baby and not tell us?" she said playfully and kissed

Nella on each cheek. She seductively checked Sosa out at the same time.

Glenda chimed in with a bright smile. "Yeah, bitch, how you not tell us out of all people? Where they do that at?"

Sosa handed Glenda the fresh-smelling newborn, and she began to coo in baby talk. Glenda was also appraising Sosa's handsome looks on the low. She started at his shoes, sized up the bulge in his jeans, inspected his fingernails for dirt, and looked him in the eyes to see if he was on some bullshit. Sosa passed her exam.

Nella was excited to see her girls. "How did y'all triflin' hoes find out where I was? I was trying my best to disown y'all, ghetto bitches," she teased and observed the way her friends were drooling over Sosa. A surge of possessiveness shot through her, but she quickly shook it off.

Brazy confessed to answering Nella's phone and telling Glenda and Lala what hospital they were at, and Sosa announced that he had some business to take care of. He was anxious to find out if Ice had heard anything on the streets about his restaurants going up in flames. Sosa was unable to call Ice last night because the flight attendants made him turn off his phone. When he landed, he hit Ice's line several times, but only got his voicemail. Earlier, Sosa had scrolled through his own call log and noticed a missed call from Ice. He cursed himself for allowing his battery to go dead and hoped that Ice didn't think he was deliberately trying to ignore him.

Before Sosa and Brazy bounced, Sosa turned to Nella and said, "You never told us what you named the baby."

Nella looked down at her beautiful son and her heart swelled with pride. "His name is Najee, of course."

Sosa raised a suspicious eyebrow before he and Brazy cut out. 'Something definitely ain't right,' he thought!

****

Lala and Glenda stayed to catch up on old times. After an hour of yip yapping and playing with the baby, Lala dipped off to the hospital's snack shop. On her way back with three Styrofoam cartons of Chinese food, she cautiously looked both ways, then fished in her Prada bag for her cell phone and a book of matches that had a telephone number scribbled across the flap.

The laid-back voice of a Hispanic Cholo answered her call. "What's crackin'?" he greeted smoothly.

"Can I speak to, Cartoon?" Lala asked in a hushed tone as a fine, dark-skinned brotha with a serious expression strolled by. Lala got a whiff of his expensive cologne. He smelled like new money.

"This is, Toon. What up, who dis?"

"Hey, handsome, this is Lala. Remember me?"

"Como Esta, mama? Of course, I remember you. You're Nella's friend, right? I hope you got some good news for us?" the Cinco Diablos hitman asked while watching ESPN and chewing sunflower seeds.

"Yes, I do, but I need to speak directly to, Benzo Al." Lala wanted to make sure she got paid for her information.

"No, you speak to me or nobody at all. If what you say is important, I'll give your message to El Señor." In one smooth motion, Cartoon expertly cracked open a sunflower seed with his teeth, extracted the kernel, and spit out the salty shell.

Lala sighed and gave in. She looked around nervously, cupped her hand over the phone, and whispered, "I got the four-one-one on, Nella."

She stopped talking when the fine, dark-skinned brotha came back her way and pressed the down button on the elevator. His vibe was different. Now he seemed cold, his look gave Lala the chills.

Cartoon turned down the volume on the soccer game and checked his stopwatch. It only took the Feds forty-nine seconds to trace a phone call, and another thirteen seconds to triangulate an unencrypted signal to within one-hundred feet of the nearest cell tower. "Look, bitch! Stop wasting my time and tell me where she is," he demanded impatiently.

"She's at Cedars-Sinai hospital checked in under the alias, Asia Wright," Lala blurted.

Cartoon sprang to his feet, snapped his fingers at one of his underlings, and instructed him to bring the satellite phone. Benzo Al's number was on speed dial. "Good work. If yo' info is valid, I'll personally break you off fifty gees. You have my word. Play it cool and stick around until me and my boys get there. Comprende?"

"Yes, I understand." Lala fantasized about the number of designer handbags and Christian Louboutin shoes she could cop with fifty bands. She returned from the snack shop baring hot food and a frosty smile. To some, loyalty meant everything, but to Lala, fidelity meant nothing.

CHAPTER 15

Supply and Demand

The sizzling sound of fried bacon and the scrumptious aroma of chorizo and scrambled eggs titillated Najee's senses and snapped him out of his slumber. He stretched his stiff limbs, wiped the crust from the corner of his eyes, and glanced at his wrist. The small hand was on the ten. The big hand pointed to the three.

"Shit!" He knew better than to fall asleep at a jumpoff's house. His initial plan was to fuck, get up, and get out by sunrise, but after sippin' yak, smoking L's, and dickin' Angela down into the wee hours of the morning, he plummeted into a tranquil coma.

Noticing that Angela was not in bed, he checked under the pillow for his strap. Cool, it was still there. His jeans were crumpled up on the floor with the corner of his wallet sticking out. He smiled to himself as he recalled pretending to be asleep while watching Angela rummage through his pockets. As long as his knot of gwuap was intact, he wasn't sweatin' it. All bitches were nosey, he surmised and returned the favor.

He snuck down the hall to the door Angela did not take him into when she was giving him a tour of her crib. He looked both ways, then quietly wiggled the gold doorknob. To his disappointment, the door was locked.

He found the bathroom, splashed cold water on his face, gargled with mint Scope to slay his dragon breath, and bailed through the mansion naked like Melvin from the movie Baby Boy. He found Angela in the kitchen whipping up some breakfast burritos. She stood topless with a skimpy pink thong running up the crack of her round phatty.

Najee felt his manhood rise. "Diz-zaam, Angela, you thick as a protein shake!" he complimented her physical attributes. He placed his gun on the marble island and walked up behind her while she was standing at the stove. He wrapped his big arms around her shoulders and twirled her brown nipples between his thumb and forefinger.

Angela turned the fire off and allowed herself to enjoy the feeling of Najee's warm, minty breath on the nape of her neck. She could feel the pressure of his long, thick dick pressing against the crease in the middle of her back.

She was a new age independent woman who usually kicked her lovers to the curb once she got her nut, but she wanted Najee to stay. There was something forbidden and taboo about his essence. It was as if she was petting an exotic animal at the zoo. She knew it was dangerous, yet she couldn't pull her hand away. She wanted to be bitten, she wanted to be ravished.

Najee was more than happy to oblige. He bent her over a marble countertop, jerked her thong down to her knees and pushed his rigid, morning erection deep into her guts. Angela's face contorted into a mélange of intense pleasure and exquisite pain. She arched her spine and threw it back at him, loving the way he energetically pounded into her.

After thirty minutes of back shots, Najee sat in a chair, and Angela straddled his waist. She bounced on his pogo-stick like a cowgirl riding a mechanical bull. They came simultaneously in a sweet gush of warm body fluids.

Angela remained on Najee's lap fully satisfied and totally exhausted. Her eyes met his, and she realized he was even sexier in daylight. She traced her finger across the *No Love* tattoo stamped over his heart. The tattoo was a reminder of all the trials and tribulations he had endured. To Angela, everything about Najee was saucy. She rocked her hips on his semi-hard penis, savoring the aftershocks of her explosive orgasm.

Najee swept a sweaty strand of frizzy hair away from Angela's face and looked her directly in the eyes. "Did you find what you were looking for when you went through my wallet last night?" he asked.

Angela blushed with embarrassment but kept it one hundred. "I'm sorry, Sinatra. I just wanted to know who you were."

"It's a little late for that, ain't it?"

Angela shrugged her shoulders and threw her hands up. "You're right, I should've played Sherlock Holmes before I let you smash. I didn't think I was gonna wake up feeling the way I'm feeling. You put it on me, and I want you in my world. However, before I can let you all the way in, I need to know more about you. So please don't be mad at me, Papi," she begged.

Najee seductively traced her full lips with the tip of his tongue. "Nah, I ain't mad at cha', but you still didn't answer my question. Did you find what you were looking for?"

"Jeez, you don't give a bitch a break, do you?" Angela playfully punched him in the arm. "To answer your question, no, I didn't. I had my peeps who work for the LAPD run the name on your driver's license, it came back clean. Too clean if you know what I mean. So, who are you and what are you hiding?" Angela tried to read Najee's face for clues, but he kept a stone expression, relieved his alias stood up under scrutiny. Before he could flip the script and begin his cross-examination, her iPhone chimed. "I gotta take this call, it's business." Angela dismounted Najee's dick and answered the phone.

After a pause, she spoke in effortless Spanish. "El tiempo esta caliente. The forecaster said that it prolly won't rain for another month."

Najee munched on a strip of burnt turkey bacon and faked like he wasn't ear hustling. He had learned Spanish, Swahili, and Arabic while doing a ten-year bid in San Quentin, but he kept the knowledge that he was bilingual close to his vest. Having the upper hand on your enemy could be the difference between a long life and a quick death.

His ears perked up when he heard Angela tell the caller that it was hot in California. It let him know that the caller was in another city, and they were not talking about the weather. It was actually raining at that very moment.

Angela's voice grew louder, firmer as she demanded twenty-one gees per kilo. "I gotta have all of mine. The price tag is veintiuno for each book. Take it or leave it!" she delivered the ultimatum like a boss bitch.

Najee's spider senses began to tingle. Her whole steelo had changed from a poodle to a bulldog in a matter of seconds. He got dressed, tucked his pistol, and met Angela back in the kitchen. She hung up the phone and hand-fed him another piece of bacon.

"Sorry about the interruption," Angela apologized and kissed Najee's greasy lips.

Najee hit her with a knowing wink-wink. "It's all good, baby. Money don't wait."

Mounting his lap again, Angela wrapped her arms around his neck. "It looks like you know a thing or two about gettin' money yourself."

"Whatchu' mean by that?" Najee swallowed the turkey bacon, impressed that she wasn't cooking with swine.

"Game recognize game, Sinatra. I know you're a drug dealer, too," she accused with certainty. "I peep the way you move and the way you talk. Or shall I say, the way you don't talk. Most black men who have a lil' bit of change love to run their mouth about how much dough they're getting as if a bitch like me is supposed to be impressed."

She paused and stroked a long French tip fingernail across the old bullet wound on Najee's torso. "But you're different," she insisted. "For instance, your timepiece is hella fly, but it's not all gaudy and iced out like you're a wannabe rapper. In fact, there's not one diamond in the bezel, but I bet my left titty you didn't pay less than forty bands for it. People know what a Jacob's watch is, but most of them can't even pronounce Audemars Piguet."

Najee nodded his head in agreement. "True dat, true dat." The watch was a gift from Nella. She always had lots of class.

Angela was wrong about Najee pushing poison, but everything she said about his people talking reckless, putting trifling hoes in the mix, and being too flossy was on point. He had made a lucrative career off dope boys who committed such foolish transgressions.

He was about to up his piece, shove the snub nose down Angela's throat, and demand the combo to the safe, but her cell phone lit up again. This time, she didn't say that the call was business. She said it was urgent, hopped off Najee's lap, and stepped into the next room.

Najee figured it was her nigga. That was Gucci with him. The interruption gave him the opportunity to wipe down anything he may have touched just in case she didn't open the safe and he had to twist her lid off.

Najee didn't despise drug dealers. *Who am I to knock the next man's hustle?* he surmised. Nevertheless, he did hold them in contempt because they raped the hood like the Europeans raped Africa. They put profit over people but never gave back to the land. He put his back against the kitchen wall and quietly crept closer to the living room hoping to decode Angela's oblique conversation.

"Is everything set up, Benzo Al?" Angela queried. "Cool, that's what's up. Those vatos are becoming a major problem. It's about time they got dealt with," she declared vibrantly after a short pause.

Najee's jaw muscles tightened and the big vein on his neck twitched. The name Benzo Al scorched his eardrums. He wanted to rush into the next room and start blammin', but he held his anger in check, inspected the six brass slugs in the cylinder of his flamethrower and continued listening to Angela's convo.

"I'm down to ride 'till the bloody end," Angela affirmed her loyalty. "Get Puppet to arrange the transportation. We need ballistic grade armored SUVs and some heavy artillery." Los Cinco Diablos was preparing to make a major move on another crime family. Angela nodded her head while receiving further instructions from Benzo Al, and then she asked, "By the way, how is Juan? I heard he got burned pretty bad at the chop shop."

Her comment really put Najee on pins and needles. He cursed himself for not putting a slug in Juan's cantaloupe. "Oh, so his condition is stable now?" Angela confirmed after hearing the good news. "Thank God he pulled through. I'm gonna swing by Cedars-Sinai with a sketch artist. Hopefully, Juan can describe this, puto. You and the committee think Najee is dead, but I disagree. I can feel his presence. He's close," her words broke off, and a chill tiptoed down her spine.

131

Last night she dreamed that Najee had broken into her home and was standing at the foot of her bed staring at her with his cold, penetrating eyes. She snapped awake and gasped for air as if she was being held underwater. She was relieved to find Sinatra by her side, his strong body pressed closely against hers, his eyes swallowing her sexiness like a piece of sweet potato pie. She felt safe and secure in his arms as he slid into her wetness from the side and made love to her one last time.

Benzo Al debated Najee's existence for several minutes before Angela finally hung up and salsa danced her way back into the kitchen with a joyous smile. The drought was about to be over, and Benzo Al had a plan that would ensure Los Cinco Diablos' dominance over the drug trade.

Looking cool and nonchalant, Najee stood posted up against Angela's stainless-steel refrigerator. She got on her tippy-toes and rewarded his patience with a slow, sensuous tongue kiss. "Sorry about the interruptions, Sinatra," she said when their lips unlocked.

"It's all good, do you," Najee replied indifferently. Now that he knew Angela was plugged, he was going to exploit their relationship until he penetrated the core of Los Cinco Diablos. He pulled her closer to him. "I need a big favor, Mami."

"Whatcha' need?" Angela fondled his manhood through his jeans.

"Can you get your hands on fifty bricks?" Najee asked without blinking.

Angela took a step back. "Hold up, fifty kilos? You movin' them thangs like that, Papi?"

"Can you supply me or not?" Najee retorted bluntly. He had no patience for a verbal sparring match.

Angela hesitated for a brief moment. Fifty yams were equivalent to a life sentence in a federal USP. She was positive Najee was not a cop, but she didn't know if he could hold his own if he got jammed up. Against her hustler's intuition, she accepted the challenge. "Yeah, I got access to that type of weight, but I don't know you like that. I'll serve you five, and we'll see how it goes from there."

"That's lightweight," Najee countered. "I can move a lot of work, I just need a steady connect. If you can't get that many bricks, cool. Let me holla at your boss," he knew his words would strike a nerve.

The temperature in the room dropped and Angela's cordial chitchat became glacial. "I'll do ten, take it or leave it. But I'm warning you, Sinatra, I play with the big boys in the big leagues. If you want to be successful in this game, you best come correct, keep ya' mouth shut, and make your payments on time. If break any of those rules, I'm personally gonna zip you up in a body bag," her words were not an idle threat, they were a deadly promise.

Najee faked a smile and pulled Angela back into his arms. One of her small hands traced the length of his growing erection. It took all of his will power to push her fingers away. "It's MOB on this end, baby. From here on, we gotta separate business from pleasure. Feel me?"

Angela squeezed his dick one last time and boasted, "Have it your way, but I bet you start having withdrawals when you start missing this addictive panocha." She fed Najee another strip of bacon. "I have to dip outta town for a couple of days. I'll hit you up when I get back. Have your pesos ready."

"That's what's up. I'll be ready, but speaking of coming correct, I ain't paying twenty-one gees for a key. I can get a lower price from the Armenians."

His discipline and take-charge attitude left a positive impression in Angela's mind and between her legs. She was so caught up with lust that she didn't realize Najee understood Spanish.

Najee playfully slapped her on the ass, got dressed, and bounced out. He weaved in and out of the congested West L.A. traffic until he pulled into Cedars Sinai Medical Center on Beverly and San Vicente. He had found a way to infiltrate the nucleus of Benzo Al's criminal enterprise, therefore, Juan had to be exterminated before he revealed that Najee was still alive.

Larry D. Wright

CHAPTER 16

Cedars Sinai Medical Center: Beverly Hills, CA

Najee hated the sterile smell of hospitals. He wanted to get in and out of the facility for the sick and near-dead as quickly as possible. He made his way to the doctor's lounge on the first floor and purposely bumped into a busy, West Indies heart surgeon as he rushed out of the private break room.

"Oops, excuse me, Doc," Najee apologized politely while cuffing the identification badge he picked from the doctor's pocket. The badge had an RFID chip embedded inside the plastic, which gave him unrestricted access to the secure medical supplies.

Najee came upon a windowless door with a blue and white sign that read, *AUTHORIZED PERSONNEL ONLY*. He ignored the warning and swiped the stolen ID badge across the square security pad. The lock clicked open, and Najee snuck inside.

A scrawny, red-headed pharmacy technician who resembled Harry Potter adjusted his thick bifocals and rose from his cluttered desk. "Excuse me, sir, but you can't be in here. This is a restricted area."

"Oh really?" Najee upped the trey-eight and jammed the black hole against the pharmacy tech's pale cheek. Warm piss leaked down his leg and puddled up at his orthopedic shoes. "Keep calm, and I won't hurt you," Najee reassured. "All I want is a hypodermic syringe and a vial of potassium chloride." He pushed the terror-stricken vic towards a row of locked medicine cabinets.

"Are you insane?" the pharmacy tech asked incredulously. "If you inject someone with potassium chloride, they'll go into cardiac arrest."

Whack!

Najee smacked him upside the head with the pistol. "Yo' bitch ass better start worrying about your own health. Now get my shit before I get impatient."

Armed with a small bottle of the clear, deadly concoction, Najee struck the pharmacy technician in the back of his head with

135

the butt of the .38, knocking him unconscious. Next, he crept to the intensive care unit located on the fourth floor and wandered into the burn victim recovery wing. There were no Diablo goons guarding Juan's private suite. Looking both ways to make sure he was not noticed, Najee slipped inside the door.

Two pillows were propped behind Juan's back, and a shiny ointment lathered his legs, arms, and chest. His skin bubbled with blisters and boils. A Spanish soap opera played on Telemundo, but his eyes were tightly closed.

Living up to the *No Love* tattoo branded over his heart, Najee quietly tiptoed to the side of the hospital bed and drew several CC's of potassium chloride into the syringe. He held Juan's wrist and eyed the throbbing vein traveling along his hairy forearm.

Juan felt the presence of evil towering over him. He opened his eyes just a Najee was about to jab him with the long, sharp needle.

He immediately recognized his attacker and screamed for assistance. "Help!"

Startled, Najee fumbled the syringe. He attempted to cover Juan's mouth, but Juan bit his fingers. "Help!" Juan yelled loudly, his lungs working at full capacity. "Helpmmph!" Najee placed his left palm over Juan's mouth and smothered his third plea for help.

He used his right hand to stab Juan in the neck with the diabolical needle. Juan's pupils bulged and his body stiffened. The cool toxic fluid squirted into his jugular vein. The liquid traversed through a maze of arteries and rushed to Juan's heart. Juan grimaced and braced himself for an anticipated agony that never came. That was the beauty of potassium chloride. It stopped the heart quickly and painlessly.

Najee's method of assassination was pain-free, nevertheless, cruel. Juan's body jerked once, twice, and then ceased to move. Najee snatched the syringe out of his neck and kept it groovin' without a hint of remorse.

"Fuck 'em," he grumbled as he exited the elevator and strolled past the snack shop. "Those cowards slaughtered everything I loved. It's only right that I make the world feel my pain."

His murderous rant was interrupted by the sight of a sexy, Hershey colored vixen talking in a hushed tone on her cell phone. She had curves like a Coke bottle and stood over six feet in her come-fuck-me, Prada high heels. Najee did a doubletake. The thick stallion was Nella's best friend, Lala. He doubled back and pretended to wait for the elevator, but he was actually eavesdropping on her conversation.

"I got the four-one-one on, Nella," Lala sold her disloyal soul like it was a worthless trinket at a trailer park yard sale. "She's at Cedars Sinai hospital checked in under, Asia Wright."

Najee peeped how Lala covered the phone with her hand and looked at him sideways. To avoid suspicion, he stepped onto the crowded elevator when it opened. All thoughts of hurting Nella evaporated. She was his earth, his Cleopatra, his Nefertiti, and he was prepared to lay his life on the line to protect her.

Larry D. Wright

CHAPTER 17

DEA Headquarters: Major Crimes Division

Agent John Sullivan sat in his small cubicle at the DEA headquarters in Los Angeles. A wooden picture frame held a photo of his lovely wife and their two-year-old daughter, Hailey. Since taking his current assignment, he was seeing his family less and less.

He stretched his arms and let out a long yawn in spite of draining two cups of espresso that morning. He and an African-American field agent named Ronald Wilson had prowled the streets all night trying to track down Najee. The citywide search was unsuccessful, so he prepared himself to get chewed out for letting a person of interest slip through the dragnet.

His desk phone jingled. It was the dreaded call he was expecting. He took a deep breath, exhaled, and picked up the receiver. "Agent Sullivan speaking."

"What the hell is going on, kid?" Blondie fumed with anger. "I go outta town and leave you in charge for five minutes, and just like that, everything goes to shit!"

"But, sir!"

"But, sir, my ass!" Blondie cut in. "You blew your cover. I instructed you to move with extreme caution. The perp we're dealing with is not an amateur, he's a professional. Did anything come back on the Facial Recognition Software?"

"No, the FRS database was a dead end. The photos we took were low resolution and didn't have a clear shot of his eyes."

"What about ALPR? Every traffic light has a camera these days. Maybe we can track his vehicle?"

"The Automatic License Plate Recognition program was useless. The suspect had phony plates."

"Figures!" Blondie retorted. He was at the Atlanta DEA headquarters exchanging his civilian clothes for tactical gear. He spent the combination to a locker and traded his faded UCLA T-shirt for a blue, bulletproof vest. "We need to get a lead on this guy pronto. I think he's a Cinco Diablos hitman."

139

"*Hitman?*" Agent Sullivan questioned. "I thought the motive for the 187's in Hawthorne was a robbery?" He pulled a manila folder from his file cabinet and thumbed through the wrinkled pages.

"That was my first impression, too, but think about it. We're in the midst of one of the worst cocaine droughts since Pablo Escobar was eradicated. Yet, the assailant killed the Haitians and didn't take any of the drugs, just the money. I believe he was there to deliver a death message from, Benzo Al."

Agent Sullivan agreed. "It's a big stretch, but you may be onto something. The coke was worth at least a quarter of a million on the streets. The perp had to have known that." The gravity of his blunder finally set in.

Blondie's accusatory tone didn't help matters. "Precisely, but thanks to you and that black prick, Wilson, we'll probably never know his connection to Sosa or Los Cinco Diablos."

An uneasy silence commandeered the line. Blondie didn't mean to come down so hard on the rookie. Agent Sullivan's heart was in the right place. He just needed to be schooled by a vet. "Sorry to bust your chops, kid," Blondie apologized. "But I'm having a shitty day. On top of hearing about our suspect shaking you guys, I also learned that my CI, Alex Munoz, fucked around and got himself killed this morning."

Agent Sullivan tossed the manila file folder on his untidy desk. "Apology accepted, sir. Do you have any leads on the Munoz murder?"

Blondie held the cell phone against his ear with the help of his shoulder and strapped on his body armor. A tactical unit consisting of fifteen DEA agents cocked and locked their assault rifles and coordinated their watches and walkie-talkies to the same channel.

"I don't have anything solid. The last call on Alex's cell phone was from a BBE member name, Ice. I have a team gearing up now. We're gonna kick in some doors and crack some heads until we get some answers."

Agent Sullivan took a sip of espresso and combed through the notes he had compiled on BBE. "I wish I was there for the action. Did you gather any new intel on, Sosa?"

"No," Blondie answered begrudgingly. "While I was off questioning, Alex Munoz, Sosa gave our field agents at the hotel the slip. I'm not surprised, he's an elusive bastard."

Agent Sullivan felt better knowing he wasn't the only person who had screwed up.

Blondie strapped a backup pistol to his ankle. "My CI mentioned a possible connection between that Los Cinco Diablos chop shop fire in Compton and that elite crew called the Body Snatchers who were terrorizing drug dealers across the country. One person was injured in the fire, but he survived. His name is Juan Valesquez, get over to Cedars Sinai Hospital and see what you can find out. Also send a forensic team to the Vista Condos, ASAP. Dust everything for prints, even the metal handle on the toilet. I want to know who this schmuck is by happy hour."

Agent Sullivan cringed. He detested being the bearer of bad news. "I hate to be the one to tell you this, but there was a terrible fire in the perp's condo, so we were unable to lift any prints. The whole place was obliterated."

"Shit!" Blondie punched a dent in the metal locker. He regretted not bringing the perpetrator in for questioning when he had the chance. "Let me take a wild guess, the accelerant used to start the fire was ether, right?"

Agent Sullivan raised a suspicious eyebrow. "That's correct. How did you know?"

Blondie didn't answer. He hung up the phone and slammed his knuckles into the locker again. The possibility of capturing Sosa and Benzo Al was fading with each day.

Agent Sullivan logged off his computer, clipped his gold shield onto his belt, and set out for Cedars Sinai Hospital in order to interrogate Juan.

Larry D. Wright

CHAPTER 18

Los Cinco Diablos Hideout: MacArthur Park, CA

Cartoon hung up the phone with Lala, tucked a loaded Beretta into each slot of his leather shoulder holster and put on a Ben Davis jacket to conceal the bulky weapons. "Everybody strap the fuck up and let's ride out. This is a TOS mission for, Benzo Al. Terminate on sight and don't screw up. You know how El Señor feels about mistakes. If one of us fucks up, we're all dead, ese," he instructed his crew of gunslingers through a mouth full of sunflower seeds.

A shooter named Dreamer pulled a black and gray Raiders jersey over his head, pushed a thirty-two-shot clip into the bottom of an AKM, and dipped the tip of a Newport 100 into a baby food jar filled with sherm. He used another cigarette to light the tip so that the flammable PCP wouldn't flare up and burn off his eyebrows. He took a deep pull, exhaled three rings of smoke, and passed the monkey piss to a large, menacing convict named Puppet.

Puppet crammed a Desert Eagle down the front of his blue Dickies, adjusted his blue and white Dodgers jersey to hide the lump, and eagerly accepted the happy stick from Dreamer. His arms, chest, and neck were blasted with Indian ink, but the tattoo he admired most was the Old English letters splashed across his stomach proudly proclaiming his allegiance to Los Cinco Diablos.

They arrived at Cedars Sinai with the quickness. "Check it out, homes," Cartoon began as the three shermed up Cholos piled out of a blue, 1978 Monte Carlo sitting on gold hundred spokes. "We go in, we take care of this shit, and we come right out. Pop a cap in any gringo muthafucka who wants to play hero. Comprende?"

Dreamer dropped the laced Newport in the parking lot and crushed out the flame with the toe of his black, Nike Cortez. "What about that chica, Lala?" he asked.

Cartoon's reply was cold and heartless. "Murk that bitch, too. Los Cinco Diablos doesn't do business with snitches. If she betrayed her own people, whatcha think that backstabbing puta would do to us?"

****

Najee was ducked off in the cut by the hospital's vending machines. He peeped the three Latino gang bangers pile out of a blue MC on gold Ds. They moved with a mechanical purpose like Navy Seal Team Six embarking on a covert mission. The automatic glass doors swept open as if trying to avoid the menacing trio.

Cartoon's roaming retinas smoothly canvassed the overcrowded waiting room to assess any potential threats. He trained his eyes on a subdued white man sporting a buzz haircut and a well-pressed, tan blazer.

The white man stood waiting by the elevator, legs shoulder length apart, gun and badge inconspicuously bulging against his jacket. The name on his government credentials read, *Special Agent* John Sullivan. The crew of professional gunslingers wisely bypassed the elevator and trotted up two flights of steps to the maternity ward. Najee was right behind them.

Cartoon spotted Lala pacing nervously in the hallway. "Psst, señorita, over here." He waved urgently.

Lala expelled a tense sigh of relief. "I'm glad y'all got here fast. Nella's friend, Sosa, was charging his phone and left it on the nightstand. He's on his way back. So, you better get the info you need from her quick."

"What room is she in?" Cartoon pulled out a Beretta and screwed a four-inch noise suppressor onto the barrel. Dreamer and Puppet mimicked his actions.

Lala's eyes swelled. "Why you come strapped? I thought you just wanted to ask her some questions about her ex-boyfriend, Najee," she muttered while backing away from the loaded weapons.

"Get over here!" Cartoon grabbed a handful of Lala's Yaki weave and jabbed the silencer against her rib cage. "Scream and I'll blast you right here, puta." He warned in broken English and shoved her towards the maternity suites. "Show me where that bitch is at." Lala's disloyalty and fetish for designer labels had placed her life in imminent danger.

The elevator announced its arrival with a loud ding. Sosa and Brazy stepped into the hallway just as the Cinco Diablos hitmen stormed into Nella's room. Glenda was the first to get it. Cartoon clenched his crooked teeth and squeezed off. Teflon shells whistled through the air and slammed into Glenda's sternum. Two gaping holes disfigured her C-cup breasts. Dreamer's AKM coughed up fiery bullets and unmercifully chopped through Glenda's abdomen, spilling her guts onto the rug.

After Nella was raped, she vowed to never get caught slippin' without her piece again. She reached under the pillow and came up dumpin' a chrome .380. The wild slugs missed their intended target but gave Sosa the opportunity to get off.

Sosa snuck up quietly and pressed his stinger against the back of Puppet's shaved dome. Puppet felt the icy, steel barrel against his brown skin and heard a haunting click. Sosa let off at close range. The foe-five slug split Puppet's wig and left powder burns on his flesh, warm blood and bone fragments gushed on Lala's shirt and face.

Caught off guard, Cartoon and Dreamer swiveled around simultaneously and retaliated with a barrage of rapid gunfire. Six of the bullets hit Brazy. The most lethal shell struck him in his left pectoral, perforating his lung, heart, and liver before chiseling an exit through his back. His body relinquished his condemned spirit, and he collapsed.

Sosa looked down at the dead soldier. Brazy's lifeless eyes stared back at him. Rage boiled in Sosa's plasma. He blinked back salty tears and charged toward Cartoon and Dreamer. "BBE fa' life!" he yelled, and finger fucked the trigger until the clip was empty. The thunderous booms sounded like a muffler backfiring.

Dreamer took one to the neck. The tumbling slug ripped through his trachea. He dropped his gun, fell to his knees, and clutched at his throat in a frantic attempt to stop the rapid flow of blood skeeting from his windpipe. Nella let her .380 bark with murderous intentions. Two of the stray bullets left deep craters in the drywall, missing Cartoon's melon by inches, but the other three hollows drilled Dreamer in the back. He fell face first in the hallway.

The stench of death and gunpowder was overwhelming. Cartoon grabbed Lala in a tight headlock and used her body as a human shield. He popped three shots at Sosa in the process. The sizzling lead struck Sosa in the arm and snapped his humerus bone. Sosa winced in pain and dove into Nella's room, landing on his stomach.

Lala kicked, screamed and struggled to break free, but Cartoon was too strong, too determined. He needed a hostage in order to make his escape, and she was it. He dragged her to the elevator. The doors dinged open, and he forced the panicked passengers out at gunpoint.

Najee couldn't get off a shot without getting caught up in the crossfire, however, once the shooting ceased, he ran to make sure Nella was straight. He was expecting to find her helplessly confined to a wheelchair, but Nella had defied the odds. Witnessing his wifey walk on her own accord was exhilarating. He was proud of her, but something was wrong.

Nella scrambled toward the baby's bassinet. Her heart pounded in her left titty. The baby's face and clothes were soaked in reddish-brown blood. "Ohhh, noooo! God, please no!" Nella cried out. Her son was motionless.

Tears cascaded from her eyes like a ruptured dam. She gently scooped the baby's limp body into her arms and cradled him against her lactating breast. "Why, God? Why spare me but take away an innocent baby? I hate you! I hate you! I hate you!" she screamed. Her blasphemous words were bitter and sharp.

As if the heavens were playing a cruel joke on her, the baby slightly opened his sleepy eyes and smiled up at his mother. He was oblivious to the chaotic and violent world he inherited. Nella broke down and wept happily. She checked his body for wounds. He was not injured. The fresh blood on his face and clothes belonged to Glenda. A mixture of relief and grief seized Nella's soul. Her baby was alive, but she had gotten one of her closest friends murdered.

"Forgive me, my Lord. I'm sorry for doubting you," she repented sincerely.

Sosa crammed his smoking pistol down the front of his pants. The hot shaft felt warm against his belly. "We gotta raise up, shawty," he proposed. "This spot is 'bout to be crawling with Five-O."

His words snapped Nella out of her trance. She went to Sosa. His shirt was drenched in blood, and his left arm dangled painfully by his side. "Sosa, you're hit!" she gasped. "You need to see a doctor!"

"No, not here. I know a veterinarian who specializes in gunshot wounds. She'll patch me up on the low for a couple of gees. What about you and the baby, are y'all good?" He placed his good arm around Nella and the infant.

Nella appreciated Sosa's compassion and bravery. She raised her chin and covered his lips with her own. They shared an overdue, intimate French kiss. A squadron of police cars and armored tactical vehicles secured the perimeter of the hospital. The annoying melody of loud sirens brought Sosa and Nella back to reality.

"We gotta bounce," Sosa reminded Nella.

Nella composed herself and opened her eyes. She looked over Sosa's shoulder and froze. Najee stood in the doorway. His lips were turned upside down into a lascivious frown. His countenance was grim, his fists were clenched, and the thick vein on his temple throbbed angrily.

"Najee!" Nella called out, but Najee turned and mobbed off on rubbery legs. "Najee, wait! It's not what you think, baby!"

Nella attempted to run after Najee, but Sosa grabbed her by the wrist with his good arm. "You trippin', shawty. Najee is dead."

"No, he's not, I just saw him!" She yanked her arm free and ran after Najee, but by the time she made it into the hallway, he had vanished. More tears trickled down her cheeks.

Sosa walked up behind Nella. The pounding pain in his arm was excruciating. He had lost a lot of blood and was feeling nauseous. "You're in shock, Nella. Najee is resting in peace. Pull it together and let's bounce before the po-pos run up on us. Plus, those were Benzo Al's soldiers. We gotta get you somewhere safe because they won't stop until you're dead." He painted an accurate portrait of the truth.

****

Agent Sullivan arrived at Cedars too late. Juan was dead. There was no evidence of foul play, but he had his suspicions, especially after learning that a vial of potassium chloride had been swiped from the medicine supply room. He ordered a thorough autopsy and was on his way back to headquarters to write up his report when a fierce gun battle erupted. Panic-stricken patients and hospital personnel dashed towards the nearest exits. They pushed and trampled over each other like a Black Friday sale at Wal-Mart.

"Who's in charge?" Agent Sullivan questioned a battalion of underpaid and undertrained security guards who were gathered by the main elevator.

A smug, ex-military type stepped forward and hooked his thumbs through his belt loops. "The name is, Malone. Sergeant Malone, I'm in charge." A wad of tobacco bulged in his cheek.

"Not anymore." Agent Sullivan flashed his government credentials. "Where's the action?"

"In the maternity ward on the second floor, sir," the head security guard replied, feeling out trumped.

"Darn it!" Agent Sullivan brushed his tan blazer aside and withdrew his service weapon. "Let's split up. Secure the stairwell and the main elevator. I'll cover the freight elevator," he directed and sprinted toward his post.

Najee stepped off the freight elevator and collided into the young, DEA emissary. They stared each other up and down, their eyes unwavering. Agent Sullivan had been studying surveillance photos of Najee for the last twenty-four hours, so he immediately recognized him and drew his sidearm.

"Put your fuckin' hands in the air, do it now!" Agent Sullivan shouted. He had the drop on Najee.

Najee complied and slowly raised his hands in the air. "What's going on, officer? What did I do wrong?" he inquired innocently.

"I'll ask the questions," Agent Sullivan retorted. "Why did you murder, Juan Valesquez?"

Najee remained silent, pleading the fifth.

"You're a Los Cinco Diablos hitman, aren't you?" Agent Sullivan insinuated.

Najee laughed then frowned. "Are you crazy? I'd rather shovel shit with a teaspoon than work for the Cinco Diablos."

"Deny it all you want, but you're still going down," Agent Sullivan assured. "We know you robbed the Haitian, killed him in cold blood and gave the money away. My question is why? Are you some sort of vigilante?"

The Feds knew too much. Najee concealed his worry and kept a stony mug on his grill. "That's a good question, but you're not gonna get an answer today. Look behind you."

Agent Sullivan turned to find Cartoon aggressively leading Lala towards the front entrance with his heat pressed against her melon. Agent Sullivan turned back to Najee and found himself looking down the pitch-black barrel of his tool.

Najee held the strap sideways and grinned. "Never turn your back on a suspect, rookie. I could murk you, but I got a feeling you're a good cop. Go home to your family, and stay out of my way," he advised with his finger firmly on the trigger.

Agent Sullivan held his ground. Letting Najee get away a second time was not an option. The two unyielding men stood face to face, guns aimed in a classic crime fighter versus villain standoff.

Agent Sullivan broke the silence. "You're under arrest. You have the right to remain silent."

"You'll never take me alive," Najee vowed.

"Anything you say can and will be used against you," Agent Sullivan continued.

"You got it all wrong, officer. I'm not a bad guy. I just do bad things to my enemies."

Agent Sullivan ignored him. "You have the right to an attorney. If you can't afford an attorney, one will be—"

"The person you really want is getting away," Najee reasoned, pointing to Lala. "Would you rather arrest me or save that poor girl's life? Remember this, the enemy of my enemy is my friend."

His words made Agent Sullivan pause. Should he serve, or should he protect? He was indecisive. He did not want to tell Blondie that the mysterious perp had slipped through his grip again, yet, he could not ignore a hostage situation. Lala's scream nudged him out of deliberation. Protect was the verdict.

"This ain't over. We'll meet again," Agent Sullivan promised, and raced after Cartoon.

He missed Sosa and Nella creeping out of the West wing stairwell, but Najee didn't. He watched from afar with rage in his heart and his finger on the trigger as Sosa, Nella, and the baby melted into the sea of people evacuating the building. Their problems were only beginning.

CHAPTER 19

Juárez, Mexico

Los Cinco Diablos Headquarters

Benzo Al pounded his bowling ball-sized fists on the round, oak table. The loud boom reverberated throughout the conference room. All except one of the men in attendance flinched. "There will be no merger with the Nogales Cartel. Not now, not ever!" He slowly looked directly at his comrades one by one in order to emphasize his point.

He resembled a pissed off Rottweiler dressed in a black Versace shirt. His bloodshot red eyes radiated with homicidal tendencies.

Benzo Al's stepbrother, Carlos Manuel Guzman, remained calm and reserved. He adjusted the knot in his Ralph Lauren Purple Label tie and retorted in the same stern manner. "Fortunately, the choice is not yours alone. Uniting the cartels is good for business. Times have changed, mi hermano. We cannot have senseless bloodshed and prosperity at the same time. Ase es la vida. Such is life."

The five ruthless leaders of Los Cinco Diablos were assembled at a highly secretive meeting in Juárez, Mexico, a border city opposite El Paso, Texas. It was a rarity to see all of them together in the same room. They were wanted men, international criminals with a priceless bounty on each of their heads. Under the cloak of darkness, each member was escorted into a fortified compound on the outskirts of Juárez. They were not allowed to bring any cell phones, just one heavily armed guard.

Don Julio, the oldest member of the clandestine clan, twisted the ends of his handlebar mustache and nodded his head in agreement with Carlos. A custom-made Michael Kors suit and a head full of silver hair gave him a distinguished appearance. He oversaw a number of high stakes gambling houses that stretched from

Oakland to Manhattan, but his underground casinos were in danger.

The Mexican drug cartels had been locked in a deadly, cataclysmic battle for far too long. It was time for peace. It was time for reconciliation. When Don Julio spoke, you could hear the infinite wisdom in his words.

"We are on the brink of extinction. Look what happened to the Chinese triads, look what happened to the Italian mafia. They stole all the fruit off the trees but did not plant seeds. They became masters of war and slaves to greed. We must prevent this from happening to Los Cinco Diablos. Peace is the only path to prosperity." He paused to make sure he had everyone's attention.

Carlos liked what he was hearing so far. With Don Julio on his side, the leverage was in his favor.

Don Julio coughed coarsely, regained his composure, and continued speaking, "However, I am categorically against a merger with the Nogales Cartel. Aligning ourselves with those barbarians would weaken Los Cinco Diablos. I say feed them to Chupacabra." Chupacabra is a hideous, mythical creature that many Mexicans fear.

The old man cast his vote and reclined in his large, leather-backed chair. His decision blind-sided Carlos. A look of despair and disappointment registered on his face. Each executive on the Cinco Diablos committee had equal status and authority, therefore, in order for a decree to be official like a referee whistle, you needed the majority number of votes. Benzo Al and Don Julio were vocally against an alliance with the Nogales Cartel. That was two votes against his one. Carlos turned towards Roberto 'The Farmer' Vargas for support.

The Farmer was a very simple man who lived on a modest horse ranch in Mexico. Aside from the beefy foot soldiers patrolling the perimeter of the hacienda with Skorpion assault rifles, you would never have guessed the humble crop grower was responsible for millions of dollars in counterfeit goods making it to U.S. shores from Shanghai. Even now, while the other men sported

Italian shoes and silk ties, he wore a simple wool poncho and an old sombrero.

The Farmer lit a thick cigar, puffed, exhaled, and began speaking in fluent Spanish. "Gentlemen, thanks to Carlos, we don't have to stash our dinero under the mattress anymore. He has established relationships with some of the most prestigious banks in the world. Major corporations beg us for venture capital, and we are in a position to put him in the governor's seat. We're strong, which means we don't need the Nogales Cartel to be successful—" He paused to take a hit off the cigar.

A condescending smirk appeared at the corners of Benzo Al's lips. It appeared as though he had won. Carlos's shoulders sagged in defeat.

The Farmer stubbed out his Havana on the table and resumed making his point, "However, the other families have recognized the errors in their ways. If the Los Zetas form a peace treaty with the Sinaloa and Gulf Cartel, the Tijuana and Juarez Cartel will join their alliance. Then they will make war against us. I have already spoken to our friends, El Chango from the Michoacana Cartel, and the Beltran brothers. They are waiting on us to make a move. I vote yes to the merger. Billions are at stake." He leaned back and folded his arms.

Carlos perked up and smiled. Benzo Al glared at the Farmer and shook his head in disappointment. The ballot was two yays and two nays. Fernando 'Shadow' Rivera held the swing vote. Shadow was a burly, boisterous man who drank fine whiskey and entertained the crowd with vulgar sex jokes. Today he was uncharacteristically quiet. All eyes were on him, he shriveled under their penetrating gaze and sweat-dampened the collar of his shirt. The mastermind behind a lucrative, international sex trafficking ring was fidgeting in his seat like a piñata filled with penny candy.

Two days ago, Shadow was certain of which way he was going to cast his vote, but then he received a disturbing message, one that would ultimately seal the fate of the all-mighty cartel. He looked at each poker-faced board member as his thoughts drifted back forty-eight hours. He had dismissed one of his new recruits with a playful slap on her ass, poured himself a healthy shot of whiskey, and told his most trusted driver, Chico to prepare the limo. Chico ran a long, aluminum pole with a round mirror attached to the end under the limo. When he reached the front passenger side, he noticed a white envelope taped under the wheel-well.

Chico immediately began to bark orders into his walkie-talkie. Three more troops who were policing the perimeter rushed to Chico's location with their M-240 machine guns eager to spill blood. Chico whispered a short prayer, slid under the limo on his back, and carefully detached the envelope. The note was addressed to Shadow. Chico ran into the villa and handed the letter to his boss.

"What the hell is this?" Shadow held the envelope up to the light and examined its contents.

"It's a letter, patron, I found it under the limo."

Shadow cautiously opened the seal, inched the letter out of the envelope, and read the bold, black words as if he had seen Satan. The note simply said, *Boom*! The message was warning him that despite surrounding himself with security, he could still be touched.

Right on cue, Shadow's office line rang. He stared at the phone like it was a coiled-up rattlesnake basking in the sun. Grunting angrily, he waved everyone out of his office. "Get the fuck outta here!" He waited until the door closed before reluctantly answering the call. The voice on the other end was another Cinco Diablos member.

"Paga tus deudas. Pay your debts." The caller gave the order and hung up the phone. Shadow had made a deal with Satan, now it was time for the devil to collect his dividend.

Benzo Al's husky voice snapped Shadow out of his trance. "We don't have all day, Shadow. Cast your vote." It was Benzo Al who had sent the threatening ultimatum.

Shadow swallowed hard and stated his position. "Mi amigos, we control the routes along the Rio Grande River. We also have two high-level U.S. Customs officers at the San Pedro port on our

154

payroll. So, we don't need the Nogales Cartel in order to move our cocaína. They need our drug tunnels and semi-trucks to move their marijuana, therefore, I vote against the merger," his words tasted like bitter vinegar.

Once again, Benzo Al had outsmarted his younger brother. A master strategist and a student of Sun Tzu's Art of War, Benzo Al believed in absolute power. Importing cocaine into the United States was Los Cinco Diablos' most lucrative operation, and Benzo Al ruled his kingdom with an iron fist concealed inside of a velvet glove.

He knew that his stepbrother was watching the throne. He also had a suspicion that Carlos was secretly conspiring against him with the leader of the Nogales Cartel. The merger would have diluted Benzo Al's growing power.

Benzo Al stood up and addressed the council. "You vatos are growing soft," he admonished, his voice snapping like a swift whip. "Have you forgotten how Los Cinco Diablos came into power? Through fear." He turned towards Carlos and resumed, "As you all know, I hate my father, he was a coward. It was my mother who taught me that corruption is about control, not cooperation."

He snapped his fingers and his guard left the room and returned with three Mexican men who were handcuffed and blindfolded. "On your knees, puto!" The guard lined them up in a row and kicked them in the back of their knees.

Benzo Al pointed his finger. "Here are our three problems. The Attorney General of Mexico, the director of the Border Patrol, and I'm sure that Carlos recognizes Pablo Estrada, the leader of the Nogales Cartel. I have replaced two of these men with people who are more sympathetic to our cause. After today, the drought is over, and Los Cinco Diablos is back in business." Staring at Carlos, Benzo Al upped a long, Colt .45 revolver loaded with six Teflon widow makers.

Blamm! Blamm!

He double-tapped the trigger, and the government official's head exploded. Blood and mushy pulp left and oval splatter mark on the wall behind him. Next, Benzo Al pressed the warm barrel between the Border Patrol agent's eyebrows and squeezed off. The slugs bounced around in his skull like ping pong balls before carving an exit through the back of his cranium.

Benzo Al slowly faced Carlos. All the hatred he reserved for his father, he also shared for his illegitimate stepbrother. He slid the smoking revolver across the table. "Your turn, ese. Prove your loyalty to la familia."

Carlos stared at the murder apparatus. His hands trembled nervously. He was a cunning and unscrupulous businessman but far from a killer. Don Julio recognized this and stepped in to save Carlos from further humiliation.

"Three more dead bodies won't solve our problems, carnale," Don Julio pointed out in his hoarse voice. "If it were that easy, I would kill this peasant myself."

The meeting adjourned. As the cartel bosses prepared to leave, Benzo Al's guard stood behind Pablo Estrada. Benzo Al nodded his head, giving Angela the green light. The heartless killer, Spanish guillotine in hand, viciously wrapped the sharp, piano wire around the Nogales Cartel leader's neck. His eyes bulged behind the blindfold, and the red veins in his pupils popped.

The stonehearted assassin's top teeth grinded against the bottom as both ends of the crude, Spanish guillotine were pulled tighter. The serrated wire cut into the skin. The Nogales Cartel leader desperately wheezed for oxygen. His arms thrashed, but he ultimately succumbed to the will of death. His body went limp and his bowels let loose. The conference room reeked of fear and feces.

Benzo Al, Don Julio, The Farmer, and Shadow made a quick exit, but Carlos couldn't move. His eyes were transfixed on the three dead bodies and the repercussions that were to come.

"My brother needs to be stopped, but how?" he contemplated. He grabbed the pistol off the table and vowed that Benzo Al would die by his own gun.

Angela unwrapped the lethal murder weapon from around the vic's neck, gave Carlos a deadly wink, and brushed past him on the way out of the foul-smelling conference room. A black bullet-proof Chevy Suburban waited at the curb. A machine gun-toting chauffeur opened the rear door.

Angela climbed in next to Benzo Al and called him a liar in Spanish. "Mentirozo! Why did you lie to the board members? You're gonna get us both killed. Those three dead bodies are not our only problem. If Najee is not alive, then who hit the stash house in Hawthorne and murdered the Haitian? Who burned down the chop shop? And what about his bitch? She dropped two of our soldiers in Amsterdam and two more of our best men at the hospital. If Carlos finds out—" her voice trailed off, and she gazed out of the window. The custom SUV sped through a small village populated with mud-brick houses and proud Mexican natives.

"Calm the fuck down, Angela! I got this shit under control," Benzo Al guaranteed. His hand slithered under her Valentino leather mini, and he massaged her phat monkey through her skimpy red panties.

"Cash rules everything. A large shipment of coca is waiting for us by the docks along with ten million for the election. When I put the next power move in play and the money starts flowing again, the board members will thank me. Just like I'm thankful to have you. You're the deadliest woman I know, and the best thing about it is that no one outside of Los Cinco Diablos knows who you are. I'm proud of you, mi amor," he whispered sweetly in her ear and kissed her softly on the neck.

Angela rebuffed his sexual advances and scooted closer to the passenger door. Not to be rejected, Benzo Al frowned and angrily forced two of his pudgy fingers knuckles deep into her dry vagina. "What's wrong, Angela, why you trippin' so hard?" he asked coarsely and worked his thick digits in and out of her pussy.

Angela winced in pain. "Nothing is wrong. I've just decided to start separating business from pleasure. You should try it sometimes," she found herself quoting Sinatra.

Benzo Al roughly yanked her long hair and crammed another thick finger into her tight pussy. "I guess you're too good for me now that you found a new lover." He frowned wickedly. "Don't deny it, I smell him on you. If you want him to stay alive, I suggest you start showing me a little bit of respect. You don't make the decision 'round here, you nigger loving whore. You do as you're told. Do I make myself clear, puta?" He called her a bitch and rammed his hand deeper.

Angela's mouth fell open and she raised her sexy hips off the leather seats to meet his probing fingers. This time, she moaned in delight, not discomfort. "Ay, Papi, I understand! Hurt me until it feels good."

Benzo inserted a fourth finger. Angela could smell the musky scent of her own arousal, pain was her secret pleasure, and only Benzo Al knew how much of a freak she was. He flipped her over onto her stomach, ripped her panties off, and spanked her colorful butterfly tattoo with the palm of his callous hands, leaving red marks on her cheeks. Angela squeezed her eyes tight and came hard as she fantasized about Sinatra.

CHAPTER 20

In Cold Blood

DEA agents armed with an arsenal of high-powered artillery and search warrants set out to conduct simultaneous raids throughout Atlanta in an orchestrated effort to dismantle BBE. Two Chevy Tahoes screeched to a halt in front of Ice's baby mama house. The midnight sky camouflaged the vehicles' Navy Blue paint and dark tinted windows. Six anxious DEA agents piled out and surrounded the modest, single-family home.

Blondie ran up to the front entrance lugging a heavy, steel battering ram, and swung it at the door. The wood molding splintered, and the door came off its brass hinges. A second DEA agent tossed two flash grenades into the compound. They exploded with an earsplitting *kaboom* and oozed shrouds of gray smoke.

"DEA, everybody on the ground, now!" Blondie demanded. He and two other agents stormed into the house. They fanned out in a V formation. Their loaded AR-15s aimed angry red beams searching for potential suspects.

Ice snapped out of his slumber and reached for his chopper. His movements startled his baby mama. Qnesha knew he stayed strapped but witnessing him rack a slug into the AK frightened her.

"What's wrong, Ice?" Qnesha asked, her sagging, 44Ds exposed.

A booming voice coming from the living room supplied the answer. "Federal agents! We have a warrant to search the premises. All occupants come out with your hands in the air!" The back door crashed in. Broken glass clanked on the kitchen floor. Three more DEA agents cautiously entered the spot.

"Shit!" Ice slipped on his jeans and a pair of first edition MJs. He wondered how the Alphabet Boys found out where he lay his head at night. A shortlist of names flickered through his mind. He posted his back against the wall while holding the chopper and peeked out of the curtains like Malcolm X. Red and blue swirling lights illuminated the dark sky.

"Allah have mercy," he groaned, but it was too late for prayer.

"Isaac Miller, we know you're in there," Blondie announced, using Ice's government name. "Make it easy on yourself and come out with your hands where I can see 'em."

Silence!

"All righty then, kick it in," Blondie ordered and stepped aside.

A brave young agent used the heel of his steel toe boots to kick the plywood door open. Ice responded with a short burst of gunshots. Yellow flames spewed from the muzzle, casting off just enough light so all could see the valiant DEA agent tumble backward. His bulletproof vest caught four slugs. His handsome face ate the rest.

Using tactical precision, three of the agents dropped to one knee and retaliated. Their fierce ammo sliced through the baby crib and shattered the bedroom window. Although the infant was at his grandmother's house, Qnesha screamed at the thought of her son being riddled with bullets.

"Hold your fire! Hold your fire!" Blondie yelled after over thirty shells had been recklessly expended. "Did anyone get a visual on the suspect?" he asked with his own weapon ready to spit.

"Negative, sir," Agent McCoy answered.

Blondie moved into position next to the bedroom door. "This is your last chance, Miller. We have the place surrounded. Give yourself up, now!"

"Fuck you!" Ice retorted to the familiar voice. Jail was not an option. He held the chopper at waist level and let off again.

The agents replied with more retaliatory slugs. The rapid automatic gunfire sounded like a whole pack of firecrackers igniting. "Fall back! Everybody fall back, damn it! He has a hostage!" Agent McCoy barked.

Ice appeared in the doorframe. Red beams crisscrossed Qnesha's breasts like polka dots. Ice gripped her by the neck and pressed the K against her cheek. Tears streaked her face. "Er'body drop yo' guns and clear the fuck out, or I'ma body this bitch," he warned. Not only was he a grimy nigga, but he was also narcissistic. He only cared for himself.

"This is not gonna end well for you, pal." Blondie insisted from the shadows. "Let the girl go, and I won't have to pop a cap in your black ass." Crisis management was not his forte.

Ice shoved his baby mama out of the room using her as a human shield and sprayed his last ten bullets in Blondie's direction. Blondie returned fire. His polymer tip, .223 ammo tore into Qnesha. Her body jerked side to side like she was doing the Harlem Shake. The force of the blast kept her upright until finally, the shooting stopped and she crumpled into a heap of bloody flesh.

Ice retreated, diving headfirst through the shattered window. Bullets zipped over his head. He landed with a painful *thump*, quickly collected his barring, and scattered over the neighbor's wooden fence. An angry Rottweiler's razor-sharp fangs nipped at his heels. Ice back kicked the charging dog without breaking his stride and vaulted over another rickety fence. His heart thumped rapidly.

He spotted an old Ford F-150, smashed the driver's side window with a large rock, and reached inside to open the door. The horn blared loudly, and the headlights flashed off and on, but Ice was not deterred. The factory alarms on early model Fords made them the easiest vehicles to peel. He swiftly popped the hood, ripped out the horn's wiring harness, and disengaged the alarm. The annoying noise ceased.

Next, he checked the bed of the truck. Sweet. There was a toolbox. He retrieved a flat head screwdriver and jabbed the steering column until the plastic cracked. He inserted the screwdriver into the neck of the steering column and clicked the ignition switch. The rusty, F-150 croaked to life. Ice was gone in sixty seconds.

****

Yellow crime scene tape roped off Qnesha's home. Blondie and two DEA agents towered over her mangled corpse. Her legs and torso were inhumanly twisted. Type B blood stained the hardwood floors.

"Jeez, Rossetti, how are we gonna explain this one?" Agent McCoy asked, staring down at the unarmed, deceased body. Each time he went on an assignment with Blondie, he received a reprimand on his otherwise pristine record.

Blondie unstrapped the throwaway pistol he kept in his ankle holster and placed the grip in Qnesha's right palm, making sure her fingerprint was on the trigger. "We're gonna explain it like we always do, so listen up. This is what we tell headquarters and the Fulton County PD." Blondie's voice became a conspiring hiss. "We identified ourselves with a knock on the front door. When we didn't get an answer, we breached the main entrance. An unknown male and female suspect accosted us with their guns drawn. We demanded that they drop their weapons, but they didn't comply. Instead, one of them opened up on us, and we returned fire. It's that simple, guys. Any questions?" He looked each man in his eyes.

Agent McCoy shifted uneasily. "I don't know about this one, sir. Maybe we should just tell the truth. You didn't follow protocol when we learned that the assailant had a hostage. We should have talked him down," he accused.

Blondie pointed his index finger as if it were a loaded machine gun. "My version is the truth, you schmuck. Do you think we're gonna get guns, dope, and bad guys off the streets by following some bullshit, bureaucratic protocol?"

He walked up on Agent McCoy and poked him in the chest with his finger as he lectured. "This is a war on drugs. It's us against them, and sometimes there is collateral damage. Besides, she isn't some innocent Cosby kid. She lives with a known drug dealer who sleeps with an AK-47 for Christ's sake. An AK-47 that took out one of your colleagues, I might add. So, get with the program or you're gonna be on administrative leave while a bunch of Black Lives Matter protestors loot and burn down the city."

As Blondie completed his sermon, one of the agents who were thoroughly searching the home rushed toward the debating men. "Sir, I found something that I think you're gonna want to see."

Blondie spun on his heels and followed the excited agent into the kitchen. His smile beamed upon seeing a pile of duct-taped blocks and three stacks of cash with bank bands sitting on the counter. "Whew!" Blondie whistled. "That's a lotta coke. Does anyone else know about this?" he quizzed, eyeing the money and the dope.

"No, sir, not yet. I wanted to alert you first."

Blondie patted the young agent on the back. "Good job, Agent Cox. I'll take it from here." He tallied up the twenty kilos and fanned one of the stacks of money. "It's a damn shame that these assholes have this type of cash lying around while the good guys like us are struggling to pay our mortgage."

Blondie was baiting Agent Cox in. He did not trust any cop that wasn't just as dirty as he was. His new partner, Agent Sullivan, was squeaky clean and went strictly by the book. That made Blondie nervous, real nervous. For months, he had been trying to get the rookie on the take, but Agent Sullivan always refused. Now he hoped he could entrap Agent Cox.

Agent Cox watched Blondie fan a second stack of money with his thumb. "I agree, I'm glad to have a job and all, but it just doesn't seem fair. Wendy and I are up to our necks in student loan debt."

Blondie liked what he was hearing. He looked over his shoulder. The other officers in the living room were still wrangling over the details of the shooting. He lowered his voice and whispered, "Listen close because this is gonna go real quick." He pushed all three stacks of money toward Agent Cox. "Take this money, buy your wife something nice, and put the rest up for a rainy day."

Agent Cox resisted. "Thanks but no thanks, sir. Me and Wendy will be just fine."

"Stop being a proud redneck and take the money. I won't say anything." More police officers spilled into the house. Voices inched toward the kitchen. "You better make up your mind quick and do what's right for your family," Blondie insisted, and stuffed the twenty birds into a garbage bag.

Agent Cox gave in to temptation and crammed two of the money stacks down the front of his pants. He loosened the Velcro on his bulletproof vest and stuffed the other stack under his armpit.

Blondie calmly strolled past the profusion of medical technicians and Fulton County police officers who had arrived and were now busily scouring the compound. After close to two decades in law enforcement, Blondie was no longer delusional. He understood that there was no difference between a cop and a criminal. Both breeds wallowed in the mud of corruption.

He sat in the Tahoe and flipped through the names and addresses Alex had given him. One name, in particular, stood out. Before cranking the engine, Blondie inspected one of the kilos. Something about the tightly wrapped brick looked odd. He removed his Swiss Army knife, punctured the package, and tasted the white substance on the tip of the blade.

"Jesus friggin' Christ!" Blondie frowned and banged his fist on the steering when he realized that the tightly wrapped brick was fake. Nothing was going his way.

****

Ice dipped to Boulevard and banked a left onto Outlaw's street. To his dismay, the block was hot. Swirling police lights and reporters with digital cameras mounted on their shoulders camped out on the lawn of Outlaw's honeycomb hideout. An ABC News reporter jammed a microphone into a stoic looking U.S. Marshal's face. He waved off her rapid-fire questions with the standard no comment response and ducked under the crime scene tape.

Ice pulled over, killed the lights, and watched everything go down with his seat reclined. The Alphabet Boys roughly led Gutter and Escobar out of the house by their elbows. Minutes later, EMS workers rolled a gurney out of the spot. Ice sat up. His heart thumped rapidly. Outlaw laid stretched out on the cold slab of metal. The U.S. Marshal compared Outlaw's face to a Polaroid photo and confirmed the *Game Over* tattoo on his eyelids. The streets would have applauded the way Outlaw went out with two Glocks blazing and screaming fuck the law.

Ice's bottom lip trembled. "Rest in paradise, my nigga," he mourned the fallen soldier.

Blondie spotted Ice in the stolen Ford. He rolled past the vehicle, bent the first corner, and parked. He stealthy crept along the passenger side of the truck to avoid detection. Grievous tears blurred Ice's vision, so he did not notice the seasoned agent. Blondie withdrew his Smith & Wesson, opened the passenger door, and slid in next to Ice.

"What da' fuck?" Ice gasped.

Blondie shoved the thumper against the side of Ice's neck and snarled, "Shut the fuck up, asshole!" He kept his weapon trained on Ice and used his other hand to do a quick pat search. Satisfied that Ice was not packing, Blondie whacked him with the pistol. "What the hell were you thinking? You almost killed me tonight!" he sternly chastised his newest informant.

"My bad, Blondie," Ice apologized while dabbing his head to make sure the blow didn't open his stitches. "On the reals, I didn't even know you was in town. How come you didn't let a nigga know that the Red Dogs was gonna roll on me?"

"How come you didn't let a white boy know that you were gonna roll on, Alex Munoz?" Blondie countered, enjoying the dumbfounded look splashed across Ice's face. He holstered his service weapon and continued, "I thought we had a deal. You were facing double digits when I knocked you on that homi in Decatur. I risked my career and reputation getting rid of the burner with your fingerprints on it. All I asked in return was that you debrief and divulged all the intel you had on Sosa and BBE. But no, you wanted to play both ends against the middle."

Ice vehemently denied the allegation. "I wasn't playing you. I told y'all everythang I know."

"You're a horrible liar, dick head. I learned the location of the BBE stash houses from Alex. Furthermore, I stuck to my end of the bargain. I hit your line several times in order to give you a heads up about the pending raids, but you didn't answer any of my calls. If I didn't know better, I'd think you were deliberately trying to avoid me." His disgruntled scowl expressed his frustration.

Ice shivered under Blondie's cold glare. "My bad, I put my cell phone on silent so my BM wouldn't trip if one of my other hoes called. Then on top of that, I popped too many Vicodins and passed the fuck out."

Blondie examined the bloodstained gauze wrapped around Ice's head. "You look like shit. What the hell happened to you?"

Ice squeezed his eyes tight, half hoping that when he opened them his misfortunes would magically disappear. "Keeping it real, I was trickin' off last night and got set up by a stripper bitch. Her people stuck me for half a ticket. That's why I had to burn, Alex." The confession tasted like placing your tongue on a 9-volt battery.

Blondie shook his head. From the jump, he didn't trust either of his Atlanta informants. He was testing Alex and Ice to see which CI he could depend on. Both of them failed miserably.

He unclipped his handcuffs and clamped silver shackles around Ice's right wrist. "You're useless to me, Ice. I'm taking your black ass in for the murders of Alex Munoz, Qnesha Hubanks, and Special Agent Carl Zimmerman."

Blondie could almost feel Ice tremor. Years on the front lines of the battlefield had taught him the secrets of physiological warfare. He knew that fear was a man's Achilles heel. Threaten a human being with his or her worst phobia and that person's moral compass would bend to your will. He fastened the left cuff onto Ice's wrist and resumed speaking, "You may be Billy Bad Ass when you have a gun in your hands, but we're gonna see how tough you are when a 250 pound Aryan smells your pussy and rapes you in the showers."

Ice's eyes widened. "Wait! Wait!" he protested. Perspiration saturated his underarms.

"I'm tired of waiting, and I'm tired of cleaning up your sloppy mess," Blondie scolded. "You stepped in a deep pile of elephant shit tonight. Those skinheads are gonna love that tight black booty of yours. I may be able to straighten out this debacle, but I need something in return."

All the bitch leaked out of Ice's pores. "Anything you say, boss-man. I ain't tryna' go back to jail. Just tell me what you need me to do."

"Our deal hasn't changed. If you want to keep your freedom, bring me, Sosa. I can't frame him on a trumped-up homicide or trafficking charge. His Jewish lawyers will have the case thrown out before the ink on the indictment dries. I need wiretaps and surveillance footage that'll be irrefutable in court. I need you to do your friggin' job."

"I'm tryin', I put that on my momma," Ice swore. "I've been doing everythang under the sun in order to lure Sosa back into the game. I even paid some of them Louisiana boys to torch his restaurants so that he would be hurting for cash, but Sosa is sticking to his word. He ain't fucking with that cola no mo'."

Upon hearing this new revelation, Blondie swiftly swiveled towards Ice. His scowl deepened. "Back up a second. Are you telling me you're the one who's behind the restaurant fires?"

"Yeah! Pretty clever idea, huh?" Ice smiled broadly. His diamond teeth twinkled under the full moon. He was hoping his perfidious efforts to coax Sosa back into the game would impress Blondie, but his unconscious acts of arson only infuriated the officer.

Blondie smacked Ice on the back of the head. "You brainless, schmuck," he denounced angrily through tight lips. "Are you aware that an innocent, sixteen-year-old girl perished in one of those fires? Give me one good reason why I shouldn't book your black ass for capital murder?"

Ice started talking faster than the rapper *Twista*. At the end of the secret conversation, he was placed on a red-eye flight to LAX. His mission: bring down Sosa by any means necessary.

Larry D. Wright

Blood Out

"If there was no consumption, there would be no sales."
El Chapo – Sinaloa Cartel

Larry D. Wright

CHAPTER 21

Cocaine Fever

The human psyche is fragile. Crush the weakest man's spirit, and he will still find a way to prevail, however, break the strongest man's heart, and he will be devastated for a lifetime. Najee's quest for vengeance was for a worthy cause, but his bloody crusade had turned him bitter and brutal. If that wasn't bad enough, witnessing Nella kiss Sosa amplified those pernicious feelings. There was no hope for him now. He had crossed the dark abyss and found himself on the evil side of innocence.

He rented a nondescript car, jumped on the 405 Freeway, and arrived at Venice Beach. He fed eight quarters into a greedy parking meter on Rose Street and mobbed one block to the Venice boardwalk donning a pair of white Balenciaga shorts, a white Balenciaga shirt, and a pair of matching Balenciaga Yacht shoes with no socks on. Although the bikini-clad snow bunnies were jockin' his swag, he felt ridiculous in the linen ensemble. The outfit reminded him of Detective Tubbs from Miami Vice.

Despite Najee's blasé demeanor, anxiety besieged his soul. He was about to transform from a stick-up kid to a dope man and make his first drug buy. The one hundred and fifty bands he carried in a duffel bag only weighed 6.5 pounds, but the money seemed to grow heavier with each lumbering step.

He wiped the trickling sweat off his cleanly shaved dome and paused for a moment to get acclimated with his surroundings. Neither the street vendors who enthusiastically hawked their handcrafted wares nor the energetic tourist in colorful Hawaiian shirts noticed the slight bulge on his hip or the way his alert eyes shifted nervously behind tinted Roberto Cavalli lenses.

He spotted Angela sitting alone beneath an umbrella at the famous Side Walk Cafe. Although the noon temperature was blistering, she looked cool wearing an oversized straw hat, big framed Dior shades and a tight-fitting, gold, Salvatore Ferragamo bikini.

Najee sat in the empty seat across from her and dropped the duffel bag next to her pedicured feet. "It's all there," he said, looking around so he could see who could see him.

Angela lowered her shades. The $2,300 rose gold frames rested on the bridge of her nose. She tilted her head down and openly ogled Najee's chocolateness before her smile faded. "Are you loco? Not here in the open. Follow me." Her tone was all business. She stood up and walked away without waiting to see if Najee was behind her.

Najee was thrown off by Angela's aloofness but remained on his square. He grabbed the duffel bag and followed her scantily clad, tattooed backside into the dimly lit restaurant. He could have sworn he saw a big, red, handprint on her ass cheek.

They skirted past the bar and strolled into the kitchen. Two brawny Latinos named Nacho and Syco Mike greeted them. They had thick necks, mean mugs, and cold souls. Najee immediately noticed the sharp meat cleavers clutched in their beefy fingers.
Angela spun toward Najee. Her face was void of emotion. "Strip down, we have to search you."

Najee protested. "Nah, fuck that! A striptease wasn't part of our deal. Either you trust me and we do business, or I'm out this bitch."

He turned to leave, but the Cinco Diablos henchmen blocked his exit. Syco Mike folded his arms across his wide chest, and Nacho cracked his knuckles, eager to put in some work.

Angela called off her obedient guard dogs and sauntered up to Najee. Her protruding nipples brushed against his chest. "It's just a precaution. My people don't know you," she stated calmly, her lips seeking his.

Najee twisted his head to avoid her kiss. "I'm doing business with you, not your people," he clarified. His hand slowly inched toward his heat.

Angela gently touched his wrist. "Don't do nothing stupid, Sinatra. We're not trying to take your money, we just need to check you for a wire."

"*A wire*? Bitch, do I look like a snitch?"

172

Syco Mike and Nacho flexed up, but Angela kept her cool. "Listen, ese, this is how Los Cinco Diablos gets down. You asked to play with the big boys in the big leagues. I'm just granting your wish," her tone was stern. During each meeting, Najee was getting a glimpse of her dark side.

Najee was familiar with how the Cinco Diablos handled their B.I. He was only playing hardball because he didn't want to seem too eager. His frown softened into a smile. He tossed the duffel bag to Syco Mike and joked, "Make yourself useful and count this bread while I entertain the lady." He handed Angela his 357 Python, took off his shirt, and dropped his Balenciaga shorts down to his ankles. No wires, just hard muscles, prison tattoos, and battle wounds.

Syco Mike unzipped the bag. His anger receded and his eyes danced excitedly upon inspecting the crisp big faces. "Wassup with all these bloodstains on the money, homes?" He dumped the cheddar on a wooden John Boos butcher's block and quickly counted the bundles with the swiftness of a bank teller.

"I cut myself while shaving," Najee responded with a straight face.

Syco Mike couldn't contain his laughter. "I like this vato. He's funny, he has heart, and his money adds up." He turned to Nacho and instructed him to grab the work. "Go get the cocaína, homes."

The acidic tension in the atmosphere dissipated. Angela handed Najee his clothes and Nacho handed him a duffel bag containing ten kilos with the Cinco Diablos' seal of authenticity stamped on them.

"You handled yourself well, Sinatra. I'm proud of you," Angela complimented. Seeing him naked again made her pussy moist. She wondered how long she would be able to separate business from pleasure.

Najee slung the strap over his shoulder, shook Angela's hand, and tried to bounce before she heard his heart pounding in his chest. He was almost out of the restaurant when Angela stopped him.

"Aren't you gonna check the quality of the coke?" she asked suspiciously.

Najee cringed. He had made an amateur's mistake and needed a quick come back. "Unlike some people I know, I trust those I do business with."

Angela flinched, and Najee knew his guilt trip was effective.

He stepped onto the Venice boardwalk and whistled a long sigh. "I did it, I'm in!" He celebrated, with his head held towards the clear, blue sky. "Just a little bit longer, mama. Benzo Al is going to suffer for what he did to you, Boulevard, and Angel. I promise." After that ominous vow, he climbed into the Avis rental and pushed out. He had finally infiltrated the Cinco Diablos, but his problems were just beginning.

Najee wrestled with the thought of slangin' poison to his own people. He initially intended to cop the first batch of dope from Angela, flush it down the toilet, and use his own money when it was time to re-up. However, he sadly discovered that Nella had raided all six of his Greyhound lockers, took the dough, and left a dead rose in its place. Now he needed to figure out how he was going to sell ten slabs of coke, an almost impossible task for an inexperienced drug dealer with no clientele.

He began contemplating which hood he could invade and set up shop, but he ultimately crossed each block off his list for one reason or another. As he banked a left turn by the check-cashing spot on Rose and Lincoln, he had an epiphany and remembered what Spade had told him about taking over the projects. A smirk appeared on Najee's lips as he concocted his next move.

His mind was settled. He decided to take over the Bungalows, a housing project more dangerous than both the Cabrini Greens in Chicago and the Nickerson Gardens in Watts combined.

However, in order to do so, he needed to put together a team that was just as savage. He pressed the pedal to the metal and headed towards Mount Nevaeh Church to recruit his first soldiers.

****

Angela's phone buzzed in her Ferragamo clutch. Although the number was blocked, she knew who the caller was. "Como estas, Papi?" she greeted Benzo Al.

"Bien, señorita. Have you been watching the news?" Benzo stared at the 10-inch monitor mounted in the headrest of his car. "They found Cartoon's body in the Tombs near our meat factory."

"I know, I saw the story on KTLA this morning. Did you green light him?" She sprinkled a pack of Sweet-N-Low into her iced tea.

"Of, course, I did. He fucked up the hit at the hospital, but the Nogales Cartel got to him first. They carved a big N in his chest to send me a message."

"This is what I feared most, another war. We underestimated Najee and the Body Snatchers. We can't make that same mistake with the Nogales Cartel. Have you spoken to Carlos and the committee?"

"I don't answer to Carlos, and as far as Najee is concerned, if he's still alive, we'll find out sooner or later. There's not a cave on earth that he and his bitch can hide in."

Angela moved away from the Cafe and walked on the beach to get more privacy. The warm sand was soothing under her feet. "I'm glad you came to your senses. There have been too many incidents involving our stash houses and ether. Wherever Najee is hiding, it won't be too long before he makes his move on us. When that time comes, we must be smart and lure him into our trap."

"I agree," Benzo Al grumbled. "By the way, how did everything go with the new customer?"

"Smooth, everything went down smooth. We meet again next week." Angela felt a familiar tingle in her vagina. Seeing Sinatra's black meat stretch down his leg left her hot and bothered.

"I see." Benzo Al stroked his salt and pepper goatee. There was a hint of jealousy in his voice when he spoke, "I advised you against bringing him in. The Jamaicans and the Haitians are loyal, but the African-Americans are unpredictable and unreliable. You say he's good people, so I'll take your word for it. Just remember, if he becomes a liability to the organization, it's on you." He rolled a string of Catholic rosary beads between his fingers as he lectured.

His warning didn't go unnoticed. "You don't have to threaten me. I know the protocol. I brought him in, so I would have to take him out."

Benzo Al's chauffeur respectfully presented him with a wooden box of Cuban cigars. Benzo Al selected one of the tightly rolled delicacies, snipped the end off, and lit the tip with a gold, butane lighter. He took a puff, exhaled, and relaxed in the backseat of his Brabus Mercedes Benz. "Never let love or money cloud your vision, mamacita. Both are deadly illusions. I can tell that you like this vato. But do you trust him?"

Angela hesitated. The silence seemed to linger on forever. She had asked herself the same question a hundred times. Her heart always supplied the same answer. "Yes, I trust him!" For some reason, the words stung rolling off her tongue.

"I hope so." Benzo Al cocked his foe-five. "Because if he fucks up, I will make you pay for his mistakes with your life. Sangre dentro, sangre afuera. Blood in, blood out." The line went dead.

CHAPTER 22

Hell Is Hot

The small white chapel that Najee was visiting had a clever name. Nevaeh is heaven spelled backward. Despite its celestial title, Mount Nevaeh Baptist Church was located on the East Side, right in the heart of the hood. The graffiti littered liquor store next door pushed alcohol, the Tam's Burgers across the street peddled high blood pressure, and the prostitutes and drug dealers sold everything else in between.

In spite of being positioned in the midst of such sin and debauchery, the church was bustling with devoted parishioners. Najee wondered would they still flock to the humble house of worship if they knew their pastor was a cold-blooded killer.

He sat in the parking lot and stared at the huge, gold cross that was perched on top of the church's sloping steeple. As a child, his hustling parents rarely took him to Sunday service. The only deity they worshipped was the almighty dollar.

He adjusted his Polo shirt to conceal the bulge of his bulky weapon and slipped inside the church unnoticed, or so he thought. A Rastafarian with a soul blacker than the tailored suit he wore watched Najee closely.

A strong volt of conviction surged through Najee as he passed a large mural of Jesus painted on the colorful, stained glass. It was as if those piercing blue eyes could see through his flesh. When he moved to the left, they followed him. When he moved to the right, the eyes were right there judging his heart and reading his sinful intentions. He was about to turn and abort the mission, but his lust for vengeance pushed him on. He sat in the back of the church, hoping his hellish ways didn't set the wooden pews on fire.

The congregation was decked out in their Sunday's best. The men sported pressed suits and shiny black shoes, the women rocked floral dresses that were a little too tight and elaborate hats that were a little too big.

Clapping hands, joyful shouts of Hallelujah, and cries of Amen made the flimsy roof levitate off its hinges. Ironically, the biggest gossipers and worst sinners sat in the front row, as if being closer to the alter somehow brought them closer to God.

The Bishop, his three-piece suit the brightest and most expensive of them all, paced across the stage with the light-footed agility of Muhammad Ali. His smooth, cappuccino colored skin and toned physique made him appear younger than his fifty years. He spit scriptures into the microphone, hooking the receptive congregants like a rapper performing at Summer Jam.

"And the Lawd Jesus said in John fourteen, verse six, 'I am the way, the truth, and the life. No one comes to the Father except through me.'"

"I tell you my friends, the hour of the Apocalypse is upon us. You must decide which army you're gonna be a part of. Repent now! Turn from your sinful ways or be cast into the fiery pits of hell."

Najee felt as though the Bishop was looking and speaking directly to him. A voluptuous, almond skinned sista rose to her feet. She jumped up and down excitedly every time the preacher made a point. Her huge breasts bounced beneath the taut fabric of her yellow dress, threatening to escape the stuffy confines of her bra.

The Bishop used a paisley printed silk handkerchief to pat the gleaming sweat off his forehead and continued preaching salvation into the mic without missing a beat.

An elderly woman who was sitting in the front row suddenly fell out in the middle of the aisle and began to convulse. Her lips spewed a stream of foreign gibberish. Najee moved in to help. He thought the flopping woman was having a seizure, but the old black lady sitting next to him assured that she was okay.

"Don't worry 'bout Sista Jones, honey chile'," she said as she folded a church program in half and used it as a fan. "She just caught the Holy Ghost."

Najee chuckled and used the distraction to his advantage. He dipped down a long corridor to the back office, jacked a slug into the chamber, and waited patiently for the Bishop.

He did not have to wait long. After the collection plates circulated, the congregation dispersed. Playful laughter announced the arrival of the Bishop and the voluptuous sista in the yellow dress. The Bishop pinched her on her wide rear end, and she giggled with delight. They stumbled into the well-furnished office with their arms entwined and their lips locked in a feverish tongue kiss. Neither of them noticed Najee sitting in a chair in the corner with his legs crossed.

The Bishop sat in his large, coffee-colored, leather chair. The voluptuous sista lifted the hem of her dress and straddled his lap. He pulled the top of her strapless dress down, and her big yellow titties flopped free. The Bishop suctioned one of her dark brown nipples into his warm mouth. Her red lips formed an O, and a low moan escaped from her belly.

Najee cleared his throat, "Umm, uh hummm, I don't mean to interrupt this little party, but I need to holla at the Bishop."

His presence startled the couple. The embarrassed sista jumped off the Bishop's lap and awkwardly tucked her yellow titties back into her yellow dress. The Bishop reached for the pistol he kept taped under his desk. He grabbed it with lightning speed.

"Who da' hell are you?" he questioned. His eyes focused on the nickel-plated trey-five-seven resting on Najee's thigh.

Najee stood up. "You might as well put that banger away, I already took the bullets out." He opened his fist and ten shells fell out of his palm. He was dealing with a butcher, so such precautions were necessary.

The Bishop watched the slugs hit the hardwood floor. A lesser man would have panicked, but he remained cool. He calmly laid the useless ratchet on the desk and leaned back in his chair. "Patience is not my virtue, so if this is a hit, let's get it over with." He had been in the game long enough to accept whatever fate Jehovah had ordained for him.

"I didn't come to take your life," Najee responded coolly.

"Ah, a professional, I like that. No sense of turning a simple robbery into a homicide, right? The safe is behind that portrait of the Virgin Mary. The combination is six-six-six."

"This ain't a robbery either."

The Bishop cocked his head to the side with skepticism. "Then what do you want?"

Najee gripped the handle of his stinger. "I want Benzo Al dead and so do you."

A deafening silence enveloped the room. The Bishop made a head gesture to his mistress, shooing her away. "Give us a lil' privacy, baby girl, and go check on Sista Jones." He waited until she left the room before he spoke, "There's only one person who wants Benzo Al's head worse than I do, but he's dead. So, who da' fuck are you, and why should I stop my mans from blowin' a hole through ya' chest?"

Najee looked down at his Polo shirt. A red dot covered the horse logo just above his heart. His eyes followed the threating beam. The Rastafarian in the black suit stood outside the office window aiming a WinMag rifle equipped with a Vortex sniper's scope.

The iron curtain had been pulled back, and the Bishop's true nature was unveiled. He was a gangster extraordinaire, the last of a rare breed. In the early 90s, he ran a crew of murderers for hire called the Kill Squad. Their bloody services were favorites of the Irish Mob and the Chinese triads. These organizations had their own killers on the payroll, but when they had a sensitive job that needed to be handled delicately, they outsourced the contract to the Kill Squad.

The Kill Squad was meticulous and loyal. Once a hit was in motion, nothing or no one could call it off, not even the person who hired them. In many cases, hardened hoodlums would slit their own wrist once they learned that the Kill Squad had a sheet of paper with their name on it.

The crew consisted of four ex-militiamen who met in Mogadishu while training a brigade of Al-Shabaab fundamentalist near the Somalian border. Their code names were the Pope, the Bishop, the Deacon, and the Altar Boy. When they were not hunting their prey, they found sanctuary in the church, convincing themselves that they were God's angels of death cleansing the world of evil.

They had a successful run until they accepted a contract from Benzo Al. They received twenty-five bands upfront, a sheet of paper with a name on it, and the promise of seventy-five gees once the assignment was complete. The task seemed easy enough, but nothing is simplistic when dealing with the likes of Benzo Al.

The crew of assassins strapped up and set out to purge the world of another wicket soul. They tracked their victim down to a Catholic school in Beverly Hills where they quickly learned that the target was a young Mexican girl.

Her father's construction company had dug a network of drug tunnels for Los Cinco Diablos. The underground passages started in Mexicali and stretched as far as San Diego and Douglas, Arizona. In order to keep the locations of the clandestine tunnels a secret, the immigrant miners who completed the excavation projects were murdered.

The girl's father knew too much and feared that his life was in danger as well. He contacted the Feds and agreed to testify before a federal grand jury in exchange for immunity. He was seized into protective custody, so Benzo Al couldn't kill him. Instead, he settled on the next best thing—his daughter.

The Bishop and the Deacon refused to do the hit. They did not want the blood of an innocent child on their hands, but the Pope and the Altar Boy were heartless. Their veins pumped molten lava, and they didn't care if the target was six or sixty.

The four men bickered bitterly. Guns were drawn, shots were fired, and blood was shed right in front of the little girl as she was being released from class. In the end, the Bishop and the Deacon prevailed, but a part of them died as well. They blamed Benzo Al for their loss and still hated him until this day.

Najee removed his Cavalli shades. His eyes were the gateway to his soul. He moved closer to the Bishop's large, maple desk. Outside, the Deacon raised his rifle and aimed the red beam at the center of Najee's forehead in response. His trigger finger itched. It had been years since he felt the exhilarating sensation of taking another man's life. He was about to squeeze off, but the Bishop raised his fist, signaling for him to stand down.

The Bishop moved from behind his desk. Najee and he stared at each other. "I don't recognize ya' face, Soulja, but your mannerism and demeanor seem familiar. Do I know you from somewhere?"

Najee tucked his burner and extended his palm for the Bishop to shake. "Candy is my mother. She brought me to you to be baptized."

The Bishop was thrown back and his skin turned pale. "Najee?" he whispered as if saying the name out loud would conjure up an evil spirit. "I thought you were dead!" He rejected Najee's handshake and embraced him in a tight hug instead.

"I die hard," Najee boasted. "It's gonna take an army to kill me."

The Bishop released Najee. His tone grew serious. The stress lines in his forehead deepened with concern. "Los Cinco Diablos is an army. Do you think you can shoot a hundred muthafuckas with one gun and not get caught or shot in the process? Com' on, young Soulja. You're not like one of those characters in a badly written urban novel. You do this for reals. What kind of foolish bravado possessed you to take on the Diablos by yourself? A lone wolf is easy prey."

"I wasn't by myself. I was rockin' with the Body Snatchers."

Najee's machismo pride left the Bishop salty. "Oh, yeah, where's your crew now? Because of your selfish vendetta, Yung Zay is dead. Rio is dead. Maceo is dead. Juice is dead, and you might as well put a gun to Nella's head yourself because she's as good as dead too. The streets are talking about the shootout at the hospital. It's only a matter of time before they track her down."

The Bishop's truthful admonishment incensed Najee. The vein on his temple pulsated with icy rage. "My selfish vendetta?" he retorted. "Those punk muthafuckas made me watch while they butchered my whole family. I saw Boulevard get hit three times in the chest. I can still hear his lungs wheezing for air as he took his last breath. I witnessed my momz take two slugs to her spine. I can still hear her gargling on her own blood. I was forced to watch a grown-ass man viciously rape a fourteen-year-old virgin.

I can still hear her brains splatter on the headboard after he shot her in the face at point-blank range. So, you damn right I'm holding a grudge. I don't need a sermon from a hypocrite like you to know that." Najee turned to leave. "Maybe the Pope and the Altar Boy were right, you've grown soft."

The Bishop angrily grabbed Najee by the collar and forcefully drove his back into the wall. The portrait of the Virgin Mary slipped off its bracket and crashed on the floor.

"The only thing soft about me is my dick after I bust a nut from killing a man with my bare hands," the Bishop spewed. "I play the murder game fo'real. While you were getting drunk off breast milk, I was fighting wars in Third World countries that make South Central seem like Disneyland, so don't lecture me."

He released Najee's shirt collar and his voice softened. He cared about Nella and Najee, that's why he was riding him so hard. "Haven't you learned anything from my mistakes, young Soulja? I haven't gone after Benzo Al yet because revenge is an art. You can't go at it like a hothead. That's why they say revenge is a dish best served cold."

The Bishop was about to finish lacing Najee with jewels, but he felt something hard pressed against his stomach. He looked down. Najee had his .357 Python pressed against the Bishop's belly button. The Deacon still had the infrared beam trained on Najee's skull.

When there were multiple killers on the scene, anything could pop off. Someone had to be the peace broker. The Bishop placed a firm hand on Najee's shoulder and looked him squarely in the eyes. "We're old friends, Najee. Let's call it a draw."

Najee overstood that the Bishop was not backing down. In that brief moment, he learned another valuable lesson from the veteran. Soothing words are more powerful than speeding bullets. Najee put away his thumper and all was forgotten. The two street warriors embraced in another brotherly hug and engaged in a civilized conversation.

"How is, Katrina?" Najee inquired.

The Bishop shrugged his shoulders. He had met Katrina's mother when she ran from her pimp in Milwaukee. Katrina was a young girl when her mother checked into the Bishop's shelter for battered women. He raised her like she was his own, but now their relationship was a sore topic.

"I'm only hard on Katt because I love her. She's as wild as ever and still won't listen to me, but that's still my little princess. Last I heard, she hit a lick in Atlanta for five-hundred K and was layin' low in the Big Apple." He paused to reminisce for a moment and then laughed. "Matter of fact, didn't you use her when you pulled your first move?"

Najee joined the laughter. It felt good being in the company of family. "Man, that girl is something else. After I shot Twan, I started ransacking his crib looking for the paper he owed Hoova Blue. When I went back into the living room, Katt was taking off this nigga's watch and diamond earrings. She's a beast fa' real. She taught me a lot about the game."

"I taught her what she taught you and everything else she knows. That's why I feel so guilty. I created a monster." The Bishop zoned out for a saddened moment, then cheered up. "Hey, did she teach you how to unlock handcuffs?" He pulled a pair of practice cuffs from his drawer and tossed them to Najee.

"Nah, but I want you to show me. That skill may come in handy one day." Najee was always eager to soak up new game.

The Deacon rushed into the office out of breath. He was a big man, 6'3' with rich, dark skin the same hue as African soul. His thick, lustrous dreads were parted down the middle and rested on his wide shoulders. He was handsome with a mellow deposition but behind the docile facade, evil hibernated in his soul.

He looked at the Bishop and Najee quizzically. "What da' hell is goin' down? First, yah pulling pistols on each other, now yah laughing like old friends." His hypnotizing Jamaican dialect revealed his Kingston roots. "Me no understand ya' Yankees."

The Bishop made the introductions. "Deacon, this is my godson, Najee. Najee, this is my Rafiki, the Deacon."

Najee had heard of the Deacon through Mufasa. They locked grips in a firm handshake and exchanged pleasantries. The Bishop sparked a Black N Mild, inhaled a toke through the plastic filter, and got down to business. "I know you didn't come out of the woodwork just to trade old war stories, so tell us why you're really here."

"I think I finally found a way to get at, Benzo Al," Najee announced. "But I need your help."

"What's in it for me?"

"Revenge!"

"*Revenge* is expensive." The Bishop dislodged a gray stream of cigar smoke.

Najee grinned. "That's why we're also gonna steal ten million from Los Cinco Diablos!" Now he had their full attention.

The Deacon and the Bishop exchanged a knowing look between themselves. The Deacon's yearning for revenge had been lying dormant for years. He sensed that the hour of retribution was near. The Bishop gave the nod okay, and the Deacon smiled. It was one of those smiles that an alligator gives its prey before it attacks.

The Deacon removed a thick Bible from the bookcase and pressed his thumb against a biometric security pad. His fingerprint was authenticated, a titanium bolt slid back and the bookcase swung open revealing a hidden, 9x12 chamber. The concrete room was no larger than a prison cell. Chrome racks holding military-grade assault rifles and other untraceable firearms were mounted on the walls.

Najee's eyes widened. There were choppers with clips longer than his forearm, and handguns that were designed to spit like fully automatics. He was happier than Dracula at a blood bank, but there was one weapon in particular that piqued his curiosity.

Najee picked up the black, plastic device. It was lighter than he expected. "What's this?" he turned to the Deacon and asked.

"Yah holding it upside down, youngin'. Here, let me show ya' how it works." The Deacon took possession of the device. "Jah heard of a street sweeper, right? Well, 'dis is a block shaker."

Najee smirked. He admired all of the deadly artillery on the walls, but it was going to take more than firepower to bring down Benzo Al. It was going to take brains, heart and a clever plan. Najee had all three. "Huddle up and let me lay out how we gon' get this bitch!"

The possibility of them succeeding was slim. Najee was in control for now, but he would soon spindle out of control.

CHAPTER 23

Death Around the Corner

Gotti was chilling low key at his baby mama's house on 132nd and Purche, right in the heart of Shotgun Crips hood. His BM went to Gardena High with most of them, so they had given Gotti a ghetto pass as long as he didn't come through their turf flamed up.

The precious moments he spent reading bedtime stories to his three-year-old daughter, Lexus and making love to his wifey helped take his mind off the killing, backstabbing, and constant drama that went down in the Bungalows.

The coke drought had stalled his hustle, but he had a lil' sumpin' sumpin' in the stash and was prepared to make a power move once the cartels blessed the streets with product. He was primed and ready to be a boss.

The house phone rang, stirring him out of his thoughts as he lounged on the couch with his baby mama. She had fallen asleep on his chest while watching a bootleg DVD. No one had the number to his landline, so Gotti hesitated before picking up the phone.

"What's brackin'?" he grumbled into the receiver.

"I see you're a family man. I like that, dawg," a menacing voice on the other end complimented. "I would hate for little Lexus to have to grow up without a father. So, stay out of the Bungalows today. Something big is about to pop off. I'm letting you live because I want you on my team, feel me?"

"What, you lettin' me live? Who the fuck is this, Blood?"

"This is your warning!" The caller hung up.

Gotti slipped on his white Chucks, grabbed his strap, and sprinted out of the house. If the police were going to raid the Bungalows, he needed to give his crew a heads up. He hopped in his SS Camaro and smashed up Rosecrans headed to the freeway. The chameleon paint flipped colors in the gleaming sunlight. He hit Sincere's line, but the call went straight to voicemail.

Gotti hung up and called a YG named Remy. Remy did not pick up either. Frustrated, Gotti shifted gears and pushed the V8 engine to the limit. When he was almost to the hood, he hit up Sincere again. This time, his comrade answered.

"What's crackalackin', Gotti? I see yo' baby mama finally let yo' sprung ass come outside," Sincere teased.

Gotti heard laughter in the background but let the comment ride. He had more important matters to tend to. "Y'all niggas need to be easy. I think the po-pos finna run-up in the jects today."

Sincere sucked his teeth. "Nigga, are you pinching off yo' dope sack? When was the last time the one-time rushed the Bungalows? Them white folks don't give a fuck about us. They hoping we kill each other so they can turn the projects into a fancy high-rise for rich people like they doing up in Harlem."

Sincere was a hot boy, but sometimes he made a lot of sense. Gotti merged onto the off-ramp and relaxed a little. "Yeah, you right, my nizzle." He chuckled nervously. "But still bick back and be bool. Somebody just called my tilt and left a brazy ass message."

"Word, what they say, fam?" A commotion drew Sincere's attention to the front of the projects. A crowd of people huddled around a silver Escalade sitting high on 30-inch DUB floaters.

"I'll put you up on game when I get on the deck. I'm right 'round the corner," Gotti told him.

Sincere shoved his way through a cluster of dope fiends. "You betta' hurry up, Mr. Stuntastic is back in the jects about to give out some mo' money. He must think we sweet or sumthin'. Ain't no ghetto pass tonight, though. I'm about to strip this nigga."

"You talkin' 'bout Blood in the Porsche truck? What if homie plugged?"

Sincere upped his TEC. His two cohorts brandished Glock-9s. "Nah, he ain't connected. Remy hollered at his fam in Carson and his people in East Oakland. Ain't nobody heard of a cat name, Sinatra. Ol' boy is fair game."

'*Damn!*' Gotti thought to himself.

He liked what Sinatra was doing for the streets and was hoping to link up with him. He parked down the block and met up with Sincere, Remy, and Dolla just as they ran up on Najee and pressed the iron to his medulla.

"Break yo' self, fool!" Sincere twisted his lips sideways. His eyes were narrow angry slits. "Hand over that duffel bag and run them jewels while you at it."

Najee felt the steel pressed against his head but remained cool. "You got it, playa. Just don't kill me. I got a three-year-old daughter at home." He looked directly at Gotti as he made the comment.

Gotti smacked Najee with the pistol. "Don't talk, just cooperate, nigga." He peeped the custom-made Audemars Piguet on Najee's wrist and unfastened the platinum buckle. "Now this what it do! I've always wanted an auto-mars!" he quipped, pronouncing the brand's name wrong. He was swept up in greed.

They stuck Najee for his watch, Jesus piece, and duffel bag. Before hopping into the Escalade, Gotti pistol-whipped Najee and made him lay it down in the middle of the street. Sincere climbed behind the wheel, Gotti rode shotgun, and their accomplices rode in the back. Adrenalin laced laughter and congratulatory high-five circulated inside the luxurious Cadillac truck.

Sincere was geeked up. Before they were even off the block, he turned to Gotti and said, "Whatchu' waiting on, nigga? Open the bag and let's see what fammo twerkin' with."

The duffel bag felt hefty. Gotti placed it on the center counsel and pulled back the zipper. His mood soured. "What da fuck?" He held up a rubber band stack of newspaper that was cut out to look and feel like real money. "Bust a U-turn, Blood! That slick nigga played us!"

Sincere slammed on the brakes. "On what?" He peered inside the duffel bag. There were fifteen more stacks of fake money. He could not believe his eyes.

Gotti's iPhone buzzed, he placed the caller on speakerphone and answered angrily. "Who the fuck is this?"

The same menacing voice from earlier was on the line. "I was your warning. Now I'm your nightmare. I could've used a rider like you on my squad, but greed was your Achilles heel. Enjoy the watch in hell, comrade." Najee ended the call and used his cellular signal to trigger the device that the Deacon had equipped him with earlier.

The timer inside the duffel bag began to beep loudly. Gotti rummaged through the sack and pulled out a black box with a row of red LED lights on top. The lights blinked rapidly.

Five, four, three, two!

A rancid feeling curdled in the pit of Gotti's gut. He only had one second to live. His last vision was of Najee. His last thought was of his daughter.

Kaboom!

As promised, the block shaker shook the block. The centrifugal force of the explosion lifted the 5,100-pound SUV four feet into the air. The metal frame buckled like plastic, and the windows shattered outwards, ejecting sharp pieces of glass-like shrapnel. The blast killed all four doomed passengers instantly. Their heads exploded like ripe watermelons being smashed with a sledgehammer. Red pulp splattered on the leather seats and wood grain.

The Los Angeles Fire Department arrived and extinguished the smoldering Escalade, the bomb squad scoured the area with K-9s searching for additional explosive devices, and ATF agents in white hazmat suits and latex gloves collected evidence.

The only recognizable remains left were Gotti's charred arm. The authorities showed the custom Audemars watch on the eleven O'clock news hoping someone would come forward and identify the victim.

Benzo Al's stepbrother, Carlos Guzman, was at a $1,000 per plate black-tie affair. He smiled when he received a Twitter tweet about the explosion. The Cinco Diablos had long ago begun to finance political campaigns in exchange for favors when the official was elected. Now, however, they wanted one of their own in a position of power. Carlos Guzman was that man, and his ambitious eyes were on the governor's mansion. The rampant lawlessness in the Bungalows would give him ammunition to go after the current governor.

Carlos set down his glass of Chardonnay and called his aide to set up a press conference. It was time to unveil his anti-crime initiative

Angela saw Najee's burnt watch on TMZ and broke down in tears. She blew up his phone back to back fearing he was dead.

Spade laid in the cut on the side of the building. The street-lights had been shot out long ago in order to shroud the illegal activities that afflicted the projects. The darkness helped him blend in with the shadows. He clutched a can of 211 beer concealed in a brown paper bag and watched Najee slide into the passenger seat of a blue, Cadillac CTS driven by the Bishop. Spade had witnessed everything pop off in real-time. A proud smile washed across his lips. Sinatra had taken the throne and crowned himself king.

Larry D. Wright

CHAPTER 24

Hollywood Hills, CA

Najee loved cruising solo through his city at night. There was no place like L.A. The brisk night air was fresh, and the streets were alive with electricity. He pushed the CTS up the Sunset strip smoking on Moonrocks and vibin' off the eclectic mix of young people who seemed to never sleep. He felt no remorse for the murders he committed earlier that day. His only regret was not having Gotti on his team.

Angela had been blowing up his line all night long. He swiped the ignore icon each time she called. It wasn't because he wasn't feeling her, it was because he was feeling her too much. The thought spooked him. Falling in love with a loca who was heavily plugged with the Cinco Diablos would only complicate matters.

He thumped the ashes off his Dutch Master and breezed through the green light at Sunset and La Brea just as Angela hit him up again. He contemplated ignoring the call for the umpteenth time, but temptation strong-armed his will power.

"What's up, beautiful?" his voice was rough yet smooth. If a lion could speak, it would sound like Najee.

"Oh, my gosh, Papi. Where are you? I've been calling you all night long." Angela paced back and forth in her huge bedroom. Her tight boy shorts and sports bra left nothing to the imagination.

"Whoa! Hold up, lil' mama, don't be interrogating me about my whereabouts. I'm a grown-ass man." He checked Angela while checking his rearview mirror. An LAPD squad car dipped in traffic.

Angela stopped pacing and placed a manicured hand on her sexy hips. "Geez, Sinatra. Why you so hard on a bitch? I was just worried about you, that's all. I haven't heard from you since we made that move at the beach. Then tonight I saw your watch on the news. That was your watch, wasn't it?"

Her inquiry was more of an accusation than a question. Najee stiffened but remained mute. His silence confirmed her suspicions. She was relieved he was not hurt. She sat on the edge of her bed and painted her toes with blue nail polish, Najee's favorite color. She could not understand why she was feeling him so much. The thought of her lover thuggin' in the streets made her horny.

"Are you okay, Sinatra?" she asked after a long silence.

Najee stubbed out the cannabis and watched the one-time with his strap in his lap. The black and white patrol car swooped past him and flashed their lights on a Dodge Challenger. Najee relaxed and focused on Angela.

"Yeah, I'm straight, baby. I haven't forgot about you. Keeping it trill, I've been thinking about yo' fine ass all day. I've just been busy in these streets trying to build my empire. Know what I mean?" He banked a right turn and ascended into the Hollywood Hills.

Najee's comment warmed Angela's heart. "I've been thinking about you too, Sinatra. Come over, Papi. I need to see you."

"Why you want me to come through and blow yo' back out?" he joked.

"Boy, you nasty," Angela blushed. It had been years since a man made her giddy like a high school freshman.

"Do you want to see me or not?" Najee checked the time on his Franck Muller watch. It was 1:20 A.M. Going to Angela's spot would serve three purposes, he decided. It would help him take his mind off Nella, give him an alibi, and most importantly, allow him to siphon information from her about Los Cinco Diablos.

"Of, course, I want to see you." She strolled into her walk-in closet and picked out a strapless Prada mini dress.

"Then open your gate."

"You're here already? Stop playin', Sinatra," Angela gushed with excitement. She ran to the window, pulled back the curtains, and smiled. "How long have you been waiting for me?"

"All my life, baby. All my life."

Angela opened the tall, iron gate with her remote, and Najee drove through. She watched him back into a parking space that allowed for a quick getaway if necessary. Her father was the same way. Whenever he went into a building, he scouted for exits and positioned his seat to face the front entrance. Najee's gangsterism made her nipples and clitoris tingle. In her world, paranoia, intellect, and ambition were the traits of a good boss.

She met Najee in the foyer of her mansion. No words were spoken. Their body language communicated their lascivious thoughts. Angela fell into Najee's arms. Her warm breasts pressed against his cold heart. Their eyes met briefly before their starving lips locked like prison bars in Attica.

They did not make it to her bedroom. Najee stripped out of his gear, pulled Angela's sports bra over her head, and peeled her boy shorts down to her ankles. Her golden bronze skin glistened like an Aztec princess. The shaved V between her legs was phat. Najee's middle finger caressed her there.

"You're already wet," he whispered softly against her neck.

"I get this way every time I think about you. What kind of spell did you put on me?" she asked, removing his finger from her sopping wet vagina and placing it between her lips. She licked off her sugary juices before sinking to her knees.

She wanted to suck his big dick again. She looked at it first. It was smooth, rock hard, and the color of chocolate syrup. She took the head into her mouth, savoring the manly flavor and loving the animalistic groans that belched from Najee's throat. She sucked him deeper, much deeper, causing his toes to curl. Najee threw his head back and lurched his hips forward. Powerful jets of cum shot from his throbbing penis and splashed on her tonsils. Angela kept sucking until his knees buckled.

"Damn, baby! Superhead don't have nothing on you!" Najee swept Angela's long hair away from her face and watched her greedily swallow all of his babies. His libido was amazing. His erection stayed rigid, and he was ready for round two. "Let's go to your room, Angela. I want to make love to you."

He reached down and pinched both of her sensitive nipples between his fingers, soliciting a moan from Angela. The sensation made her tremble. She rose from her knees but didn't want to let go of his dick. She held onto his swollen tool and led him into her spacious, master bedroom. Once there, she crawled onto the bed doggy style and looked over her shoulder.

"I don't want to make love. I want you to fuck me hard. Put it in my ass first."

They spent the rest of the night and the majority of the next day in bed. If Angela dozed off, Najee would wake her up with a hard dick invading one of her tight holes. If Najee crashed out first, Angela would revive him by wrapping her warm mouth around his flaccid penis. When they got hungry, they ate food off each other's bodies. The room reeked with the sultry scent of sweat and unadulterated sex.

****

Loud screams, gunshots, blood. More screams, more gunshots, more blood. Najee drifted asleep and his harrowing nightmares haunted him. The grim images jostled him awake only to find Angela straddling his midsection cowgirl style and clamping a handcuff around his left wrist. She secured the other cuff to a wooden post on her headboard.

Najee's eyes widened alert. He sat up in bed and grabbed her by the throat with his free hand. "Bitch, are you crazy? Uncuff me before I break ya' neck!" He didn't notice Angela moan. The tight grip around her throat made her cum.

"Chill, Sinatra, I just wanted to play a little game. You can tie me up next and do anything you want."

Najee looked around the room. Angela had brought out her secret box of toys. He spied a black blindfold, a leather whip, gag balls, nipple clamps, flavored lubricants, and an assortment of dildos ranging in size from a small vibrating bullet to a huge life-like penis. He had never indulged in anything like this before. He was down to get his freak on, but the handcuffs had to go.

"Stop playing games, Angela, and give me the key. Haven't you seen Roots? Black men and shackles don't get along well."

Angela burst out laughing and laid her head on his chest. "So, now you Kunta Kinte, huh?"

196

Najee smiled back at her. "You think it's funny, huh?" he asked playfully. "I got something for that ass, watch this."

He brought his free wrist to his mouth and used his teeth to unbuckle the leather strap on his Franck Muller watch. On many timepieces, the small silver pin that goes through the holes on the watch strap can be used to pick locks. Najee jiggled the silver pin inside the keyhole just as the Bishop had taught him, and the handcuff clicked open. The process took less than thirty seconds.

Angela was amazed. "I'm impressed." She rubbed his chest working her way down to the bullet wound on his torso. "You're a mysterious man, Sinatra. You got me head over hills, yet, I really don't know anything about you. Tell me about the person inside here." She tapped on his heart.

Najee was modest and didn't like bragging about himself. "There's not much to tell. I'm just a regular guy." He played with her belly ring.

"Trust me, you're beyond regular." She squeezed his dick to emphasize her point. "If you don't want to talk about yourself, tell me about Angel." Najee flinched and Angela felt compelled to clarify her query. "You said her name in your sleep," she added.

Najee wondered what else he might have slipped and said in his sleep. He was mad at himself for not being able to control the nightmares that plagued his nights. He rolled out of bed and took a steaming hot shower. Angela got in with him and used a sponge to soap the 'Only God Can Judge Me' tattoo sprawled across his back. The soothing hot water rained on their bodies.

"Don't take it personal, baby," Najee spoke in a far-off voice. "But some things are not meant be spoken out loud." He turned towards Angela. "Tell me about yourself. How did a nice girl like you get twisted up in this evil game?"

Angela wrapped her arms around his neck. "I feel like I can talk to you about anything. Do you want to know about my father's construction company being a front for Los Cinco Diablos, or about how as a young girl, I got turned on while watching four black men have a shootout in front of my Catholic school?"

Najee perked up when he heard this. He was anxious to find out if the details matched the Bishop's account of the regretful shootout that he and the Deacon had with the Pope and the Altar Boy. Najee lathered her toned frame with scented body wash and listened attentively as she told him about her father's death and how she was shuffled between foster homes and detention centers until she found refuge in the streets.

Najee was familiar with the story. He wanted to tell Angela that her father's mysterious death was no accident and that it was Benzo Al who had poisoned him, but he kept the information to himself, hoping he could use it later in order to turn Angela against her boss.

CHAPTER 25

Forest Lawn Cemetery

Seven Days Later

A procession of six black limos carrying the grieving family members of Brazy and Gotti inched forward in traffic at a snail's pace. A long column of Chevy low riders trailed closely behind. The stoned faced occupants of these vehicles sipped Absolut, smoked sherm sticks, and plotted revenge against an invisible enemy.

Word came down from the Cinco Diablos letting it be known that Brazy had gotten caught up in friendly crossfire during the mêlée at the hospital and that he was not the intended target. Benzo Al hit Brazy's moms off with some paper and sent her a dozen roses to express his condolence. In the mean streets of L.A., that's as close to an apology you're gonna get.

The horrific murder of Gotti was a different story. The news of him and his crew being blown to bits left niggas in the slums shook. Sinatra's name rang loudly in the streets. Not many people knew what he looked like or where he came from, so tall tales were spun, and an urban legend was created. The outlandish rumors spread throughout the ghetto like syphilis. Najee laughed at the ghetto gossip, but secretly, he relished the thought of being the bogeyman.

Sosa and Ice showed up at the cemetery to pay their humble respects to their fallen comrade, Brazy and his deceased relative, Gotti. Their black Tom Ford suits and dark Louie shades were in stark contrast to the multitude of flamed up Pirus rockin' burgundy and red attire. Damu love was in full effect.

Ice pulled a wave brush from seemly nowhere and stroked his hair. His mind was in plot mode. "What's the business, Sosa? You hear anythang on the soldiers who got nabbed by the Feds in Atlanta?"

Sosa's arm was in a sling, but he was healing well from the hospital shootout. Disguising his distaste for talking hood politics at a funeral, he answered Ice anyhow. "They gravy, I put up the bail money and hired that hotshot attorney, Robert Henak, to represent them. What's up with you, though, you straight? I heard about Qnesha and Outlaw. That shit is fucked up, my dude."

A rare jab of remorse punched Ice in the gut. "I'm straight, big homie. Outlaw went out with a bang, but they blasted Qnesha in cold blood for no reason. To top it off, that pig Blondie planted a burner in her right hand. Qnesha is left-handed, but I guess black lives don't matter." At that moment, he decided to no longer work with Blondie.

Sosa felt bad that neither he nor Ice was able to make it to the funeral. He had a lot of love for Outlaw, but the ATL was too hot, right now. "If there's anythang I can do for you and Lil' Ice, just holla," he offered. "You know I got chu'."

Ice saw an opening and went in hard. "Now that I'm doing my thizzle out here on the West Coast, too. We need to link up and do it big. I got word that Benzo Al finna flood the streets with yay. If we work together, we can put the game on click-clack."
Sosa cringed, the conversation had him noticeably irritated. This was neither the time nor place to chop it up about Los Cinco Diablos. Because of all the full-fledged gang members and drug fugitives present, he knew the Feds were not far behind. He wouldn't have been surprised if a hidden camera was concealed in one of the caskets.

His alert eyes swept over the mourners. A pretty little girl in a red princess dress placed a bouquet of white roses on Gotti's coffin. Sosa turned to Ice and let him have it.

"Pride breeds fools, but wisdom is found in he who seeks advice. Take this free jewelry to the pond shop, nephew, because I'm about to tell you some real shit. I'm not looking for a crime partner. The dope game is dead. Secondly, the Nogales Cartel and the Los Cinco Diablos are at war. Trust me, you don't want to get caught in the middle. You ain't ready!"

Ice opened his mouth to respond, but Sosa's cell phone rang, stealing his attention. Sosa answered with a smile, leaving Ice frowning bitterly.

"Wassup, ma? How is the baby doing?" Sosa's mood lightened. He loved spending time with Nella and could talk to her all night long, but out of respect for the dead, he kept their convo brief. "That's all good. I'm glad my two favorite people are straight. You need anythang from the sto'?"

Sosa detected shade coming from Ice but dismissively brushed off the warning signs. His lack of discernment would come back to haunt him. He confirmed Nella's short grocery list and rushed her off the phone. "Some diapers and some Good Start formula? A'ight, shawdy, I'll slide through later and dump it off."

Sosa hung up and turned to resume speaking with Ice, but Ice had already mobbed off and was mingling with a group of Bloods. No one noticed the police drone soaring high above. Two tech savvy detectives from the L.A. Gang Task Force lounged in a catering truck parked three blocks away. They sipped stale coffee while watching the funeral on their tablets.

****

Ice politicked with the Damu's and liked the page they were on. He never did understand why brothas banged over red and blue when it was obviously about that green, nevertheless, after the funeral, he found himself chillin' with a female Blood named Redbonez. They cruised through the West Side in her red six-trey Impala and kicked it at a picnic in the Jungles. When darkness cloaked the city, she took him to a house party in Denver Lane hood. It was here that Ice learned just how connected Redbonez was.

"Peep this, Blood, you 'bout to enter a different world. When we step up in this joint, try not to stare and don't talk too much," Redbonez warned. "We just lost one of our family members, but the G's ordered us not to retaliate until the heat dies down and the enemy is slippin'. The wolf pack don't understand this war strategy. They thirsty for blood and ready to set trip, so be smooth."

As soon as Ice walked into the spot, he ignored Redbonez warning and couldn't stop staring. Plush red carpet and blood-red walls greeted him when he strolled into the tan-colored house on Imperial Highway.

The leather couch was red, and the curtains were fashioned out of large, red bandanas. Two red piranhas swam in a fish tank filled with red water, and a red nose Pitbull with a red spiked collar guarded the front door. Young men and women dressed in various shades of red sipped a strong red liquid out of red plastic cups. The only thing that wasn't crimson in color was the bountiful amount of lime green weed that circulated liberally. Ice was amazed at the allegiance these hardened gangsters had for their nation.

The mere presence of Redbonez livened the party. Her swag was saucy, and her vibe was mellow. Everyone went out of his or her way to greet Redbonez with a respectful handshake, a tight hug, or a head nod. They held her in high esteem. It was obvious to Ice that she was a rider, and this was her family.

Redbonez wasn't overly attractive, however, her sparkling smile was captivating, and her shapely body was bangin'. Ice liked the way her white CK Jeans showed off the contours of her fat ass. He wondered why they called her Redbonez when actually her skin was the color of coffee with a splash of cream.

His thoughts were abruptly interrupted when Lunatik from Pasadena Lanes blessed him with a thick, chocolate Philly and a red cup. Ice hesitated and looked around the smoke-filled room before taking a cautious sip.

"Shizz, the way these niggas is banged out, I hope this ain't no real blood they drinking," he told himself and swallowed the strong red liquid.

He tasted Belvedere and cranberry juice. Ice chuckled nervously at his own paranoia and hit the blunt hard, letting the THC exhaust collide with his lungs. The powerful Humboldt County herb made him cough until he folded over and tears welled up in his eyes.

Redbonez patted him on the back. "You gotta sip not guzzle. This that real Cali weed grown in California soil under that California sun. Some niggas think they smokin' on Kush, but they don't know no better. On the West Coast, we call hydro pretendo. Ya' feeling me?"

She had a point. Ice tipped his cup, downed the Belve, and grinned. Diamonds twinkled in the dim room. It quickly became apparent that he was not from those parts. Ironically, his syrupy, Dirty South accent worked in his favor. The men stopped sizing him up with hard stares, and the hood rats started throwing the P his way.

Out of respect for Redbonez, he played his position and looked but didn't touch. He had told her that he was in L.A. trying to link up with a new plug, and he didn't want to jeopardize making hundreds and fifties for some ass and titties.

Redbonez, however, was not trippin'. She called over two of the baddest chicks at the party. They looked like they stepped off the pages of a Phat Puffs magazine. In a brass display of dominance, Redbonez snatched the slimmer of the two by her long, flowing hair and tongue kissed her deeply. The chocolate brick house standing next to them joined in, and the trio of women engaged in a wet, three-way kiss.

Redbonez broke the erotic ménage and introduced her friends to Ice. "These are my two bitches, Cinnamon and Spice. They're gonna hold you down while I handle a little business. Play ya' cards right, and I might introduce you to some people that can change ya' life." She surprised him and slipped her skillful tongue down his throat as well. The night was getting interesting, and there was more to come.

Ice languished on the red leather couch sandwiched between two beautiful bombshells. He watched Redbonez enter one of the closed doors at the back of the house. It looked like a party inside of a party. However, the gangsters in this room were a bit older, their hearts a bit colder, and the stress of years of war with the Hoovers and the Raymond Crips showed on their valiant faces.

A huge figure draped in a black and gold Versace button-up sat at the head of a round poker table. Rubber band stacks of big blue faces were piled in front of him like a king's feast, but there were no cards or poker chips. An unlit cigar bobbed in the corner of his lips. Redbonez pulled out her Bic lighter and respectfully lit the Zino.

The flame illuminated the hulking figure's face. He motioned for Redbonez to sit at the opposite end of the table. Business was in motion. Ice crammed his head to get a better view, but an old pimp with a red feather tucked in his black fedora mean mugged him and slammed the door.

One hour, two blunts, and three red cups later, Redbonez emerged from the conference room followed by the large man in the gaudy, Versace shirt. Two Hispanic bodyguards flanked his left and right shoulders.

Ice immediately recognized Benzo Al and stood up to salute the boss of all bosses. "Benzo Al, what it do, my man? How has life been treating you?" he greeted, extending his palm.

Both of Benzo Al's bodyguards upped heat and pointed the bangers at Ice's face. Benzo Al gave them the nod to lower their weapons. "Let him through, Ese." He squeezed Ice's outstretched hand tight. A little too tight. "Muy bien, life is good, mi amigo. How is, Sosa?" he asked with acid in his voice.

Redbonez stepped back with a hand on her hip and one eyebrow raised curiously at Ice. "Wait a minute, you already know Benzo Al?" Her interest and respect for Ice shot up to ten.

Although Ice was chopped, he picked up on the smoke between Sosa and Benzo Al. He ignored Redbonez and used the simmering animosity to his advantage. "I don't fuck with that mark ass nigga no mo'! I'm solo, ambitious, and looking for a new team." He held his chin up and maintained steady eye contact as if he was on a job interview.

Benzo Al liked what he was hearing. He was very familiar with BBE and Ice's reputation of being one of the premier street goons in Atlanta. Los Cinco Diablos was embroiled in battles on all fronts, so Benzo Al decided to use Ice as a pawn in his war games.

"You drinka tequila, no? Let's take a ride, have a drink like gentlemen, and discuss business," his offer was more of a demand than a suggestion.

They were ushered into the back seat of Benzo Al's cocaine white Brabus Mercedes. He poured Ice a stiff shot of Mescal tequila. A dead worm floated at the bottom of the glass. They clicked cups in a toast, and Benzo Al began to lay out his unthinkable plot.

"So, tell me about Sosa and this chica he just had a baby with," he instructed.

Ice returned Benzo Al's devilish smirk. "I can do better than tell you, I can show you!"

Larry D. Wright

CHAPTER 26

Money Controls Minds

Najee was only 5'7', but he mobbed through the Bungalows with the audacious bravery of Goliath. He had eliminated the opposition and inaugurated himself as king of the projects. As he strolled through the courtyard, men, women, and children saluted him with the admiration and reverence reserved for an emperor. It didn't hurt that he had the loyalty of the Bishop and the Deacon on his side. Although the Kill Squad had been out of commission for years, the old heads recognized game and showed respect where respect was due.

Najee returned the love. He shook hands with the men and women and flagged down a passing ice cream truck that had no intention of stopping due to fears of getting robbed. Najee handed the driver a roll of crisp, fifty-dollar bills and bought out all the ice cream for the shorties. Little gestures like that make a big impact. The neglected ghetto kids surrounded Najee and cheered happily.

The bombing incident sent chills through the asphalt jungle and made national headlines. Eager reporters from local news stations, as well as a journalist from major media outlets like CNN and MSNBC, bum-rushed the projects with microphones and cameras. The headline thirsty paparazzi were hoping to get footage of the anarchy and felonious activity that the Bungalows were notoriously known for.

However, they got nothing. Najee suspended all drug dealing, prostitution, robberies, gambling, and loitering. After several crime-free days, the disappointed media packed up their news vans and chased the next big story.

Najee gave the kids at the ice cream truck some dap on the fist, encouraged them to stay in school, and then entered the five-story brick mansion through a heavy, metal door. His nose was immediately aroused by the various odors of the ghetto.

The delicious smell of crispy fried chicken seeped from under the door of a black family on the second floor, and the scrumptious scent of tortillas and pinto beans floated from the stove of a Hispanic household on the third level. These soulful aromas would have normally made Najee hungry, however, the stench of stale piss and vomit in the hallway ruined his appetite.

The Deacon hit the up button on the elevator. The old boxcar creaked and croaked until its rickety doors squeaked open on the main level. One look inside the filthy elevator made the men opt for the pissy stairs instead.

Najee jumped over a puddle of urine and made his way to the first floor. He was welcomed by more heartbreak and despair. A door to one of the apartments was open. The sparsely furnished unit had an old couch that had seen better days and a big, floor model TV from the 90s. Even though the television was decades old, the owner had the nerve to be stealing cable. The white walls had turned a dingy yellow from cigarette smoke, and roaches feasted on the leftover scraps inside a greasy pizza box.

Najee became distraught by what he saw. A nappy-headed black toddler appeared in the doorway. He sucked the air out of an empty baby's bottle, working in vain to satisfy his hunger pangs. Day old piss and shit made his Huggies diaper sag. His shirt was off, revealing the worst protruding bellybutton Najee had ever seen. It was as if the doctor said fuck it and sent the kid home without paying proper attention to his navel.

The kid's unfit mother was slumped at the kitchen table nodding off with a rubber tourniquet around her forearm and a syringe dangling from her vein. The harsh reality of poverty saddened Najee. Reluctantly, he turned his back on the misery and kept it moving to the next floor.

The Bishop noticed Najee's sudden mood shift and placed a comforting hand on his shoulder. "Your purpose in life is bigger than your beef with, Benzo Al, my man. The Lord brought you here as an instrument of His divine will. He wants you to make this a better place for kids like him."

Najee sighed and looked towards the chipped paint on the ceiling. "I don't know if I can do it. What if I make things worse? What if these cats want war?"

"You can do it," the Bishop encouraged. "There's about twenty, cold-hearted brothas waiting for you outside. Those youngsters are lost in triple darkness and desperately seeking guidance. Speak to them like a leader, not a tyrant, and they will follow you through hell and back."

"I don't know, man. I may have bitten off more than I can chew. It's impossible to just waltz up in the projects and take it over."

"I agree, but you've studied the Art of War, have you not? Battles are won with brains, not bullets. Use this up here." He tapped on his temple. "And make a difference in these brothas lives."

Najee marinated on the Bishop's statement. He was a sinner and knew without a doubt that he would eventually die a violent death and spend eternity in Hades, but the Bishop's words inspired him. "I'd rather be feared than loved," Najee declared. "But you're right, I think I can make a difference. All of us can make a difference. Just keep your eyes open and watch my back when we get out here. We don't know if these soldiers are going to get down or lay us down."

The three killers trotted back down the pissy flight of stairs and bailed side by side to the playground where all the players, hustlers, and gang bangers congregated. Nerves were on edge as the trio approached. All eyes were on Najee. They had heard many rumors about Sinatra and were surprised that he wasn't taller and scarier looking.

Najee scanned each face through his Google glasses. The foolish youth these days lived out their lives on social media, posting pics with guns and money, broadcasting their business, and inadvertently divulging their locations via geotagging. Simply visit their Facebook, Instagram, or Youtube accounts, and you could easily find out everything about them. Najee used this to his advantage. He stood on top of a park bench and held court.

"For those who don't know me, my name is Sinatra, and I'm a muthafuckin' problem!"

Disgruntled murmurs interrupted him. The Bishop shook his head with a disappointing sigh. Najee held up his hands to calm the legion of thugs. "Hear me out, my niggas. Hear me out." He decided to take the Bishop's advice and switched tactics. "I didn't come to pull y'all down, I came to pull y'all up. Get it in with me, and I can get you paid. We all can ball if you give me the opportunity to lead you."

At the mention of money and leadership, the mumbles ceased. Real street niggas respected structure and currency.

"You got my attention, speak on it," a lanky, shifty-eyed hustler with an ugly keloid scar across his left temple spoke up.

The Deacon hit Najee with a supporting wink, prompting him to continue, "From here on out, this is how it's gonna go down 'round here. The first thing we're gonna do is take over the whole fifth floor. One apartment will be used for drugs, one will be used for prostitution, and another will be for gambling. All illegal activities will happen up there, or it don't happen at all.

"Next, we gon' give back to the community starting by sanitizing this bitch 'till it's clean. And every month we're gonna have a food drive to make sure these kids got something in the frig to eat. We're also gonna open a boys and girls club where the current, rundown recreation center is located."

The group of outlaws nodded their heads in agreement and gave each other some dap. They liked the idea of doing something good for the shorties. It was a shame that the children had to see dirty needles, used condoms, and drug dealing on their playground.

Najee lit a blunt, took two puffs, and passed it to a slim, dark-skinned gunslinger who was dressed fresh to death. The soldier nodded his gratitude, and Najee resumed lacing his new crew with game.

"Security will be our number one priority. We gotta make sure our S is on point twenty-fo-seven—" He paused and pointed to the slim, dark-skinned gunslinger who he had passed the blunt to.

"Crunchy, you know who's who 'round here. I want you to work closely with the Deacon and put together a topnotch security team."

Crunchy's smile widened. He appreciated being given an important leadership position. Sincere and Gotti never believed in his abilities and treated him like a send-off. He was beginning to like Sinatra more and more.

Najee noted the positive change in Crunchy's disposition and carried on speaking. "The elevators are for the residents only. A soldier will ride on there at all times to escort people to and from their perspective floor. Show some project love and help the women and old people with their grocery bags and shit like that. We want to create an atmosphere where the residents need us. If they have something to gain, they won't risk losing it by calling the police on us. Feel me?

"The stairs are strictly for our use. I want a guard strapped and posted up on each floor. Nobody gets in the Bungalows unless they live here or they one of us."

Najee took a moment to single out the hustler with the long keloid scar gracing his temple. "Casino, you about getting that paper. I want you to link up with the Bishop. Y'all will make sure the yayo empire operates smoothly. And from now on, we move in secrecy. No more pushin' packs in the open and serving fiends in the courtyard. It's about to get real hot 'round here. That punk ass politician, Carlos Guzman, is tryna' make a name for himself at your expense, so dead that shit. I have a better way."

Najee jumped off the bench, making himself accessible to his troops. His voice lowered a few decibels. The goons leaned forward to hear his stealthy plot. "We need to put lookouts with pre-paid cell phones on the ground here, here, and here." He pointed to specific, strategic locations. "Money collectors will be posted up there, there, and there. The money collectors will handle the cash and signal the fifth floor with how much dope the custie copped. A soldier on the fifth floor will stick a long water hose out the window and blow the package down to the hype. If we jam like this, nobody in the clique will get knocked by the jakes. If five-O try to raid, we simply move the work to another apartment before they can even get into the building. Any questions?"

The murmurs continued, but this time the legion of thugs buzzed with a positive vibe. Crunchy pushed his way through the crowd. "Yeah, I got a question. How you know my name?"

Najee lowered his Google glasses and smiled at Crunchy. "Simple, I read your Facebook page."

The Bishop and the Deacon opened large duffel bags and began to distribute guns, burnout cell phones, and packs of dope. A new era was beginning.

****

It was not an easy endeavor, but within a couple of months of implementing his master plan, Najee had the projects crackin'. Word quickly spread about the high quality, white flake his crew was pushing, causing hypes to travel from near and far in order to cop a euphoric blast of ready rock.

It wasn't just the dope fiends on Najee's line. Hustlers who had suffered severe losses in the drought were seeking a new plug. Najee's visits to Angela become more frequent. He bought weight wholesale and flipped it retail. His prices had the dope boys going crazy. Sinatra was the man.

The inhabitants of the Bungalows prospered as well. Despite the heavy volume of traffic, the crime rate had decreased dramatically, the elevator and hallways ceased smelling like vomit and urine, and a well-stocked food pantry was placed in an apartment on the first floor. No man, woman, or child went without a nutritious meal.

As promised, the shorties now played safely in their new recreation center. Because Najee believed that education was a springboard that could catapult the inner-city youth out of the ghetto, a portion of the rec center was transformed into a small classroom and equipped with laptop computers. He even set up an after-school program so that struggling students could get help with their homework. Surprisingly, Crunchy turned out to be an excellent minister of security as well as a patient tutor.

On the surface, the gears of Najee's money machine churned smoothly, but the pats on the back and accolades started to go to his head. He lost focus of his main mission and embraced the mentality of a drug dealer. It became increasingly evident that he liked being Sinatra more than he liked being Najee.

Larry D. Wright

CHAPTER 27

Diablos Hideout: Calabasas, CA

Benzo Al's massive estate made Angela's mansion look like a studio apartment. Heavily armed Cinco Diablos goons safeguarded the compound with machine guns, and sexy Latina housekeepers in skimpy French maid outfits catered to his every need.

Benzo Al, Ice, Angela, and an audio-visual technician lingered around a bank of security monitors. Grainy footage from the hospital shootout played on one of the six screens.

"Stop right there," Benzo Al ordered. The technician pressed pause. Benzo Al pointed a chubby finger at the monitor. "That's Sosa. Do you recognize the chica with him?"

Ice squinted his eyes to get a better view. "Nah, I don't recall seeing her around, but at the same time, Sosa is a player. He always kept a different hoe on deck."

Benzo Al stroked his goatee. It was his habitual habit. "Her name is Nella Jackson. She has cost me a lot of time, money, and grief." He flicked the gray embers off his cigar. "She has to pay for her transgressions. Do you think you can find her for me?"

Ice nodded his head. "If she's with Sosa, I can track her down. He's been spending a lot of time with Larry Wright, the CEO of Baller Belly Entertainment. All I gotta do is wait until he leaves the studio and follow him to her crib. What's the business, do you want me to snatch the bitch up and bring her to you?"

Benzo Al liked Ice's treacherous ambition, but he had other plans. "No, I have something else in mind. Something that will let all my enemies know that the devil is real, and hell is hot." He laid out his sinister intensions in vivid detail, then questioned Ice's ability to carry out such a heinous task. "Do you have the balls to do what I ask when the time comes?"

Ice wavered. "I don't know, Benzo. I got heart, but—"

"Being a boss ain't about having a heart, it's about being heartless."

Ice brushed his waves. He had done a lot of dirt in his time, but the evil that Benzo Al proposed wasn't on his resume. "I, um—I don't think it's a good idea," he stuttered badly.

Benzo Al blew smoke at Ice. "Luckily, I don't pay you to think." He crushed out the cigar and stood closer to Ice. "I'm a man of great wealth, power, and influence. If a man like me owed you a favor, it would be more valuable than a blank check from Warren Buffet," he boasted.

Angela stepped in to add her two cents. "Remember what you said about African-Americans being unpredictable and unreliable? Well, I don't trust this vato. He doesn't make eye contact with me, and he smells like a rat," she spoke unfavorably about Ice as if he wasn't in the room. "But as much as I hate to admit it, he's right. The crime you're suggesting isn't a good idea. It's bad for business."

Benzo Al hit Angela with an icy, *shut-the-fuck-up look*, and ignored her. "As I was saying, men like you and me know the importance of favors, but more significantly, mi amigo, we know the importance of fidelidad— loyalty. If you want to be a part of this organization, you must prove your loyalty. Sangre dentro, sangre afuera. Blood in, blood out."

Ice weighed his options. Benzo Al was essentially offering him the keys to the city. He wondered what unspeakable act Sosa had to commit for the privilege of sitting at the table with the crime boss.

Surahs from the Holy Quran tumbled through his head. He hadn't been to Juma'h or gotten on his prayer rug and made salat towards Mecca in months, yet Allah tugged at his conscience.

Ice opened his mouth to decline, but the allure of money, power, and respect was victorious. He accepted the task. "I'll do it!"

"Muy bien, compadre. You made a wise decision. Let's go have a shot of tequila to celebrate." He placed a friendly arm around Ice's shoulders and led him to the bar room. If you looked closely, you could see a pair of devil horns sprouting on top of Benzo Al's head.

****

Angela stared Ice down with an intimidation glare. She didn't like his ill vibe. The feelings were mutual. Ice didn't trust her either. He deliberately bumped into her on his way out of the room.

The audio-visual technician began to rewind the footage, but a blurry image caught Angela's eye. "Wait, hit play!" She moved closer to the wall of monitors.

The audio-visual tech pressed the play button, and the video rolled again. Angela could not see what took place inside of the hospital room, however, the surveillance camera in the hallway captured the shootout. The bloody clash only lasted a few seconds, but it was fierce and brutal, leaving combatants from both platoons dead.

"Okay, press pause, and zoom in on that guy right there," Angela pointed a trembling finger. The audio-visual tech manipulated the footage, and Sinatra's face filled the screen. Angela's heart sank, and her intestines twisted into a tight knot. She had to catch her breath before she spoke, "Did Benzo Al watch the entire video?"

"No," the audio-visual technician answered a little too quickly. "He was only interested in the frames that included Sosa and the girl."

'*Good*,' Angela thought. "Detective Gowdy is working on Juan's homicide. Did he give us the footage from the hospital's burn unit?"

The audio-visual tech flipped through several DVD's and selected a silver disc labeled, Sinai Burn Unit. "Here we go. The boss didn't watch this one either." He slid the disc into a Blu-ray player.

Sinatra came on screen and glanced both ways before slipping into Juan's room. He ran out a few minutes later looking guilty. Angela had seen enough. She felt used, played, and betrayed. She hit the eject button, confiscated the DVD, and angrily stomped out of the mansion, almost breaking one of her Jimmy Choo heels in the process. Hell hath no fury like a woman scorned, and Angela was hotter than an incinerator. Her malignant wrath was aimed at Sinatra for toying with her emotions.

She climbed behind the wheel of her black and pink Range Rover and cursed herself for falling so hard so quickly. She zipped through rush hour traffic with her Jimmy's pushing the throttle, her finger dialing Sinatra's number, and her mind contemplating his murder.

****

The audio-visual tech waited until Angela left, and then rushed into the bar room. Benzo Al and Ice watched the surveillance monitors as Angela sped off the compound with a depraved look in her chestnut-colored eyes.

Benzo Al threw back a shot of Cuervo and addressed the technician. "Did you follow my instructions and tell Angela that I hadn't watched the videos?"

"Si, señor," the audio-visual tech confirmed. He was petrified of Benzo Al and was anxious to pack up his equipment and leave. "I told her you were only interested in Sosa and the chica, and that you didn't watch the second DVD at all. What happens now, patron?"

Benzo Al opened the electronic drapes with a small remote and admired the cluster of glass mansions nestled into the mountainside. "Now we wait to see if she does the right thing." He attempted to conceal his growing distrust in Angela, but the lines of distress crisscrossing his face divulged his doubts.

Ice had never seen Benzo Al so unsettled and vulnerable. He figured his troubles had something to do with the surveillance footage. He downed his tequila and leaned against the long, wooden bar. "That guy in the video is smooth as silk. What is he, some type of assassin?"

Benzo Al rubbed his wooden rosary beads and gazed out of the window. "What he might be is unimportant. Who he might be has me worried!"

218

****

Najee was chillin' in the Bungalows smoking purple harem, sipping Grand Marnier, and politicking with his new troops. He had sauced up one of the apartments on the fifth level by installing bamboo hardwood floors, white leather furniture, African artifacts, and flat-screen TVs.

Every night was a liquor and lust-filled party. The Deacon didn't see any harm in letting the hardworking hustlers unwind, the Bishop, on the other hand, was troubled by Najee's injudicious behavior. The more Najee took on the persona of Sinatra, the less prudent and disciplined he became. The Bishop tried to pull Najee's coat on several occasions, especially about the ill vibe he felt drippin' off Casino, but the sapient counsel landed on deaf ears.

Najee's cell phone lit up. He smiled at Angela's phone number. She had promised to cook for him tonight. He was looking forward to dining on her home-cooked cuisine then devouring her sexy body for dessert.

"What up, lil' ma, I was just thinking 'bout you." He set his glass of cognac on the marble table and stepped into the hallway for privacy. Crunchy was posted up by the door sporting a bullet-proof vest and gripping a South African R4 with a 50-round magazine.

Angela rolled her eyes. "Cut the bullshit, Sinatra. Where are you?"

Her inquisition blew his buzz. "Here we go again. What I tell you about interrogating me? What's next, are you gonna waterboard me too? I'm where I'm always at, knee-deep in the gutter trying to get this butter."

Angela swooped up to her crib, punched in her security code, and sped through her iron gate. "Is that all you've been up to?" she asked curtly. "Because from my experience, brothas who talk slick act slick."

Najee couldn't understand why Angela was so insecure. She was beautiful, rich, and an excellent lover. She could have any man or woman she wanted. Najee decided to be diplomatic and dead the argument before it escalated.

Misdiagnosing her fury for jealousy, he attempted to smooth things over. "Listen, Angela, I don't want no static, especially not tonight. I just want to get off the block, eat some frijoles, watch some old gangster movies, and make love to my woman." He could almost taste the chicken, rice and sazon seasoning.

Angela's heart fluttered, he called her *his* woman, aggressively claiming the pussy as his own. She longed to hear those affectionate words instead of being treated like a slut by Benzo Al and a string of meaningless one-night stands. If she was wearing panties, they would have been wet.

"You still there, lil' ma?" Najee inquired, snatching Angela out of her thoughts.

She wanted to surrender to Najee's charm, but visions of him at the hospital made her bitter. He was up to something foul. She brought him into the game, so she had to take him out or her own life would be in danger.

She hardened her heart and forced a fake smile. "I'm here, and I will continue to be here as long as you treat me right." She ran game. "I want to see you, Papi."

"That's wassup, I'm on my way," Najee announced. "But my car is out of gas, I need to re-up."

"On what? You just re-upped a few days ago. Are you sold out already?" For a moment, concern for her cousin Alex entered her mind. She was holding twenty chickens for him, but he never called back.

"Don't talk so reckless on the phone, lil' ma," Najee admonished. "Like I said, my whip is outta gas and I need twenty gallons to fill my tank. How you lookin'?" He had just offed his last slab to his homie C-Dogg from Compton and his clientele from the Jordon Downs and the Nickerson Gardens were blowing up his line. They were feeling the way he cleaned up the Bungalows and wanted to do the same thing in their projects.

Angela liked the way Najee kept her on her toes. He was one of her best customers, and Benzo Al was beginning to take notice. She pondered Najee's last request and said fuck it, might as well take his three hundred gees before taking his life. "I got you covered, Sinatra. How long will it take to get your pesos ready?"

Najee glanced at the face of his watch. "Gimme about forty-five minutes. I'm dying to see you," he stated, giving no thought to his ominous prediction about dying.

Angela hung up the phone and retrieved her Spanish guillotine. The blood-stained, coil wire was sharp and lethal like its villainous owner.

Crunchy stopped Najee in the hallway. "Where you headed, big bruh?"

"I got a little B.I. to handle. Why, what's poppin'?"

"It ain't my place to say it, but you shouldn't be making moves dolo. You too big in the game to be rollin' by yo' self. Every nigga on the other side of this brick mansion is gunning for your head."

Najee was touched by Crunchy's genuine concern. "It's all good, loved one. I can handle myself." He patted the trusty heat on his waist.

"But ain't this why you got soldiers? So, you wouldn't have to handle everything by yourself?"

Impressed by Crunchy's wisdom, Najee propped himself against the wall and chopped it up with him for a moment. "I've been checkin' your stello. You got a wise dome. Why do you allow yourself to be stuck in the slums?"

"Sometimes you get buried under so much shit, even when you come from up under it, the stench is still on you. The streets are the only place that would accept me. The streets is all I know."

"I can dig that," Najee related. "If you could be anything, what would it be?"

"A rapper," Crunchy replied instantly. A bright light gleamed in his eyes when he spoke about music. "I haven't been trickin' my money off like the rest of these lames. I've been stackin' up to buy some studio equipment so that I can get Mack-A-Hoe Enter-tainment jumpin'."

"I can dig that, too, but don't limit yourself. Dream bigger, not only can you be a rapper, you can be a rap mogul." Najee gave Crunchy a pound on the fist and headed towards the stairs.

"Sinatra," Crunchy called out. "I don't see you trickin' off dough either. What are you saving your money for?"

"War!"

Najee hopped into Bishop's CTS and pushed out. Blondie and Agent Sullivan were not too far behind.

"What I tell you, rookie?" Blondie unraveled a stick of spear-mint gum and started the engine. "I knew we would find him back in the projects. Criminals are creatures of habit. They always re-turn to the crime scene. Let's see what Sinatra is up to today. Hopefully, his movements will give us a clue about his connection to Los Cinco Diablos."

****

It took Najee longer than expected to go to his stash, count out three-hundred bands, and drive cautiously to Angela's tilt. It was dark outside by the time he arrived. The tall, black gates parted, and Najee drove onto the well-maintained property. He observed the curtains move in Angela's room as he found a new place to park.

A candy blue Maserati Quattroporte occupied his favorite spot. Najee didn't sweat it. He figured the whip belonged to one of the beefy Mexican goons who accompanied Angela when she made moves.

He adjusted his New Era hat, made sure his fit was on point and strolled confidently up the cobblestone walkway. He stood on the porch for a moment half-expecting Angela to come down and greet him with a juicy kiss like normal. When she didn't come to the door, he wiggled the gold knob, it was unlocked.

He cautiously pushed the door open and stepped inside the breath-taking foyer. An eerie sensation seized him. His right hand instinctively reached under his Givenchy shirt and clutched the ivory grip of his banger. He checked the kitchen, empty. Next, he made his way into the domed ceiling living room and called Angela's name over the loud reggaeton music.

"Angela, where you at, girl?"

"I'm in the bathroom, bae. Come up here," she invited.

Najee relaxed and hustled up the extravagant spiral staircase. The Latino rapper Don Omar was blasting through the Bose surround sound speakers. Light shined from under the bathroom door at the end of the hall. Najee turned the knob and walked in, but something wasn't right. There was no sign of Angela. He snatched open the shower curtain and froze. The tub was lined with clear plastic. This precaution allowed assassins to clean up their bloody work and dispose of the body easier.

The fine hairs on Najee's arms stood up. He reached for his thumper and slowly back out of the bathroom.

Angela crept up behind him with her Desert Eagle aimed at the back of his neck. "Don't even think about pulling that gun, pendejo," she warned and pressed the tool against his skin.

Najee remained still. "What's all this about? You thirsty, you tryna' jack me, bitch?"

Angela raised the big, heavy gun and whacked him on the back of his head. Najee winced and saw white static. A second blunt blow drove him to his knees.

"Shut the fuck up! I'm asking the questions!" Angela shouted. "Why did you kill, Juan Valesquez?"

"Who? You got me fucked up. I don't know nobody named, Juan," he denied the allegation.

Whack!

Angela struck Najee again. The blow almost knocked him unconscious. He touched the growing lump on the back of his head, then looked at his hand; his fingers were red.

Angela tossed the surveillance disc marked, Sinai Burn Unit, onto the bathroom tiles. "Don't make this worse than it has to be, Sinatra. I saw the video footage of you at the hospital. Tell me the truth, and I'll let you die quick."

Najee read the white label on the DVD and grimaced like he had bitten into a sour lemon. His mistakes had caught up to him. He should have let Juan die at the chop shop instead of biting the forbidden fruit of murder twice. He looked at the plastic lining in the tub and began to sweat. Vivid images of his tumultuous life flashed before him in chronological order. Childhood, manhood, fatherhood.

"*Fatherhood*?" he silently questioned, perplexed by how God communicated with him in mystifying ways during the most unusual circumstances. A power greater than himself told Najee that his mission in life was not complete.

He slowly rose to his feet with his hands in the air. "If you care anything about me, Angela, you'll let me tell my side of the story," Najee proposed calmly.

"I said don't move, mufucka!" she screamed, holding the gun in both of her trembling hands.

Najee moved closer. "If you gon' shoot, then shoot, but I didn't kill Juan."

"Mentirozo!" she screamed in Spanish. "You're a liar! I saw you on camera going into his hospital room."

"You got it twisted. I wasn't there to kill him. Juan was my plug. I was there to check on him," Najee lied with a straight face. "But he was already dead by the time I arrived. Check the surveillance footage closer. The killer was most likely disguised as a nurse."

His fabricated theory sounded convincing, yet Angela applied more pressure on the trigger. "I don't believe you. I also saw you on the same floor as Sosa and Nella. What's your connection to them?"

Hearing Nella's name made Najee's ankles weak. He almost stumbled backward and fell into the plastic-lined tub, but he held on to the towel rack for support. No matter how hard he tried to shove Nella out of his mind, her beautiful face persistently invaded his conscious. He hoped Angela didn't notice his falter.

He composed himself and continued to lay it on thick. "When the drought hit, my pockets started hurting, so I turned to the murder game for some quick paper. A heavy hitter from the Bungalow projects had a hundred and fifty bands on Nella's head, so I took the contract."

"Why did he want her dead?" Angela asked.

"I don't ask questions. I was more concerned with getting paid, but someone beat me to the punch. By the time I got there, some crazy-ass Mexicans were already letting her, and Sosa have it. I didn't want to get caught up, so I bounced. I didn't want to give the money back either, so I planted a bomb on the cat who hired me, used the loot to cop ten bricks from you, and took over the projects." Najee moved closer to Angela. His lips touched hers. "Real eyes realize real lies. I know you believe my truth."

His persuasive tale disarmed Angela. The deep furrows in her forehead softened, her breathing became easy, and the pressure she applied on the trigger slackened.

"What am I doing?" She lowered the gun and apologized profusely. "I'm so sorry, Sinatra. Please forgive me!" She reached out to hug Najee, but he rebuffed her.

"Nah, fuck that, get off me!" He shoved her away and charged out of the bathroom.

Angela laid her pistol on the bathroom sink and chased after him. She stopped him at the top of the stairs. "Please don't leave me, Sinatra! I know I fucked up but let me make it up to you. I'll do anything you want me to do."

Najee turned to face Angela. Black rage shrouded his handsome features. He had never hit a woman in his life, but her actions warranted his wrath. He reached back like Iceberg Slim and slapped the taste out of her mouth. Angela's left cheek turned rosy red. Before she could fully recover, he grabbed her tightly by the throat.

"Listen good, punk bitch. Don't eva' pull a mufuckin' weapon on me again!" He squeezed her neck tighter. "If you do, I'll put my Air Force One's so far up yo' ass, you'll be shittin' out Nike signs for a year!" His fingers dug deeper into her skin, restricting her airflow.

Angela's pupils rolled back and her plump, cherry glossed lips ousted a lustful moan. "Iy, Papi, choke me harder. Make me cum!" She got off on the sensation of asphyxiation. Sometimes when she was alone masturbating, she would choke herself until she reached an intense climax.

"What the fuck?" Her request shocked Najee. To Angela's dismay, he released his grip, leaving a red handprint wrapped around her petite neck. "Does pain turn you on?" he asked curiously.

Her reply came in the form of a promiscuous moan. Najee reached under her short, Dior skirt. She wasn't wearing panties. The smooth lips of her vulva were warm, and her pink tunnel was dripping wet. "Damn, bae! This pussy on fleek!"

He slipped two fingers deep inside of her and used his thumb to massage her stiff clitoris in a counter-clockwise motion. Angela's entire body convulsed, and she came on his knuckles. Her orgasm was powerful and exquisite, the kind that makes you want to smoke a cigarette afterward.

They made love right there at the top of the staircase. Angela mounted Najee's stiff dick and held on to the wooden handrail as she rode him like a mechanical bull. Najee flipped her over and buried himself between her inviting legs. His penis drilled in and out hard and fast, fast and hard like a steel piston on an oil well. He came deep inside of her, confident that she was on the pill.

CHAPTER 28

Ridin' Dirty

Midnight found Angela and Najee entangled under her silk sheets. She snored lightly, exhausted from getting dicked down properly. Najee made sure she was asleep, then he crept out of the bed. He snooped through each room of the mansion opening drawers, lifting pillow cushions, and looking behind the expensive paintings on the walls, all in hopes of finding a clue that would lead him closer to Benzo Al.

After striking out in the game room, he grabbed a butter knife from the kitchen and tiptoed to the mysterious locked door. As usual, it was tightly secured. He carefully stuck the knife in the doorjamb and tried to pry the lock open without scratching the oak molding. He was so engrossed in his task that he did not hear Angela sneak up behind him.

"Uh, hmmm," she cleared her throat, "Need some help?" She stood with her hands on her hips and her lips poked out in displeasure.

Najee's skeleton damn near jumped out of his skin. He was busted. He had no choice but to turn the tables on her. "You brought this shit on yourself, Angela. You don't trust me, so I don't trust you either."

"You got the audacity to blame me for your paranoia? That's just like a nigga." Her smile softened the comment. "If you wanted to know what was behind that door, all you had to do was ask?"

"A'ight, what's behind that door?"

"If I tell you, then I gotta kill you," she teased.

Najee couldn't tell whether she was playing or if she was serious. After the earlier incident, he realized that he didn't know her like he thought he did. He had looked into her eyes and saw what he saw when he looked at himself in the mirror. The dark soul of a killer.

Angela laughed at his indecisiveness. "Relax, Sinatra, you're wound up too tight. Forget what's in the room. Let me show you what's outside."

She led him onto the front porch and dangled an elegant, Maserati key before his eyes. "Surprise, I bought you a new car!" She cheerfully grabbed him by the hand and led him closer to the $80,000 gift.

Najee appraised the bold trident logo mounted onto the front grill. The chrome, three-prong, Maserati emblem was a symbol of vitality, wealth, and social status.

When he was serving a dime piece in San Quentin, he would flip through the Robb Report and DuPont Registry dreaming of owning such a well-crafted, Italian machine. He vividly pictured himself whippin' through the hood, the kids saying that's my car, and the women screaming let me ride.

By the time he hustled up enough bread to cop one, his name was too hot in the streets. He could afford the vehicle, but he couldn't afford the attention that came with it. It was for those same reasons that he politely declined Angela's gift.

"Thanks for the car, baby. I'm hella flattered, but I can't take it. I'm too hot, and the thirsty niggas would have my head on a sushi platter if they saw me pushin' a Maserati through the ghetto."

Angela felt hurt and rejected. "Maybe that's the problem. You care too much about the ghetto. You're a phoenix, Sinatra. Rise out of the ghetto ashes and re-brand yourself. You're on another level now. It's time for you to stop hanging on the block wearing jeans and Jordan's and start rockin' Tom Ford and networking with the right people."

Najee was offended by her comment. "By the right people, do you mean some stuffy, old, white men at the country club who wouldn't give a fuck about me if they didn't need me to invest my dirty money? I'll pass, my people are in the ghetto. At least I know they're real."

Angela wrapped her arms around Najee's neck and kissed him under the moonlight. "You're so wise, yet so naive, Papi," she said when their lips detached. "It's always about the money and always will be. The ghetto doesn't care about, Sinatra. It cares about what it can get from, Sinatra. Once the money stops, the love will stop, and the ghetto will turn on you. Mark my words."

She was hitting Najee with some real shit. The truth hurts, so he changed the subject. "I have some business to take care of. Do you got them thirty birdies I asked for?"

"Thirty?" Angela raised a brow. "I thought you only needed twenty?"

"Like you said, I'm on another level now. And from here on, I want to deal directly with your boss. No more middleman wheeling and dealing. Feel me?"

Angela released her embrace and stepped back. This was the third time he had tried to pressure her into meeting Benzo Al. She was growing suspicious. "I—I—can't introduce you to him," she stuttered badly. "Like I've already told you, he lives in Mexico, and he's not fond of meeting new people."

Najee lifted her chin with his finger. It was his signature move when he wanted to look into a woman's soul. "Stop trying to spin me, Angela. Mexico is no longer a safe-haven for kingpins. Not even El Chapo was safe. I like doing business with you, but if I can't deal directly with the Don, I have no choice but to shop with El Feo's crew."

Angela would hate to lose a client to El Feo. As dangerous for his dark temper as he was for his good looks, El Feo took over the cartel after she strangled their leader at the merger meeting in Mexico.

A full-fledged war was raging between the two factions, yet Angela struggled with the thought of introducing Najee to Benzo Al. Her trust in him was beginning to dwindle, and she couldn't jeopardize the organization.

"I'm sorry, Sinatra, but my hands are tied. I can't introduce you to my boss, but I can hit you with the twenty bricks on consignment. That's a D-Boy's dream."

Najee folded his arms and voiced his agitation. "The only thing that comes to a dreamer is sleep, and that front shit is punk shit." He popped the trunk to the Caddy. "Let's swap it out for the twenty pigeons so I can hit the slab while traffic is light."

"I thought you would never ask. The car is not just a gift, it's an investment in you because you earned it." Angela pressed the Maserati keys into Najee's right palm. "The coke is stashed in your new ride. Turn the ignition key backward, pull up the emergency brake, and turn on the hazard lights. A secret compartment in the trunk will slide open. There's also a smaller stash box under the center counsel for your gun." She moved back into his arms and kissed him softly on the cheek. "I don't know if you're a saint or a sinner, but one day you're gonna have to choose a side. If you make the wrong choice, it could cost you your life. Drive carefully, Sinatra."

****

Najee dipped off in the Maserati. He pressed the clutch, punched the gas, and felt the exhilarating jolt of 406 pounds of torque rushing from his foot up to his hand on the chrome shifter knob. The 22-inch Savini rims and Kuhmo tires hugged the winding roads. The speedometer threatened 100MPH. Sinatra was loving it, Najee was hating it. His two personalities clashed.

The Maserati descended from the Hollywood Hills and rolled to a jerky stop on Sunset. The wiser Najee took control, reminding his reckless alter ego that a life sentence was car-pooling in the trunk. Although he turned onto the main drag following all traffic laws, an LAPD squad car busted as wild U-turn, slid up to the Maserati's rear bumper.

Wuap! Wuap! The siren made Najee cringe. The twirling red and blue lights made his stomach queasy. "Damn!" he hissed and glanced into the rearview mirror. "Did that bitch Angela set me up?" he wondered.

Reluctantly, Najee pulled over and cocked his heat. As the officers in the squad car were running the Maserati's plate numbers, a maroon Chevy Malibu pulled up. There was a letter E on the license plate, signaling that it was a government vehicle. The driver, a strapping blond man in a rumpled suit, got out and whispered a few words to the boys in blue. The officers nodded their understanding, turned off their emergency lights, and eased back into traffic.

Najee watched the tall blond man through the side rearview mirror. He moved with a cocky swagger. Najee had met men like him before. All of them were veteran cops with a lot of juice. Najee decided to hide his Glock in the stash box and wait to see how the situation panned out.

Blondie crammed a fresh stick of gum in his mouth, tossed the foil wrapper on the asphalt, and approached the driver's side window. This was his first face-to-face encounter with the infamous, Sinatra. He was anxious to see what all the street buzz was about.

Blondie stuck his head into the driver's side window. "Well, well, well, I finally get to meet the one and only, Sinatra. Step out of the car, asshole. My partner and I need to have a chat with you."

Agent Sullivan unbuckled his gun holster and advanced to the passenger side of the car. Najee recognized him from the standoff at the hospital. The two men made eye contact and exchanged corrosive frowns.

"Com' on, let's move it!" Blondie ordered impatiently. "And don't make any sudden moves. I would hate to have to kill you before we got better acquainted."

Najee eased out of the ride and assumed the position with his hands on top of the car. "Why did y'all pull me over?" he demanded to know.

"We racially profiled your black ass because we didn't have anything better to do," Blondie remarked sarcastically and kicked Najee's legs wide apart. "Are you carrying any sharp objects that could cut me?"

"Just my brain," Najee returned the cynicism.

"A smart ass, huh? We're gonna get along just fine." Blondie turned to his partner. "Sullivan search this schmucks car. Make sure you tear it up real good."

Najee voiced his objection, "I know my rights. You don't have probable cause to search my vehicle."

Blondie clapped his hands mockingly. "Where did you learn that in the prison law library while searching through Lexis Nexis? By the way, I thought you would be taller." He laughed at his own joke and fished out Najee's wallet. "Demetrius Madlock, huh?" He read the name on the California driver's license and tossed the ID into the middle of the street. "It's probably a fake from Mac-Arthur Park, so I won't even bother running it."

Next, he dug a roll of money out of Najee's pocket and stuffed it into his own. Najee knew better than to protest.

Agent Sullivan thoroughly searched inside of the car, in the trunk, and under the hood. He didn't find any signs of drugs or weapons. What made him curious were the DMV papers he found in the glove compartment.

"*If Sinatra didn't like the Diablos, why was he at the mansion of a suspected cartel assassin, and why is he driving a car that is registered to their chop shop?*" he questioned himself and reported that the vehicle was clean.

"You sure?" Blondie asked, keeping one eye on Najee.

Agent Sullivan didn't like being second-guessed. "Of course, I'm sure. The car is brand spanking new. Not even an ash in the ashtray."

Blondie was disappointed that he didn't catch Najee riding dirty. "Looks like tonight is your lucky night, Sinatra. But be warned, every cop in this city is on your ass, so put some money away for canteen."

Najee chuckled arrogantly. "I've heard a lot about you, Blondie, but yo' crooked ass don't pump fear in my heart. You don't have shit on me, and even if you did, I'm never going back to jail. I'll die first, bitch!" He hawked a wad of thick phlegm at Blondie's shoe, climbed back into his whip, and smashed.

Agent Sullivan flexed up and rushed Najee, but Blondie held his arm out to stop him. "Easy, partner, we don't want to blow our case," he reminded. "He's right. We don't have anything on him, not yet."

"But, sir, he just spit at on officer. That at least justifies taking him down to the station."

"And then what? We spend the next four hours filling out unnecessary paperwork?" Blondie removed a handkerchief from his breast pocket and wiped Najee's spit off his shoe. "My way is better. Did you attach the GPS device under the hood?"

"With all due respect, we could get in trouble if we invade a citizen's privacy without a warrant."

"Did you do it or not, Sullivan?"

Agent Sullivan reluctantly nodded his confirmation. "Yes, I attached it by the radiator like you suggested." He had been racking his brains for weeks trying to decode the hidden meaning behind Najee's obscure message, "The enemy of my enemy is my friend." The tracking device was illegal, but at least it would bring him one step closer to untangling the riddle, he justified.

"Good job." Blondie used the handkerchief to collect Najee's saliva and placed the specimen into a clear evidence bag. "Pretty soon we'll know his every move, and thanks to his hot-headed arrogance, we also have his DNA. I need you to get his sample down to the forensic lab first thing in the mornin'. Have Special Agent Wade run it through the CODIS database so we can discover who this asshole really is. Meanwhile, I'll hit the Bungalows and give one of Sinatra's workers an incentive to talk. I have the perfect candidate in mind." His sneer broadened as he plotted flipping another informant.

****

The brief encounter with Blondie and Agent Sullivan was not fortuitous. There was no such thing as an accidental meeting with the Feds. Najee glanced in the rearview, side mirror, and over his shoulder searching for the jakes. Every pair of headlights had him 'noid.

At first, he regretted accepting the car from Angela, but after the run in with them peoples, he appreciated her generosity and ingenuity. The custom stash boxes saved his life. He shifted gears, switched lanes, and called the Bishop. Getting no answer, he was forced to link up with the Deacon at the Fat Burgers in Hollywood.

The men exchanged no words, just a head nod and a duffel bag full of coke.

Still feeling wired after the drop, Najee headed to Pasadena. By the time he reached Colorado Boulevard, he was more at ease. He pulled onto Allen Avenue, a quiet residential street. Quaint single-family homes with manicured lawns lined the peaceful block.

Najee parked in the same spot that he had been parking in every night for the past month. The vantage point gave him a clear view of Nella's house. He detested seeing Sosa's QX80 Infinity truck in the driveway. At 1:00 a.m. in the morning, there was nothing open except legs and the drive-thru at Jack-N-The Box.

Najee pulled his strap out of the stash and fiddled with the stainless-steel trigger. He was on one and contemplated kicking in the front door.

****

DEA Headquarters:

Major Crimes Division

Early the next morning, an old Konica fax machine that stood in the corner of the Major Crimes Task Force's cramped office hummed as it received a copy of an FBI field card. A DEA agent looked around the office suspiciously, confirmed that his colleagues were busy pecking away at their keyboards, and slipped the sheet of paper from the tray.

The agent read the message three times to make sure his eyes were not deceiving him. After memorizing the profile, he sent the document through the paper shredder and made a quick exit with his phone to his ear.

"Let me speak to, Benzo Al," he insisted to the grumpy Cinco Diablos lieutenant who answered. "I don't give a damn who's giving him a blowjob. Tell him that Najee is still alive!"

CHAPTER 29

Cocaine, Cars, and Caskets

The sun doesn't discriminate. Without prejudice, it shines its phosphorescent rays on both the sinners and the saints. Today it hung over the Bungalows like a shiny Christmas ornament adorning a pine tree.

It was the first of the month, so the mood in the projects was festive. In the hood, the poor celebrated the first like the holiest of holidays. Many of the tenants were hanging their nosey heads out of their open windows or loitering in the courtyard waiting on the mailman and his blue satchel full of government checks.

Spade, who considered himself a grill master, slapped another slab of beef ribs on the charcoal and then flipped the jerk chicken. The young hoochies who had developed big booties and full titties over the winter wore cheap flip-flops and tight shorts, shamelessly flaunting their newfound sexuality. The D-boys were making it do what it does, while the energetic kids played in the cool water gushing from an open fire hydrant. They giggled and danced happily through the spouting water, forgetting the pain and poverty that dominated their world.

The timeless tunes of Marvin Gaye flowed through an old boom box, but his soulful voice was drowned out by the spitfire rap music emanating from a row of slick cars frolicking in the parking lot. Everybody who was somebody brought out them big boy toys and campaigned in a masculine display of show and tell.

Candy paint sparkled, chrome rims gleamed, and diamond jewelry blinged. All eye was on them until Najee pulled up in his ocean blue Maserati and shut shit down. Heads swiveled in his direction, and prying eyes strained to see who was behind the tint.

Najee drove through the projects slow, taking careful inventory of the jealous frowns and phony smiles. "Fuck 'em, let 'em see me. Let 'em hate on me." Each day he was changing, slipping deeper into the persona of Sinatra. His quest for revenge, coupled with his broken heart, had made him a volatile and dangerous man.

235

He found an empty parking space, pulled in backward, and emerged from the whip. Black LeBrons touched the pavement followed by black jeans, a black wife beater, black Jesus piece, and a black Crooks & Castles fitted cap pulled low over his ears. Woodgrain Cartier frames hid his eyes.

A hood dreamer named Keisha ran her pierced tongue over her glossy lips. She was a thirty-six-year-old welfare recipient who still tried to fit her stretched marked stomach and cellulite thighs into her sixteen-year-old daughter's clothes. In spite of being a hot mess, she was hella cool, and everybody in the projects loved her.

"Mmm, mmmm, that short nigga is fine," Keshia remarked while watching the love Najee received from his team as they shook up and exchanged salutations. "I'll drop and give him fifty, right now. What about you, Tanika? Could you see yourself swervin' with, Sinatra?"

Tanika rolled her green contacts. "I don't know 'bout all that. He makes me nervous," she replied, her eyes devouring Najee's swag.

Tanika was a stuck-up project chick who thought she was better than everyone else because she had a job as a CNA. She walked around with her ass tooted in the air like her shit didn't stink even though her credit was bad, and she was one piss test away from getting fired.

"From what I heard from, Casino," Tanika continued the gossip she heard during pillow talk. "He's the worst kind of killer. He does it for fun. Just look at him wearing all that damn black in this hot ass sun. Who does that?"

Keisha sucked her front gold tooth. "Girl, please. You frontin', I see how you look at Sinatra when he comes through. You nervous 'cause he made them panties wet!" she teased.

Tanika blushed at the truth and changed the subject. "Anyways, stop talking about my panties and finish telling me why CPS took crack head Tammy's kids." She passed the blunt to Keshia and plucked a piece of barbeque off the grill.

Najee traded fist pounds, shoulder bumps, and head nods with his team. At the same time, he took in the scene. The projects reminded him of an episode of Good Times. "I love to see black people eat and be merry. When was the last time there was a block party in the jects?"

Crunchy and Casino gave each other a knowing look and laughed. "We ain't never rocked out like this, fam. I haven't had to bust my iron in weeks," Casino replied.

"That's one-hunnit, big bruh," Crunchy agreed. "Everybody gettin' money, we taking care of our community, and Gotti's people don't want no smoke. We was strapped up and ready after his funeral, but none of his niggas was willing to ride for him."

"You mean willing to die for him!" Casino interjected. He poked his chest out trying to impress Najee.

Truthfully, Casino had never murked nothin' in his life. The Bungalows were in disarray when he stepped on the scene, so the hood embraced him on the strength that he talked slick and had an ugly scar across his face.

Najee saw straight through Casino and damned himself for not vetting him better prior to giving him a slot on the upper tier of his organization. The blunt error made Najee realize that he was slippin'. His jaw muscles tightened as he did the math on the other mistakes he may have made while masquerading as Sinatra. He had a sudden urge to holler at the Bishop to see if he felt the same vibe.

Before mobbin' off, Najee noticed the lack of security and cautioned his crew about getting too relaxed. "The opposition is rockin' you niggas to sleep. Just because you can't see them, doesn't mean they can't see you. The streets are always watching. With that said, while y'all down here drinking, smoking and jaw jacking, who's holding down the spot? Who's guarding the stairs and the elevator? Who's on point watching for the Jakes?"

The embarrassed soldiers stuffed their hands into their pockets and looked down at their shoes. Najee became upset. "Where the hell is the Bishop!" he asked, looking around.

Crunchy hated that he had let Najee down and vowed to stay on point. "The Bishop has been MIA all day, but the Deacon is posted up over there." He directed Najee's attention to the front entrance of the projects.

The Deacon stood guarding the heavy metal door with his big arms folded across his chest and his nappy dreads hanging in his face. Despite looking like a menace, he too was in a festive mood.

"Bless up, Soulja Boi, I like the new ride." He hailed Najee with a rare smile. The aroma of jerk chicken and weed smoke gave him a contact high.

Najee and the Deacon hit elbows, and their arms formed an X. Their salute was more than an elaborate handshake. It was an oath to never cross each other.

"Thanks, comrade. All is well for now, but I had a wild night. Remind me to tell you about that crazy bitch, Angela," Najee suggested. "By the way, have you heard from the Bishop? I hit his line last night and this morning, but he didn't holler back."

"I haven't spoken to him either. Don't sweat it, though. He probably swung by the church to check on something."

"By something, do you mean that thick yellow bone I caught him with?"

The Deacon's sly wink was confirmation. Before Najee could express his reservations about Casino, a brown Buick Regal swerved around the corner and stopped. A tall figure with a blue flag concealing his face like a bandit got out of the passenger's side and yelled something inaudible. Similar to the carnage in Najee's nightmares, loud gunfire crackled followed by screams and blood.

"That's right, run bitches, run!" the shooter taunted and squeezed off shots. Slugs from his HK MP5 stalked victims like heat-seeking missiles.

Three bodies dropped like dominoes. First Keisha, then Crunchy, and sadly, the toddler with the protruding belly button. Najee recalled seeing the baby on his first day touring the Bungalows. A bullet struck the kid above his left eyebrow and exited by his right ear. His brains gushed on the asphalt. During the pandemonium, the baby's limp body was trampled by the stampeding crowd.

The civilians ran away from the gunshots, and most of the D-Boys took cover. Najee and the Deacon bravely charged toward the shooter with their weapons extended. Flames spit from their barrels as well as their hearts, but the shooter remained poised and squeezed off five rounds at Najee and the Deacon.

They hit the ground in order to duck the whisking bullets and came up dumping, banging the shooter twice in the chest. He stumbled backward, but his body armor kept him on his feet. He retreated towards the getaway car blasting off wildly until his magazine was empty.

The getaway driver got out of the Regal, pumped a sawed-off Mossberg, and provided cover fire. Lead buck shots pelted the BBQ grill and left a circle pattern of small holes. Spade attempted to flee, but the getaway driver drilled him in the spine. Blood spurted from Spade's mouth, and he collapsed face-first onto the concrete. He died with a frozen scream on his face.

The first shooter fumbled with the new cartridge, giving Najee and the Deacon the opportunity they desperately needed. They blasted back, their faces forming askew frowns as they let off.

The first shooter finally chambered a round, but it was too late. Fate accosted him in the form of hot ammo. Najee's bullets hit his left kneecap, shattering his patella. The Deacon's kill shot struck him in the center of his blue bandanna. The shooter fell flat on his back and began to convulse.

The getaway driver kept dumping off. Red shotgun shells ejected with each stroke of the trigger. Najee and the Deacon sought cover, giving the getaway driver a chance to escape. The Buick Regal spun off. Najee chased the fleeing vehicle down the street screaming profanities and blasting his hammer until his clip was depleted. The car screeched around the corner and vanished.

"Fuck!" Najee roared and ran back to the courtyard to evaluate the damage. In less than sixty seconds of combat, five bodies were stretched out. He met up with the Deacon who was standing over the deceased shooter. The Deacon reached down and peeled back the blue rag.

Najee took a good look at the shooter and a cyanic taste filled his mouth. "He's only a kid." Guilt and grief nibbled at his soul.

Making a crucifix sign across his chest, the Deacon whispered a short prayer for the damned and made an important observation. "Something ain't right, Soulja Boi. He's wearing a blue flag, but the bum bloodclot who was shooting the twelve-gauge had on red Chucks."

Making no attempt to disguise his worry, Najee's shoulders drooped. "That's not good news, but it doesn't surprise me that the Damus and the Locs linked up to come after me. I heard Gotti had family on both sides of the color lines. Plus, both parties would benefit if I got knocked off."

"How so?" the Deacon asked.

Najee covered the ivory grip of his thumper with his T-shirt. "For one party it's about the money. For the other, it's about respect. The Bloods benefit by getting revenge for their dead homie. The Crips benefit by finally taking over the Bungalows." Najee was about to mention that he thought the person rocking the red Chucks was a female, but a piercing yell rattled his ears.

The Deacon and Najee quickly turned around. The woman who was nodding off at the kitchen table with a syringe dangling from her arm cradled her dead baby closely to her chest. Anguish was etched into her features.

"My baby! Lawd Gezus, have mercy. They done kilt my baby!" her sorrowful wail poured from the hole in her broken heart.

Najee rushed over to console her. "It's gonna be alright, sista," he promised and rubbed her shoulders. "I'm gonna take care of the funeral and make sho' you're compensated for yo' loss."

"Get cho' fuckin' hands off me! I don't want your blood money." The woman pulled her hair and spazzed out on Najee. "You did this. It was you they were after. It's you who's pumping the white man's poison into the black community. You're not,

Sinatra. You're Satan!" she screamed and hugged her slain baby closer to her bosom.

Her words stabbed Najee in the heart like a double-edged dagger. He was speechless. He staggered away with shame fogging his vision. In his haste, he stumbled into a crowd forming a circle around one of the dead victims. Crunchy laid prone with his arms extended as if he had been nailed to a cross. His Hi-Point .9mm was still clutched in his palm. His index finger was still curled around the trigger.

Najee struggled to stay strong and emotionless. "Only mortals cry," he tried to convince himself, yet tears swelled up in his eyes. Out of all his new recruits, he had bonded with Crunchy the most. They had spent many nights on the fifth-floor smoking blunts, freestyling, and discussing ways to make the ghetto a better place. Crunchy was a real nigga, and several spray-painted murals dedicated to his life would soon grace brick walls in the hood.

Three black and white patrol cars and a SWAT van pulled up, but it was the tall blond man who exited a navy-blue Tahoe who concerned the Deacon the most. Federal agents rarely troubled themselves with the mundane task of investigating random drive-by shootings. Their presence told the Deacon that there was more at stake. He tugged Najee by the arm trying to pull him away from the bloody body.

"C'mon, comrade, we gotta rotate. Dem pussy boi jakes are here."

"Fuck 'em, let's go to war." Najee kneeled beside Crunchy, closed his open eyes, and pried the nine-millimeter out of his grip.

"Not here, not now," The Deacon wisely advised. "Don't forget our main mission is to lure the lion out of his den."

"It's over, Deacon. Benzo Al is untouchable. I've tried to get at him from every angle, even stooping as low as buying his poison and feeding it to my own people." Najee pulled the pistol's shaft back slightly and confirmed that it was loaded.

"Like yourself, I'm a mercenary who would rather die on the battlefield than in my sleep, but if yah die today, everything yah worked for, killed for, and bled for would have been done in vain.

We can't surrender and give Benzo Al the victory, so exercise control over self. A Soulja should never let anger and emotions consume him."

Blondie looked at his cell phone screen and ignored Agent Sullivan's call. He was tired of the rookie's *goody-two-shoes* attitude. Real police work entailed getting down and dirty when needed, Blondie rationalized, and Agent Sullivan was just too squeaky clean. He adjusted his Ray-Bans, pulled a search warrant from his breast pocket, and strutted confidently towards the front entrance of the Bungalows.

Najee mused over the Deacons wise counsel and snapped into action. "You're right, I'm gonna find out who was behind the shooting, but first things first. I'm headed to the fifth floor to clean up. Rally the troops, and don't let Five-O in the building until you see a warrant. By law, it must specifically state which apartment they're authorized to search. Once you find out, hit me on the hip so I can move the coke."

"Ten-foe, let's move out!" The Deacon was back in military mode. He rounded up fifteen hard bodies and cut Blondie and a squadron of officers off at the front entrance. Young black men wearing Du-rags, wife beaters, and granite faces confronted the boys in blue. Everyone was present except Casino.

Grinding on a stick of nicotine gum, Blondie stepped forward with the warrant in hand. He stopped in front of the Deacon and hooked his thumbs through his belt loops like a cocky cowboy. "What's this, the welcoming committee?" he questioned sarcastically, and disrespectfully spit his gum on the ground.

The band of hardened thugs were ready to turn up and become unruly, but the Deacon raised his fist and urged the troops to remain calm. "Yeah, we're a committee, but pigs ain't welcome." He kept his composure and smoothly rebuffed Blondie.

Blondie's pale skin turned a shade redder. He unfolded the two-page legal document and shoved it in the Deacon's face. "I have a no-knock warrant that says otherwise. Now move your black ass outta of my way before I have you and the rest of these jigaboos booked on obstruction of justice charges."

242

Blondie's words antagonized the crowd, and they began to get buck. The standoff was on the brink of becoming a full-scale riot. The Deacon tried to stall for more time, but both sides started pushing and shoving. He had already accomplished his objective of getting a copy of the warrant, so there was no need to subject the residents to more bloodshed, he decided.

He scanned over the document quickly and noted that a federal magistrate had authorized the search and seizure of any narcotics, drug paraphernalia, drug ledgers, or guns discovered in apartment number 501. Confident the Feds wouldn't find anything incriminating in unit 501, the Deacon ripped the warrant in half and handed it back to Blondie.

Blondie eyed him contemptuously before turning to address the other officers. "Secure the front and back entrance, pronto. No one gets in or out of this roach motel unless they're wearing a badge or in a body bag."

Larry D. Wright

CHAPTER 30

Bullets and Betrayal

Najee had a five-minute head start, but he needed to move quickly. His nervous fingers fumbled with the keys as he tried to enter unit 502, the spot where they stashed the weight. He tried key after key until finally, the last one on the ring slid into the doorknob effortlessly. He rushed inside, grabbed a trash bag, and began throwing triple beam scales, money counter machines, Benzocaine bottles, and plastic baggies inside.

Next, he went to the safe and punched in the combination, 807. August 7 is the date of Nella's birthday. He grabbed the twenty bricks he had copped from Angela last night and rushed into the bathroom. He punctured one of the tightly wrapped kilos with a knife and dumped the white powder into the toilet. Rising coke fumes stung his nose and eyes.

He tried to flush the toilet, but the Feds had shut the water off. "Ain't this 'bout a bitch!" He jiggled the chrome handle to no avail.

The Deacon still hadn't called. Najee paced back and forth in the living room. "Come on, my nigga hit my line," he coaxed.

Every second was critical. Without knowing which apartment, the Feds were going to raid left him in a pickle. They could very well be targeting the unit he was standing in, yet, if he switched apartments, he was faced with the same conundrum.

Throwing caution to the wind, he risked calling the Deacon. He pulled his phone out of his pocket, looked at the screen, and his jaw drooped open in disbelief. He didn't have a signal. He cursed himself for using a janky Cricket phone. Their service was horrible. He moved around to different areas of the apartment trying to get a signal, but no small bars appeared in the right-hand corner of his screen.

"Fuck it!" Najee cursed and decided to switch apartments. The spot he was in was too hot. He tossed the remaining nineteen slabs into the trash bag and decided to post up in unit 501. The crew never stored money, drugs, or guns in their party house, so he figured the crib wouldn't be the Feds' primary focus. He couldn't have been more wrong.

Entering apartment 501 was easier. The key he selected opened the lock on the first attempt. He pushed through the door and froze. Casino stood in the middle of the living room pointing an eight-shot .22. His hands shook nervously, and a wet spot soaked his underarms.

Najee smelled fear, but it wasn't his own. "What the fuck you on, Cuzz?"

Casino turned the ratchet sideways and asked, "Did you really think you could take over the Bungalows with no opposition? Did you think niggas who been waiting in line for the throne was just gonna bow down? Shit ain't that sweet in the projects, fool ass nigguh."

A tornado swirled in Najee's veins. "I knew you was a bitch."

"I got yo' bitch," Casino replied. "Stop rappin' and drop that bag, niggah"

Najee tossed the trash bag to Casino. At the same time, he reached for the banger tucked by his pelvis, but the butt of the gun got tangled in his shirt. His clumsiness almost cost him his life. Thinking fast, Najee turned and ran while trying to free his pistol.

Blaw! Casino fired a shot. Missing badly, he chased after Najee and blasted twice more.

"Ahhh, shit!" Najee groaned as he felt a stab of pain. Without looking, he extended his arm backward, pulled the trigger, and continued running down the stairs.

Slugs knocked the wind out of Casino. He clutched at his stomach and grunted before stumbling backward into the apartment. On the fourth level, Najee heard the crackling static of walkie-talkies approaching from the third floor.

"Shots fired! I repeat, shots fired! Secure all levels, now!"

Najee veered off onto the fourth floor and desperately pressed the elevator button five times. He could hear the old elevator creaking up slowly, but the Feds were moving quickly. He was trapped.

"Psst, Sinatra, over here," a woman's voice called.

Najee turned with his nine-mil ready to spark off, but he saw Tammy in her doorway waving frantically for him to come to her. He was relieved to see a familiar face. He staggered inside of her small apartment, closed the door, and slid the deadbolt into place. "Good lookin'," he expressed his gratitude and labored to catch his breath.

Tammy slid the chain on its hinge. "Have a seat, Sinatra. You don't look too good."

Najee felt unusually exhausted and light-headed. He took her advice and plopped down on her faux leather sofa. Tammy disappeared into the kitchen and reemerged with a cool glass of water. Najee spotted a roach leisurely walking across the wall and kindly declined.

Tammy followed his eyes. "I don't blame you," she admitted, embarrassed. "You've made a lot of positive changes in the projects, and I'm proud of you. But what you need to do is call an exterminator up in this bitch." She laughed.

Her giggle was light-hearted and carefree, yet, there was a mixture of sadness in her glee. She had a white chip from Narcotics Anonymous proudly proclaiming that she was thirty days clean, however, her sobriety came thirty days too late. Her newborn baby was born addicted to crack, so Child Protective Services sequestered all her children and placed them in foster care.

Najee tried to join in on the laughter but grunted in pain, something was wrong. He raised his shirt and checked his torso. A red and pink laceration extended across his ribcage. He tried to lower his shirt before Tammy saw it, but it was too late.

"Oh, no, you're bleeding, Sinatra!" Tammy sat next to him. "Let me see it, I used to be a nurse."

"It's all good," he refused treatment. "The bullet only grazed me."

Tammy shook her head. "You talk like getting shot at is normal. Do you ever get tired of that life?" she questioned and retrieved a bottle of rubbing alcohol and a bag of cotton balls from the medicine cabinet.

Najee pondered the question before answering honestly. "A soldier in fatigues can't afford to get fatigued. He has to keep running whether he's running to his destiny or running from his adversaries."

The borders of Tammy's lips unfolded into a smile. "That was very poetic," she complimented.

Najee lifted the hem of his T-Shirt, and Tammy drenched a cotton ball with alcohol. She gently dabbed the deep gash, making sure the wound was clean.

"The bullet didn't penetrate you, and the blood is dark red, which means it didn't hit any arteries. Raise your shirt a little higher," Tammy requested, her secret motive was to see more of his chiseled body.

Najee lifted his shirt higher. Tammy regarded the quarter-sized scar on his back, then she studied a similar scar on his stomach. The old bullet wounds were familiar. She saw them the first time she made love to her high school sweetheart.

Najee felt Tammy staring at him. "Is everythang straight?"

Tammy dropped the bottle of alcohol and screamed. The officers in the hallway heard her loud shriek and assembled on the fourth floor. Tammy ran for the door, but Najee caught her by the arm and slammed her against the wall.

He covered her mouth with his palm to stifle her yell and pressed his gun against her temple. "What the hell is yo' problem? You tryna' get me popped off?" Tears mixed with black mascara cascaded down Tammy's cheekbones. Najee loosened his grip on her lips. "I don't want to murk you, but if you scream again, I'll splatter your brains all over this wall." The foreboding glare in his black pupils bolstered his threat.

Tammy gasped and sucked in fresh air. "I'm afraid of ghosts," she whimpered.

"Ghosts?" Najee asked, puzzled. "Are you still smoking that shit?"

Tammy shook her head no. "Najee is dead, I even brought flowers to his funeral, yet, I'm looking at you. I'm touching you."

She reached out and caressed his cheek. "Oh, my gosh! What did you do to your face?"

Najee dismissed her accurate observation with a nonchalant chuckle. "You buggin', Tam-Tam."

Tammy almost fainted, but Najee caught her in his arms. Her eyes may have been deceiving her, but not her ears. "I can't believe you're still alive. Najee is the only person who calls me, Tam-Tam."

There it was, the truth was out there. Najee's silence corroborated Tammy's assumptions. A battle raged in his heart. The good in him squabbled with the evil, waging war over killing Tammy in order to keep his identity concealed.

He stepped back, gripped his iron in both hands, and aimed the gun at her chest, but he couldn't do it. He wouldn't do it, he decided. There was already too much innocent blood on his hands. Their haunting faces were the jurors who would decide if he was worthy of redemption.

Tammy didn't realize that she was holding her breath until Najee lowered the gun. "Thank you. Thank you, Najee! I mean, Sinatra!" She fell forward and hugged him, her tears wetting his shirt. "Your secret is safe with me," she guaranteed.

A hard knock on the door grabbed their attention. It was one of those assertive knocks that screamed police.

Najee put the gun up to his lips and shushed Tammy. "Shhhh, don't move! Don't say nuthin'!" His roving eyes sought a hiding place, but the small apartment offered no such sanctuary.

Blondie and his men took position on both sides of Tammy's door. As usual, Blondie was in full control. "There's a dead body on level five. The perpetrator could have heard us coming, made a detour on the fourth floor, and taken a hostage. That would explain the yell we heard from the woman." Heads nodded in agreement with his assessment. "I'm gonna knock one more time. If we don't get an answer, we go in hard."

Blondie pounded on the door again. Receiving no answer, he signaled for Officer Pulaski to come forward. The young SWAT team member swung a heavy, metal battering ram at Tammy's door. The thin plywood yielded to the blow and swung open. The doorknob left a dent in the drywall.

"Police, come out with your hands up!"

Tammy rushed out of the bathroom with a white towel wrapped around her body and another twisted around her head as if she had been taking a shower. "What's going on, officers?"

Embarrassed, Officer Pulaski turned his head and apologized. "Sorry, ma'am. We thought we heard screams coming from your apartment."

"That must have been my TV." Tammy pointed to the scary movie playing on her flat screen. It was the only item of value she hadn't taken to the pond shop in one of her crack-hazed stupors.

Blondie pivoted on his heels prepared to leave, but the tan curtains flapping in the breeze piqued his interest. Against Tammy's protest and demands to see a warrant, he shoved her aside and looked out of the window. He spotted Najee quickly scampering down the fire escape.

"Holy shit!" Blondie blurted out and barked orders into his radio. "Ten-Thirteen to all available units. Be advised, a black male suspect wearing all-black attire is fleeing down the fire escape on the East side of the building. Don't let him get away!"

Najee looked up and saw Blondie sticking his head out of the window. The cop's golden hair and alabaster white skin was an incentive to move faster. Najee scampered down the shaky, black steps. The rusty fire escape squeaked under the pressure of his weight. From his aerial view, he spotted two uniformed cops bend the corner.

The officers noticed Najee and ran towards him with their weapons unlocked. Najee looked down and calculated fifteen feet between him and the cement below. He had to either jump or be boxed in. Najee chose to take a leap of faith. He let go of the black railing and propelled himself off the fire escape. He landed awkwardly, stumbled, and twisted his right ankle. The pain was worse than the bleeding wound on his ribcage.

"Freeze, nigger!" one of the officers demanded.

Najee launched flames their way. He was off-balance, so the slugs missed. The trained officers dropped and returned fire. Bullets whizzed by Najee's ears. He kept it gangsta and kept it moving. As he ran, he imagined runaway slaves, bruised, beaten, and petrified, yet, strong and determined.

Najee was hurt badly, but he wouldn't give up. He summoned the strength and perseverance of his African ancestors and pushed harder. He jumped on top of a large, green trashcan and vaulted over a brick wall that led to a graffiti cluttered alley.

He landed hard again, stumbled, fell, and aggravated his injured ankle. His pistol flew out of his hands and slid across the alley. He crawled and recovered it just as the two officers climbed on top of the metal trash bin. Najee saw their heads peer over the wall, and he tried to murk something. He squeezed the trigger six times. The officers ducked, and puffs of smoke ricocheted off the bricks where the bullets missed.

Najee turned and ran hard, but he wasn't moving fast. He limped towards San Pedro Street with his bad leg dragging behind the rest of his body. Screaming police sirens closed in, and the ghetto bird's whirling propellers sliced through the air. Even worse, he was out of ammo.

Just when he thought his problems couldn't get any worse, a black Lincoln limousine inched along beside him. The tinted windows were the color of black licorice. Najee put his head down and hobbled faster.

The rear window slowly lowered. Najee braced himself for a hail of bullets, but none came. "Get in!" an authoritative voice commanded.

Najee ignored the voice, looked over his shoulder, and kept it moving on his swollen ankle. The police were getting closer. Getting caught meant growing old and gray locked up in a federal USP.

A Latino cholo popped through the moon roof. His chest, face, arms were inked up. He wore a frown and clutched a Heckler & Koch VP .70 mm. The firing mechanism had been altered to spit six-round bursts. Najee spotted a spider tattoo on his hand. It was the trademark of the Nogales Cartel.

The limo stopped and the man in the backseat opened the backdoor. "I said get in, that's not a request, it's a direct order!"

The chauffeur stepped out of the car. His thick neck and wide chest stretched the fabric of his pinstriped suit. When he got close enough, Najee blazed him in the jaw with a powerful combination. The chauffeur walked through the solid punches, grabbed Najee by the shoulders, and slung him into the back of the limousine.

"Would you rather take your chances with me or the police?" The mysterious Mexican man in the backseat asked coolly.

Najee had questions of his own. The man looked familiar, but Najee couldn't place his grill to a name. Whoever he was, he had a lot of clout, Najee concluded. The pursuing police clearly saw him get into the limo, yet, they did nothing to apprehend him.

"Who are you?" Najee inquired.

"I'm your friend—" He paused and took a sip of Chardonnay. "—or I'm your enemy. The choice is yours to make," he spoke excellent English and wore an expensive blue suit with a purple tie. He gave off the aura of wealth, influence, and danger.

The limo picked up speed and headed into the downtown business district. A succession of tall glass skyscrapers extended into the clouds. "Where are you taking me?" Najee grumbled in distress. His sprained ankle and the laceration across his torso throbbed painfully.

The mysterious man looked Najee over and noticed that he was bleeding. "You're in bad shape. My people will patch you up. After you get some rest, we can talk business."

"What business are you talking about, and why did you help me get away from the police?"

"My new friend, sometimes strange alliances are forged to achieve a common objective."

Najee was familiar with the quote. "Ivan the Terrible."

The man smiled, growing fonder of Najee each moment. "Yes, indeed. I see you're well versed in Russian history."

"And war," Najee added.

252

The man gazed out of the window and watched the business-people mill to and fro with their briefcases. "I must admit I don't condone war. Don't get me wrong. In many cases, murder is necessary, but senseless homicides are destroying your people as well as La Raza, so I chose to invoke change from within."

"Basically, that's a fancy way of saying you're a politician," Najee quipped.

The man's smile broadened. "I was told that you were intelligent, to the point, and obsessed with killing Benzo Al. So far, you haven't disappointed me."

Hearing Benzo Al's name made Najee's adrenaline surge. He reached for the door handle and tried to jump out of the moving limo, but the Mexican man placed a gentle hand on his shoulder to stop him. "Stay, you're amongst friends. I can help you get, Benzo Al, but before I tell you how, answer your phone."

"My phone is not—" Najee stopped mid-sentence as his phone began to ring. The mysterious man chuckled mischievously. Angela's number flashed on the screen.

Larry D. Wright

CHAPTER 31

Soul on Ice

"Your nobody 'til somebody kills you," were the Notorious B.I.G. lyrics tiptoeing through Najee's mind as he laid in Angela's bed staring up at the white, stucco ceiling with his hands laced behind his head. In addition to the drama that jumped off in the Bungalows, a lot of heavy shit had been dropped in his lap today.

First, the mysterious man in the limousine offered him a proposition he couldn't refuse. Next, the Bishop recounted how Blondie visited him in the middle of the night and threatened to put a body and twenty kilos on him, and finally, there was Angela's urgent phone call.

She excitedly informed Najee that Benzo Al wanted to meet him tonight at a political fundraiser taking place at the Microsoft Theater. It was a black-tie affair, and Angela had already bought Najee a tuxedo.

At last, he would be in the same room as Benzo Al. Whatever his faults, be it savage, cold, or simply heartless, this was the reason he had turned his back on Nella. It was the reason he killed, the reason he sold death to his people, and the reason he was probably going to hell. Yet, despite his sacrifices, he was apprehensive about meeting the man who had caused him so much anguish.

He rolled over towards Angela who had just gotten out of the shower. She smiled at Najee and laid a sexy, black Oscar De La Renta dress across the bed. "Something don't add up," Najee remarked. "Why is, Benzo Al, so eager to meet me all of a sudden?"

Angela sat in a floral upholstered chair and buffed her smooth legs with baby oil. She had just thrown up for the third time that week, but despite her queasy stomach, she was looking forward to the meeting.

"You're a street legend, Sinatra. Crime bosses from Harlem to Tacoma are talking about you blowing up cars, taking over project buildings, and shooting it out with the police. Who wouldn't want to meet you? You're either a threat or an asset to their organization."

Her answer made a lot of sense. After all, his plan from the jump was to hustle hard and cause enough chaos to get Benzo Al's attention. What better way to get street cred than by flippin' pies and getting into some real gangsta shit?

Najee relaxed and blew halos of hookah smoke with Angela. In addition to getting him faded, the lime green sativa also had a beneficial medicinal effect. It soothed the wound on his ribcage and reduced the swelling in his ankle.

He put a new gauze pad on his wound, wrapped an ace bandage around his ankle, got dressed and checked his sauce in the mirror. The tuxedo fit perfectly like the tailor had sewed it onto his body. The last time he wore a suit was at his own funeral, Najee reflected and snapped a gun into his shoulder holster.

"Let's ride, Mr. GQ. We're running late." Angela jerked Najee out of his thoughts about death.

He kept facing forward and secretly watched her through the full-length mirror. She strapped a nickel-plated .380 to her black lace garter belt. Najee felt the hefty weight of his own firearm and was glad he had linked up with the Bishop and got some new heat.

For a moment, Najee began to have suspicions about the Bishop, especially since he had been missing in action for two days, however, the Bishop was loyal, Najee concluded after thinking things over. The Bishop could have thrown Najee under the bus when Blondie threatened to plant some dirt on him, but he remained faithful and told Najee about the late-night encounter. Najee was constantly strategizing on ways to stay one step ahead of his opponent, so he told the Bishop to go ahead and let Blondie think that he was a snitch. Najee planned to use Blondie's own tricks against him.

The dapper couple left the mansion and drove to the black-tie affair in the Maserati. Najee was wearing a $1,400 tuxedo, driving an $80,000 car, and had a million-dollar bitch in the passenger seat, yet, he felt cheap. Visions of the baby with his brains blown all over the cement tormented him. The mother's sharp words bludgeoned his eardrums.

Mistaking Najee's moment of soul searching for nervousness, Angela attempted to quell his anxiety. "Relax, Sinatra." She placed an encouraging hand on top of his as he shifted gears. "Benzo Al is going to love you. He started at the bottom and clawed his way to the top just like you did. As long as everything about you checks out, it should be a prosperous meeting."

"What do you mean if everything checks out?" Najee wanted to know, but the conversation was interrupted by the valet parking attendant.

Najee peeled a crisp Jackson from his gold money clip and instructed the valet to park near the closet exit. Cameras clicked and bright bulbs flashed as the handsome couple schmoozed on the red carpet with celebrities, foreign dignitaries, and the CEO's of Fortune 500 corporations. Angela seemed to know everyone already.

She leaned on Najee's shoulder and whispered in his ear, "These people are bigger criminals than we are. Los Cinco Diablos secretly finances their big budget Hollywood films and business ventures. Tonight were holding a political fundraiser for Benzo Al's brother."

Najee absorbed the info, locked his arm in hers, and quickly led her off the red carpet. The cameras and microphones were making him nervous. A hostess standing at a glass podium checked the VIP guest list on her iPad, confirmed their names, and granted them entrance through the velvet ropes.

They walked through, and the metal detector screamed. Najee winced at the unwanted attention. Two beefy security guards scuttled over. Najee recalled meeting them at the restaurant on Venice Beach when he copped his first ten bricks. He felt shade coming from the one name, Nacho. The guards acknowledged Angela with a respectful nod but informed Najee that he had to leave his gun at the coat check.

"You know the business, Ese. We have to frisk you for weapons," Syco Mike said politely.

"And for a wire," Nacho added a cheap shot.

Najee side-eyed Nacho with a threatening glare. "Are you always this crabby, or is it that time of the month?"

Nacho flexed like he wanted smoke, but Angela stepped between them. The commotion caught Benzo Al's attention. Angela calmed Najee and planted a long, sensuous kiss on his lips. When their tongues untangled, Najee opened his eyes and caught Benzo Al watching him intensely. He could feel Benzo Al peering into his soul.

"Something ain't right!" Najee spoke softly to himself.

CHAPTER 32

Welcome to Hell

Benzo Al shook hands with billionaire and philanthropist Charles Koch. Their slippery handshake solidified a masterstroke on Benzo Al's part, a coup d'état secretly snatching the governor's election right out of his brother's grasp.

The dueling siblings had different perspectives of Los Cinco Diablos' future. Carlos wanted to legitimize the organization, on the other hand, Benzo Al saw Los Cinco Diablos dominating the underworld through sheer fear and brute force. The brothers made no qualms about sabotaging the other's agenda, and the chess move Benzo Al just made with his billionaire crony maneuvered him one-step closer to a checkmate.

He reclined in his seat and watched Najee intensely. The two men made eye contact, but neither of them blinked. Benzo Al peered deeply into Najee's soul and found that he was dealing with a formidable opponent.

Najee ended the staring contest with Benzo Al. He didn't want to come across like a punk, yet, he didn't want to seem like a threat and blow his cover either. Angela hooked her arms into his and led him to Benzo Al's table. Najee scanned the venue, snapping mental pictures of the faces and exits. A black waiter, his thick dreads hanging gracefully on the back of his white tuxedo, served chilled glasses of champagne off a silver platter, and another black waiter pushed a cart collecting dirty dishes. Najee accepted a glass of Perrier-Jouët and continued looking around.

The auditorium was decorated in patriotic red, white, and blue. Latex balloons and paper ribbons were suspended over rows of round tables with white tablecloths. Wealthy donors hobnobbed under large vinyl banners that urged voters to elect Carlos Manuel Guzman for governor.

Najee took a closer look at the distinguished, middle-aged, Mexican banker posing in the posters, and then it hit him. The politician in the poster was the mysterious man from the limousine. It all started to come together.

He spotted Carlos shaking hands with a group of supporters and waited patiently until it was his turn to speak with the Cinco Diablos money launderer turned politician.

Najee shook Carlos's hand and pulled him close to his body. "Why didn't you tell me that you're, Benzo Al's brother?" he whispered. "I thought you were plugged with the Nogales Cartel."

Carlos smiled like a ventriloquist and spoke without moving his lips. "It's complicated. Anyhow, I should be asking all the questions. What the hell are you doing here? I told you not to make a move until I set up the ambush!" he stressed while continuing to smile and shake hands.

"I'm here with, Angela. Benzo Al wants to meet me all of sudden."

Carlos's smile melted. "Oh, no this is bad! You're gonna fuck up the move. Things have to be timed perfectly, that's why I told you to wait for my call."

Najee didn't like another man giving him orders. "Let's get something straight. I don't work for you or nobody else. Secondly, you need to chill. If I can kill, Benzo Al tonight both of our problems would be solved, but for now, it's just a meeting. Benzo Al has no idea why I'm here. Angela told me he simply wanted to meet the rising star of the organization."

Carlos looked around the banquet hall nervously. "You don't know who Angela really is, do you?"

"Nah, I don't. Who is she, and why you tweakin' out? You need to smoke some weed or pop a perc or something because you blowin' my buzz."

Carlos saw Benzo Al and Angela wade through the horde of partygoers, making their way towards him and Najee. Carlos shook hands with a local businessman before giving Najee one last word of caution. "Get out now, they know!" he said quickly and shuffled off.

"What did you say?" Najee asked. The loud band music and chitchatting rich people drowned out Carlos's warning. By the time Angela and Benzo Al approached, Carlos was schmoozing his way through the crowd.

Angela made the introductions, "Sinatra, meet the boss of all bosses, the one and only, Benzo Al."

Najee noticed the way Benzo Al was possessively cupping Angela's ass. He ignored the obvious attempt to make him jealous and extended his hand for the kingpin to shake. Benzo Al stopped rubbing Angela's booty and squeezed Najee's palm tight. Real tight. Najee was surprised at his power. He looked Benzo Al over as if appraising his prey. Benzo Al had grown older and grayer, but Najee didn't let that fool him. An old lion is wiser, hungrier, and more treacherous than any predator in the jungle.

"It's a pleasure to finally meet you, mi amigo," Benzo Al greeted cordially. "I've heard a lot of things about you."

"The pleasure is equally mutual." Najee's grip tightened to match Benzo Al's strength. "I've heard a lot of things about you, too." It took all of Najee's strength to restrain his hate for the man in front of him.

Benzo Al released Najee's hand and gazed towards his brother. "It looked like you two were having an interesting conversation. Do you know, Carlos Guzman?"

Najee was quick on his toes. "No, not unless you count the hundreds of political ads that are polluting the airwaves. I'm curious. Why does Los Cinco Diablos support politicians who run their campaigns off the promise of being tough on crime? Isn't that counterproductive?"

Benzo Al led Angela and Najee back to his table. The waiters served Black Angus steak and Maine lobster. "You don't know how the dope game works, do you?" Benzo Al asked as he laid a white cotton napkin in his lap. "Why do you think they call the houses we hustle out of the trap?"

"I've never thought about it, enlighten me." Najee took a sip of champagne to disguise his nervousness.

"Because it's just that, a trap."

"What do you mean?"

"Think about it," Benzo Al began as he sliced into his medium-rare tenderloin with a steak knife. "Who do you think funds DARE and all of those, '*This is your brain on drugs,*' commercials? The cartels, that's who!"

"Why? That only validates the politicians' arguments in support of stiffer penalties for drug cases." Najee maneuvered himself between Benzo Al and Angela.

"Precisely," Benzo Al confirmed. "The greater the risk, the greater the rewards. Stiffer prison sentences for manufacturing and selling narcotics increases the value of our cargo, or at the very least, keeps the prices stable. In fact, the drug trade affects every facet of commerce."

"Especially the prison industry," Najee spat bitterly. "Now I see how it works. More people going to jail equals more jobs for law enforcement and corporations like CCA, which build concrete plantations. The people who benefit from mass incarceration thank the politicians in the form of union votes and donations. In return, the bureaucrats thank Los Cinco Diablos in the form of political favors once they're elected."

"Correct again," Benzo Al admitted.

Najee placed his hand under the table. His fingers slowly inched their way up Angela's skirt without Benzo Al noticing. Angela bit her bottom lip and suppressed a moan. Najee stroked her pussy as he spoke, "Thanks for enlightening me on how the game really works. Now I understand why the Nogales Cartel is trying to take over your cocaine operation. They know that every state is eventually going to legalize marijuana, and if marijuana is legalized, they have no illegal crop to profit from."

The lights dimmed and Carlos took the stage to give his speech. Benzo Al grinned. It was time to end the games. "You always did catch on fast, Najee. I guess those lessons you learned while riding in Boulevard's Cadillac have paid off."

Najee heard his real name and his back stiffened. He had walked into a trap. Several Los Cinco Diablos soldiers moved into position. Their guns bulged beneath their black suits. Adrenaline rushed through Najee's arteries, making his heart thump like Congo drums.

Benzo Al leaned forward. The pompous look of victory beamed in his evil pupils. When he spoke, his voice was laced with absolute revulsion and disdain, "I know that's you hiding behind that mask, Najee. You've been a thorn in my side for many years. So, I'm going to enjoy peeling off your new face with a machete."

Najee felt the heavy presence of the Cinco Diablo henchmen standing behind him. "Who ratted me out?" he asked, stalling for time.

"Your arrogance," Benzo Al jabbed Najee in the middle of the forehead with his index finger. "The thing about living a double life is that you gotta know when to turn on and turn off. You started believing in your own illusion. You thought you were untouchable like Nino Brown. But this ain't New Jack City, homie. It was a bad move to spit at that pig, Blondie. I had your DNA profile before he did."

Najee clenched his lips, he had sold his soul for this very moment. To be close enough to squeeze the life out of his enemy. He openly rubbed his hand between Angela's thighs, showing Benzo Al that he now owned his prize possession.

"You took away everything I loved," Najee told his adversary. "On your order, my family was slaughtered. So, when I kill you and make no mistake about it, I will kill you. I'm going to murder you slow and savor each bite like a wolf devouring bloody meat."

Benzo Al leaned in even closer to Najee. His eyes were cold and dark like black ice. "Even when your foot is caught in a trap, you're still making idol threats to a legendary boss. I need to teach you some manners, Chavito. We're gonna see how gangsta you are when my butcher cuts you apart while you're still alive and make you watch as he feeds your arms and legs into a meat grinder."

Najee was unmoved. "Do it look like I'm spooked? My cause is worthy, so my death will be honorable."

"If this was a movie, I would be rooting for you. I mean, who wouldn't move mountains in order to avenge their mother's death? But you got it all wrong, Ese. I didn't order the hit on your jefita."

"Don't—don't fuck with my head," Najee stuttered. "I was there, I saw Cheddar squeeze the trigger with my own eyes."

"Then there you have it. Your family's blood is on Cheddar's hands, not mines. Boulevard and Candy were worth more to me alive than dead. Boulevard owed me one hundred and eighty bands, and killing your mother was a waste of good pussy. I still get a hard-on thinking about the times I had my way with that black whore," he intentionally provoked Najee.

All of Najee's inner demons simultaneously demanded blood. He suddenly grabbed a sharp steak knife and stabbed Benzo Al in the hand. The blade sliced through his palm, and the tip lodged itself into the wooden table.

"Aghhhh!" Benzo Al yelled.

Before his scream fully left his lungs, Najee swiftly reached under Angela's dress and unsnapped her .380. His mind was set on giving Benzo Al the business. He brought the pistol up and fingered the trigger three times.

Click! Click! Click!

The thumper was empty. Najee looked at the gun in shock. Three Cinco Diablos goons upped heat. Najee stared down the dim tunnels of the deadly trinity, but it was the lethal darts launched from Angela's teary eyes that stabbed him the deepest.

"Are you really, Najee?" Angela asked. Her voice quivered as she sniffled back tears. "Answer me, muthafucka'!" she screamed. "Is it the truth or a lie?" Najee's silence supplied the answer. "Pinche pendejo!"

Angela reeled back and slapped Najee across the cheek. "You don't have to say it, I feel it. I've felt your presence all along. That's why I used the same trick on you that you used on Rio."

Najee's eyes widened. "How did you know about—" Then it dawned on him. "You killed Juice, didn't you? You're the female assassin who uses the Spanish guillotine to murk people."

Tears seeped from Angela's eyes and rested in the corner of her lips. "You're not the only one who was hiding something. The only difference is that your secret is gonna cost you your life."

Benzo Al yanked the knife out of his hand and wiped the bloody blade on Najee's tuxedo. "I warned you not to fall for him, Angela. Love blinds the eyes and softens the heart."

Angela grabbed a .40 Cal from one of the Cinco Diablos henchmen. "I know what I gotta do. Sangre dentro, sangre afuera!" she declared, and pressed the barrel against Najee's left eye socket.

Najee thought about the hit that was placed on Angela's father and tried to use the info in order to turn her against Benzo Al. "I'm not your enemy, baby gurl. Benzo Al is. Your father didn't die from some mysterious illness, Benzo Al had him executed."

Angela laughed. It was one of those laughs that you hear in an insane asylum. "You fool, Benzo Al didn't kill my father. I did, I hated him. That sick bastard used to come into my room every night when I was a little girl. So, when Los Cinco Diablos offered to rescue me, I gladly accepted the vial of poison and sprinkled it into his tequila. He was my first kill. There were many more bodies after him, but I'm going to enjoy murdering you the most." She pressed the gun deeper into Najee's eye socket.

The waiter balancing the platter of champagne glasses bumped into one of the Cinco Diablos goons and spilled alcohol on his suit. "Excuse me, I'm so sorry," he apologized and upped a .9mm. He pointed the heat at Benzo Al and looked at Angela. "I wouldn't do that if I were you!"

Angela clicked the hammer back anyhow. "Well, you ain't me." She glanced over her shoulder and saw the caterer who was serving champagne.

The Deacon was cleverly disguised in a white waiter's uniform. His famished eyes were hungry for homicide but turning his back towards Nacho was a crucial mistake. Nacho made his move and silently slithered behind the Deacon. He pressed the muzzle of his gun against the Deacon's dreads. "Drop your pistola, puto!"

The two groups of outlaws were entangled in an intense stand-off. Angela kept her teary eyes and her strap on Najee, the Deacon kept his flame aimed at Benzo Al, and Nacho kept the muzzle of his burner flush with the Deacon's scalp.

The busboy stopped collecting dirty dishes. He was Najee's ace in the hole. The Bishop maneuvered his metal cart closer to the action, reached under the cart, and came up waving a big boy military toy with 7.62 caliber ammo capable of knocking your heart through your back. The barrel of the Kalashnikov seemed to point at everyone at the same time.

Najee's rigid shoulders and tense facial muscles relaxed as his contingency plan came together. The Bishop was in position to chop everybody down Columbine-style, but instead, he aimed the high-powered automatic weapon at Benzo Al's Adam's apple.

"You got two loaded guns pointed at you. We can call this a stalemate or a suicide mission. The choice is yours, Alonzo." The Bishop's voice was even and smooth. His trigger finger was calm and steady.

Benzo Al was not used to hearing his government name. He nursed his bleeding hand with a cloth napkin and studied the Bishop's face closely. Finally, recognition set in.

"Welcome to hell, Bishop. They say if you don't burn your trash, it'll just be recycled into something new. I should have killed you and the Deacon when I had the chance."

The Bishop chuckled at the threat. "Ye though I walk through the valley of the shadow of death, I shall fear no evil, especially coming from a bitch like you. So, stop jacking and squeeze off or speed off," he spit bars like he was still preaching in the pulpit.

Several campaign donors who were listening to Carlos's speech noticed the disturbance. A white woman twisted in her chair and saw Mexican and black men with guns. She screamed loudly, setting off a domino effect of events. Confused, rich Caucasians erupted into a frenzy. Elbows flung and designer high heels broke as they skedaddled towards the front exit fearing that ISIS had invaded the building.

Benzo Al was furious. His plan failed, but he didn't let it show. The war was on, and he had every intention of being victorious. He knew things about Najee that Najee didn't know about himself. This information gave him the advantage.

Benzo Al gripped the bloodstained steak knife and faced Najee. "I underestimated you again, but this ain't over. I will make you come to me again, but instead of using a machete to carve off your new face, I'm gonna use this steak knife."

Using the flick of his wrist, Benzo Al slashed Najee across the left cheek with the serrated blade. Najee flinched in pain as his face opened and exposed pink flesh. He grabbed his silk handkerchief and applied pressure to the wound.

Benzo Al gloated and admired his handy work. "Now we both have blood in the water. May the best shark win!" Each group backed away slowly never taking their eyes or aim off the enemy.

****

After barely escaping with his life, Najee dropped the Bishop and the Deacon off at Mount Nevaeh Church, then he headed to Watts in order to pay a visit to the Voodoo Lady. The Voodoo Lady, an old Jamaican witchdoctor who treated everything in the hood from Chlamydia to gunshot wounds, brewed some special herbal tea for his ankle, stitched up the gash on his rib cage, and applied a coat of antibiotic ointment to the cut on his cheek. The scaring would be minimal, she informed Najee, but her good tiding did not soothe the blow to his pride. His plan to exterminate Benzo Al had backfired, causing him to get snared in the tarantula's deadly web.

Najee counted his blessings as he smashed to the city of Hawthorne with sour diesel smoke drifting through the moon roof and murky thoughts floating through his mind. What bothered him most was Benzo Al's nonchalant demeanor. It was as if Benzo Al knew something Najee didn't know. Something that gave him the upper hand.

Najee blew smoke through his nose and collected his thoughts. He needed to find out what Benzo Al and the Feds knew about him. If anyone had that type of intel, it was his old pal, Detective Mark Brooks. Detective Brooks was now retired and running his own private investigation firm, but his tenor on the force, including a seven-year stint as an LAPD/DEA liaison, kept him in the loop about many things. Najee planned to visit the detective tomorrow.

Ejecting a deep sigh, he smashed up Imperial and bent a left onto Eucalyptus Ave. The Maserati coasted slowly through his old stomping grounds. Names that Najee didn't recognize were boldly spray-painted on the huge, cement plant holders at the dead end. The fresh graffiti announced a new generation of Eucalyptus Gangster Crips who were marking their territory and continuing the perpetual cycle of reckless violence, prison, and death.

Najee was deeply saddened by the notion that a young black man who lived in the ghetto only had a life expectancy of twenty-four years. He was supposed to be doing something about that. He was supposed to be a poor, righteous teacher handing jewels to the youth and making the hood a better, safer place, he scolded himself. Instead, he was on the block packing heat, moving weight, and murdering anything in his way just like them. The only difference was that he knew better.

Najee was lost. His spirit was grasping in triple darkness trying to find something to hold on to. He had to find himself before he could step into the dawn and be a light to his brothers.

There was one person who could give him that balance. Like a magnet drawn to steel, Najee found himself making the journey to Nella's house. He parked in his usual spot and watched her and Sosa through the open curtains. As always, bitterness set into his heart when he saw them together.

CHAPTER 33

Nella's Hideout: Pasadena, CA

Nella liked her new hideout. The two bedrooms flat had just enough room for her and Lil' Najee. It was also in a quiet neighborhood and had a spacious kitchen. The kitchen table is where she and Sosa spent most of their time talking and building with each other.

Nella loved the way Sosa smiled at her. He made her feel as if everything was going to be okay. After the shootout at the hospital, they went to her condo in Marina Del Rey only to find that the place had been ram shacked by the Cinco Diablos. Benzo Al's goons ripped her Brinks safe out of the wall and made off with the 1.2 Million dollars that she took from Najee's safety deposit boxes. Nella was devastated, but as always, Sosa was there to help her hold it all together. Even the baby was bonding with him.

Nella set down her wine glass and turned on the stereo. R&B crooner *John Legend* serenaded the couple. "I'm tired of the life," she began to reflect deeply. "The game has no heart, so the streets have no love. I should have seen the knife in Lala's hand before I allowed her to stab me in the back, but I didn't want to believe the warning signs. Don't make the same mistake with your homie, Ice. That nigga is foul, I can feel it."

Sosa brushed off the comment. "It ain't even like that, Ice cool. I found him in the slums and let him eat with me. He owes me his life."

"That may be true. Just don't let him repay his debt with your blood."

Sosa knew better than to ignore a woman's intuition. A hungry wolf would gnaw off its own leg. Nella had him second-guessing his instincts, but he would never let a woman turn him against his crew.

"You're right, the game is dirty, but my niggas is loyal 'till death do us or the Fed's unglue us."

The conversation made him feel uneasy. He double-checked the deadbolt on the front door, hooked the brass chain onto its latch, and looked out of the front window. The Cadillac CTS was not there tonight, but a suspicious Maserati was in its place. The carrot-orange glow emitting from the tip of the driver's blunt allowed Sosa to see inside the car.

The driver of the Maserati saw Sosa peering through the curtains and quickly pulled off. Sosa got a quick glimpse of the driver and realized that the person behind the wheel was the same mysterious player who he had seen in the Porsche truck. Now the fires at his condo and restaurants didn't seem like an accident anymore.

Nella walked over and stood next to Sosa. "What's wrong?" she asked, her nostrils inhaling his intoxicating, Armani cologne.

Sosa pulled the drapes closed. "Nothing, I'm good." He had noticed the Cadillac about a week ago but didn't want to alarm Nella.

He turned around and found her standing behind him, all five-feet-five inches of her. Her silky hair was wrapped in a French bun. A pair of Pucci jeans clung to her curvy assets and melted into a pair of butterscotch colored Coach boots. Sosa caught a whiff of her Chloe perfume and grabbed her by her thin waist. Their eyes met, their lips touched and their tongues clashed.

Sosa drew her body closer to his broad chest. He could feel her heart beating rapidly. His large hands slowly slid down her spine and rested on her ample backside. He kissed her deeply and squeezed her booty. It was so soft yet so firm.

Nella felt the lump in Sosa's pants swell to an unimaginable dimension. Her nervous fingers massaged the length of his massive tube of meat. It grew and grew and kept growing. She wondered could her tight pussy take all of him.

Sosa helped her unbutton his $1,200 Robin's Jeans. Nella's eyes widened, and she gasped when his huge dick sprang free. It stuck straight out from his body and bounced up and down like a diving board. A pulsating vein traveled down the length. The sight of his long, thick equipment scared Nella, yet, her pussy secreted sticky feminine juices into the crotch of her Fredrick's of Hollywood panties.

Sosa's fingers invaded her tight jeans. He couldn't believe how smooth, phat, and wet her coochie was. One of his probing digits sank inside of her. Nella's legs wobbled like boiled Ramen noodles. It had been over a year since a man had touched her there.

She yearned to feel Najee's strong hands caressing her body. She missed him so much that her clit ached. On humid nights, she had to sleep with a pillow between her legs to soothe the pain.

She wanted to feel all of Sosa's throbbing monster buried inside of her neglected pussy, but the thought of another man making love to her made her feel guilty. She quickly sobered up and pushed Sosa away.

"I—I can't, I can't do this. I'm sorry for leading you on, but I just can't," Nella apologized and tried to walk away.

Sosa pulled her even closer to him and sucked on her neck. Nella's eyes rolled into the back of her head. "I want you so bad, shawty. Don't shut down on me now," Sosa appealed. "Look what you started." He guided Nella's hand to his stiff tool.

Nella's small fingers barely wrapped around his thickness. It pulsated in her grip. "I want you, too, but I can't. My heart still belongs to, Najee."

"Najee is gone, Nella. I ain't a hater, and I most definitely can't tell you when to move on, but I'm the one who's been holding you down, making sure you straight, making sure you safe. Feeling me? I deserve some of that pussy."

Nella giggled at his mannish comment. "No, you didn't go there. Put that thing away before you put somebody's eye out," she joked.

"You think it's funny, but I'm serious, girl," Sosa announced with a hint of frustration, and concealed his disappointed penis.

"I know you're serious. Just be patient with me while I work out my issues. I promise that—"

Boom! Bang! Bam! Three hard kicks on the doorknob made the front door crash in. Four menacing figures wearing black mechanic overalls stormed into the crib. Three of them wore scary

Obama Halloween masks. One wore an evil Hillary Clinton mask. Each of them brandished HK MP5 submachine guns with 30 round magazines.

Infrared dots danced on Sosa's chest. He slowly looked towards Nella. A similar red dot was aimed at her forehead as if she was Hindu. Another was aimed at her stomach.

The Hillary Clinton masked intruder stepped forward, seized the derringer that Sosa kept strapped to his ankle, and back slapped him. "You know the drill, light-skinned ass nigga. Lay yo' mufukin' ass down!"

The intruder turned to Nella next. "You too, dick teasing tramp. Stop looking at me sideways like you ain't never seen a thoroughbred gangsta bitch and lay yo' punk ass down, too."

Nella was shocked that it was a female calling the shots. Sosa wondered how one of the gunmen knew he kept a derringer in his ankle holster. Sosa and Nella were outnumbered and outgunned, so they wisely complied and laid face down on the carpet.

Nella had been on countless kick door missions. She knew that as long as the vics remained calm and cooperated, they would be safe. "The money is in the freezer," she offered. "Take it and leave."

The female intruder signaled to one of her accomplices, and he dashed off to find the cash. He returned with a shrink-wrapped block of hundred-dollar bills and handed it over to the leader.

"Good lookin'." She tossed the package up and down, feeling its weight. "This feels like fifty or sixty gees." She passed the bundle to the lone gunman who was guarding the door. He was the only assailant who didn't speak. It was as if he didn't want anyone to recognize him by his voice.

The female intruder trained her weapon on Sosa and Nella. "Thanks for the gwuap, but that ain't what we came for."

Two of the masked men dashed into Nella's room and snatched the sleeping baby out of his crib. Lil' Najee immediately began to cry.

Nella rose to her feet and rushed the kidnappers. "No! Not my baby!" she screamed.

272

The Hillary Clinton mask seemed to grow more menacing as the intruder slugged Nella on the back of the head with the assault rifle. Nella saw blurry images before finally passing out. Sosa jumped to his feet and caught the female attacker with a round-house to the jaw. Her head snapped back, and she toppled sideways, dropping the HK.

Sosa dove for the chopper. He came up, finger on the trigger, darting eyes seeking a target, but the quiet gunman who was guarding the door tackled him with a solid shoulder to the midsection. He drove forward until Sosa's spine collided with Nella's large fish tank. The glass shattered sending water and tropical fish to the floor.

The hard collision knocked the wind out Sosa and he dropped the gun. Recovering quickly, he kneed the masked man in the stomach. The man grunted, and Sosa followed with a left-right-left and a stiff uppercut to the chin. He grabbed the assailant's mask attempting to rip it off, but one of the other thugs stepped forward and drew down.

"Don't make me outline you in chalk, nigga! Put cha' dick beaters where I can see 'em." A red decimal point sized up Sosa's temple. One of the men escaped with the baby cradled under his arm like a football.

Sosa reluctantly put his hands in the air. The quiet gunman regained his composure and aimed his chopper to Sosa's face. Sosa was certain that it was game over.

Death was inevitable, but one of the kidnappers stood between Sosa and the barrel. "Chill, homie. Chill the fuck out. This is business not personal. Stick to the script and let's rollout, Blood." He pulled the dazed female intruder to her feet, put her arm over his shoulder, and helped her limp out of the house.

The quiet gunman sneered at Sosa before clobbering him in the face with the hard stalk of the HK. Blood leaked from Sosa's nose, and he crumpled next to Nella.

****

The four intruders piled into an old, Dodge van and peeled out. Ice took off his hot Obama mask and checked on Redbonez. "You a'ight back there?"

Redbonez ripped off her sweaty Hillary Clinton mask and rubbed her sore jaw. "Y'all should've bodied that fuck nigga for putting his hands on me, but as long as we got the gwuap and the baby, I'm bool Blood. What's next, Ice?"

Ice watched one of his accomplices strap the baby into a car seat. "We split the dough and take the kid to the meat factory. Benzo Al has a score to settle."

Mystified by the plan, Redbonez asked, "Why didn't he just green light her? We could've laid everybody out and been done with it."

"I feel you, but Benzo is on some whole other shit. He has plans for the baby. I guess shawdy and her dude was part of that stick-up gang that was puttin' it down a couple of summers ago."

"I thought Sosa was her dude?" Redbonez wondered.

"He prolly is fucking the bitch now. Her other nigga supposedly took buck shots to the face at one of Sosa's spots in Atlanta. Everybody thought he was dead, but it turns out that he faked his death and came back reincarnated as that new nigga, Sinatra."

Redbonez stopped playing with the baby. The expression on her face grew serious. "You telling me that Sinatra and Najee are the same person?"

"Yup, why you look so worried?"

"Najee is a beast in these streets and not to be fucked with. I got a taste of what that nigga working with when me and Gotti's relative, C-Real, wiped shit down in the Bungalows. Blood wasn't ducking action. He and one of them brazy ass Jamaicans kept coming like they was bulletproof. If this is his seed we kidnapped he ain't gon' stop until we're dead."

"You sound shook," Ice teased. "That nigga bleed just like us. Benzo Al proved that tonight."

The driver echoed Ice's sentiments and stopped the beat-up van at a red light. A smoke gray Dodge Magnum sat idle at the intersection waiting on the signal to turn green. Two bullet holes were in the back door.

Ice gazed out of the passenger side window. "On my life, I know that hoe!" he exclaimed excitedly and rolled down the dingy window to get a better look. "Her name is Katrina. I'm finna twist her weave sideways." He instructed the driver to follow the Magnum when the light turned green.

The name Katrina inflamed Redbonez. "Is you talkin' 'bout Katt, the Dominican stripper who be settin' niggas up? She got my nigga Twan X'ed out and was tryna sell his jewelry. I'm at that bitch on sight." Redbonez strained her neck to get a good look a Katrina.

Oblivious to the dangerous minds plotting her demise, Katrina dialed the Bishop's number, lit a Newport, and allowed the call to flow through the Bluetooth on her Kenwood radio. The music stopped, and the phone rang through the speakers.

She was almost relieved when her stepfather's voicemail picked up. Leaving a message was easier. He didn't approve of her lifestyle and constantly preached to her whenever they spoke. The last time they had a decent conversation was when her mother died from lupus two years ago. However, now that she was back in L.A. and pursuing her lifelong dream of squaring up and opening a beauty salon, she wanted to mend the broken ties.

The Bishop's deep voice directed the caller to leave a message at the beep. Katrina let out a deep breath and began to spill her heart. "Hi, papa, it's your little princess, Katt."

Redbonez put on her Halloween mask, swung the side sliding door open, and jumped out with the chopper. She was about that action and exemplified the notion of shoot first ask questions last. Using calculated intentions, she marched up to the car and banged on the driver's side window.

The loud knock startled Katrina, and she dropped the Newport between her legs. The fiery tip singed her inner thigh and burned a hole in the leather seats.

"Goddammit!" She lowered her head and searched for the cigarette. As she recovered the square and looked towards Redbonez,

Katrina's eyes widened with fear. The terrifying Hillary Clinton mask had dark eyes and a permanent evil grin. Katrina screamed and mashed the gas pedal. White smoke shot from the spinning back tires and the Hemi engine howled through the intersection.

Redbonez aimed and squeezed off, spraying the fleeing vehicle with lead. Katrina heard the rear window shatter and ducked low. Not again, she thought to herself before fire ripped through her collarbone and broke her clavicle.

A second bullet torpedoed through the back of the headrest and split her skull. The Dodge Magnum fishtailed, spun out of control, and smacked head-on with a McDonald's pole. Katrina's forehead slammed into the steering wheel, and she lost consciousness. The call was still on speakerphone.

Ice watched in awe before angrily jumping out of the van. He ran up to Redbonez just as she peeked inside the mangled car to confirm the kill. Blood and pulp stained the windshield and dashboard.

"Damn, Redbonez, why you off the bitch? She stuck me and my dudes for five hundred bands. The plan was to follow her home and torture her ass until she reunited me with my merch. Now I'll never get the money back."

Redbonez shrugged her shoulders. "My bad, Ice, but this is why they call it Killa Cali. We terminate opposition on site." She stood on her tippy toes and offered Ice a consolatory kiss on the lips. "Don't sweat it. You got a thorough bitch on yo' team, and after kidnapping that kid for, Benzo Al, you earned the trust of the Diablos. We'll make that paper back and then some, but right now, you need to get back in the van, boo. The Department of Transportation recently installed traffic cams at every intersection." She pointed to the stoplight.

Ice looked directly at the tented bubble mounted on top of the traffic signal and cringed. "Fuck! Fuck! Fuck!" he chanted. He had forgotten to put his mask back on before jumping out of the van. The surveillance camera captured clear footage of Ice's face. The Bishop's voice mail recorded the vile murder.

CHAPTER 34

All or Nothing

Worry obscured Nella's natural beauty. She bit her fingernails and paced nervously back and forth in the living room. Every now and then, she glanced at the telephone, praying that the landline would ring.

"I'm about to flip the fuck out. It's been twelve hours, Sosa. Somebody should've called with a ransom request by now." That was the tenth time she repeated the same statement. She picked up the phone to make sure there was a dial tone and then resumed pacing the floor.

Sosa stood up and gave Nella a comforting hug. "It's gonna be okay." His big arms enveloped her tightly. "Everything in life is about money or power. If this was about money, I would be worried. But the kidnappers wasn't trippin' over the gwuap you gave them. They specifically came for the baby. Somebody is about to make a power move, and they plan to use Lil' Najee as collateral, but in order to do that, they gotta keep him alive, or they have no leverage. Feel me?"

His consoling words did not alleviate Nella's affliction. The woe in her heart was just as heavy as the puffy bags under her eyes. "But it's been twelve hours." The grieving mother sobbed into Sosa's chest. "If an abducted child isn't found within the first twenty-four hours, they usually end up dead."

"There's still time left, have faith, shawty."

Nella suddenly pulled away from Sosa and picked up the house phone. "Faith without works is dead. We can't sit around and do nothing. We gotta call the police. They can put out an Amber alert, or something." She began to dial 911.

"Nah, hold up!" Sosa quickly pressed his finger on the hangup button. "We can't call Five-O. I'm on the indictment list, and you're a wanted fugitive. Remember?"

"I don't care about me. I care about my son. I'll give you a fifteen-minute head start, but after that, I'm calling them people. That's my son we're talking about."

Sosa placed both of his hands on Nella's shoulders. She avoided his eyes and tried to hold back her tears. "Look at me, Nella. Have I ever let you down? Not only are we gonna get your son back, but we gon' murk the fuck boys who took him."

Even as the reassuring declaration escaped his lips, Sosa knew there was a possibility that the baby was already dead. Power is a volatile powder keg shit could go either way.

Nella digested what Sosa said and hung up the phone. She saw the bigger picture. "Okay, I'm with you, but we need to hit the streets and put some gun barrels down some nigga's throats until one of them starts bumpin' their gums." The old Nella was back. After she was shot on the church steps, she shunned violence, but now she was a mother bear protecting her cub. "Who do you think is behind this?"

This time it was Sosa who averted his eyes. When he spent time at the Baller Belly studio, he usually left chopped, potentially giving the jack boys an opportunity for a quick come up. He had to tell her the truth. "To be honest, somebody I know may have caught me slippin' and followed me to your crib last night. One of the kidnappers even knew that I kept a strap in my ankle holster."

"Who in your circle is shiesty enough to cross you? Was it, Ice?"

Sosa was thinking the same thing as breaking news flashed across the television. He grabbed the remote and turned up the volume.

The news anchorwoman shuffled her cue cards. "We have new information regarding the melee that erupted at the Microsoft Theater late last night. A credible source, who chooses to remain unnamed, has positively identified one of the suspects."

A grainy photo of a Najee rushing out of the Cedars Sinai burn unit appeared in the right-hand corner of the screen. *"This man is a high-level drug dealer who is not only responsible for the disturbance at the political fundraiser for governor hopeful, Carlos*

Manual Guzman, but he's also wanted in connection with the bombing deaths of four men in the Bungalow housing complex and a recent shootout with federal authorities that left one suspected drug dealer dead. If you see this individual, please do not approach him. He is armed and extremely dangerous. I'm Ashley Oliver for ABC News, we now return you to your regular program."

Sosa and Nella stared at the TV. Each had their own reasons for the sudden silence. Sosa spoke first. "Nah, it wasn't Ice, it was that nigga!" He pointed at the flat screen. "I saw that same man at my condo before it burned down. Then I saw him again last night before Lil' Najee was snatched." Sosa grabbed his AK-47 off the coffee table and pushed a 50-round cartridge into the bottom. "Strap up, we 'bout to smash through the Bungalows and sweat something."

"What? Wait!" Nella had to catch her breath. "You saw him here last night? Are you sure it was the same man?"

"Positive!"

Nella recalled the many nights she had felt the essence of her soul mate in her proximity. "It wasn't him," she stated with certainty and flopped down on the couch. "If that man wanted to hurt us, we would be dead already." Scrolling through the contact list in her cell phone, she highlighted Detective Brooks' phone number and pressed send.

Sosa racked the chopper. "I got a feeling you ain't been keeping it one-hunnit with me. No more secrets, Nella! Do you know that nigga?"

"Yes," she answered. "I know him better than anyone on earth. Sinatra is Najee!"

****

Najee drove a low-key rental to Detective Brooks' office in Century City. They met in the lobby and exchanged pleasantries before Detective Brooks escorted Najee up to his office suite.

"Nice!" Najee whistled as he took in the expensive decor. "This is a far cry from the small cubicle you called an office at the Firestone Division."

Detective Brooks was a large white man. Even in his late sixties, he stood strong and vibrant. The only sign of him aging was the comb-over haircut, which he sported to hide his bald spot.

He grew attached to Najee after investigating the murders of Candy, Boulevard, and Angel. His daughter, renowned Beverly Hills plastic surgeon Renee Brooks, was the doctor who performed Najee's facial reconstruction.

Using a hand gesture, Detective Brooks offered Najee a seat and poured him a glass of Scotch. "Thanks for the compliment, business is good." He lifted Najee's chin with his finger. "What happened to your face, son? You get into a scrap with a cat?"

Najee stroked the scab on his cheek. "Yeah, a big cat. Me and Benzo Al met face to face last night. I left him with a parting gift as well."

Detective Brooks poured himself a shot of Scotch and the old friends clicked glasses. "I heard about the standoff. Your new face is all over the news."

"That's what I came to holla at you about. The Cinco Diablos knew my real identity. I need to know which cop leaked that information."

Detective Brooks tossed a manila envelope on the desk, leaned back, and crossed his legs. "The information you need is all there. It's been so hard to catch this guy because he's a freelancer. He doesn't work for one organization. He contracts his services out to the highest bidder."

Najee opened the envelope and reviewed its contents with a surprised look on his face.

"There's more." Detective Brooks leaned forward and lowered his voice. "Those two dicks, Blondie and Sullivan, planted a GPS device in your car."

Najee raised an eyebrow. "When? How?"

Detective Brooks poured up another round of Scotch. "It's the oldest trick in the book. I used to do it all the time. My partner and

I would pull over a perp, and while I gave the guy a hard time, my partner would pretend to search his vehicle."

Najee finished the detective's narrative, "And while I was being hassled by Blondie, Agent Sullivan planted the GPS device in my car."

"Exactly. My team can remove it and sweep your stash spots for bugs and mini surveillance cameras. Just say the word."

Najee declined the offer. "Good lookin', but I want to leave it in. It just may save my life." He dug into his pocket and pulled out a brown, unlabeled bottle of pills that he had cuffed from Angela's medicine cabinet. "By the way, how soon can you get a lab report back on these? I think Los Cinco Diablos is coming out with a new designer drug."

Detective Brooks pushed down and twisted the white cap off the bottle. He looked at the pills and laughed. "You're wrong, my friend. These are not a party drug. They're fertility pills. Whoever's taking these is trying to get pregnant."

The receptionist buzzed in and informed the detective that he had an important call on line three. "Excuse me, Najee, I have an urgent call," Detective Brooks apologized and accepted the call. "Badger Investigative Services, how can I help you?"

"It's, Nella, I need to call in a favor."

"I'm listening."

"I need you to put me in contact with, Najee." Her voice was soaked with desperation.

Detective Brooks hit the conference button and placed the call on speakerphone. "Sorry, Nella, but I don't know where he is."

"Bullshit, don't front on me. I know how close the two of you are. Tell him that it's me. Tell him that I need to see him."

Najee thought about spotting Sosa's ride in Nella's driveway on the late-night tip and hardened his heart. He frowned and ran his finger across his throat, silently telling the detective to kill the call.

Detective Brooks understood the message. "I'm sorry, Nella, but I don't know if that's enough. Najee doesn't want to be found. I have to go now."

"Wait! Don't hang up! Tell him—" She sniffled and wiped away tears. "—tell him that his son has been kidnapped!"

CHAPTER 35

A Woman's Worth

Najee, the Bishop, and the Deacon wasted no time getting to Nella's house. Najee jumped out of the Lincoln Navigator before the SUV stopped rolling and leaped up the steps onto the porch. He banged on the front door as the Bishop and the Deacon caught up to him and flanked his broad shoulders. No smiles, they were all business.

Mid knock, Nella answered the door. She stood in the archway with her hands on her hips giving Najee black girl attitude. She had lost the baby weight and was still just as beautiful as he remembered her. The only change was puffy bags under her red eyes, which marked her stress.

Najee didn't realize how much he missed his queen, his earth, until now. He opened his arms wide and invited wifey back into his heart, back into his life, but Nella rebuffed him. She reached back like a baseball pitcher throwing a fastball and slapped him across the cheek. Her palm landed on the opposite side of his scar.

Najee's head whipped to the side, but he took the blow. He deserved it. Nella's small fist pounded on his chest as she cussed him out. Najee stood strong and allowed her to vent. When she was exhausted from punching him, he pulled her into his warm embrace.

Nella tussled, she didn't want to forgive him so easily, but finally, she succumbed to love. Her body went limp in his arms and she sobbed.

Najee kissed away Nella's tears and consoled her with the words she yearned to hear. "It's okay, baby. Let it all out, I got chu'. I love you," he declared.

"Then why did you leave me? Do you have any idea what I've been through?" Nella fired off.

"I didn't just up and leave you. I left a long letter explaining everything."

"What letter?" Nella raised an eyebrow.

Najee held her at shoulders length and looked into her eyes. "Hold up. Are you telling me that you didn't get the letter I left on the pillow in Amsterdam?"

"No, I didn't get it. What did it say?" she asked curiously.

"It doesn't matter now. There's no excuse for leaving you. I was wrong, baby. Keeping it real, I've been wrong about a lot of shit lately, but I'm back. The real Najee is back, and I'm not going anywhere." He was about to continue, but a male voice made him look up.

"Is that the best you can do? Is that all you have to say after everythang you put her through?" Sosa rolled up his sleeves as he made his way onto the porch. Tension infiltrated the atmosphere.

The Bishop and the Deacon upped heaters ready to sweat something, but Nella stood between Sosa and Najee.

Najee gently nudged her to the side. "Fall back, I got this." The Bishop and the Deacon put their guns away, and Najee mobbed up on Sosa. "I should put a trey-eight slug in that S on yo' chest, nigga. I asked you to look out for my woman, but instead, you snaked me. Get yo' own bitch, Cuzz, and stay the fuck out my bidness!"

The taller Sosa remained vigilant. "I don't chase, I stay on base. If you was here handling yo' business, then yo' bitch wouldn't be choosin'."

The slick diss incited Najee's anger. He shoved Sosa in the chest, sending him crashing against the side of the house. Sosa knotted his fist and charged forward, but with the swiftness of Butch Cassidy, Najee brandished the snub nose and aimed it at Sosa's heart.

"Today is a good day to die if you ready to die over a bitch." Najee spent the cylinder. The drum clicked like the tumblers in a combination lock until a bullet lined up with the barrel.

Sosa drew his own heat, but Nella stepped between the guns. "Hello, I'm right here and both of y'all are calling me all kinds of bitches like I'm invisible." She rolled her neck towards Najee. "And not that it's any of your business who I sleep with, but I wanna let it be known that me and Sosa are not fuckin'," she said her piece and stomped into the house.

Sosa shook his head when Najee didn't follow her. "How come you ain't going after her?"

Najee tucked his burner and watched Nella's backside sway with the gracefulness of a Gypsy belly dancer. "I don't chase either, homie."

Sosa put away his cannon. "You have a lot to learn about women, whoady."

"Amen," the Bishop agreed.

Sosa leaned against the wooden rail and folded his arms. "Nella is worth chasing. She's loyal, and she loves you to death, my nigga. I can't lie and say I didn't try to smash, but she wasn't goin'."

"So, nothing happened?"

"Nothing!" Sosa told a white lie.

Najee thought about the situation for a moment and then extended his hand. "Good lookin' for taking care of Nella while I was gone, and I apologize for pulling a strap on you. That's not my style or character."

The two men shook up and gave each other a solid shoulder bump. "Apology accepted. It takes a real man to admit when he's wrong, I respect that. We can settle our differences later, but first, we gotta get, Lil' Najee back."

"She named the baby after me?"

"Of, course she did, you're his father."

Najee walked into the house and found Nella in her room kneeling at the edge of the bed with her head bowed in prayer. It had been a long time since Najee prayed. After seeing so much death and despair, he sometimes questioned if God even existed.

A white ray of divine sunlight splashed through the parted curtains and shined directly on him. It was as if the Lord was beckoning him to call upon His name. Najee fell to his knees next to Nella and joined her in prayer. He was humbled when her hand reached out for his. She firmly squeezed his palm, letting him know that she forgave him.

"They took our son!" Nella wept when she opened her eyes.

Najee noticed a gold picture frame sitting on the dresser. "Is that him?"

"Yes." Nella handed Najee the picture, and they sat on the edge of her bed.

Najee rubbed a finger across the photo. "He's handsome."

"He looks like you," Nella's voice lowered. "But I hope he doesn't grow up to be like you."

Najee overstood where she was coming from. Her words were not an insult. They were maternal instincts. Every mother wants what's best for her child.

"I feel you, I want a better life for our son as well. I'm gonna get him back and murk whoever did this. That's my word."

Nella softly stroked the scar on Najee's cheek. "The Cinco Diablos did this to you, didn't they? I believe they kidnapped, Lil' Najee, too."

"Why you say that?"

"I feel it. This is how they get down. They did something else, too."

Najee lifted Nella's chin. "What, baby? Talk to me."

Nella sunk her head sadly. "One of them raped me in Amsterdam." Shame stirred inside of her like a big black pot of boiling stew.

Najee's heart crumbled. "What, they violated you?" He stood up ready to kill. "Let's ride!" he roared. "Let's ride, right now!" The Bishop and the Deacon rushed to his side.

Nella grabbed her gun. "I'm coming with you."

"Nah, little mama, it's too dangerous. This whole thing is a setup. The Cinco Diablos doesn't plan on letting me, you or the baby live. Stay here and I'll get Sosa to call in some of his troops to help me."

Nella fell into Najee's arms and kissed him. Their tongue fluttered like butterfly wings, causing sparks to shoot through her nipples and clit like she had touched an electric fence. "I know the Cinco Diablos is playing for keeps, Najee. That's why I'm not letting you out of my sight. I'm afraid this may be the last time I see you."

Sosa appeared in the doorway and cleared his throat. "You may have to let him go alone!" He held an envelope and black velvet box lined with red satin. He gave the box to Najee and handed Nella the letter. "A kid on a bike just delivered this. He said a Mexican lady paid him one-hundred dollars to drop it off in your mailbox."

Najee opened the velvet box. Through a cloudy film of tears, he studied the tiny thumb inside. The fingernail was blue, and dried blood coagulated where the limb had been chopped off. He stuffed the box in his pocket, hiding it from Nella.

Nella read the letter in silence, and then she broke down and cried.

"What does it say?" The Deacon accepted the letter from Nella and read it out loud, "*Today his thumb, tomorrow his whole hand. For each day that Najee doesn't turn himself in, we will send you a piece of your baby until there's nothing left to bury except his dick. Yours truly, Angela.*"

The room fell completely silent. The ticking clock sounded louder than a church bell. "Who is Angela?" Nella asked.

Najee ignored her and asked a question of his own. "What do you remember about the kidnapping?"

Not easily snubbed, Nella demanded, "Who the fuck is, Angela?" Her eyes pinned Najee against the wall.

Najee's face remained blank. "Nobody, just another name on my hit list."

Nella side-eyed Najee but calmed down. "I remember that one of the kidnappers was a female. She had on a pair of red Converse," she offered.

The Deacon and Najee gave each other that look. One of the shooters in the Bungalows was a female wearing a pair of red Chucks.

Sosa spoke up, "Before they even patted me down, they knew I had a strap in my ankle holster. Plus, one of the kidnappers had to remind his crime partner that this was business not personal. That leads me to believe that they knew me."

Najee rubbed the stubble on his chin. "That's good to know. The only crew with enough heart and guns to help me bring drama to Los Cinco Diablos is BBE, but it sounds like you need to weed out a few snakes."

Sosa lit a blunt, puff-puffed, and passed it to Najee. "Snitches and snakes always get exposed. In the meantime, I got some real niggas that will ride with me." He exhaled smoke and started calling Block Boy Empire soldiers from Texas, Detroit, Milwaukee, and Miami.

"By the way," Najee continued after taking a toke. "Last night Benzo Al threatened to cut me up and feed me into a meat grinder. The only killer I know who gets it in like that is the Butcher. He's a Jewish guy who has a kosher meat factory somewhere in the Tombs. I bet that's where they're hiding the baby, and it's probably where they're gonna take me."

The Tombs were a dangerous subsection of South- Central Los Angeles. Some believed that the borough earned its haunting title because of the rundown factories that lined the block, but in actuality, it was given the name because of the number of dead bodies that are dumped there each year.

"There's at least two dozen factories in the Tombs," Nella pointed out. "If you turn yourself in, how are we gonna know which one they're holding you and the baby at?"

Najee thought hard and then came up with a clever solution. "Yo, Bishop, did you convince Blondie that he flipped you?"

The Bishop stopped looking out of the curtains. "Yup, I even put him up on a gun lick just to earn his trust."

"Okay, cool. Get on the horn and call him. Tell him that a big deal is going down tonight between BBE, Sinatra, and Los Cinco Diablos, but you don't know where. That outta get his crooked ass salivating."

The Bishop parted the curtains again and scrutinized a passing car. "Why call Blondie? How is he going to help us?"

"Just follow the breadcrumbs. He'll lead you right to me." Najee pulled Nella into his arms and kissed her passionately for what may be the last time.

****

DEA Headquarters

Major Crimes Division

Agent Sullivan rushed to Blondie's desk and handed him a document with the Transportation Security Administration's official seal on the letterhead. Blondie bit a chunk out of a bagel and examined the sheet of paper. "What's this?"

Agent Sullivan sat on the edge of the desk and blew on his hot cup of coffee. "The TSA just put out a new threat bulletin. Several confirmed BBE members are migrating from all-across the country and are converging at LAX. Something big is going down, and we're in the dark."

"That's what bothers me." Blondie wiped Philadelphia cream cheese from the corners of his lips. "My CI's have their ears glued to the pavement, but the streets ain't talking."

"Maybe someone on the inside could gather some intel. What's the four-eighty on your informant, Ice Pick, or whatever his name is?"

Blondie fought the urge for a cigarette and settled for a sip of Red Bull instead. "No go, I got Ice's papers transferred to Los Angeles for the sole purpose of helping the agency bring down Sosa, but he fell off the grid after his baby mama's funeral. For some reason, he blames me for her death. Anyhow, last night he stepped in another pile of shit, and his name came up in the murder investigation of, Katrina Santana. He'll be calling me soon, and when he does, I'm gonna fuck him over with no Vaseline."

Blondie's desk phone rang, and he answered. After listening for a moment, he pulled an ink pen from behind his ear and scribbled on a yellow *Post-it* Note. He hung up in a better mood. "Good news! That was the new informant I flipped. They call him the Bishop. He has some solid intelligence on BBE, Sinatra, and Los Cinco Diablos."

"Isn't he the preacher who was suspected of training AL-Shabaab soldiers in Mogadishu?"

"That's him, he's also one of Sinatra's—err, should I say, he's also one of Najee's top lieutenants. He just told me that there's a major drug deal going down tonight, but he doesn't know the location of the meeting. Supposedly, Sosa, Najee, and Benzo Al will be in the same room."

Agent Sullivan jumped to his feet, almost spilling coffee on his tie. "That's the break we've been waiting for. Let's get a tactical unit together, suit up, and crash their little party."

"I'm one step ahead of you." Blondie opened the GPS App on his iPad and logged in. A red dot on the map identified the location of Najee's Maserati traveling southeast.

****

Ducked off a half a block from the DEA headquarters, a black Lincoln Navigator with tinted windows idled at the curb. The Bishop was behind the wheel, Sosa rode shotgun, and Nella and the Deacon occupied the rear. From their position, they could see the front entrance of the building. Everyone sat up at alert when Blondie and Agent Sullivan dashed out wearing bulletproof vests. They hopped into a maroon Chevy Malibu and dipped into traffic.

Sosa watched their taillights twist around the corner and vanish. "Why we still sitting here? Let's follow them."

"Patience, my comrade, patience. Blondie is a vet. He'll spot us as soon as we get behind him," the Bishop advised.

Three armored tactical vehicles pulled out of the garage and raced in the same direction as the nondescript Malibu. The Bishop smoothly fell in behind the convoy.

It all became clear to Nella. "This is what Najee meant when he said follow the breadcrumbs. He must have discovered that the

Feds put a GPS tracker in his car. They're gonna lead us right to him."

Najee's plan was brilliant. A feeling of hope swept through the SUV. They followed the fleet of DEA vehicles into the Tombs. The palm trees and sunny skies were replaced with smog discharging from the chimneys of industrial plants and crumbling brick buildings.

The Deacon spotted Najee's Maserati parked in a no-parking zone. A greasy tow truck driver hooked a steel cable onto the undercarriage and pulled it onto his flatbed. A group of DEA agents stood on the curb and watched with frustration on their faces.

As the Lincoln Navigator slowly drove by, Nella lowered her window and caught a snippet of Blondie's conversation.

"Gott'damnit'! The tow truck driver said a black male parked here and three Chicano gang bangers snatched him into a white van. They could be taking him anywhere." Upon hearing this, Nella put her face in her hands. Disappointment snuffed out her optimism.

Larry D. Wright

CHAPTER 36

Killing Season

The trail was cold, so the crew headed back to Nella's crib in order to regroup. They drove in silence, each lost in pessimistic thoughts. Every now and then, a low beeping sound pierced the quietness.

"Somebody pleeeze put on their seatbelt. That beeping noise is annoying." Nella was disappointed and wanted to lash out at anything. Her baby was gone. Najee was gone, and she was losing her mind.

"My bad. That's my phone reminding me that I have unchecked messages," the Bishop confessed.

"Please listen to them before that beep drives me cray-cray."

The Bishop ranted about new technology and CIA spies while checking his voicemails. Suddenly, his shoulders sagged as he listened.

The Deacon had known the Bishop for many years. They had fought many wars in the same trenches, so he could sense the dark change in the Bishop. They caught each other's eyes in the rearview mirror, and a diamond-like tear slithered down the Bishop's cheekbone.

'*This is a first*,' thought the Deacon. "Is everything irie?" he questioned in his Jamaican twang.

For an answer, the Bishop pulled over onto the shoulder of the freeway. He sat motionless for a tenuous moment, and then banged his clenched fist on the steering wheel. "My princess! They murdered my little princess! Somebody gotta die!" he yelled.

"Katrina, your daughter Katrina?" The Deacon couldn't believe his ears.

"Yes, Katrina. They killed her last night," his voice cracked with sorrow.

The name Katrina sounded vaguely familiar to Sosa, but the Katrina he knew lived in Atlanta, so he didn't speak on it.

The Deacon took the cell phone from the Bishop's hand and listened to the message himself. His jaw muscles constricted, and his eyebrows came together forming a wicked V. He had carried the same scowl as he trekked across deserts in foreign lands seeking out the enemy.

"I have good news and bad news," he announced and placed the voicemail on speakerphone.

"How could any good news come out of this?" Nella wanted to know.

"The bad news is that I know who kidnapped your son," the Deacon stated.

Sosa heard Ice's name on the voicemail and he too became enraged. "The good news is that Ice and Redbonez won't live to see tomorrow. Get off at the next exit. I know where he and that bitch is laid up at."

****

The cockpit of the Navigator reverberated with the clank of gunmetal as Nella, Sosa, and the Deacon crammed bullets into banana clips.

The Bishop kept his steel toes on the gas and his callous knuckles wrapped tightly around the steering wheel. He regretted not making amends with Katrina and sending her roses while she was still alive. Now he would have to put the flowers on her grave. He wouldn't be able to mourn properly until her killers paid reprimands with their blood.

Sosa spotted Redbonez's six trey Impala parked at a hotel off La Brea Avenue in the city of Inglewood. "Make a left right here and park all the way in the back," he instructed.

The plan was to lay low while a plump housekeeper made her rounds, but Nella had no patience for being patient. She jumped out of the SUV with the Glock 40 and ran up on the maid. A black, skintight bodysuit hugged her figure like cellophane. A pair of camouflage Giuseppe boots rode up to her knees and matched the camouflage bulletproof vest on her chest. She was literally dressed to kill.

Sosa, the Bishop, and the Deacon pulled black Jason hockey masks over their faces and followed her lead. The housekeeper heard the determined click-clunk of Nella's Giuseppes, but before she could look over her shoulder, Nella pressed the steel against her coconut.

"Don't scream. Don't look back. Just do as I say, and I might let you live."

The housekeeper's bottom lip quivered. "Please don't hurt me, Mademoiselle!" Her broken English had a hint of a French accent.

There was something familiar about the housekeeper, but Nella pushed the thought off the cliff in her mind and stayed on her three-sixty. "Use your key to open the door," she ordered, ignoring the *Do Not Disturb* sign.

The housekeeper's jittery fingers produced a universal key card that worked in all the hotel room doors. She inserted the white, plastic card, and the lock opened. The clicking sound brought back painful memories that Nella had tried hard to suppress. Visions of the rapist on top of her, his crooked, tobacco-stained teeth grinning at her displeasure, made her fizzle like shaking a can of Pepsi.

She was the first to crash through the door. Her Glock and her eyes moved back and forth in unison. She counted three bodies tangled under the sheets playing a game of erotic Twister. The smell of weed, sex, and cheap perfume filled the room.

Redbonez parlayed on a pile of hundred-dollar bills. As she lounged on her back, a pair of soft lips sucked one of her chocolate nipples, and a long tongue slowly slithered across the pink slit between her legs. The sudden intrusion startled her, but she quickly regained her composure and reached under the pillow for her ratchet. However, before she could blast off, Nella was in her chin like an ingrown hair.

"Stop looking at me like you ain't never seen a thoroughbred gangster bitch and put cha' hands in the air," Nella ordered. It felt good hitting Redbonez with her own words.

Sosa snatched the covers back hoping to find Ice, but instead, he found Redbonez's two bitches, Cinnamon and Spice. The Deacon shoved the maid inside, and she fell to her knees next to the queen size bed. The toilet flushed, putting the crew on high alert. They aimed their weapons at the bathroom door.

Ice emerged from the bathroom with a white towel wrapped around his waist and a cigarillo pinched between his fingers. "Don't nobody go in there for about forty-five minutes. That McDonald's gave me the bubble guts," he joked before feeling the overwhelming aura of death looming above him. "Awww, shizz!" he gasped at the four guns aimed at the tattoos on his chest. He scattered into the bathroom like a roach and slammed the door.

Sosa was on it. He kicked the flimsy door off its hinges and spotted Ice with the upper half of his body scrambling out of the bathroom window. Sosa grabbed him by one of his dangling ankles and yanked him back inside. Ice fell on the cold tile floor.

Sosa jammed the AK against his cheek. "What happened to, 'till death do us or the Feds unglue us?"

Ice instantly recognized the gravel voice behind the hockey mask and started pleading for mercy. "I'm sorry, Sosa, but they made me do it. The Cinco Diablos said they was gonna kill me if I didn't help them kidnap the baby."

"Bitch made nigga, people warned me you was a snake. If you thought the Cinco Diablos was going to kill you, what did yo' monkey ass think I was gonna do once I found out?"

Ice weighed the irrational logic of his excuse and switched tactics. "See—what happened was—Redbonez planned the whole thing, dawg. Benzo Al paid her a hundred racks to snatch the shorty. On my momma, I didn't know what was poppin' off until it was too late."

Sosa kept the stick trained on Ice as he cautiously backed up and peeked his head out of the bathroom door. "Is that true?" he interrogated Redbonez.

Even though Ice had thrown her under the bus, Redbonez kept it trill. "I ain't no rat like this busta, so fuck you, you, you, and you!" she spat defiantly. "I ain't scared of death. The devil is the founder of the Bloods, and I'm looking forward to going to hell so I can kill Big Tookie the right way."

Her bold statement made everyone pause. Eight beating hearts pumped like a marching band at a Macy's parade. Nella lowered her gun and directed the Bishop and the Deacon to do the same.

"Put your guns down, fellas." The Bishop objected, but Nella assured him she had everything under control. "This is a bad bitch, I'm liking her style." Nella licked her middle finger and seductively traced the contours of Redbonez's lips. "Youz ah bad bitch, ain't chu'?"

Redbonez let her eyes lustfully scan Nella's bangin' curves. The black bodysuit made her look like Cat Woman. "Fa sho'!" Redbonez answered confidently and sucked on Nella's finger.

"I thought so, I can use a murder mami like you on my team. Get dressed." Nella tossed Redbonez her clothes. "You're in the midst of some real killers, apex predators at the top of the food chain. The world is ours, and it could be yours, too. All we ask is trust."

Redbonez had heard about Najee and Nella putting it down from coast to coast. They were the millennial version of Bonnie and Clyde. Tales about their shootouts, high-speed chases, and million-dollar heists were legendary. Redbonez wanted in on the action. She ignored the shade coming from the Bishop as she gratefully accepted the invitation. "Fuck it, I'm 'bout that life. What I gotta do?"

"You can start by telling me where Benzo Al is hiding my baby."

Redbonez dillydallied with the buttons on her blouse. Snitching was not in her blood. The Bishop tapped the face of his watch, warning Nella that they were running out of time.

Nella raised the gun, her aim was steady. "Look, bitch, I could've turned you over to my alligators, but I let you live because you got heart and you're smart. Don't start acting stupid."

Cinnamon and Spice were petrified. They had the sheets pulled up to their necks trying to hide their naked bodies. "Just tell her where the baby is at so they can leave." Cinnamon sobbed.

"Who told you to speak, bitch?" Redbonez plopped down in a chair, grabbed a half-smoked Optimo out of the ashtray, and relit it. She had a bad feeling in her gut as she spilled the beans. "You didn't hear this from me, but the Cinco Diablos is holding the baby and Najee at their chop shop in Bompton off of Rosecrans and Wilmington." To Redbonez relief, Nella lowered her gun.

"That wasn't so bad, was it?" Nella said and turned to the Bishop as she strolled out of the hotel room. "She's all yours."

The Bishop pointed his chopper at Redbonez's medulla. "Nah, hold the fuck up!" Redbonez griped. "What happened to me being on the team and all that other good shit?"

Nella spun around, the smile was gone. In its place was a glare more menacing than the black hockey masks. "Dig this, dyke bitch, if it was up to me, I would kill you for disrespecting the big homie, Tookie and for putting your greasy hands on my baby. But I can't deny my associate the honor of avenging his daughter's death."

The housekeeper sniffled and asked, "What about me? You said you would let me live."

"Correction, hoe. I said that I might let you live. Then I realized where I remembered you from." Nella grabbed the housekeeper by her ponytail and pressed the Glock against her temple. "I always wondered how those Diablo soldiers got the key to my hotel room."

The housekeeper's mouth dropped open. Flashes of recognition twinkled in her teary eyes. Nella was no longer confined to a wheelchair, but the same tenacious spirit that she exhibited in Amsterdam was on full display.

The housekeeper hugged Nella's legs and begged for her life. "Pleeeze don't kill me! I didn't know they were going to hurt you. They told me they were thieves who stole from American tourists when the tourists were out sightseeing. I swear, I only gave them the key because I thought you left with your fiancée. When the

Cinco Diablos found out that I helped you escape, my life was in danger too, so I used the money you gave me and fled to America."

"Well, your life is still in danger, bitch!" Nella clenched her teeth and pulled the trigger, striking the housekeeper in the chest.

Ice screamed, and Sosa crammed the AK into his mouth. "I know it was you who burned down my restaurants, and I know why you was trying so hard to lure me back into the game." His finger applied pressure to the trigger as he spoke. "You can be powerful, or you can be pathetic, but you can't be both. Till death do us, nigga." Sosa squinted his eyes and let off. The back of Ice's head exploded. Slimy chunks of his skull splattered all over the mirror and porcelain sink.

Redbonez knew that kidnapping the baby would only bring her bad karma. Now it was time to make atonement for her transgressions. She held her chin up proudly and didn't close her eyes. She wanted to see it coming.

The Bishop aimed, smiled, squeezed. *Bang!* "Ashes to ashes, dust to dust," he chanted.

Nella watched Redbonez fall out of the chair, and then she turned to the Deacon. "No witnesses!"

The Deacon licked his parched lips. His demented soul craved blood. "The wages of sin is death," he quoted *Romans 6:23* and sprayed the mattress with the fully. Cinnamon and Spice jerked as a torrent of burning bullets shredded through their flesh. The killing season had begun.

Larry D. Wright

CHAPTER 37

Los Cinco Diablos Chop Shop: Compton, CA

The room was black, pitch black. It was the type of blackness that made evil spirits shiver, however, Najee thrived in darkness. The nocturnal blackout reminded him of summer nights in the ghetto where he would pen poetic syllables under the celestial starlight because the electricity in Sugar's house was shut off. But he was no longer in the ghetto, he was in hell.

"Despierta lo," a baritone voice ordered a Cinco Diablos minion to wake Najee.

Nacho splashed a bucket of ice-cold water on Najee's face, bringing him back towards the light. Najee jerked awake and gasped, "Where am I?" The drowning sensation made him feel like he was being waterboarded.

He struggled against the restraints, his lungs expanding and constricting as he guzzled desperate breaths of air. Once his breathing became normal, the pain set in. His entire body ached, and blood seeped from the deep slit in his bottom lip. He strained to open his eyes, but he could only see blurry images out of one of them. His right eye was purple and grotesquely swollen shut.

Hushed voices schemed in Spanish, and a baby cried in the distance. Despite his anguish, Najee's lips formed a faint smile. Knowing that his seed was still alive gave him reason to live.

The oppressive heat and the grungy smell of motor oil told him that he was not trapped in a freezer at the meat factory in the Tombs. When his vision cleared, he spotted a floor jack, power tools, and several stripped exotic automobiles. It was then that he realized that he was sitting in a chair at the Cinco Diablos chop shop with his wrists handcuffed behind his back.

His pounding headache intensified as he thought about his botched plan. Instead of the cartel goons taking him to the Jewish butcher, they knocked him unconscious and brought him to a different location.

Benzo Al stepped from the shadows, rolled up his sleeves, and pulled a pair of black leather gloves over his thick fist. He greeted Najee with a stiff punch in the stomach. To his delight, Najee folded over and coughed up dark red mucus. Benzo Al followed with a right cross to the jaw, making Najee groan as his neck snapped back. The sulfur taste of blood filled his mouth.

Benzo Al's laughter echoed off the walls of the dark, dank garage. "You should've never crossed me, you pinche chango. Only a foolish man digs a deep hole for his enemy but falls in it and breaks his own neck."

Nacho joined the laughter. He stood by the door wearing an Oakland Raiders jersey and packing a TEC-9.

Although it looked like Najee was defeated, he still had a lot of fight left in him. He collected phlegm in his throat and hocked a wad of bloody spit on Benzo Al's Stacy Adams. "I'm going to pull you apart piece by piece until you collapse like a Jenga puzzle. Then I'm going to kill you with your own gun."

Benzo Al's laughter morphed into a frown. "You hear this vato? Homey thinks he got big balls. Instead of cutting off his face, I'm gonna cut off his huevos."

Keeping a close eye on Najee, Benzo Al retrieved a DeWalt power tool equipped with a circular saw blade that's used to cut through metal. The round disk had razor-sharp edges like a shark's teeth. Benzo Al flicked the power button, and the deadly blade began to spin.

Najee squirmed in his seat. His hands worked anxiously behind his back, and the thick vein on his neck pulsated in rhythm with his pounding heart.

Benzo Al revved the throttle and moved closer, so close that Najee could feel wind breezing off the buzzing blade. Benzo Al swiped the power saw between Najee's legs just as Carlos Guzman burst through the door.

"Estúpido! What are you doing?" Carlos barked, and brushed past Nacho.

Benzo Al stopped mid-swing. The jagged teeth of the saw nearly ate through Najee's denim jeans, leaving him castrated.

Benzo Al spun towards his stepbrother and warned, "Mind your own business, homes!"

"Los Cinco Diablos is my business," Carlos snapped back.

Benzo Al sucked his teeth, "You don't know shit about power, ese. This mayate disrespected Los Cinco Diablos. We have to make an example out of him."

Carlos looked at Najee's critical condition and hoped that he was healthy enough to complete the mission. Najee was to play a pivotal role in his bid to overthrow his stepbrother and take over Los Cinco Diablos.

Carlos walked up and stood toe to toe with Benzo Al. "You're making the spot caliente, hermano. This is not your personal torture chamber. It's a place where we conduct business. A large shipment of cocaína is in route, and the committee wants the product on the streets esta noche."

"Don't tell me how to do my job, Ese. I know the shipment is supposed to be on the streets tonight because I set the fuckin' schedule. In case you forgot, I do this shit for reals, homes. If you can't take the heat, go play in your air-conditioned office while I get back to business."

Carlos brushed off the diss and moved aside in order to give Benzo Al a clear view of Najee. He pointed and said, "The only thing that's getting played is you. You were always good at checkers, but you never grasped the complexity of chess. You didn't bring Najee here. He brought you here."

The parable confused Benzo Al. "What are you talking about?"

For a split second, Carlos felt pity for his stepbrother. "I'm sorry, but I had no choice. The committee green-lighted you."

Just as the revelation soaked into Benzo Al's brain, Najee loosened his watchstrap, wiggled the small silver pin inside of the lock on the handcuffs, and opened them. Free from his restraints, he charged at Benzo Al with the steel cuffs wrapped around his fists like brass knuckles. He caught Benzo Al by surprise and clocked him with a bone-shattering right hook. A left, right, left, right hook followed. The blows knocked loose one of Benzo Al's wisdom teeth and drew blood from his nose.

Benzo Al buckled under the staggering punches. He dropped to his knees and groped on the ground for the power saw. Najee pounced on him. He attempted to kick Benzo Al in the teeth, but Benzo Al caught his foot and twisted his sore ankle sideways.

Najee stumbled and landed on the greasy concrete. Benzo Al seized upon the opportunity. Exposing the swiftness of a cheetah, he was on Najee's back. His big forearms clutched Najee's neck in an NYPD chokehold.

"Shoot this motherfucker, Ese!" Benzo Al commanded. Nacho aimed the flame, but he couldn't get off a clean shot.

"*It's now or never,*" Carlos persuaded himself. It was time to make his bones. If his brother thought he was soft, then he would show him. Carlos upped the Colt .45 revolver that Benzo Al had slid across the table at the Cinco Diablos meeting in Mexico. Carlos had vowed to himself that his brother would die by that very same gun. His hands trembled, but he managed to bust a cap at Nacho just as Nacho got a clear shot at Najee.

Hot metal rocked Nacho in the chest, throwing him against the wall. As Nacho's legs gave out, he sprayed wild bullets in Carlos's direction. Carlos sprinted and attempted to duck behind a stolen Ferrari, but a violent flow of hollow points sliced through his upper body. He slumped over the hood of the Ferrari. The Colt .45 fell out of his hand, skidding towards Benzo Al.

Drool drizzled out of the corners of Najee's mouth as he struggled to stay conscious. His fingernails frantically groped for Benzo Al's eyeballs, but Benzo Al's python sized forearms squeezed his windpipe and sapped his energy. Najee was on the verge of blacking out but hearing his son's cry gave him willpower.

He gathered all the strength he could muster and elbowed Benzo Al in the gut. Benzo Al belched out a grunt, and his grip loosened. Najee reached back, grabbed Benzo Al by the neck, and flipped the drug kingpin over his shoulder. Benzo Al's body twisted in the air, and he landed on his back with a crack.

Najee dove for the Colt .45, but Benzo Al reacted quickly, grabbed him by the ankle, and tugged him to the ground. Out of breath and laboring heavily, both exhausted men tussled for their lives. It was Najee who broke free first. He lunged for the foe-nickel, swooped it up, turned, and fired.

Blamm!

The powerful handgun recoiled in his grip. Blood rushed from the hole in Benzo Al's left shoulder and saturated the sleeve of his white dress shirt, yet, he struggled to his feet refusing to accept defeat. Najee remained in a seated position. A squiggly stream of smoke drifted from the gun barrel.

Blamm! Najee fired again. "That was for touching my son." A bullet ripped through Benzo Al's hand.

Blamm! "That was for violating my queen." Najee was aiming for his dick, but the bullet punched Benzo Al in the gut instead. Even with sizzling slugs lodged in his shoulder, hand, and stomach, he continued to stagger towards Najee.

Blamm! "That was for my mama, Boulevard, and Angel." Benzo Al's left kneecap exploded, and a bloody bone poked through his black slacks. His burly body finally collapsed and slammed hard against the concrete.

Najee stood up. This was the moment he had been anxiously waiting for. He wobbled on weak legs, but his spirits were strong. He looked down on his enemy and used his foot to roll Benzo Al onto his back. Benzo Al tried to mouth defiant words, but he gargled on his own blood.

Najee pulled his black hoody over his head and aimed the revolver at Benzo Al's face. "Look at me!" he ordered. Their eyes met. One man smiled in victory, the other groaned in defeat.

Blamm! "That was for redemption!"

Larry D. Wright

CHAPTER 38

Guns and Dead Roses

Angela arrived at the chop shop and heard the rapid crackle of automatic gunfire followed by five thunderous booms. She pulled out her own gun and warily approached the two heavily armed henchmen who were in the lobby guarding the door that led to the garage bays.

"Where is, Najee?" she asked Syco Mike. She had an important message to give Najee before Benzo Al drove a bullet through his forehead.

Syco Mike took a drag off his cigarette and flicked the butt into a can. "By now he's dead or close to it. Benzo Al wants his death to be slow and painful." He high-fived his Diablo cohort.

Their cocky confidence did not tranquilize Angela's apprehension. Najee was crafty and calculating. She had witnessed the consequences of underestimating him and didn't want to make the same mistake twice.

The eerie silence on the other side of the door made her uneasy. She wiggled the locked door handle. "Are Benzo Al and Najee alone?"

Syco Mike attempted to calm her worries. "Chill out, ay. It's all good. Nacho and Señor Carlos are back there, too. Besides, Najee ain't going nowhere. We got him handcuffed."

"*Handcuffed?*" Angela's eyes widened in disbelief. "Cabrón, I told your dumbass to tie him up with rope. Najee knows how to break out of handcuffs. I've seen him do it with my own eyes."

Without hesitation, she aimed and fired at the lock. The blasts knocked two oval chunks out of the wood. Angela stood to the side, and Syco Mike lowered his shoulder and rammed the door. It crashed open. A revolting whiff of blood and gunpowder stung their lungs.

Three bodies were slumped on the concrete. A close-range slug to the mug left a deep crater where Benzo Al's nose used to be. A pool of crimson fluid surrounded his head. A trail of blood leaked into a nearby drain.

A gamut of emotions cart-wheeled through Angela's shaking body. "Alonzo!" she screamed and ran into garage bay number three.

"Angela, wait! Don't go in there!" Syco Mike warned, but it was too late.

She dropped to her knees next to Benzo Al's warm corpse, and Najee emerged from the shadows like a ghostly vapor. Red rage smoldered in his heart, Nacho's blue steel TEC-9 fit perfectly in his grip.

He pointed the muzzle at the back of Angela's neck and pulled the trigger, but the gun misfired. He checked the chamber and spotted a gold-colored slug jammed in the feed shaft. His intestines curled into a sailor's knot as he worked feverishly to clear the jam. The clank of a gun bolt racking made him look up. Three barrels were aimed at his chest.

Bang!

****

The only certainty in life is death, but if you're as fortunate as Najee, there's divine intervention. An eighteen-wheeler pulled up to the side of the chop shop. Its airbrakes hissed as the African American driver glanced at the shipping manifest attached to his clipboard and confirmed the delivery address.

A tall, chain link fence parted, and a guard armed with an M-16 approached the driver's side door. "Where's Mono, the regular delivery man?" The guard's alert eyes bobbed in his head.

The driver shrugged his shoulders. "He's sick, so they sent me instead."

The guard leveled his M-16 at the driver's dreadlocks. "Mono doesn't get sick, homie." His actions drew the attention of two more Cinco Diablos hooligans. They surrounded the truck. "Get out of the cab, now!"

The driver remained calm under pressure. "Look, man, all I know is that I'm supposed to deliver this trailer to this address. If you don't want the cargo, that's cool with me. I'll just take it back to the San Pedro docks." He put the truck in reverse and prepared to leave.

The armed guard thought about it, looked the driver over carefully, and decided to let the delivery through. "Okay, pull to the back, but stay in the truck. My people will unload the pallets."

The driver drove to the loading dock and was directed to pull back into garage bay number three. A Los Cinco Diablos thugs detached the trailer. Once complete, the driver handed the clipboard to the main guard. "You mind signing this?"

The Cinco Diablos guard examined the fake shipping label with a confused look. "What's this?"

"Your death-certificate." Holding the thumper sideways, the Deacon aimed and blew his wig back. *Bang!*

****

Inside of the chop shop, the loud gunshot was the divine intervention Najee needed. Reacting quickly, he leaped over the trunk of the stolen Ferrari and took cover. Syco Mike and his partner stalked him across the dark garage. Najee waited patiently, and then he came up dumping, finger fucking the trigger until both men had smoke rising from their lungs.

Outside by the loading dock, the rear door of the trailer opened. The two pallets containing two-hundred kilos of Los Cinco Diablos coke had been confiscated by BBE and loaded onto three tour buses that were headed to Houston, Detroit, and Miami. The Deacon was heated because there wasn't any money on the rig as anticipated. As a precaution, Benzo Al had decided to stash the ten-mil elsewhere.

Mono was curled up in the fetal position with his wrists, ankles, and mouth wrapped in duct tape. His bulging eyes tried to warn his crew, but the remaining guards were caught flat-footed.

Sosa, Nella, the Bishop, and several Block Boy Empire goons were hiding in the back of the trailer. The white BBE letters on Escobar's black T-shirt glowed in the dark as he pumped his sawed-off street sweeper. A lethal array of steel ball bearings collided with one of the Cinco Diablos guards and knocked him on his back. "That's what it do!" Escobar celebrated.

The last Cinco Diablos guard swung his M-16 in the direction of the trailer, but Gutter, a wild, syrup sippin' BBE soldier, squeezed the rubber grip on his hefty pistol and let the guard have it with the whole clip.

"Block Boy Empire gang, bitch!" he repped his hood as the forty-five spit lead demons.

Two more Cinco Diablos ruffians ran across the roof. Nella spotted them first. "Watch your back! Snipers on the roof!" she yelled, but the *ratta-tat-tat* sound of bullets chewing through the trailer drowned out her alarm.

Gutter's body twitched as ammo cruelly cut him down. Sosa immediately struck back, catching one of the guards as he ran across the roof. AK shells zipped through his calf muscles. The guard stumbled, fell off the roof, and landed on his side. Sosa finished him off with a shot to the grill. "You fuck niggaz gon' respect my gangsta!" he declared as he pumped the trigger.

More bullets rained from the rooftop and whizzed in the direction of the trailer. Nella was in the direct line of fire. Sparks jetted from the ventilated muzzle of the shooter's M-16 as he aimed at Nella's forehead.

"Watch out!" the Bishop shouted, and courageously tackled Nella to the floor of the trailer. Famished slugs chomped through his back. His body landed on top of Nella, keeping her safe.

The Bishop's eyes were open, but Nella knew he was dead. In fact, he died the moment he found out that his daughter was murdered. Nella rolled him onto his back and closed his lifeless eyes. "Thank you!" she whispered gratefully.

The Deacon stepped from the cab of the truck with his banger on blast. He caught the shooter on the roof with two slugs to the jaw, knocking the gold fillings out of his teeth. The shooter dropped his M-16, fell forward, and took a nosedive off the roof. In memory of the Bishop, the Deacon towered over the dying Cinco Diablos guard, quoted a Bible scripture, and popped him in the face.

****

Garage door number three rose up. Nella hit the floodlights and found Najee and Angela squared off. Their facial expressions were serious. Their guns were aimed at each other.

Nella stood by her man and pointed her own weapon at Angela as well. She couldn't believe it, but she and Najee were back together again, standing side by side with the tools of their trade ready to detonate. The Deacon, Sosa, and Escobar played the background with their choppers ready and willing.

Angela whispered a prayer to Jesús Malverde, the patron saint of assassins. She knew death would come for her sooner or later, but the uniformed shadows creeping behind the would-be killers told her that death would be later. "Hello officers," she said and raised her hands in the air.

"DEA, everybody, freeze!" Blondie ordered.

Escobar gazed towards Sosa. "It was good knowing you, big homie. Till death do us!" he declared, before jacking the street sweeper and letting loose. Buckshot made the DEA agents scatter. Agent Sullivan took cover and returned fire. A bullet smacked Escobar in the chest leaving a bloody hole in the letter E of his BBE shirt.

Escobar's valiant sacrifice gave the crew a chance to escape. Najee hit the floodlights and the garage fell pitch black again. He turned to Nella and said, "Grab Lil' Najee and bounce, he's in the office."

Nella remained steadfast. "I'm not leaving without you."

"Go!"

"No!"

Najee sighed, but a faint smile found his lips. He pulled Nella into his arms. "I love yo' hard-headed butt," he pronounced and turned to the Deacon. "Take the Ferrari and get Nella and my shorty out of here safely. I'll meet up with y'all at the church."

Ignoring Nella's objections as the Deacon pulled her away, Najee popped off at the Feds until the magazine clicked empty. Blondie and Agent Sullivan retreated and took up tactical positions. More DEA agents and U.S. Marshals moved into place.

Najee wiped his fingerprints off the empty gun with the hem of his hoody, tossed it to the side, and pivoted in Sosa's direction. "Nella and the Deacon are not gonna make it without a distraction. Give me the K and get out of here. I'll hold 'em off for as long as I can."

Sosa shoved a new cartridge into the base of the AK. "You go, I got this."

"This ain't the time to play hero and fall on the grenade, Cuzz. The one-time about to run up in this bitch. There's a secret escape shaft in the office that leads to the junkyard next door. Just remove the air conditioner vent and crawl through. If you leave now, you can make it."

Sosa declined and waved the AK like a water sprinkler. He got off twenty rounds, making the cops temporarily retreat. "I can handle myself, but Nella and Lil' Najee need you. Jest' get me some bail money, a passport, and a private jet headed to a tropical island with no extradition treaty, and I'll be straight."

There was no more time to argue. Najee smiled knowingly. "I know just the place." He firmly shook Sosa's hand. "Only a true soldier would forfeit his freedom in order to save his team. Years from now, somebody is gonna write about us in a book. The fake niggas ain't gon' understand that loyalty is royalty, but the real gon' recognize real. I'll holla at you when we meet up in Marshall Islands."

Just as Najee finished his words, the Ferrari launched out of garage bay number one. Its engine purred like a feline, rapidly zooming from zero to 60 in under four seconds. The Deacon drove like Mario Andretti, easily losing the procession of pursuing police cars within the first few blocks.

Najee pried open the air conditioner vent and crawled through the small space. A sense of jubilation swept through his aching bones as he emerged from the manhole and found himself in a junkyard full of wrecked cars. He used the Uber App to arrange for a ride, which took him to pick up his '64 Impala from a storage facility. There was more murder on his agenda, and he had an idea where he could find the ten-million dollars.

The Feds made their move and rushed the loading dock. Agent Sullivan tossed a smoke grenade canister into garage bay three. Looming gray smoke shrouded the law enforcement's synchronized advancement. A wave of police officers wearing black body armor and Kevlar helmets with clear shields accosted Sosa.

Sosa chucked the AK to the side and raised his arms in the air. "Hands up, don't shoot," he chanted as he surrendered.

"Arrest him," an eager U.S. Marshal instructed Agent Sullivan.

Blondie approached Sosa. A condescending smirk stretched sideways across his face. "I told you I was gonna nail your black ass," he gloated and turned to Agent Sullivan. "Here, you can use my handcuffs."

"Gladly!" Accepting the cuffs, Agent Sullivan suddenly slammed Blondie against a chopped-up Aston Martin. "It's you who they want me to arrest! Special Agent Steven Rossetti, you have the right to remain silent!"

"What the hell is this? Get your fuckin' hands off me!" Blondie demanded.

Agent Sullivan twisted Blondie's arm behind his back. "Anything you say can and will be used against you in a court of law. You have a right to an attorney."

"*Attorney*?" Blondie asked flabbergasted. "Are you bullshiting me? Will somebody tell me what the fuck is going on?"

Agent Sullivan clamped the cuffs tightly around Blondie's wrists, spun him around, and got directly in his face. "I'm not with the DEA. I'm with the Federal Bureau of Investigation. I was sent undercover at the behest of the Department of Justice in order to bring you down."

Stunned, Blondie's mouth dropped open and his eyes widened. "You piece of shit! I'm gonna rip your skull open and piss on your brains!" he threatened and lunged at Agent Sullivan, but two officers roughly restrained him by the elbows.

Agent Sullivan stepped aside and began issuing orders. "Get him out of here, put Sosa in the paddy wagon, and put Angela Rodriguez in the backseat of my squad car."

CHAPTER 39

Blood Out

Agent Sullivan pulled his squad car through Angela's tall, black, iron gates. "You have a beautiful home," he complimented the immaculate property.

"Thanks," Angela responded from the passenger's seat. "And thanks for taking care of, Blondie. He was getting too close. Los Cinco Diablos has been trying to bribe him for years, but he wouldn't bite. I guess some cops have integrity after all." She cut her eyes towards Agent Sullivan. "By the way, how much did the committee pay you to sell out and help me escape?"

Agent Sullivan let the jab about integrity slide. He had lost his conscience when he accepted his first bribe. In a world of corruption, the temptation for fast cash was irresistible. His All-American looks and by the book persona helped him stay off the radar for years. "They didn't pay me to help you escape," he confessed.

"What do you mean?"

Agent Sullivan put the car in park and poked Angela in the ribs with a rusty, throwaway .9mm. Angela never considered that if the cartel put a green light on Benzo Al, then they would also green-light his closest lieutenant.

"You and Benzo Al were standing in the way of the merger with the Nogales Cartel, so Los Cinco Diablos didn't pay me to help you escape. They paid me to kill you."

Bang! Bang! Two bursts of loud gunfire sent a nest of pigeons flying from the trees.

"Aaaghh!" Angela closed her eyes and screamed hysterically. The side of Agent Sullivan's head exploded. Chunks of his scattered brains splashed into her mouth. She gagged and spit the salty clumps of pulp onto the floor mat.

Reaching through the shattered window, Najee popped the lock and pulled Angela out of the car by her hair. "Move, bitch!" He shoved her in the back, directing her towards the house.

Angela stumbled on the cobblestone path and broke one of her heels. "Why didn't you let, Agent Sullivan, kill me?" she asked as she limped up the walkway.

Najee jammed his gun against Angela's spine and pushed her forward. "Don't play stupid. You know he sold Los Cinco Diablos my true identity. Besides, I'm gonna kill you my damn self," Najee revealed and guided Angela up the red granite steps leading to her door.

He marched onward with an intense purpose and punched in her security code to disarm the house alarm. Surprised that he knew her code, Angela asked, "How long have you been planning this?"

Najee smirked. "Toda mi vida. All of my life."

His fluent Spanish floored Angela. "Hablas Español?"

"Of course, I know Spanish. I love Mexico," he responded in her native tongue, but foolishly forced her inside of the house without frisking her for a weapon.

Looking around cautiously to make sure they were alone, he steered Angela towards the mysterious locked door on the first floor. "No more questions, I know this is where you keep the safe, so stop bumpin' yo' gums and open this fuckin' door."

Angela felt Najee's gun pressed firmly against her backbone. She slid a key into the lock and twisted the brass doorknob. "Is this really about the safe, or did you come back because you're sprung on this pussy?"

"Bitch, Please," Najee responded, and physically shoved her inside.

He followed her into the room. Confusion tangled his mind into a knot as his eyes took in the decorations. A luxurious cherry wood baby crib rested in the corner. Fresh paint and colorful pictures of toys and cuddly teddy bears adorned the walls. An expensive wardrobe that could fit either an infant boy or a newborn girl hung on hangers in the walk-in closet.

"You got a baby?" Najee managed to utter.

"Not yet, but I will in about seven months." Angela proudly rubbed her growing belly. Najee had blessed her with a gift and a curse.

Najee got the bubble guts and lost his equilibrium. Keeping his weapon trained on his target, he leaned against the wall for stability. "You told me you was on the pill!" he roared. "I should blast ya' triflin' ass for lying to me!"

"Both of us told lies, so I guess we even." She walked closer to Najee, his gun barrel only inches away from her perky breasts. One of her French tipped fingernails seductively stroked the side of his face.

"I hate you, but I love you much more, Papi. What's even crazier is that I'm sad for you, too. You're like the twilight. You're suspended between darkness and light. The darkness representing evil, the light symbolizing good. I told you one day you would have to choose a side. Today is that day. Either you kill me, or you let me go."

Najee's trigger finger trembled indecisively. His heart raced like Usain Bolt.

Leaning forward, Angela kissed him softly on the lips. She knew that killing a child went against every code he stood for. "Put the gun down, Najee. You can't kill me."

Chik! Chik!

"But I can, bitch!" Nella cocked her Glock and was ready to rock.

Her sudden presence caught Najee by surprise. "How long have you been standing there?" He wanted to know how much she had heard.

"Not long." Nella never took her eyes or her gun off Angela. "Your face is all over the news, babe. Detective Brooks has a plane, passports, and new identities waiting for us at a private airstrip in Bakersfield. Let me shoot this tramp so we can bounce."

Najee lowered his gun and sighed deeply. "I can't let you shoot her, Nella."

Nella frowned. "Why the fuck not? Look what Los Cinco Diablos did to your family. Look what they did to me. Look what they did to your son. Hell, look what they did to you. This bitch gets no love." Nella's finger compressed the trigger.

"Wait, wait! You trippin', baby girl! I'm begging you not to shoot!" Najee took a step closer.

Nella took a step back. "Why?"

Angela threw hot coals on the kindling fire. "Tell her, Najee. Tell her what you already know in your heart. Tell her that I'm pregnant with your baby."

"*Your baby?*" Tension filled Nella's veins and anger welled up in her throat. "Ain't this about a bitch! I knew you were lying when I asked you about, Angela. Turns out you was fucking Becky with the good hair while I was faithful, worried sick, and crying myself to sleep every night. I thought you loved me, Najee?"

Najee made a sincere appeal to Nella. "I do love you. Angela don't mean shit to me. I put that on my dead homie, Derrick Smith. I was just doing what I had to do in order to get, Benzo Al." He lifted her chin and gazed lovingly into her eyes. "The only woman I need in my life is you. You're not my number one. You're my only one."

Nella's heart softened, but her eyes hardened. "Then prove it. Shoot this bitch. Not for me, do it because she's going to teach that baby to hate you. One day he'll be in your nightmares, the next he'll be at your front door with a gun."

While Nella and Najee argued, Angela quietly eased her pistol from the small of her back. Najee continued to be the voice of reason. "If that's my fate, then so be it, but I can't murder my own seed."

"Then I will."

"I won't let you," Najee stepped between Angela and Nella. "Please don't let the desire for vengeance consume you like it did to me. You'll never be able to sleep in peace again."

Nella disregarded his words and raised her gun.

Najee raised his gun.

Angela raised her gun.

Blucka! Blucka! Blucka! Screams, gunshots, blood. One body hit the rug with a *thud*.

The Saga Continues...
The Streets Made Me 3
Coming Soon

Submission Guideline

Submit the first three chapters of your completed manuscript to ldpsubmissions@gmail.com, subject line: Your book's title. The manuscript must be in a .doc file and sent as an attachment. Document should be in Times New Roman, double spaced and in size 12 font. Also, provide your synopsis and full contact information. If sending multiple submissions, they must each be in a separate email.

Have a story but no way to send it electronically? You can still submit to LDP/Ca$h Presents. Send in the first three chapters, written or typed, of your completed manuscript to:

LDP: Submissions Dept
Po Box 944
Stockbridge, Ga 30281

DO NOT send original manuscript. Must be a duplicate.

Provide your synopsis and a cover letter containing your full contact information.

Thanks for considering LDP and Ca$h Presents.

The Streets Made Me 2

Coming Soon from Lock Down Publications/Ca$h Presents

BOW DOWN TO MY GANGSTA

By **Ca$h**

TORN BETWEEN TWO

By **Coffee**

THE STREETS STAINED MY SOUL **II**

By **Marcellus Allen**

BLOOD OF A BOSS **VI**

SHADOWS OF THE GAME II

By **Askari**

LOYAL TO THE GAME **IV**

By **T.J. & Jelissa**

A DOPEBOY'S PRAYER **II**

By **Eddie "Wolf" Lee**

IF LOVING YOU IS WRONG… **III**

By **Jelissa**

TRUE SAVAGE **VII**

MIDNIGHT CARTEL III

DOPE BOY MAGIC IV

By **Chris Green**

BLAST FOR ME **III**

A SAVAGE DOPEBOY III

CUTTHROAT MAFIA II

By **Ghost**

A HUSTLER'S DECEIT III

KILL ZONE **II**

BAE BELONGS TO ME III

A DOPE BOY'S QUEEN II

By **Aryanna**

COKE KINGS V

KING OF THE TRAP II

By **T.J. Edwards**

GORILLAZ IN THE BAY V

De'Kari

THE STREETS ARE CALLING II

Duquie Wilson

KINGPIN KILLAZ IV

STREET KINGS III

PAID IN BLOOD III

CARTEL KILLAZ IV

DOPE GODS II

Hood Rich

SINS OF A HUSTLA II

ASAD

KINGZ OF THE GAME V

Playa Ray

SLAUGHTER GANG IV

RUTHLESS HEART IV

By **Willie Slaughter**

THE HEART OF A SAVAGE III

By **Jibril Williams**

FUK SHYT II

By **Blakk Diamond**

FEAR MY GANGSTA 5

THE REALEST KILLAS

By **Tranay Adams**

TRAP GOD II

By **Troublesome**

YAYO IV

The Streets Made Me 2

A SHOOTER'S AMBITION III
By S. Allen
GHOST MOB
Stilloan Robinson
KINGPIN DREAMS III
By Paper Boi Rari
CREAM
By Yolanda Moore
SON OF A DOPE FIEND II
By Renta
FOREVER GANGSTA II
GLOCKS ON SATIN SHEETS II
By Adrian Dulan
LOYALTY AIN'T PROMISED II
By Keith Williams
THE PRICE YOU PAY FOR LOVE II
DOPE GIRL MAGIC III
By Destiny Skai
CONFESSIONS OF A GANGSTA II
By Nicholas Lock
I'M NOTHING WITHOUT HIS LOVE II
By Monet Dragun
CAUGHT UP IN THE LIFE III
By Robert Baptiste
LIFE OF A SAVAGE IV
A GANGSTA'S QUR'AN II
By **Romell Tukes**
QUIET MONEY III
THUG LIFE II
By **Trai'Quan**

Larry D. Wright

THE STREETS MADE ME III
By **Larry D. Wright**
THE ULTIMATE SACRIFICE VI
IF YOU CROSSM ME ONCE II
By **Anthony Fields**
THE LIFE OF A HOOD STAR
By Ca$h & Rashia Wilson

Available Now

RESTRAINING ORDER **I & II**
By **CA$H & Coffee**
LOVE KNOWS NO BOUNDARIES **I II & III**
By **Coffee**
RAISED AS A GOON I, II, III & IV
BRED BY THE SLUMS I, II, III
BLAST FOR ME I & II
ROTTEN TO THE CORE I II III
A BRONX TALE I, II, III
DUFFEL BAG CARTEL I II III IV
HEARTLESS GOON I II III IV
A SAVAGE DOPEBOY I II
HEARTLESS GOON I II III
DRUG LORDS I II III
CUTTHROAT MAFIA
By **Ghost**
LAY IT DOWN **I & II**
LAST OF A DYING BREED

The Streets Made Me 2

BLOOD STAINS OF A SHOTTA I & II III

By **Jamaica**

LOYAL TO THE GAME I II III

LIFE OF SIN I, II III

By **TJ & Jelissa**

BLOODY COMMAS I & II

SKI MASK CARTEL I II & III

KING OF NEW YORK I II,III IV V

RISE TO POWER I II III

COKE KINGS I II III IV

BORN HEARTLESS I II III IV

KING OF THE TRAP

By **T.J. Edwards**

IF LOVING HIM IS WRONG…I & II

LOVE ME EVEN WHEN IT HURTS I II III

By **Jelissa**

WHEN THE STREETS CLAP BACK I & II III

THE HEART OF A SAVAGE I II

By **Jibril Williams**

A DISTINGUISHED THUG STOLE MY HEART I II & III

LOVE SHOULDN'T HURT I II III IV

RENEGADE BOYS I II III IV

PAID IN KARMA I II III

By **Meesha**

A GANGSTER'S CODE I &, II III

A GANGSTER'S SYN I II III

THE SAVAGE LIFE I II III

CHAINED TO THE STREETS I II III

By **J-Blunt**

PUSH IT TO THE LIMIT

Larry D. Wright

By **Bre' Hayes**
BLOOD OF A BOSS **I, II, III, IV, V**
SHADOWS OF THE GAME
By **Askari**
THE STREETS BLEED MURDER **I, II & III**
THE HEART OF A GANGSTA I II& III
By **Jerry Jackson**
CUM FOR ME I II III IV V
An **LDP Erotica Collaboration**
BRIDE OF A HUSTLA **I II & II**
THE FETTI GIRLS **I, II& III**
CORRUPTED BY A GANGSTA I, II III, IV
BLINDED BY HIS LOVE
THE PRICE YOU PAY FOR LOVE
DOPE GIRL MAGIC I II
By **Destiny Skai**
WHEN A GOOD GIRL GOES BAD
By **Adrienne**
THE COST OF LOYALTY I II III
By Kweli
A GANGSTER'S REVENGE **I II III & IV**
THE BOSS MAN'S DAUGHTERS I II III IV V
A SAVAGE LOVE **I & II**
BAE BELONGS TO ME I II
A HUSTLER'S DECEIT I, II, III
WHAT BAD BITCHES DO I, II, III
SOUL OF A MONSTER I II III
KILL ZONE
A DOPE BOY'S QUEEN
By **Aryanna**

The Streets Made Me 2

A KINGPIN'S AMBITON
A KINGPIN'S AMBITION **II**
I MURDER FOR THE DOUGH
By **Ambitious**
TRUE SAVAGE I II III IV V VI
DOPE BOY MAGIC I, II, III
MIDNIGHT CARTEL I II
By **Chris Green**
A DOPEBOY'S PRAYER
By **Eddie "Wolf" Lee**
THE KING CARTEL **I, II & III**
By **Frank Gresham**
THESE NIGGAS AIN'T LOYAL **I, II & III**
By **Nikki Tee**
GANGSTA SHYT **I II &III**
By **CATO**
THE ULTIMATE BETRAYAL
By **Phoenix**
BOSS'N UP **I , II & III**
By **Royal Nicole**
I LOVE YOU TO DEATH
By Destiny J
I RIDE FOR MY HITTA
I STILL RIDE FOR MY HITTA
By **Misty Holt**
LOVE & CHASIN' PAPER
By **Qay Crockett**
TO DIE IN VAIN
SINS OF A HUSTLA
By **ASAD**

Larry D. Wright

BROOKLYN HUSTLAZ

By **Boogsy Morina**

BROOKLYN ON LOCK I & II

By **Sonovia**

GANGSTA CITY

By **Teddy Duke**

A DRUG KING AND HIS DIAMOND I & II III

A DOPEMAN'S RICHES

HER MAN, MINE'S TOO I, II

CASH MONEY HO'S

By Nicole Goosby

TRAPHOUSE KING **I II & III**

KINGPIN KILLAZ I II III

STREET KINGS I II

PAID IN BLOOD **I II**

CARTEL KILLAZ I II III

DOPE GODS

By **Hood Rich**

LIPSTICK KILLAH **I, II, III**

CRIME OF PASSION I II & III

By **Mimi**

STEADY MOBBN' **I, II, III**

THE STREETS STAINED MY SOUL

By **Marcellus Allen**

WHO SHOT YA **I, II, III**

SON OF A DOPE FIEND

Renta

GORILLAZ IN THE BAY **I II III IV**

TEARS OF A GANGSTA I II

DE'KARI

TRIGGADALE I II III

Elijah R. Freeman

GOD BLESS THE TRAPPERS I, II, III

THESE SCANDALOUS STREETS I, II, III

FEAR MY GANGSTA I, II, III IV

THESE STREETS DON'T LOVE NOBODY I, II

BURY ME A G I, II, III, IV, V

A GANGSTA'S EMPIRE I, II, III, IV

THE DOPEMAN'S BODYGAURD I II

Tranay Adams

THE STREETS ARE CALLING

Duquie Wilson

MARRIED TO A BOSS… I II III

By Destiny Skai & Chris Green

KINGZ OF THE GAME I II III IV

Playa Ray

SLAUGHTER GANG I II III

RUTHLESS HEART I II III

By Willie Slaughter

FUK SHYT

By Blakk Diamond

DON'T F#CK WITH MY HEART I II

By Linnea

ADDICTED TO THE DRAMA I II III

By Jamila

YAYO I II III

A SHOOTER'S AMBITION I II

By S. Allen

TRAP GOD

By Troublesome

Larry D. Wright

FOREVER GANGSTA

GLOCKS ON SATIN SHEETS

By Adrian Dulan

TOE TAGZ I II III

By Ah'Million

KINGPIN DREAMS I II

By Paper Boi Rari

CONFESSIONS OF A GANGSTA

By Nicholas Lock

I'M NOTHING WITHOUT HIS LOVE

By Monet Dragun

CAUGHT UP IN THE LIFE I II

By Robert Baptiste

NEW TO THE GAME I II III

By **Malik D. Rice**

LIFE OF A SAVAGE I II III

A GANGSTA'S QUR'AN

By **Romell Tukes**

LOYALTY AIN'T PROMISED

By Keith Williams

QUIET MONEY I II

THUG LIFE

By **Trai'Quan**

THE STREETS MADE ME I II

By **Larry D. Wright**

THE ULTIMATE SACRIFICE I, II, III, IV, V

KHADIFI

IF YOU CROSS ME ONCE

By **Anthony Fields**

THE LIFE OF A HOOD STAR

330

The Streets Made Me 2

By Ca$h & Rashia Wilson

BOOKS BY LDP'S CEO, CA$H

TRUST IN NO MAN

TRUST IN NO MAN 2

TRUST IN NO MAN 3

BONDED BY BLOOD

SHORTY GOT A THUG

THUGS CRY

THUGS CRY 2

THUGS CRY 3

TRUST NO BITCH

TRUST NO BITCH 2

TRUST NO BITCH 3

TIL MY CASKET DROPS

RESTRAINING ORDER

RESTRAINING ORDER 2

IN LOVE WITH A CONVICT

LIFE OF A HOOD STAR

Coming Soon

BONDED BY BLOOD 2

BOW DOWN TO MY GANGSTA

The Streets Made Me 2